CROSSFIRE

HEIDI HERMAN

CROSSFIRE

HEIDI HERMAN

Cover design by KAM.design
Edited by Vanessa Lebans
Formatting by F + P Graphic Design

Pink Viking Press, a division of Hekla Publishing LLC
1603 Capitol Ave
Suite 310-A431
Cheyenne, Wyoming 82001
www.pinkvikingpress.com

ISBN Paperback: 978-1-947233-17-1
ISBN eBook: 978-1-947233-18-8
Library of Congress Control Number: 2025922332
First edition | Printed in USA

crossfire *noun*

a: in combat, a situation where firing occurs from two or more points, causing the lines of fire to intersect.

b: in business or politics, an instance when opposing forces or interests meet, cross, or clash.

c: in communication, a rapid or heated exchange of words.

d: in rodeo [team roping], an illegal maneuver by the heeler, occurring when they throw their rope hastily, before the header has fully controlled the steer and made it change direction.

1

Twelve million dollars. Moirin Garrett nodded and scrawled her signature at the bottom of the page, approving the request. It was a good investment. The hydropower division had a solid team, and she was confident they'd soon achieve marketable results. She flipped through the sheets, approving several more requests before straightening the pile and sliding the entire stack to the corner of the desk.

She ran her hand along the edge of the sleek walnut surface. Commissioned by her grandfather, it was a work of art, eight feet across and four feet wide, inlaid with Colorado aspen and juniper with hand-tooled leather panels. She was the third generation to sit at the desk where piles of work rarely existed. They signified a backlog and inefficiency. Right now, the incriminating stack screamed for attention. The corner office was the pinnacle of prestige, the payoff for a lifetime of effort, but no one ever mentioned how much work it took to keep it.

The shrill ring of the landline telephone cut through the silence of the office, echoing through the executive floor that had long since emptied. She glanced at the caller ID and sighed, picking up the receiver. "Mother."

"Don't *Mother* me. Edgar has the limo downstairs waiting. He called and said you're not answering your cell."

"I'm just finishing up a few things."

"It won't do to be late. It simply won't."

"Mother, I know. I'm hanging up now to change. Tell Edgar I'll be down in ten minutes."

She put the receiver back on the cradle and opened one of the desk drawers. Withdrawing a tablet computer connected to her home security system, she paused to let the screen brighten, showing the image of her living room.

Orson sat, staring at the camera, his crooked tail twitching. Waiting. When he saw the light come on, his petulant meow resonated in the empty condo. She smiled as she pressed the microphone button to activate the speaker.

"Sorry, buddy. It will be a few more hours before I come home." She switched to the food dispenser app on her phone, tapped it, and watched the camera as Orson tore off toward the kitchen, drawn by the sound of treats clinking into the bowl. She closed the tablet and returned it to the drawer.

Moirin crossed the office to her private bathroom, which included a closet and shower. Her schedule demanded convenience and efficiency. This wasn't the first time she changed from business suit to evening dress at the office. Within minutes, her hair, makeup, and attire were suitably altered, and she took the elevator to the lobby.

"Good night, Sam." She raised a two-finger wave to the security desk as she passed.

"Good night Ms. Garrett."

Edgar stood at the open rear door of the town car, waiting to close it after she slid into the back seat. Twenty minutes later, the car stopped, and the door reopened. She took a deep breath, nodded at Edgar, then exited the vehicle.

Moirin surveyed the room filled with donors and supporters drawn here by the mission of environmental preservation. The annual People for Earth Preservation Foundation gala was a major society event that Moirin typically avoided. This year, her mother insisted that association with the group would counteract the criticism and judgment Moirin often received for her role in running a wildly successful international energy company. She didn't think changing public perception would be as easy as that, but the effort seemed to please her mother.

The Board of Directors of PEP, as they were known, had wanted the gala to be immersed in nature. The Nautilus Ballroom at the Denver Aquarium fit the bill, shimmering like rippling bands of water, its elegant tones of blue and gold blending together like a warm sunset over the ocean. Exhibits of marine life and freshwater creatures in various habitats surrounded the attendees, providing a vivid glimpse at the life they worked so hard to preserve. Muted notes of classical music softened the conversations around her, the actual score unrecognizable over the human voices.

She walked to the bar and ordered a whiskey highball. A drink to avoid the femininity of a wineglass, the appropriate color of a man's drink, but tempered with ginger ale. Another concession for public appearances. She took a drink, mentally reviewing the talking points for the evening. There was a narrow focus for the event, and she intended to stay on topic.

Moirin didn't need to circulate through the crowd because everyone in attendance sought her out. A pose for a photo, pitch a plan, voice a criticism, ask a favor… everyone wanted something. Her long career had made her recognizable to many, both in the Energy sector and amongst environmentalists. The PEP marketing team had made full use of the press release announcing her attendance at the event.

"Ms. Garrett. What a tremendous honor to meet you. I mean — I heard you would be here tonight, but I didn't believe it. After all, you, with this crowd, but here you are." She wasn't the first one to point out the incongruity of a corporate energy executive's attendance at the annual environmental gala.

Moirin turned and faced the thin, willowy girl, taking in the sparkling eyes and flushed cheeks. She remembered those days when the world was exciting and full of promise. For a moment, she would have given anything to switch places with the young corporate groupie. Then again, the thirty years of hard work and sacrifice she'd spent building a career would still be ahead of her.

"Thank you," she said, smiling as she clasped the girl's outstretched hand between both her own. "You have a lot of passion. Is that for business, the environment, or both?"

"I, well, I guess, both. I'd like to be an environmental attorney one day. I'm one of the interns for PEP this summer. I'll start my junior year in the fall." A quick calculation put the girl's age at around twenty years old. Had she made different choices in life, Moirin may have had a daughter that age, perhaps even several children. She brushed the odd thought aside to encourage the girl with a nod.

"Good for you. Summer internships are an excellent experience."

"Excuse me, ladies. Moirin, hello." A white-gloved hand tapped on her forearm.

Moirin glanced in the direction of the new voices. The young girl's slim hand pulled out of her grasp, backing away as she spoke. "Anyway, Ms. Garrett, I want to thank you. You're my inspiration — a role model of how women can succeed in this field. I just wanted to tell you." As quickly as she appeared, the girl blended into the crowd.

Moirin found herself surrounded by a trio of aging society matrons. Each was garbed in elegant, understated evening wear, but glittering with jewels. They were major benefactors of the foundation, pillars of the Denver community, and the figureheads of her mother's ladies' group. Each of them was here to see and be seen, solidifying relationships with those in power and establishing ones with the up-and-comers.

She faced them, suppressing a sigh, and mustered one of her cultivated smiles: courteous but distracted, designed to deter prolonged interaction. "Ladies, good evening." She nodded to each one in turn. "Mrs. Eldrich, Mrs. Myerson, Mrs. Devonshire."

"Hello, dear. We were thrilled to hear from your mother that you would be announcing your company's support for this. Such a worthy cause." Eliza Eldrich spoke for the group, her companions nodding in enthusiastic agreement.

"Yes, it is, isn't it? It's so good to see you all here tonight as well. If you'll all excuse me." She cocked her head toward the bar and lifted her empty glass. The trio of ladies tittered and nodded, releasing her from further social obligation.

Her drink refreshed, she scanned the crowd for the enthusiastic intern. She could use more of the girl's energy, but Moirin couldn't spot her. Instead, a flurry of activity caught her attention. In the opposite corner of the room, a round, squat figure in a dark suit gestured emphatically at one of the uniformed hostesses. The hostess's features were drawn with an expression somewhere between extreme patience and complete frustration.

Moirin recognized both the emotion and its origin. Gregorian Plankett. An odious narcissist with more money than principles, his hefty contributions didn't make his personality more tolerable. The hostess seemed to be losing whatever battle they were fighting, shifting from one foot to another and glancing away, possibly looking for reinforcements to manage the situation.

Moirin grimaced and searched for a suitable focus for her attention. One of the mayor's aides stood with his wife alongside a congressman whose arm was firmly in the grasp of a porcelain-faced blonde. Perfect. Before she could step in the direction of the group, the event manager materialized, blocking her path.

"Ms. Garrett. It is wonderful having you here tonight." He spoke in a slow, calm manner, his voice hushed.

"Thank you. It's a lovely event." She inclined her head to the center of the room.

"You're too kind. I hate to bother you, but I need your assistance with a small item." He cleared his throat and twisted his long, elegant fingers before clasping them securely, almost prayerfully, together. "I am so sorry to ask, and it is indelicate, but we have a bit of a dilemma."

"Oh?" She massaged her neck before running a hand over her hair, ensuring it was still tucked into the elegant chignon. The once-vivid flame color had mellowed over the years to a deep auburn, now touched with a few strands of gray, but appearance was still important. She wrenched her expression into a smile, digging deep for the illusion of energy she didn't feel.

"With a reservation event of this type, dinners and seating are set in advance, and last-minute changes are difficult to accommodate. Mr. Plankett seems to have brought two guests tonight instead of one."

"That is unfortunate." She narrowed her eyes, hoping he would ensure Plankett remained someone else's problem.

"Yes, well," he cleared his throat before his words came out in a rush, "um, each of our special invitees received a guest ticket. Pardon my presumption, but I don't believe I've seen you with a companion or escort tonight…" He paused, his eyes pleading for her to answer the unasked question.

Someone slid up next to her. Without warning, Gregorian Plankett slapped the underside of her elbow, driving her arm up, sloshing her drink from its glass. "She never has a date to these things anymore. What's the problem? Just sit my cousin next to her. It'll give him a thrill to be at the head table, and everyone will think she's a cougar now with a handsome young buck next to her. Win-win." He smirked.

Moirin kept a firm grip on her composure, dabbing the spilled drops from her hand with a napkin. She turned away with a tight smile, swishing the soggy napkin through the air as though to playfully slap his forearm, but stopping short of direct physical contact.

"Oh, Mi-ster-Plan-kett." She drew out his name, accentuating each syllable. Any bystander overhearing her might think she was tolerant and accommodating, possibly even indulgent, even as Gregorian's smirk faded; her rebuff was evident in her body language and expression. She had honed a look she used as effectively in business negotiations as in personal conflicts. Unfortunately, unlike her normal negotiations, she had no play here. Concession was her only option.

She turned her back on him and smiled at the event planner. "Yes, of course. Mr. Plankett's additional guest may be accommodated. There is an unused dinner place setting at our table." Direct and forthright as always.

Without a backward look, she walked away with slow, measured steps, relying on her appearance to be all the armor she needed. She knew the shimmery, sheer fabric of her bronze-colored ankle-length gown followed her body's curves without clinging, accented by a daring neckline and modest side slit. A woman in her early fifties was on a fashion tightrope, walking that fine line between sexy elegance and becoming gossip fodder of what-was-she-thinking-wearing-a-dress-made-for-a woman-half-her-age. The attitude when wearing such a dress made all the difference.

She took a deep breath, ignoring the sidelong look of empathetic pity she caught in her peripheral vision. Mr. Plankett's comments had been heard by several attendees standing nearby. Moirin refused to reveal any outward evidence of embarrassment or the disquiet that churned in her chest. There was nothing about her life to be pitied. Certainly not her single status. She smiled tersely and continued toward the congressman's group.

When they were seated for dinner, she was relieved to see Mr. Plankett's party was on the opposite side of the circular banquet table, out of earshot. Moirin herself was seated between two engaging PEP board members, one a marine biologist and the other an attorney. A retired marine biologist, seated at her right, who specialized in whales, porpoises, and dolphins, proved to be an entertaining storyteller. She enjoyed the levity he brought to the evening.

It was especially welcome after she learned that Plankett was actively involved in the PEP foundation, and she would be subject to continued interaction with him throughout the project. That information made her want to back out right then and there. Of course, she couldn't do that. The long-term benefits for Garrett were too important. Her own inclinations would take a backseat to the company, as usual.

After the tofu twist on a rubber chicken meal, the Foundation's President made opening remarks, and Moirin stepped up to the podium to deliver a few words they had requested before the keynote speaker.

"Good evening. I'm Moirin Garrett, Chief Operations Officer for Garrett Diversified, an energy company founded by my great-grandfather. He came to Colorado after the discovery of oil in Cañon City. He had big dreams back then. Like many prospectors at the time, he didn't see success right away; fortunately, he persevered. Since then, the philosophy of diversification and eco-friendly energy solutions we've followed isn't just our family's legacy; it's our mission.

"I'm proud to be joining with the People for Earth Preservation this year for a ground-breaking effort. The esteemed members of the Board are spearheading an impressive Climate Change Impact Study that I'm pleased to announce Garrett Diversified will be taking part in. The focus of the study is the impact of human energy resource procurement on the environment. Our area of the study will include sites where oil drilling, fracking, wind turbines, solar collection, and harnessing hydroelectric power have been done."

As she looked over the crowd, Moirin saw the young intern she had met earlier sitting at rapt attention, poised on the edge of her seat. Moirin imagined her own face held much the same look years before when her father told her the stories of his grandfather's struggles that she shared with this crowd tonight. She looked at the girl and nodded, smiling, realizing she hadn't asked her name.

"The very talented and respected environmentalist Riggs Robinson has been chosen to lead the project. He's here tonight with the research team he's assembled. I am honored to be joining, if only in some small way, a study that may provide guidance for our ongoing efforts to ensure a clean and healthy planet for generations to come. I've been told that due to the overwhelming response from all of you and supporters throughout the world, they've secured the entire funding goal for the five-year study."

As the audience applauded, Moirin glanced at her copious notes. Prior to tonight, she had never met Riggs Robinson and knew only the broad strokes of the study.

"For our small part, Garrett Diversified will be providing access to six sites here in Colorado for testing. Our philosophy of transparency and commitment to the environment aligns with PEP's mission. We are proud to be an industry leader and trailblazers for eco-friendly solutions. By participating in this study using some of our own properties, we can demonstrate that it is possible to be both responsible and profitable. By doing this, we hope to share with others in the industry that a balance can be struck between environmental responsibility and corporate profitability."

She double-tapped the podium with her forefingers as she nodded, smiling again at the audience. Her face ached.

Polite, scattered handclapping increased measurably as Riggs crossed the stage to join her. They shook hands briefly, Moirin stepping back as he took her place at the podium. "Now, I'd like you to meet the PEP team."

The room erupted with applause. The audience was captivated by the handsome and gregarious scientist as Moirin slipped back to her seat. She snuck a glance at her watch. *Another hour at most.* She tried to paste on an interested smile, struggling against the urge to massage her stiff neck, waiting for the night to end.

2

The quiet Sunday mornings in her condo were usually productive. To her annoyance, today had not been.

Her eyes darted from the road to the dashboard clock of her Lexus. Time was moving too fast. Her day began before dawn, but hours later, the pile of paperwork hadn't diminished to her liking. Her habit of needing to finish one more note, check one more email, and do one more task before moving to her next appointment often resulted in breathless last-minute arrivals. It seemed that today would be no different.

Sunlight cut through the branches of lush green trees as Moirin sped through her parents' Cherry Hills neighborhood. Her mother had a standing reservation for Sunday brunch and hated when Moirin was tardy. The trendy restaurant had limited parking, and arriving late often meant she was forced to park several blocks away, increasing the delay. They offered valet, but she availed herself of the service only on those Colorado days when stinging snow or bone-chilling winds made her loath to be outside. Today, only a few fluffy white clouds lazed across the vivid blue sky, allowing the sun to shine brilliantly. She was almost disappointed to find an available spot a few steps from the restaurant's front door. Her mother, on the other hand, would be pleased.

The old-English stone cottage design was out of place among the modern downtown shops, but the parking lot and grounds were in keeping with the quaint countryside theme. The valet stand stood under an arched entry that extended out to allow two lanes of automobile traffic, but the stone columns covered in hanging ivy looked more suitable for receiving horse-drawn carriages. Hedges on either side of the cobblestone sidewalks were trimmed with expertise worthy of royal English gardens.

She walked inside, nodding to Márcio, the maître d'. He smiled and looked down, moving his finger across a computer tablet. His black suit, crisp white shirt, gray vest, and ascot tie gave him the look of a proper English butler.

A hug from behind pulled her attention. "Hello, Gingersnap, you're looking beautiful." She turned and smiled. Only her father and his sister used that nickname for her.

"Hi, Dad." She leaned in, kissing his cheek. She took a step further. "Mom." She kissed the air, barely brushing close enough to feel the warmth of her mother's face.

"Hello, sweetheart."

They made an attractive couple. Charles Garrett was exactly six feet tall, his posture still straight despite his seventy-eight years. His closely cropped steel-gray hair revealed sunglass tan lines at his temples, evidence of hours on the golf course. He could have posed for a retired lifestyle magazine if not for the dark smudges under his sunken eyes.

Standing next to him, Iris Garrett had nearly an identical shade of steel-gray hair in a cropped style almost as short as her husband's. The top of her head came to his shoulder despite her high heels, and she stood just as ramrod straight. Expertly applied makeup gave her a lightly tanned, flawless complexion. A few bits of gold and diamond jewelry, paired with a sleeveless dress, created her trademark look of understated elegance.

Moirin slipped her arm around her mother's waist, giving her a sidelong hug. "Fabulous dress, Mom."

"We have your table ready now." The maître d' stepped past them to address a couple sitting on a bench nearby. "Right this way, sir, ma'am."

"Oh, please, don't call me ma'am," the woman said, smoothing her unwrinkled tennis skirt as she stood. "It makes me feel a hundred years old."

"My apologies, Mrs. Babbich…"

"Oh, no, not that either. Mrs. Babbich is my mother-in-law." She shrieked. "Call me Bitsy."

"Elizabeth, please, you're creating a scene." The man seated next to her stood up and guided her firmly toward the maître d'.

Iris huffed as she watched the couple disappear through the archway into the dining room. "No sense of decorum in that one. I'd say she married a few steps above her breeding." Her words, though whispered, were articulate, clipped in her customary style.

Moirin covered her mouth, clearing her throat to suppress a laugh. She'd bet any amount of money that her mother's childhood had been more impoverished and lacking in etiquette education than Bitsy's. The only difference was that her mother had learned how to fit into the ranks of high society even before she married Charles Garrett.

"Iris, now, you know Babbich is thrilled to be with such a beautiful woman. He had all that propriety in his first two wives, and look where it got him." Charles's low tone was just over a whisper. "Let the man indulge his happiness."

"It's just bad manners." Iris sniffed. "I won't apologize for saying so."

"Maybe you should reach out to him, Dad, see if she plays golf. Eighteen holes as a foursome would give Mom some time to influence Bitsy." An impish impulse to rankle her mother more came over her. Moirin enjoyed pulling her father into rousing debates and discussions on various topics. His open discourse was a stark contrast to her mother's more uncompromising viewpoints.

"Oh, you think?" He turned his head, raising one eyebrow.

"Sure. Just don't call her Mrs. Babbich," Moirin said.

"I would definitely avoid that." Charles' laughter dissolved into a coughing fit. "Pardon me." He shook his head, pushing away her concerned hand. "Just a frog in my throat, honey."

"Such nonsense," Iris hissed. "Please stop, you two. You're both being ridiculous. It gives me a headache to listen to you go on like that."

Moirin exchanged a conspiratorial grin with her father.

Marcio approached them and inclined his head. "Mr. Garrett, ladies. We have your table ready. If you'd follow me."

Charles allowed his wife and daughter to move first. A few steps later, he touched Moirin on the shoulder. "I'll join you in a moment. I need a moment to speak with someone." Moirin watched him approach an older gentleman with graying hair, who leaned heavily on a cane as he stood at the edge of the dining room.

Moirin sat down with her mother, each accepting a cup of coffee as it was offered, Iris nodding to the server. No menus were offered or requested; their standard order was placed with that small signal. Simply, elegantly, in the way her mother preferred all things.

"So, I received a glowing report yesterday from Eliza Eldrich about you and the gala Friday night." She spread the linen napkin across her lap with a smooth, practiced motion before looking up at her daughter.

"How nice. Yes, I saw Mrs Eldrich with Beatrix Myerson and Catherine Devonshire. We spoke briefly. Of course, I made the rounds and spoke to many of the attendees."

Iris laughed. "Yes, well, I understand those three can be a bit overbearing, but they are quite influential. I am pleased you agreed to take on a more involved role in the foundation. It should be quite good for your personal reputation."

"I did it because it's good for the company. It's an excellent endeavor, and being associated with the foundation that can certify our energy production sites aren't destroying the environment is, of course, good for Garrett."

"I'm so glad your father insisted you take the leading role instead of Ian."

"That's true. Oh, speaking of, Uncle Ian asked me to let you know Felicity will be calling to set up a foursome."

"Um, yes, she did leave me a message," Iris said, her tone noncommittal. She sipped her coffee in silence.

"Oh, Mother, be nice." Moirin chuckled. "Felicity didn't campaign for president of the arts council—she was appointed. It's a volunteer position anyway, and you would have hated it." For years, the arts council had been her mother's pet charity, although she kept her support purely financial.

"Yes, well, I should have been asked first." Iris raised her empty cup, catching the attention of a nearby waiter. He responded with a nod and hurried off for the coffeepot.

"You would have declined, and everyone knew it. There was no offense intended. You know Felicity didn't undermine you, so stop punishing her for it."

Iris sighed. "I suppose you're right. The pending litigation I'm working on now demands all my time, anyway."

"Do you think you'll be able to settle, or are you going to trial?" Moirin felt her jaw tighten. Her mother pushed herself too hard. Iris had an illustrious career as a corporate attorney, and she showed no signs of slowing down, despite being seventy-seven years old. Her expertise was still in such high demand that she often turned away clients. Meetings, filing, and negotiations were one thing, but the stress of a trial for a woman her mother's age was troubling.

"I'm sure we'll settle. The documentation against the employee is quite incriminating, but my client will obviously want to keep this quiet. Corporate fraud can be dicey, and there's a lot of evidence we wouldn't want to present in open court."

Moirin nodded. She would feel the same if one of her employees attempted to share trade secrets with competitors. Consequences were better meted out in the privacy of closed-door meeting rooms, not in an open courtroom where the details needed to be shared.

"I'm sorry, my dear. Arthur does tend to go on and on." Charles sat down across from Iris, pulling a linen napkin across his lap. "Legacy," he chuffed.

"Excuse me?" Moirin said to her father.

"Arthur," Charles said. "He's completely consumed with his endowment to the university and the scholarships. He determined to have education of future generations be his legacy."

"That's wonderful. Very generous of him."

"Yes, well, he never had a family. Worked hard, made good investments, nice guy by all accounts. That's his niece and her husband with him. Sad his family name ends with him." He pursed his lips, tapping on the linen tablecloth with his forefinger.

"His name will continue because that's his legacy," Iris said. "He has a building at the university named after him, plus an entire foundation with several annual scholarships. His name is linked to a lot of good press." She set her coffee cup down. "I think this environmental effort will help Moirin with that sort of thing as well, don't you agree, Charles? She could be remembered for doing good."

A server dressed in black arrived, sliding dishes before each of them. It was their standard Sunday brunch fare; each week, an identical meal of perfectly prepared eggs Benedict, lemon poppyseed crepes, and seasonal fruit was served.

"Of course, dear, but I expect she'll be remembered for her work at Garrett Diversified. As CEO." He nodded at the waiter, then winked at his daughter.

"I hope so, Dad. I had thought I might enjoy a bit of philanthropy with this foundation, but last night I learned that Gregorian Plankett is on the Board and intends to be hands-on. Joining the effort has lost its appeal."

"That is unfortunate." Iris clucked her tongue and shook her head. "But women in business must always deal with difficult or unpleasant men. It comes with the territory. You've dealt with quite a few and have succeeded just as I've taught you. Stay focused, think two steps ahead, and never let your emotions have a part in business.

Charles speared a strawberry with his fork, then pointed it at her before taking a bite. "Keep a close eye on him. He's an underhanded, vengeful man, and he won't soon forget how you blocked his placement on Garrett's Board of Directors a couple of years ago."

"There was absolutely no way I was going to allow that. Gregorian is too shifty, always seems to be up to something. Although I've never heard of any accusations sticking, his name comes up too often regarding questionable business dealings. He would have been a disastrous influence on our Board. I wish Ian had handled it, but he still thinks business is best done either at a cocktail party or on the golf course, where Gregorian excels. He's well-connected and slick enough that Ian's blind to any red flags." Moirin's heart rate spiked, and a flush spread across the back of her neck as a few distasteful interactions with Gregorian flashed through her mind.

"Exactly why this change in leadership is long overdue, Moirin. I wish we could have pushed it through a couple of years ago, but you know how Ian pushed back then."

Iris chuffed, looking from Charles to Moirin. Moirin raised her eyebrow, waiting for her mother to comment, but Iris looked down, demurely sipping her coffee.

"I remember. I think he's ready now, and it's a good time for the company to make the change. I've been content as COO, running the day-to-day, for what, eight or nine years now? But it makes a difference when the head of the company is a woman instead of a man. I think we're in a good political climate to transition."

"Ian doesn't have a choice, now. The industry is changing rapidly now; we need a strong CEO at the helm. Someone who can be agile and pivot when needed. Man or woman, makes no difference." Charles shrugged. "You're the best one for the job."

Iris wagged her finger at him. "It does make a difference. Moirin, it's what I've always told you. Women must work harder to overcome the glass ceiling. You're in a family business, and it's a double-edged sword. If you succeed because of hard work and merit, you'll still have some people claim it was nepotism. After you've taken the promotion, you'll have to work even harder to prove you deserve it."

"I know, Mom." Moirin sighed and turned to her father. "So, you've talked to the other board members? They'll back the transition at the next meeting?"

"Yes, well, ah, yes and no. You've more than proven yourself to me and everyone else. But the company is significantly larger than it was when Ian took over after my heart attack. They do feel that standard vetting and approval is warranted, just for appearance. Just a formality, of course."

Her heart dropped, the elegant eggs Benedict souring in her stomach. Surely she heard wrong.

"Vetting and approval?" Moirin repeated the words, her voice sounding sharp in her ears. She swallowed hard, tamping down a wave of righteous indignation. Being subjected to vetting like an unknown candidate pitching a resume was humiliating.

"Charles, honestly." Iris' tone was disapproving. "I thought you quashed that."

Sexist, insulting, unfair. She pushed the words aside as they emerged, refusing to allow them to take root. She pulled in a deep, calming breath.

"I did my best, but as you said, family business has some level of expected nepotism. Unfortunately, one of the newer board members made a point that it's prudent to do more than rubber-stamp the candidate, and others agreed." Charles shrugged. "Where's the harm? You'll exceed any standard they measure, and you have no skeletons. Like I said, a formality."

Moirin had no argument. The company was significantly larger because of her work, not Ian's. How did they not see that? Her father had a valid point that it was just a formality, but the idea of an assessment – one that might find her wanting - was disconcerting.

"Of course, yes. I understand," she said. "The full support of the Board always translates well to public perception. I assume it would be some abbreviated process of vetting? They would not be considering multiple candidates, simply verifying my viability independently?"

"Exactly. It's not a competition. You really have nothing to worry about, Moirin. By the end of the summer, everything will be different. You'll be CEO, Ian will have retired, and Garrett Diversified will be one of the less than twenty percent of corporations worldwide to have a female CEO. How's that for a legacy?"

"It's quite an achievement. I suppose most people consider their children to be their legacy. I guess I'll be my own legacy. Otherwise, I should have made some children long before this." Moirin smiled wryly.

"People can fail you. Children aren't a reliable legacy." Iris scoffed. The table was silent before she rushed to clarify. "You're an exception, dear, of course. A credit to the Garrett name. You know we're both proud of you. And a female CEO of an international corporation reflects well on the community."

Moirin nodded. Of course, her mother was interested in her success only as far as it reflected on her parenting, the community, and perhaps the women's group. That made sense. She couldn't worry about that now. Her focus would be on the quick and easy approval by the board. Her father was right. She was above reproach, and vetting would be easy.

Charles reached over and patted her hand. "Not to worry, honey. This will go off without a hitch."

"I appreciate your faith in me, Dad." She'd prefer to leave her own imprint on the world, but, unless she wanted to trailblaze a new path, a daunting task this late in life, solidifying her family's business legacy would have to do.

"Keep focus on the company as you've always done. Mind your Ps and Qs. Be above reproach, and the Board will have nothing to be concerned about. And neither will we."

She pushed away the plate. *Nothing to be concerned about.* Still, the sour taste lingered in her mouth.

Monday morning, Moirin refilled her coffee and stood by the floor-to-ceiling windows, enjoying the view, one of her indulgent compensations for the sacrifice and effort it took to get here. The snow-capped peaks visible in the distance during the winter and in the summer, the blend of mossy to emerald green mixed with variegated browns, displayed the majestic panorama of the Rocky Mountains. She could see the thick stands of trees between the rocky outcroppings and imagined the wildlife moving through the brush, breathing in crisp air even as she inhaled the cold, metallic-tinted oxygen pushed into her corporate cage at regular intervals from the mechanical beast on the roof.

She took a sip of coffee and blanched, choking back a cough. Her assistant, Wanda, must have brewed this hours ago. She dumped the bitter sludge in the nearest philodendron and debated walking to the executive lounge, which might have an equally vile offering, or taking a trip down to the atrium level of the building, where a high-end coffee shop offered the best espresso downtown, but would likely have a ten-minute wait. She glanced at the clock. It was nine-thirty, and the small cafe would likely be packed. Make that a twenty-minute wait. Time she couldn't afford.

The telephone rang, pulling her attention to her desk, the top now almost invisible under the folders piled at one end, carefully arranged stacks of paper at the other, strewn paper, pens, and various notepads between. She shifted piles to find the instrument.

"Moirin Garrett."

"Moirin, it's Ted Iverson. I needed to give you a heads up on a delay I'm having getting this report together." Ted Iverson was one of her product managers in the renewable energy sector. His anxiety was evident in the whiny, breathy delivery of the words. Ted was reliably competent and conscientious, so she took his concern seriously. He explained that a glitch in the data had delayed the financials that were due for the quarterly reports.

"What do you mean by *glitch*? You're saying the data is bad?" she asked, noting down the particulars as he spoke. A problem in the quarterly report would impact the annual report, as the fiscal year was ending. If not corrected, it could delay both reports - precisely the type of operational slip she couldn't afford right now with the Board's scrutiny.

"Not yet. I'm rerunning the underlying reports to see if I can isolate the problem."

"Send me the data. I'd like to take a look. Maybe we can figure it out together. I might pull in the IT folks and see if they can shed some light."

"Great. Thanks, Moirin."

She moved behind the desk and sat down at the computer, logging into her email. Before Ted's data came in, she'd clear out some of the other topics awaiting her attention. There was never a shortage of items requiring her immediate attention. Garrett had grown from her grandfather's humble beginnings to an international concern operating in the oil and gas, wind, and solar energy sectors. They still focused on exploration, production, and transportation of oil and natural gas, but thanks to Moirin and her cousin Colin, they had grown a renewable energy division with wind and solar energy projects.

Colin was committed to renewable energy, and his reports last year had prompted Moirin to promise the Board exciting and profitable advances in the area. Unfortunately, groups such as Ted's, which focused on hydrogen research, had so far not produced the promised results. With her every move being evaluated, now was not the time for another delay or setback.

She heard the shuffle of someone entering the office and looked up. "Uncle Ian," she said.

He tangoed into the office with surprising agility, his hands in his pockets, his face beaming. An ever-present leather portfolio was tucked under his arm, tight against his body. His perfectly tailored navy-blue suit turned his portly physique into a stalwart boardroom presence. Her father's younger brother was her only boss at the company, a title Moirin considered more honorary than supervisory.

"You look like the proverbial cat that ate the canary," she said, chuckling as she leaned back.

"It's Gillian's daughter, Avery. She just told us she's expecting. Felicity's excited for another baby, but adjusting to the idea of us being great-grandparents before we hit seventy. I thought she'd reach through the phone and strangle me when I told her it's only by the skin of our teeth." He chortled at what Moirin surmised would quickly become a stale joke.

She smiled and stood up. "Congratulations all around. It's wonderful how the family is growing." Ian had a wife, children, and grandchildren. Now his grandchildren were starting their own families. She had an odd sensation. Regret? Not quite. Maybe it was sorrow. Where had all the years gone? Suddenly, she felt old and tired.

"Thank you, yes. And with Colin's oldest heading to college this fall, we'll have the next generation lined up." He rocked on his heels, looking more like a proud grandfather than a corporate executive.

"That's so good to hear. Sit down. I could use a break." Moving around the desk, she motioned to the seating area between the windows, and he settled into one of the club chairs. Moirin poured each of them a glass of water and handed one to her uncle before sitting on the couch. He settled back, tossing his portfolio on the table.

"They grow up so fast," Ian said. His grandchildren had become adults in their own right. Avery, his oldest grandchild, had been married for two years. Colin's two were in high school. Ian and Felicity had marked life milestones of weddings, birthdays, graduations, and gatherings, first their own and now through their children and grandchildren.

Moirin nodded. "I sent Ryan a graduation gift and received a nice thank-you note. In his own handwriting, no less. Colin and Brittany did a wonderful job raising him. Brittany tells me that Megan was accepted for a semester abroad. Only a junior in high school, and she speaks Italian like she was born to it." Lacking siblings of her own, Moirin thought of Colin's children more as a niece and nephew than cousins-once-removed.

Her eyes were drawn to the floor-to-ceiling bookcases behind the desk, the shelves filled to capacity. The first shelf, directly at eye level, contained a photograph of her father and grandfather. She felt like they beamed down at her in approval when she passed by, as a reminder of her responsibility to the company and to the legacy of her family. And to the future generations Ian had produced.

It was just one photo in a collection on the massive unit. The rest spanned a timeline of her own life and achievements. The earliest was her graduation day thirty years ago, posing with her parents and grandparents. Another more recent photo from Colin's graduation. Soon, Ryan's would be added. A few others were casual snapshots.

Most were professional shots of Moirin with one of two other individuals shaking hands or holding framed certificates, others where she was one of a group of three, four, or five people attired in business suits. A few were red-carpet events, where she stood next to a movie star in one, a national politician in another. One captured a wide smile as she was flanked by a rock star and a foreign dignitary. The bottom shelf featured promotional shots at ribbon cuttings and first shovel ceremonies. Memories of moments in a life lived through business functions.

"Am I right?" Her attention snapped back at Ian's voice and guffaw. She smiled weakly and whatever joke she'd missed. "It will be good to have everyone together at the graduation party. You have it on your calendar, right?"

Her cell phone rang, and she glanced at the caller ID. *Jo.* She pressed the ignore button, sending the call to voicemail, nodding at Ian. "Of course. I just sent the gift in advance on the off chance I get pulled into something last-minute or forget it at home. You know how it goes."

"Of course, of course. I'm not going to miss that aspect of this job. Benefits of retirement, eh?" He chuckled and shrugged his shoulders like a mischievous five-year-old.

"Speaking of the job, we have a C-level meeting next week." Moirin checked the calendar program on her phone. "I want to status the financials and look at the drafts for the quarterly and annual reports. Are you still good for that?" As Chief Operating Officer, Moirin met regularly with her other C-level counterparts – Chief Officers of Technology, Financial, Compliance, and the Strategy Officer. They each officially reported to Ian, but the CTO (Chief Technology Officer) and CSO (Chief Strategy Officer) worked more closely with Moirin.

"Yes. We have a few things to discuss before next month's board meeting. Colin's got some new data from R&D that might change next year's projections. Exciting stuff." Ian slapped his hands, briskly rubbing them together, his expression almost gleeful. Colin's role as CSO often dealt with the most exciting and potentially troublesome areas.

Her return smile felt wooden. She had expected the board meeting's primary topic to be his retirement and her appointment as CEO. "I'm concerned we may have oversold the Board on Colin's projections already. I'm not sure we want to add to that."

She looked down, opening her phone's memo pad, and made a note to chat privately with Colin that afternoon.

The cell phone in her hand chimed again, this time signaling a text message. She glanced at the screen. Jo again.

Are we still on for dinner tonight? Please don't cancel — I need your help!

Jo had been her friend for nearly thirty years, and such a dramatic message wasn't completely out of character. Moirin put the phone down and looked back at Ian.

"I need to prepare for a couple of meetings today and get to that never-ending stream of emails. Oh, and the PEP kickoff is this afternoon, so I'll need to review the property list we'll submit."

"One of the reasons I stopped by." He pulled a thick manila envelope and a single printed page from the portfolio. "I emailed this, but I know how things get buried in your inbox." He laughed as he stood, sliding the page on top of the envelope before holding it out. "Oh, and that package is paperwork from the Board with the vetting process they've started."

The reality hit with force beyond an emotional blow, physically pulling the air from her lungs. Vetting paperwork was real. The envelope hung in the air between them, the flap sealed with string woven around the little cardboard buttons, as if the contents needed to be restrained from escape.

She took a deep breath and exhaled rapidly, grabbing the page and envelope. Indifferently, she tossed the envelope on her desk and glanced at the printed page for PEP. "Great. I'll take a look, in case they have any questions, but I'd imagine today's meeting will be quick." The information she'd received when they agreed to the project indicated the kickoff meeting would introduce the participants and review the protocols.

Each company volunteered a property for testing and analysis to determine the business's potential impact on the environment. It seemed like a nice idea on the surface, but Moirin doubted there'd be much meat to the resulting study report. She imagined everyone's lists would be carefully selected. No one would risk outside testing on industrial property without being certain of the outcome. The thought of negative press from Garett's participation in the project was fodder for an instant panic attack. She could only imagine how that would be assessed under the Board's microscope.

"Sounds good. I'll check in with you tomorrow to see how it went." Ian whistled off-key as he disappeared down the hallway. Moirin turned to her phone, thumbing the screen to initiate a call. After five rings, she heard Jo's recorded voicemail message. She tapped her toe as she waited for the beep.

"Hey Jo. Sorry I missed you. Let's do dinner tonight at my place. We'll order up some takeout. Call me." She hung up and stared at the phone, tapping her thumb and middle finger together. The tactile sensation helped focus her thoughts. Thirty minutes ago, Jo seemed desperate to connect, and now her call was sent to voicemail.

The phone on her desk chirped, and one of the buttons flashed red. She glanced at the clock—Wanda, efficient as usual, reminding her of the next meeting on her schedule. Fortunately, it was a lunch meeting; she was starving.

She looked at the PEP site list in her hands. There was no time for review now, so she'd have to trust Ian's selections.

3

Monday morning, Moirin refilled her coffee and stood by the floor-to-ceiling windows, enjoying the view, one of her indulgent compensations for the sacrifice and effort it took to get here. The snow-capped peaks visible in the distance during the winter and in the summer, the blend of mossy to emerald green mixed with variegated browns, displayed the majestic panorama of the Rocky Mountains. She could see the thick stands of trees between the rocky outcroppings and imagined the wildlife moving through the brush, breathing in crisp air even as she inhaled the cold, metallic-tinted oxygen pushed into her corporate cage at regular intervals from the mechanical beast on the roof.

She took a sip of coffee and blanched, choking back a cough. Her assistant, Wanda, must have brewed this hours ago. She dumped the bitter sludge in the nearest philodendron and debated walking to the executive lounge, which might have an equally vile offering, or taking a trip down to the atrium level of the building, where a high-end coffee shop offered the best espresso downtown, but would likely have a ten-minute wait. She glanced at the clock. It was nine-thirty, and the small cafe would likely be packed. Make that a twenty-minute wait. Time she couldn't afford.

The telephone rang, pulling her attention to her desk, the top now almost invisible under the folders piled at one end, carefully arranged stacks of paper at the other, strewn paper, pens, and various notepads between. She shifted piles to find the instrument.

"Moirin Garrett."

"Moirin, it's Ted Iverson. I needed to give you a heads up on a delay I'm having getting this report together." Ted Iverson was one of her product managers in the renewable energy sector. His anxiety was evident in the whiny, breathy delivery of the words. Ted was reliably competent and conscientious, so she took his concern seriously. He explained that a glitch in the data had delayed the financials that were due for the quarterly reports.

"What do you mean by *glitch?* You're saying the data is bad?" she asked, noting down the particulars as he spoke. A problem in the quarterly report would impact the annual report, as the fiscal year was ending. If not corrected, it could delay both reports — precisely the type of operational slip she couldn't afford right now with the Board's scrutiny.

"Not yet. I'm rerunning the underlying reports to see if I can isolate the problem."

"Send me the data. I'd like to take a look. Maybe we can figure it out together. I might pull in the IT folks and see if they can shed some light."

"Great. Thanks, Moirin."

She moved behind the desk and sat down at the computer, logging into her email. Before Ted's data came in, she'd clear out some of the other topics awaiting her attention. There was never a shortage of items requiring her immediate attention. Garrett had grown from her grandfather's humble beginnings to an international concern operating in the oil and gas, wind, and solar energy sectors. They still focused on exploration, production, and transportation of oil and natural gas, but thanks to Moirin and her cousin Colin, they had grown a renewable energy division with wind and solar energy projects.

Colin was committed to renewable energy, and his reports last year had prompted Moirin to promise the Board exciting and profitable advances in the area. Unfortunately, groups such as Ted's, which focused on hydrogen research, had so far not produced the promised results. With her every move being evaluated, now was not the time for another delay or setback.

She heard the shuffle of someone entering the office and looked up. "Uncle Ian," she said.

He tangoed into the office with surprising agility, his hands in his pockets, his face beaming. An ever-present leather portfolio was tucked under his arm, tight against his body. His perfectly tailored navy-blue suit turned his portly physique into a stalwart boardroom presence. Her father's younger brother was her only boss at the company, a title Moirin considered more honorary than supervisory.

"You look like the proverbial cat that ate the canary," she said, chuckling as she leaned back.

"It's Gillian's daughter, Avery. She just told us she's expecting. Felicity's excited for another baby, but adjusting to the idea of us being great-grandparents before we hit seventy. I thought she'd reach through the phone and strangle me when I told her it's only by the skin of our teeth." He chortled at what Moirin surmised would quickly become a stale joke.

She smiled and stood up. "Congratulations all around. It's wonderful how the family is growing." Ian had a wife, children, and grandchildren. Now his grandchildren were starting their own families. She had an odd sensation. Regret? Not quite. Maybe it was sorrow. Where had all the years gone? Suddenly, she felt old and tired.

"Thank you, yes. And with Colin's oldest heading to college this fall, we'll have the next generation lined up." He rocked on his heels, looking more like a proud grandfather than a corporate executive.

"That's so good to hear. Sit down. I could use a break." Moving around the desk, she motioned to the seating area between the windows, and he settled into one of the club chairs. Moirin poured each of them a glass of water and handed one to her uncle before sitting on the couch. He settled back, tossing his portfolio on the table.

"They grow up so fast," Ian said. His grandchildren had become adults in their own right. Avery, his oldest grandchild, had been married for two years. Colin's two were in high school. Ian and Felicity had marked life milestones of weddings, birthdays, graduations, and gatherings, first their own and now through their children and grandchildren.

Moirin nodded. "I sent Ryan a graduation gift and received a nice thank-you note. In his own handwriting, no less. Colin and Brittany did a wonderful job raising him. Brittany tells me that Megan was accepted for a semester abroad. Only a junior in high school, and she speaks Italian like she was born to it." Lacking siblings of her own, Moirin thought of Colin's children more as a niece and nephew than cousins-once-removed.

Her eyes were drawn to the floor-to-ceiling bookcases behind the desk, the shelves filled to capacity. The first shelf, directly at eye level, contained a photograph of her father and grandfather. She felt like they beamed down at her in approval when she passed by, as a reminder of her responsibility to the company and to the legacy of her family. And to the future generations Ian had produced.

It was just one photo in a collection on the massive unit. The rest spanned a timeline of her own life and achievements. The earliest was her graduation day thirty years ago, posing with her parents and grandparents. Another more recent photo from Colin's graduation. Soon, Ryan's would be added. A few others were casual snapshots.

Most were professional shots of Moirin with one of two other individuals shaking hands or holding framed certificates, others where she was one of a group of three, four, or five people attired in business suits. A few were red-carpet events, where she stood next to a movie star in one, a national politician in another. One captured a wide smile as she was flanked by a rock star and a foreign dignitary. The bottom shelf featured promotional shots at ribbon cuttings and first shovel ceremonies. Memories of moments in a life lived through business functions.

"Am I right?" Her attention snapped back at Ian's voice and guffaw. She smiled weakly and whatever joke she'd missed. "It will be good to have everyone together at the graduation party. You have it on your calendar, right?"

Her cell phone rang, and she glanced at the caller ID. *Jo*. She pressed the ignore button, sending the call to voicemail, nodding at Ian. "Of course. I just sent the gift in advance on the off chance I get pulled into something last-minute or forget it at home. You know how it goes."

"Of course, of course. I'm not going to miss that aspect of this job. Benefits of retirement, eh?" He chuckled and shrugged his shoulders like a mischievous five-year-old.

"Speaking of the job, we have a C-level meeting next week." Moirin checked the calendar program on her phone. "I want to status the financials and look at the drafts for the quarterly and annual reports. Are you still good for that?" As Chief Operating Officer, Moirin met regularly with her other C-level counterparts – Chief Officers of Technology, Financial, Compliance, and the Strategy Officer. They each officially reported to Ian, but the CTO (Chief Technology Officer) and CSO (Chief Strategy Officer) worked more closely with Moirin.

"Yes. We have a few things to discuss before next month's board meeting. Colin's got some new data from R&D that might change next year's projections. Exciting stuff." Ian slapped his hands, briskly rubbing them together, his expression almost gleeful. Colin's role as CSO often dealt with the most exciting and potentially troublesome areas.

Her return smile felt wooden. She had expected the board meeting's primary topic to be his retirement and her appointment as CEO. "I'm concerned we may have oversold the Board on Colin's projections already. I'm not sure we want to add to that."

She looked down, opening her phone's memo pad, and made a note to chat privately with Colin that afternoon.

The cell phone in her hand chimed again, this time signaling a text message. She glanced at the screen. Jo again.

Are we still on for dinner tonight? Please don't cancel – I need your help!

Jo had been her friend for nearly thirty years, and such a dramatic message wasn't completely out of character. Moirin put the phone down and looked back at Ian.

"I need to prepare for a couple of meetings today and get to that never-ending stream of emails. Oh, and the PEP kickoff is this afternoon, so I'll need to review the property list we'll submit."

"One of the reasons I stopped by." He pulled a thick manila envelope and a single printed page from the portfolio. "I emailed this, but I know how things get buried in your inbox." He laughed as he stood, sliding the page on top of the envelope before holding it out. "Oh, and that package is paperwork from the Board with the vetting process they've started."

The reality hit with force beyond an emotional blow, physically pulling the air from her lungs. Vetting paperwork was real. The envelope hung in the air between them, the flap sealed with string woven around the little cardboard buttons, as if the contents needed to be restrained from escape.

She took a deep breath and exhaled rapidly, grabbing the page and envelope. Indifferently, she tossed the envelope on her desk and glanced at the printed page for PEP. "Great. I'll take a look, in case they have any questions, but I'd imagine today's meeting will be quick." The information she'd received when they agreed to the project indicated the kickoff meeting would introduce the participants and review the protocols.

Each company volunteered a property for testing and analysis to determine the business's potential impact on the environment. It seemed like a nice idea on the surface, but Moirin doubted there'd be much meat to the resulting study report. She imagined everyone's lists would be carefully selected. No one would risk outside testing on industrial property without being certain of the outcome. The thought of negative press from Garett's participation in the project was fodder for an instant panic attack. She could only imagine how that would be assessed under the Board's microscope.

"Sounds good. I'll check in with you tomorrow to see how it went." Ian whistled off-key as he disappeared down the hallway. Moirin turned to her phone, thumbing the screen to initiate a call. After five rings, she heard Jo's recorded voicemail message. She tapped her toe as she waited for the beep.

"Hey Jo. Sorry I missed you. Let's do dinner tonight at my place. We'll order up some takeout. Call me." She hung up and stared at the phone, tapping her thumb and middle finger together. The tactile sensation helped focus her thoughts. Thirty minutes ago, Jo seemed desperate to connect, and now her call was sent to voicemail.

The phone on her desk chirped, and one of the buttons flashed red. She glanced at the clock — Wanda, efficient as usual, reminding her of the next meeting on her schedule. Fortunately, it was a lunch meeting; she was starving.

She looked at the PEP site list in her hands. There was no time for review now, so she'd have to trust Ian's selections.

4

It seemed unseasonably hot for late May. Moirin would have preferred to stay in her air-conditioned office all day, but the PEP kick-off meeting required her presence at the Foundation's office in Boulder. Seated at the large conference table next to Riggs, along with the team members, interns, and other corporate sponsors, Moirin recognized one of the interns as the tall, willowy girl who had fawned over her at the gala. The round-robin introductions supplied her name — Steffie.

Riggs Robinson controlled the meeting with professionalism and efficiency. Her cursory assessment at the gala had pegged him wrong. His tousled blond hair, muscled physique, and golden tan made her think of an aging surfer. The easy smile, quick wit, and outgoing personality indicated playboy, but the professional profile she'd read this morning lauded his intelligence and deep commitment to the environment. She'd thought the article was written by an enamored journalist, but she saw now the assessment was accurate.

After the introductions, Riggs moved the meeting forward, walking the participants through bullet points of the study's objectives. "In a nutshell, folks, we're seeking to have an honest assessment of what works and what doesn't. Too many environmental protection efforts have been boiled down to buzzwords and empty promises. Or, worse yet, exciting new options that get implemented without proper study. I drive an electric car, but that doesn't mean I'm blind to the issues of refined lithium and EV batteries. But we don't throw the baby out with the bathwater, am I right?"

A few chuckles tittered around the room, and he continued. "We want an honest evaluation of the impact of industry on the environment from several sectors. To do that, we'll do some studies outside of Colorado. Over the next three years, we hope to complete evaluations in automotive, energy, waste disposal, wastewater treatment, and plastics production."

"That's a pretty big scope. Can you really do all that effectively for each industry?" Moirin recognized Darion Summers as the Western Regional Manager of a national waste management company.

"That's a great question, thank you. It is a major undertaking, yes, but necessary. People for Environmental Protection may be based here, but we'll network with volunteers throughout the country. I, along with a few other key staffers, will travel to ensure that samples are collected according to strict standards. We'll also handle some of the more sensitive testing ourselves."

"Riggs here is the best, we made sure of it before we picked him for the project." Gregorian Plankett's voice boomed from the foot of the table.

Riggs smiled. He nodded and shifted suddenly in his chair, pulling a cell phone from his back pocket. He glanced at it, then tapped a few buttons and stood, cupping the phone in his hand.

"Thank you for that, Mr. Plankett, but we have a great staff putting in the effort, so every success is a team effort. Speaking of effort, Steffie has assembled copies for you all of our proposed timeline and milestones." Riggs nodded at the intern. "She'll have her start explaining. I apologize, I need to take care of this, then I'll be right back."

All eyes shifted to Steffie. The girl was obviously self-conscious about the attention and scrunched her shoulders in an almost apologetic way as she gave a stiff-armed wrist pivot like an awkward beauty queen's parade wave. She stood and scooped up piles of stapled pages into her arms.

As the intern circled the room, passing out the information, she seemed skittish near Gregorian, dropping the pages on the table in front of him instead of drawing near enough to hand them over directly. The girl headed to the opposite end of the room to begin a halting speech about the project. Moirin didn't blame her for distancing herself from Gregorian.

"Okay, so you all know we are looking at the impact of industry on the environment, basically by studying the water, soil, and air. And, um, we wanted to have different sectors represented - especially major corporations. You all met briefly in the introductions, but I'll run through everyone for the project so you all know who's who from where. So, we have Garrett Industries from energy, Delvin-Smoothers from waste disposal, LGK from automotive production, and Fester & Foss from plastics. These are all household names and have properties across the US. You've each selected five locations to open for the study where we'll do the water, soil, and air testing." Steffie stopped, gulping in air. She nodded gratefully in acknowledgement as a hand went up.

"Do you have any participants from water treatment? Riggs mentioned that, but you didn't."

"Oh, yeah, um," Steffie blushed and shuffled her papers. Moirin caught a glimpse of neat columns of typed information. "Yes, the list has regional ones. That's right. We couldn't get a national company on board, so we are looking at two sites from three different regional wastewater treatment companies."

The relief was evident on Steffie's face when Riggs returned to the room and took over the question-and-answer session.

"Where are we?" He grinned and pointed at a raised hand.

Moirin tuned out the question and subsequent response. There hadn't been any surprises here, and she was confident that a minimal follow-up would be required of her. The contribution of Garrett's property list was sufficient; she and Ian had discussed locations last week, and Ian made the final selection. Satisfied that her part was finished, she busied herself making notes for the remainder of the afternoon's tasks once she returned to the office.

The meeting ended, and Moirin picked up her empty paper coffee cup and napkin, walking them to the trash can.

Through the partially closed door, she caught Gregorian's voice. "Ha. No, of course not. I handled it."

She started to back away, but the next words made her pause. "No one will ever know, trust me." Those words coming from a man like Gregorian Plankett immediately raised her distrust. The words grew fainter, as if he had walked down the hallway.

".. changed the list.. easy. They won't know...prove… regret it for sure."

Moirin took a step closer to the door, pushing it open further. The words became clear. "She's going to pay for denying me. There are consequences, and she won't see it coming until it's too late. Just watch. This will be fun."

She scowled. Last year, she'd had first-hand experience of his underhanded business practices when he'd tried squirming onto the Garrett Board of Directors. She pondered what he was plotting this time. What possible gain could he have by sabotaging an environmental study?

"Ms. Garrett?"

Moirin flinched. "Steffie, you startled me.

"Can I help with anything?"

"Oh, no, thank you, Steffie. I'm fine." She didn't want the intern to realize she'd been eavesdropping and quickly switched the focus. "By the way, you did well today." The girl's smile lacked the enthusiasm and energy she had exhibited at the gala. Moirin sympathized. It wouldn't be surprising if she were overwhelmed with her role on the project.

"Thank you. It's a lot different than school. I hope I can do a good job for Mr. Robinson and the Foundation. It could be a great reference for me."

"If today was any indication, you'll do just fine. Let me know if you ever need any help. I can't offer much in the way of mentorship for environmental studies, of course, but I am acquainted with many women who can. I could provide business mentorship if you're ever interested."

"That is an amazing offer, thank you so much, Ms. Garrett." Exuberance seemed to bubble up from a hidden emotional well, transforming the girl's face with positive energy.

"Ah, just my luck. All the true titans of industry have left." Gregorian's voice boomed as he sauntered into the room.

Steffie grimaced. Moirin glanced from the girl to Gregorian and back again. The man was truly a cretin from the dark ages. Refusing to give him the satisfaction of a response, Moirin reached over and tapped Steffie's shoulder. "Come, let me give you one of my cards. My bag is over here." She gently tugged the girl away from Gregorian.

"Oh, hey, Riggs, my man, I thought you were gone too," Gregorian said as Riggs entered the room.

"Nah, it's my new home. I'll be spending most of my time here now. Hah, I'm considering moving a cot in. The start of a new project is exciting stuff, but it really does require long hours."

"Well, I'll leave you to it then." Gregorian clapped Riggs on the back, then turned and bowed toward Moirin and Steffie. "Ladies."

The air felt lighter in the room when the large man departed. Riggs laughed. "He's a lot, isn't he?"

"I've known him through business connections for years, but I've never really warmed up to him. I was surprised to find him associated with the foundation. Philanthropy has never been his strong suit."

"I couldn't say. I've only recently met him, but he seems to be quite involved in the foundation. He serves as committee chair for this project, you know." Riggs flashed a brilliant smile. "You should join the foundation as well. We could use another corporate sponsor on the committee. I think we would do well working together. I can honestly say I'd prefer your company to Gregorian's." He winked.

Moirin laughed. It had been a long time since someone used flirting techniques to influence her. Riggs was easily eight years her junior and likely had no shortage of dating prospects. "I'm not sure I have the time to join the committee, but I would like to do what I can for the project. Let me know if Garrett can help in any way. Steffie, here's my card if you need anything."

She had plenty of responsibilities and a pile of work back on her desk demanding her attention. By the time she pulled out of the parking lot, concerns about Steffie, Riggs, and Gregorian were pushed to the back of her mind.

5

When she arrived home that evening, Moirin was drained. She closed her eyes and leaned back in her chair next to the open patio doors. Instead of relaxing, her mind scrambled from one topic to another. Mental development of a personal task list — dry cleaners, change the furnace filters, oil change for the car — was constantly interrupted by work topics.

If she were honest, concern for Jo kept her from focusing on either subject. Jo had texted she'd come over and bring food, but didn't hint about the problem she faced. It was unusual for her to ask for help. She was typically the supportive one everyone else went to for advice.

Orson jumped onto her lap, two-stepping to retain his balance, and Moirin groaned. "I suppose I need to focus on you first, right? I thought I'd take a few minutes and recharge my batteries, but I can see you disagree."

She scratched between the cat's ears. The left ear was half gone. The top of the left ear matched its right-hand mate perfectly, but the triangle shape ended there. A scar ran from his ear down over his eye, ending somewhere under his whiskers. As a result, the perpetual half-winking eye and left-side whiskers twisting upwards gave him a continual expression of wry amusement.

She'd never intended to have a pet. Never wanted the responsibility. However, Orson had chosen her. A chance stop at the grocery store with a f armer's market in the parking lot, where an animal shelter had set up a booth. As she passed the shelter's display, a long-haired chocolate-and-ivory-colored cat stared at her intently. Something compelled her to pause and reach down to pet the beautiful animal who had obviously survived major injuries. He had missing patches of fur on his back, near his chocolate-colored tail, and behind his right hind leg, due to an injury that caused a limp. The young man at the booth was stunned that the cat hadn't shied from Moirin's touch and immediately declared that Orson must sense something special in her. Three years after the adoption, she still couldn't explain why, but they'd bonded.

She looked out through the French doors and past the patio to the tall Bigtooth maple tree. It was undoubtedly chosen for its gorgeous, vibrant red foliage in the fall. As the sun sank near the horizon, the shadow from the tree crept across the chaise lounge. The leaves were a brilliant green, fluttering almost imperceptibly in the light breeze. Memorial Day had just passed, and spring growth was bursting. Crickets chirped, and a maple branch swayed as two squirrels dashed down its length in a game of chase. The cat watched them closely, his tail twitching.

"You thinking of going after them?" Moirin chucked at Orson's intensity. "How about we find you a nice, canned seafood medley instead? Let's see what's left in the cabinet."

Orson obediently followed as if fully aware of her words and anxious to find out for himself if there was indeed a seafood medley in his future. They made the trek from the patio toward the kitchen. Moirin bought the condo ten years earlier after falling in love with the generous private patio area. It was her oasis, the place where she could escape the pressures and expectations of the corporate world.

The condo itself wasn't large; a single woman didn't need much space. A two-bedroom with twelve hundred square feet, but it was a desirable end unit. The decor was crisp and clean, flawlessly executing a plan carefully created by a professional interior designer. The furniture was comfortable, inviting, and in neutral earth tones, with spots of color provided by throw pillows and small accents. The walls were painted greige, a color also chosen by her designer. The mingled tones of gray and beige virtually guaranteed that any colors added to the design palette would blend naturally, she'd been assured. A few large paintings were placed strategically on the walls, selected for their color scheme rather than subject matter. All by recognizable artists, of course.

One section of the living room was designed to display more personal images. A narrow couch table stood against the wall, covered in framed photographs. Her parents, at their fortieth wedding anniversary party, another from last year of Moirin and her parents in holiday sweaters, posed in front of a monochrome Christmas tree. The most prominent featured all eleven members of the Garrett family from last year's corporate picnic. Two shelves above the table were crowded with snapshots from vacations and social events. These were the ones she treasured. In each, she posed with one or more of the same three women: Josephine Sanderson, Leslie James, and Leslie's sister, Heather Santos. The four musketeers had been friends for nearly thirty years. Her hand brushed the frame of one as she passed by, a memento from a lake house weekend almost four years earlier.

Orson trotted beside Moirin like a canine companion as they crossed the dining room. The designer's hand was evident in the large square table that accommodated seating for eight, with two chairs at each side, ensuring that no guest was isolated from the conversation and ample space in the center for serving dishes. The visible surface was buffed to a glossy sheen, but the fine scratches and wear around the edge attested to its frequent use. If her home had a heart, it was this table.

They entered the kitchen, and Orson nosed eagerly at the feline food cabinet. The room had been customized with efficient storage and cabinets that rose to the full ten-foot height of the ceiling. The designer's touch was apparent here as well, in the well-appointed gourmet kitchen. Small appliances and gadgets lined the top shelves, much to the delight of the catering chef she often hired. Moirin could prepare basic meals, but rarely found the need for tools beyond a cutting board, a knife, or a pan.

"I'm sure we have something for you, buddy." She shooed him aside to open the door and peer inside. Orson meowed pitifully.

"See?" She said triumphantly, holding up a container. "You should have faith in me. I'm not gonna let you down." She opened the container and spread the contents into his food bowl before searching out her own treat.

She opened the thirty-eight-bottle capacity wine cooler and pulled out a Hillson Wines red, then poured a glass. Wineglass in hand, she settled on the couch and pulled printouts from her briefcase. A few minutes later, the coffee table and couch were littered with papers and notes of the glitchy data Ted Iversen had emailed. Orson sauntered in and sniffed suspiciously at each.

"We're looking for the error here, and we'd better find it fast, so these financials are submitted on time," Moirin explained. Orson was quite well-informed of the goings-on at Garrett Diversified and every other part of Moirin's life. Talking through a problem aloud helped her thought process, and it made her feel less insane talking to Orson instead of herself. As a result, he was a vault of her most closely guarded secrets and intimate thoughts.

Orson proceeded to jump awkwardly and stretch out above her head. She could hear his purring as much as feel the vibration as she slipped back into work mode. A knot of irritation and worry formed at the base of her neck. The asset allocation system had been a massive undertaking and significant investment that she had pushed. It had taken numerous case studies, illustrations, and ROI analysis to convince her father and Uncle Ian to support the project. Once she won them over, the Board's approval came quickly.

If it came out that the system wasn't performing as expected, Moirin would bear the brunt of the blame. A failed project costing half a million dollars couldn't be overlooked, especially now, when she was under the microscope. She hoped she was being overly cautious, and Ted's "glitch" was both easily explained and easily corrected.

"Nothing, nothing." She mumbled, flipping pages and picking up two lists to study side-by-side. "There must be something here, right? If I can't find it, we might be in trouble, Orson." Her stomach twisted at the possibilities. She scanned the pages, tapping her thumb and middle finger together, looking for the answer to jump out at her.

Orson mewed sympathetically.

"These numbers, here, they're inflated. The expenses can't be that high. The underlying table, let's see." She sorted through the pile again as she mumbled as much to herself as to Orson. "Yes, that. Salary, benefits, consulting fees. Okay, those match. Then the materials are where?"

Orson tapped a paw on her shoulder, his standard signal that ears needed rubbing. She leaned back as she pulled him into her lap and obliged, staring at the papers strewn on the table. "You're right, as always. I just need to outline the expense areas and have an analyst run the detailed report. I see the value of the idea." She frowned as she looked at the mess. Either her recent run-ins with Gregorian or the idea of the Board assessing her performance was making her question everything. *Get a grip.* She had yet to review the package Ian had given her for the vetting process. Now was as good a time as any to review that.

"Hi, honey, I'm home." Jo's voice sing-songed as her footsteps echoed from the small hallway. Moirin chucked. Jo's presence always had a calming effect on her, despite her habit of breezing into the house without knocking.

Moirin looked up and saw Jo holding two bulging paper bags. "And look what I have."

"Dinner. And no one had to cook. You're the best wife ever."

"Pfft, it's nothing. Besides, we have a lot to talk about. I'll grab some plates," Jo said, stopping as she eyed the mess on the coffee table. "Oh, you're working." Jo delivered the accusation in a disapproving tone reminiscent of all the lectures she'd given Moirin about being a workaholic.

Moirin flushed and dumped Orson on the couch as she swept the files into a stack. "No, not really, just researching something."

"Good. Leave that there and come with me." Jo stopped when she spied the glass on the end table. "Hey, what wine do you have open? One from your aunt's winery?" Her smile was hopeful and broadened at Moirin's nod. "Great. I'll bring the bottle and join you at the table."

She cut through the dining room, and Moirin heard her moving around in the kitchen. Cabinet doors opened and closed, then the refrigerator, followed by the unmistakable sounds of dishes clattering. It only took a few minutes for Jo to return, balancing a tray with two bowls of soup, two plates of pasta, a loaf of bread, and a glass of wine, with the half-empty wine bottle tucked securely under her right elbow.

"Thanks," Moirin met her in the dining room and rescued the teetering platter. She set it down and moved the dishes to the table. "This smells fantastic. So, sit down and tell me what's going on."

"I'm starving. Let's eat first," Jo mumbled, ducking her head and suddenly focused on the wine bottle in her hands. Her dark hair shone under the dining room light. The short, layered cut was the latest in a string of hairstyles that were all variations on the pixie she sported in college. It looked good on her, wholesome and clean, and suited her five-foot-one petite frame. As Jo sat at the table, Moirin could imagine the child she'd been, eager to please and hesitant to share a bad report card.

"Uh-huh." Moirin tsked and sat down.

As they started to eat, Moirin gave Jo time to build up to whatever was on her mind. Jo had arrived in good spirits, so it couldn't be anything horrible. But, regardless of the need, she'd help. Moirin couldn't imagine her life without her best friend, closest human confidante, the one who pushed her to stay connected with people outside of work.

Right now, Moirin could let her take her time by making casual conversation. She told Jo about her cousins, the new baby, and even her frustration with Gregorian and her wildly unfounded suspicion about Steffie.

"You think he made a pass at her?" Jo asked. "Oh, ick. He's what, thirty or forty years older than her?"

"I'm sure I caught something there. Either she's afraid of him, or just really dislikes him."

"Well, either is understandable. From what you've described, he seems like a thoroughly dislikeable fellow. Maybe she's just very perceptive."

"Maybe. I'd just hate to think there was something wrong and I didn't do anything. Then, there's what he said on the phone. He threatened someone. I distinctly heard him say he'd make her pay. And, something about changing a list."

"Well, you're not sure that it had anything to do with the PEP project, or even if he was talking about the intern, right? Shouldn't you wait until you know more, or something else happens? But then, maybe you should talk to Steffie."

Moirin shrugged. It was usually refreshing to be with Jo and take a break from the responsibilities of an international corporation that weighed on her. But sometimes Jo didn't understand the big picture. Because of her gender, Moirin didn't have the same latitude for mistakes a man enjoyed. She couldn't accuse without proof, but her conscience couldn't let go of the possibilities.

Moirin switched the conversation to lighter topics. Jo seemed unenthusiastic to talk about work or her family, but when Moirin asked about her recent yoga retreat with Leslie and Heather, Jo brightened.

"It was pretty great, actually. Leslie and Heather pitched in and paid for it as a birthday gift. There were yoga sessions, of course, but they also had wellness classes and seminars on nutrition and stress management. I wish you'd been able to come. We should plan another one for all four of us."

"Yes, I'll be sure to put that on my list," Moirin scoffed. Moirin had taken her to lunch on her birthday and had given her a high-end cappuccino machine. Something more practical and would last longer. A yoga retreat appealed to Moirin as much as binge-watching infomercials. "But I'm glad you guys had a good time."

"I needed it. It was nice to relax and get away from the stress. It was beautiful there. They had a pool and a spa, and our room was amazing. Oh, and a gourmet chef. The food was so good I couldn't believe it was healthy."

"Really? That part sounds nice. I might consider it after all. I seem to recall that vacations can be quite nice." Leaning forward on her elbows, she tried to hide a wince as a sharp pain passed through her right arm in the general area where Gregorian had walloped her a few nights before.

Jo studied her. "Are you okay? You look tired."

"Just a few long days."

Jo rolled her eyes. "With you, every day is long. You're a workaholic, and you usually thrive on it."

Moirin chuckled and tilted her head. "I can't deny that. I do thrive on the excitement of business."

"But this look here"—Jo swirled a finger in the air around Moirin's face—"is more than tired. I've known you for too many years not to see it."

"No, ah, well, just a lot on my mind, I guess." She shook off the thoughts before she got pulled in. "Anyway, this is about you. Tell me what's up. What is it you need help with?"

"I feel kind of silly now. It's nothing." Jo looked at the floor, engrossed in Orson's sloth impression as he stretched and languidly tapped a ball between his paws.

"You're the one holding out now. Whatever it is, tell me."

Jo cleared her throat and looked up. Her smile was apologetic as she shrugged, picking up a spoon and dipping it into her soup. "I'm having challenges at work and I'm not sure how to fix it."

Moirin chuckled. "Oh, workplace drama. My specialty. What's going on?"

"I love my job, but lately I've been feeling out of touch. We have more new clients, and everyone's talking about influencers on social media, creating reels, and going viral. It's hard to keep up. I'm great at marketing concepts, print ads, and product promotions. Things nobody seems to want anymore. At least none of the new clients they've been signing, anyway. This digital stuff isn't my wheelhouse. Even the young kids I'm mentoring are running circles around me."

"They love you there. I'm sure it's just your imagination. And if not, you go somewhere that your talents are appreciated."

"I just turned fifty-three, for Pete's sake," Jo said, putting the spoon down, switching to a fork to stab at the pasta. "Who do you think would want to hire someone at my age? I never thought I'd be worried about this. It's times like this I really miss Erik, for who he was, but the security of being married. A partner and, to be honest, a second paycheck."

Moira smiled and patted her hand. "Hey, you and me, we're tough, successful women. You've got this. You don't need to rely on a man to come and fix everything. You and Erik had a special relationship, partners in a way that few married couples are. You can't just replace that."

"No, you're right. But sometimes the weight of single life is overwhelming."

"Of course it is. That's why we have friends. You, me, Leslie, Heather, we're all here for each other. Well, Leslie and Heather are family, but you and me? Our real families add to our stress. Mine has professional expectations and yours, well, hon, we both know yours is crazy."

Jo's face twisted into a sarcastic smile. "You're not wrong. It's a good thing we have each other, but I'm starting to miss having a partner in life, being in love."

Moirin's heart clenched at Jo's wistful expression. Erik died nearly ten years earlier. Certainly long enough that Jo should be dating. She wouldn't voice that opinion because it would open the floodgates for Jo to nag on Moirin's unattached status.

She hadn't dated in the three years, ever since her last relationship ended. Even then, it had been uneventful, ending on a sigh instead of anguish. He had pressured her to make their relationship a higher priority, but her family and business responsibilities demanded all her energy. When he gave her an ultimatum, she chose work, so he chose someone else.

In the early days of her career, she had little time for her friends, but the sacrifice had been worth it. She had taken the company global and had branched out in ways that would ensure years of stability. It was a wonder she ever had time to date at all in the past thirty years.

Jo was different. She had majored in marketing because it was the perfect field for her. She was sociable, witty, and had an insatiable curiosity about the world. Erik had been intelligent and thoughtful but had a mischievous and playful side. They had laughed more than any couple Moirin had ever known.

"I know you loved being married, and being widowed at forty-five is not something anyone would expect. It wasn't fair, but you were good at being married."

"I was, wasn't I?"

"And I have no idea how you did it. Your childhood was weird, yet somehow commitment and family come naturally to you." Moirin was constantly impressed at her friend's devotion to her family, although she wasn't a blood relative to any of them. Her unusual childhood left her with a desperate need to be accepted, and she constantly worked to please her unappreciative family.

"I don't know. I feel like I was meant to have a big family, but that never worked out for me, huh? But I have our house and a job I enjoy. Hopefully, I can keep it. Then, maybe someday I can meet someone."

"You deserve to have someone who will love you with every part of their being, just like you would love them." For a moment, Moirin had a surreal sensation that she was speaking to herself as much as she was to Jo. Maybe when the vetting process was over, she'd have more time for a personal life.

Jo smoothed her napkin before looking up. "You should think about having a man in your life again. You can have both, you know. Women do it all the time – have success at work and a relationship."

"So you've always said. But to have one is to make sacrifices with the other. Look at my mother."

"Exactly. She's a mother, a successful lawyer, she's still married to your father, and they have a good life together. What better example could you want?"

"It's always rosy from the outside looking in. If she had focused on her career, she could have made partner at her firm years sooner. She could have been a legal legend. Instead, she had a husband and a child that kept her from being laser-focused. But as it turned out, her career kept interfering with family time, so that was a struggle for her too. I don't know how I would do that balancing act. I'd feel guilty and inadequate on both fronts."

"I think she did great. Everyone should have a mom like her. One that believes in you, pushes you to succeed, warns you when you're thinking about doing something stupid. And it's worked. I mean, look at where you are."

Moirin was quiet for a moment. She pursed her lips and shook her head. "You know what, you're right. I do owe her." Jo's own shattered childhood had left her with a deep appreciation of family and all that it meant to have blood relatives. She always managed to convince Moirin to give her mother the benefit of the doubt.

"I never had the type of career you have. What I have now is a good job, and a house that I love." Jo took several tiny bites, chewing slowly. Finally, she took a sip of wine and sighed. "I keep going over everything in my head, and I can't help but feel like I'm missing something."

Moirin felt a pull in her heart at Jo's nostalgic smile. "It's totally okay to want something more. We're both young, and we have another thirty, maybe forty years in this life. You should do more. Add a new hobby, get a more challenging job, maybe find a man. Do what you need to do to feel like you're living life to the fullest. Why not?"

"You know, you're right."

"Of course I am."

"So, what do we do?"

"We live our best life, never compromise or settle, and never forget all the great things you have."

"I think I'm going to need a more practical plan."

Moirin laughed. "We'll work on it, okay? For now, just pass me the wine."

6

The next day, Moirin left the office at five o'clock and stopped at the gym to dissolve her daily stress in a spin class, pushing herself until her body was spent and her mind clear. The locker room was jammed, forcing her to drive home feeling hot and sticky, but energized in a way only a good workout could accomplish.

The workout cleared her mind, and the short drive home allowed her to determine the steps forward. While she waited on the IT team's testing, she pondered the PEP project and Gregorian's veiled threats. Still concerned he might be targeting Steffie, she dialed Riggs' number.

"Moirin! To what do I owe the pleasure?" His upbeat tone radiated happiness. She was pleased she had caught him and didn't need to leave a voicemail.

"I've been thinking about the project. I was reviewing the packets that Steffie distributed and noticed that there wasn't a list of the locations where the study would be conducted. I was wondering if I could get a copy of that." She held her breath, hoping he wouldn't ask why. She hadn't come up with a plausible reason for asking and didn't want to share the snippets she'd overheard from Gregorian.

"Oh." Disappointment thickened his voice. "I was hoping you were calling for a more personal reason. The list, well, that's something we're trying to keep under wraps until the testing is complete. We just don't want anyone to skew our results one way or the other."

She eased the car through traffic, turning towards home. "Ah, of course, that makes sense." She hesitated. She couldn't shake the idea that something wasn't right. "I'll be honest, it is almost a personal matter. It would really mean a lot to me if I could at least see the list. It doesn't have to include the corporate names or your site summaries. I know the additional details we provided from Garrett, and I understand. I just, well, I don't want to say anything yet, but please trust me, it may be important."

"That sounds serious." She could hear the indecision in his voice. She knew it would only take a small amount of the right pressure.

"Please? I promise I have no nefarious plans, and it really is important. I would be indebted to you." A plea, a promise, and a debt. She stopped short of actually flirting.

"Aw, alright. How can I resist an appeal like that? I'll show you the list, but only if we meet for lunch. I'll bring it with me for you to look at."

"Thank you, Riggs."

They arranged the details for an early lunch the following day, and she disconnected the call. She may not find anything that would help, but at least she had tried. Parking in front of her condo, she escaped into her air-conditioned sanctuary.

After dumping her purse and briefcase at the door, she ignored Orson on her way to the shower. Once she was refreshed and dressed in sweatpants and a t-shirt, she apologized to the cat and accompanied him to the kitchen. She had filled his food bowl and poured a glass of water for herself when her cell phone rang.

She glanced down to where she had placed it on the countertop and saw the caller ID. She smiled as she answered. "Hey, Aunt Aggie."

"Hello, sweetheart. How is my favorite niece doing?" Her aunt's voice carried over the line with the warmth of a hug.

"I'm doing well, but don't let Gillian hear you say that. How are things in Wyoming?"

"Things are great. Life is good. The weather's been so nice, and my roses have come in beautiful this year."

"And the winery?" She carried the glass to the patio and settled on one of the lounge chairs.

"The vines are doing well. Of course, that's thanks to my wonderful staff. Did your father tell you we won another regional award?"

"He did, yes. I spoke to him a few days ago. He's very proud of you."

"Oh, good, good. I worry about him. Is he okay? I think when I talk to him, he lies and tells me everything is great. Whether it is or not, I don't know." Aggie sounded like a petulant child. "He thinks I fret too much. He's my older brother, but still."

"Well, you do tend to fuss over him. He's fine, Aggie. When I see him at Sunday brunch, I'll tell him he needs to drive up for a visit. That way, you can see for yourself."

"Really? Oh, that would be wonderful! Every time I try to arrange a time to stop by, there seems to be a conflict. Your mother keeps quite the busy calendar. I might drive down anyway sometime for a surprise visit."

Moirin was certain that Iris's calendar would stay full through the end of the decade if her mother thought it would keep Aggie from visiting. Her mother never gave any details, but she seemed to detest Aggie. She steered the conversation in a different direction to avoid that particular family minefield. "So, tell me more about this award." Moirin took a long drink of water.

"Oh, I was so thrilled. It's such an honor. It could be that push we need to go national."

"That's wonderful. You have worked so hard that it's nice to see it start paying off. The past few years, you've achieved a nice balance and expression. The Marquette last year, with pepper finish, was a hit every time I served it."

"Thank you so much. I was partial to that one myself. You know, you might have missed your calling as a sommelier. Unless you'd rather be a vigneron."

Moirin laughed. "A vigneron? Thank you, Auntie, but I think I'll remain an amateur wine aficionado and leave the actual cultivating to you."

"I've been happy doing it for years, but I'm turning seventy-one this year. I'm ready to start planning for retirement. Succession planning — isn't that what Charles and Ian call it?"

"That's exactly right. You should consider Avery or Megan. They're both young, just starting out. You can mold them the way you want. I already have my hands full at the company, and it will only get worse when I move to the CEO role. Plus, I'm too old to change gears now."

"Oh, posh. You're never too old for change. It's still a family business, just one that's a lot more fun."

"I have too much responsibility to think about work as fun."

"Well, okay. But Hillson Wines is not inconsequential." Aggie sounded defensive. "I have connections with a whole world of influential people. I wish you could understand what it's like to have a successful business without that terrible pressure and stress. Life's not all about work, you know. Look what it's done to your father."

"I know, I know, but Dad kept his stress bottled up. That's why he had a heart attack so young. That's not me." Moirin rubbed her finger across the rim of her waterglass. "I manage it well, and I'm sure I'll be fine."

Orson sauntered onto the patio. He sat on the flagstone, eyeing Moirin before settling in for after-dinner grooming.

"The downtown office, the home office, it's all the same. Time behind a desk working. But at least he made time to get married and have children." Aggie said.

"Please," Moirin groaned. "Not you too."

"What did I say wrong now, dear?" She could almost hear her aunt's innocent flutter of eyelashes through the phone.

"Why is the world so obsessed with marriage and family?" Moirin sighed and picked up the empty glass, walking to the living room. She waited for Orson to scamper inside before closing the door.

"Oh, honey, I'm sure it just seems that way." Her tone changed from sympathetic to curious. "The whole world, huh? Anything you want to talk about?"

Moirin huffed and sat on the couch. "I'm sure you heard about Avery. You'll have a new great-niece this year. Or early next year. I guess I forgot to ask when she's due."

"Yes, Felicity called me. I think I'm as excited as she is. The family's getting a Christmas baby," Aggie said.

"Oh, that's nice." Moirin wasn't sure what else to add. "Ian told me when we were at the office, and honestly, I didn't ask any questions."

"Sweetheart, that company is your whole world. I wonder if you don't see Ian and Colin more than your parents."

"Isn't that how it is for everyone? Except that many people spend more time with their co-workers than they do with their spouses or children. At least I don't have that guilt."

"Oh, yes, I suppose that's true. It's a bit depressing to think of it that way, though. What's got you thinking so dark?"

Orson awkwardly jumped on the couch, settling into his favorite spot behind Moirin's head, his tail curled to brush her neck. She smiled and reached up to pet him.

"Moirin, honey?"

"I'm here. Just thinking about how to answer that. It's been an odd couple of days. It's probably too many hours. First, the gala, the PEP project kickoff, and now I'm under a microscope with the Board vetting me as Ian's successor. I still have to sit down and review the package for that. Not to mention the quarterly and annual reports. I just don't want anything to fall between the cracks."

"That's a lot of weight you've put on your shoulders. I know you can handle it, Ian is still there for a while, and Colin too. Use them; it won't make you look weak. Trust me. No one would have you in charge if they didn't have faith you could handle it."

"Thanks. You're right, of course. It seems like lately everyone is wrapped up with marriage and babies, kids going off to college. Dad's thinking about his legacy, and I'm not sure what I think about beyond the company's success."

"Eh, it just seems like that. People will remember you as a person, not a job you held. Everyone lives past their own lifetime in the memories of those they touched while they were alive. Your actions, your personal integrity — that's your true legacy. Not some stuffy corporate institution."

A knot formed in her stomach. Wasn't it all one and the same? The company, her reputation, her personal integrity—they all came together as her life, inextricably tied together. If she lost one, the pieces of her life might start to come apart, like pulling a loose string and having an entire sweater unravel.

7

She met Riggs at a small bistro for lunch, situated halfway between their respective offices. He arrived before her and was seated at a corner table when she walked in.

"I appreciate you meeting me." Riggs stood and shook her outstretched hand, then waved for her to sit. "I forget how tedious it is to be cooped up in an office all day. I'm used to being in the field."

"I'm the one who should be thanking you. I know my request was unexpected." She thought it best to be direct.

"Yeah, you said it was important," he cleared his throat as his fingers fiddled with the napkin on the table in front of him. "I can trust you, right?"

Moirin worked to limit her facial expression, but felt a grin playing around her lips. "Yes, of course you can. But then, if I were untrustworthy, I'd probably lie about it."

He laughed and motioned to flag down a waitress. "Today's special, okay?" He glanced at Moirin. She nodded. "Great," he said, putting up two fingers, confirming their request to the waitress.

"So, how is everything going so far? You have everything set up to start the study?" Moirin leaned toward the table, hands loosely folded in her lap.

"We do. The team is great and we're hitting the ground running."

"I met Steffie at the gala last week, and I was impressed by her composure during the meeting. Is she your only intern?"

"The college sent me quite a few applicants, and she's one of three that will be with us just for the summer. That should get us past the initial paperwork and organization piece."

"At this point, how much interaction does the PEP Board have? Do you submit reports, or are they hands-on?"

"Um, not much interaction. I was hired to run the project and report." Riggs sat back, cocked his head to one side and folded his arms. "Why all the questions? Is there something going on I should be aware of?"

Moirin took a sip of her water. "No, of course not. After the kick-off, I realized I didn't know the full project details. When Garrett Industries joined in, it was my father's decision. He's Chairman of the Board of Directors, and the sign-off came through them. A few weeks ago, he decided that, as COO, I should also be engaged in the project. I'll admit, I'm playing a little catch-up."

Riggs smiled and leaned forward, touching her arm. "That's great then, I'm happy to answer any questions you have. Anytime."

The waitress returned, carrying two plates. She slid one in front of each of them. They ate in silence for a while until Moirin posed the one question she truly wanted to ask. "Did you bring the property list?"

Riggs swallowed, dabbed his lips with the napkin, and nodded. He tossed the napkin on the table and brushed his hands together, swallowing again. "Got it right here," he said, picking up his phone.

Moirin was disappointed. Riggs had indicated on the phone that he wouldn't bring paper printouts, but she had hoped he might change his mind. Her memory was hardly eidetic, but she accepted the device he offered and squinted at the screen. He had taken photo images of three pages. In her quick perusal, she counted ten entries per page.

"What are you looking for? Maybe I can help." Riggs leaned forward, bracing his elbows on the table. The linen tablecloth slid, shoving his plate into the water decanter and tipping it over, drenching the table in water.

Riggs swore and jumped up, narrowly avoiding the river of water that cascaded onto his chair instead of his trousers. Two nearby busboys rushed in with towels to mop up the mess.

"Jeez, Moirin, I'm sorry. Did I get you wet?" His neck was red, and the blush crept up to his cheeks.

"No, not much. I need a minute. I'll be right back." Her fingers caught the handle of her purse, and she rushed to the ladies' room.

No water had landed on her, but, at that moment, she reacted like a seasoned clandestine spy. She still had Rigg's phone in her hand. In the privacy of the bathroom, she dug her own phone out of her bag and used it to take photos of the images on Rigg's device. She needed more time to review the list and wasn't above using this convenient accident to obtain a copy to study.

"There now, no harm done," she said brightly when she returned to the table, laying his cell phone on the now-bare surface. "So, I do have to go soon and head to another meeting, but may I ask a few questions first?"

"Sure, go ahead." Riggs seemed relieved she was ignoring his blunder. He slid the phone into his pocket.

"Is your approach for the study geographical? I'm wondering if you'll need access to our sites for the entire duration of the project or if you'll finish one site and move to the next."

"Yes, great question." He was back in his comfort zone and easily answered questions she had no interest in but posed for appearances' sake.

The check came, and she insisted on paying, thanking him for his indulgence in her questions. She assured him of Garrett's ongoing support for his study, requesting he call if he needed anything. She was relieved to shake hands and exit the restaurant.

The air was oppressively hot after the air conditioning of the restaurant, but she could breathe easier. It would have been simpler to tell Riggs of her suspicions about Gregorian, but until she knew their connection, the somewhat unscrupulous charade had been safer.

Now that she had pilfered the list, Moirin hesitated. After verifying the Garett addresses were what she'd submitted, she wasn't sure of the next step.

She'd overheard a small sliver of Gregorian's conversation, which she could have easily misunderstood. She needed someone with near-encyclopedic knowledge of land, property, and contamination factors. She only knew of one person who had those qualifications.

She thumbed through the contacts on her phone until she reached Seth Masterson, hitting on it to connect the call. She had cultivated a friendship with Seth, one of the Conservation Directors, after meeting years earlier when he was starting out as an ecological analyst. He had become a valuable resource, and she had come to rely on his knowledge and insight into land management and environmental impact.

As it rang, she hurried across the parking lot. The expanse of asphalt seemed to radiate heat upward. Sweat formed, running down the back of her neck as the hair at her temples dampened.

She glanced at her watch. One-fourteen. If she were lucky, he'd be back in his office from lunch. She was panting by the time she heard a voice at the other end. She had to stop walking to catch her breath and speak.

"Seth. Good afternoon. It's Moirin Garrett."

"Moirin, hello. It's been a while." Seth's tone was friendly, and she imagined him leaning back in his chair, ready as always to chit-chat before getting down to serious business. "How's everything going?"

She shifted her purse to dig out a key fob and continued towards her car, glancing around, trying to remember where she had parked. "Good, good. Thanks. How have you and Marilyn been? I missed seeing you at the Gala last week."

"All's well, yup. So much is going on with graduation, and the kids that Marilyn wasn't up for the gala this year. But I hear it was good. A lot of buzz on that PEP project."

"That's actually why I was calling, in a roundabout way. I wonder if you might have a minute that I could stop by and get your take on something with the in-state properties that will be included in the project. I'd rather not do this over the phone." Finally finding her car, she breathed a sigh of relief as she settled into the driver's seat and cranked the air conditioning.

"I'm intrigued. Sure, I can give you a few minutes if you could come by now."

"Great. I appreciate it. I'll be there shortly."

She drove to the utilitarian four-story building, unremarkable in both design and construction, an eyesore amongst the natural splendor surrounding it. It was ironic that something so ugly would house the resources to protect the beauty it blighted. The Colorado Department of Agriculture building housed offices for aquaculture, wildlife protection, livestock health, branding management services, and several conservation programs focused on air, soil, water, agriculture, and noxious weed management. Moirin worked with staff in several of these offices but rarely visited in person.

Her heels clicked against the tile flooring, the sound echoing off the smooth stone walls. The square security desk was unmanned, so she passed by. Her steps unconsciously quickened as she saw the open elevator door. She was still a few feet away when the door started to slide shut. A hand shot out, holding it for her.

"Thank you." She looked at the only other occupant. A man, several inches taller than her own five feet six inches, stood at the back. He had a medium build but seemed to fill the space, making it feel much smaller than a normal passenger elevator.

"Ma'am," he said, tipping his cowboy hat. It was a disarming gesture, a courtesy from a bygone era. First, the chivalry to hold the elevator, now gallant manners.

He had pulled his hat off with his left hand, running the other through his thick, dark hair before replacing it on his head. It was a smooth, practiced gesture that seemed more of a habit than anything else. Moirin caught a glimpse of an attractive man with a tight smile and intense brown eyes under heavy dark brows. He pressed the button for the third floor and looked at her, questioning, his hand hovering at the controls.

"I'm going to three as well." She nodded.

They rode in respectful silence, as one often does in an elevator with strangers. The tinny notes of nearly unrecognizable songs pumped out from hidden speakers. Hard-rock eighties music reimagined as soft, flowing harmony. She couldn't stop her mind from puzzling over the song. She scoffed aloud, then, remembering the cowboy in the elevator with her, she looked at him and shrugged with a smile, embarrassed by her near-snort. *Rock and roll all night,*" she said, turning her eyes upward.

"Ah, you're right." He started to say more, then stopped, grimaced, and shook his head. Moirin laughed outright. As he smiled, his eyes softened. Suddenly, they weren't awkward strangers in an impossibly small space—they were old pals sharing a joke.

The elevator door opened, and he stood back, allowing Moirin to exit first. She smiled and turned to the left, headed for Seth's office. She came to the end of the hallway. As she reached for the glass door, a hand shot out from her right and pulled on the handle.

The cowboy from the elevator. She frowned.

"I'm not stalking you, I swear," he said, holding the door open, waiting for her to enter.

There wasn't much damage he could do in a public office, so she entered, making a mental note to be aware of anyone following her outside the building. You couldn't be too careful these days.

Moirin stepped up to the counter and spoke through the small circle cut out from the glass window, giving her name to one of the clerks, indicating she was there to see Seth. The young blond woman seemed polite but uninterested as she instructed Moirin to have a seat and then returned to the paperwork on the counter. Three other clerks— two men and a woman — were busy at their own stations. Two of them stopped to look up when Moirin spoke. The noise of clacking keyboards, paper shuffling, telephones ringing, and machinery droning leaked out from the small hole. As she walked away, the sounds faded.

One of the other clerks shouted a greeting to the cowboy who had followed Moirin into the suite. "Jace. Hi. I'll let Gordon know you're here. Shouldn't be but a minute."

Moirin turned to the cowboy, who nodded at the clerk. "You must come here a lot," she said to him. It sounded like a bad pickup line from a bar scene in an eighties movie. "Like you have a standing appointment with someone," she added awkwardly.

"Yup. True enough." He took a seat in the closest empty chair, glancing first at the closed door to the inner sanctum of the office, then up at the screen of a large television bolted to the wall. Moirin followed his gaze. The farm report was on. Statistics and current pricing for crops filled the screen.

She sat down on a tan fabric-covered couch opposite him. Jace's eyes remain fixed on each new number as the screen changed. She had an odd urge to engage in conversation, as if they were old friends inclined to sit and chat. He seemed more inclined to ignore her; their brief connection in the elevator apparently had more impact on her than it had on him. It was just as well; flirting was not her strength, and, in the moment, she couldn't dredge up a single topic for small talk.

Pulling out her cell phone, she opened the image of the list she'd pilfered from Riggs' phone. Calling Seth had been an impulse, but no one else knew more about Colorado terrain, topography, and land use. She couldn't be sure what, if anything, was suspicious. Seth was one of the few people she'd be comfortable sharing that uncertainty with, and reasonably certain he'd approach the question as a puzzling riddle to solve.

She squinted at the screen. Based on the project scope, there should be addresses of commercial or industrial sites volunteered for testing to determine a particular industry's impact. For Garrett, she and Ian had selected one site where fracking had been done twenty years prior, two with active oil wells, one a partially completed solar field, and a vacant buffer property adjacent to their largest nuclear power plant. Because they were so diverse, the water and soil testing would return vastly different results. Still, Moirin and Ian felt confident that each would be within acceptable limits and ultimately reflect good stewardship.

She scanned the list, hoping some glaring element would appear, pinpointing Gregorian's nefarious plan. The print was tiny and unreadable, affording no clues. She huffed, throwing her phone back into her purse. She crossed her arms, crossed and recrossed her legs, barely able to keep from tapping her toes in frustration.

She glanced around the room, and her attention settled on Jace. He had taken his hat off, and it hung loosely from one hooked finger. Moirin could see his features clearly. He had a handsome but weathered look. There were deep creases at the corners of his eyes, likely from squinting in the sunlight that had tanned his skin to a deep brown. The strong set of his jaw made Moirin think the pleasantries in the elevator might have been out of character for him. His mustache and closely-cropped goatee were dark, but the goatee showed signs of salt-and-pepper at the tip of his chin. Wholly engrossed in the news report on the television, he seemed unaware of her comprehensive assessment.

She had known Seth long enough to trust him, and having worked on several complex projects, she was impressed by his knowledge. This request was unusual, but not illegal or even unethical. Except perhaps the manner in which she obtained the address list, which she kept deliberately vague.

As they sat in his office a few minutes later, Moirin gave him an abridged version of her interactions with Gregorian and what she'd overheard. He listened, frowning now and then, as she laid out the limited facts.

"I know what addresses I provided, and I can make sure those are the same. I just have no way of knowing anything about the rest of them. If Gregorian's messed with the list at all, I don't know what I'm looking for."

"How do you think I can help?" he asked.

"I was hoping you might be able to take a look. See if anything jumps out at you. If not, perhaps give me an idea of what I can do? I emailed a couple of pages to you." She smiled.

"Huh." He raised his eyebrow, but proceeded to tap on his computer keyboard, bringing up the list from his email server. "At first glance, it's just addresses. I'm not sure what you think I might see." He shook his head and sent the pages to his printer.

"Would you mind printing a copy for me?"

"Sure." He tapped the keyboard again, and the printer hummed to life. He grabbed the pages from the printer and skimmed through the list.

"It might be nothing. It's probably nothing. But you know me, Seth. If it's something, I can't let it go. If Gregorian has it in for this poor intern, or someone else, I worry what it might be. He could be harming a career, or worse, deliberately manipulating the study's results. Some kind of spite or fraud? With this guy, I just don't know, but I worry about it. I don't know who to talk to or who to trust. Riggs Robinson was hired by the Foundation to run the project. Since Gregorian is on the Foundation Board, Riggs might feel a loyalty there. I'd hate to put him in a tough spot."

Yeah, I see your problem." He sighed, rolled the pages in his hand, and then tapped them on the desk as he contemplated.

The printer silenced, so he reached back, grabbed the second copy, and passed it to her. She scanned the list, running her finger down the column to highlight the text.

A sharp rapping of three quick knocks vibrated the doorframe behind her head. Moirin jerked upright in her chair.

"Seth, can you pop down to Gordon's office? I gotta get done here and go."

Moirin shifted in time to catch sight of the dark-haired cowboy from the elevator leaning in from the hallway, hat dangling from one hand as he jerked a thumb directionally down the hall.

"Oh, sorry, ma'am. I didn't mean to interrupt." His eyes flicked over her, his apology clearly insincere, as he looked at Seth, this time jerking his head in the direction Moirin assumed was Gordon's office. "Seth, can you?"

Seth nodded and stood. "I'll be right back."

She opened and closed her mouth, like a fish gasping for air, Seth and Jace disappearing before she could respond. "Sure, I've got nothing but time," she said, addressing the empty room.

Seth was gone long enough for Moirin to study the list several times over. Ten minutes later, Seth returned, apologizing profusely.

"It's quite all right." Moirin's annoyance faded, feeling gracious. "I was the one who imposed on your day, and I appreciate your efforts to assist me. I was able to take a few minutes and review the list myself."

"What did you come up with?"

"Not much, I'm afraid. I need to compare this with my original list, but I don't think all five sites from Garrett are listed here. It's odd, but we can write it off as a clerical error."

"So, do you still want me to look at this?"

"If you could, I would be grateful. Besides ours, the rest of the addresses would be test sites from other industries. There's no way to know which one might have been altered or substituted by Gregorian. I don't know what his intentions are or who might be his target if he's trying to make someone look bad."

"I can run a quick look-up and see if anything looks odd. At a minimum, I could confirm that they'd all be industrial sites or which corporations own them."

"That would be a great start." The knot in her chest loosened. She hadn't realized the twisting pressure had been building until it relaxed.

He nodded, then stood up. "I'll check into it. I'll let you know if I find anything."

"I appreciate it, Seth. Thank you." She shook his hand. She appreciated the effort, but only time would tell if he could help or not.

Fortunately, the afternoon didn't give Moirin time to think about Seth or what he might find. Once back in her office, she tossed the printed pages on her desk and moved on to the pressing demands of running an international business.

She ended the day with the IT team giving an update on Ted's data problem. She was pleased with the progress, encouraged that the initial results didn't support the idea that the database was the problem. They promised all validation would be done and Ted would be able to proceed with his reports. That would solve at least one of her concerns. The quarterly and annual reports would be completed, and that was one more item the Board could be pleased about.

It was after five o'clock when Moirin left the office, but since the sun was still shining, she felt like a kid playing hooky from school. Until recently, a twelve-hour day had been standard for her. She had to remind herself that an eight-hour day wasn't ducking work. It was ensuring mental health.

She headed for the gym, but today her timing was off, and the next spin class didn't start for another hour. Instead of waiting, she opted for thirty minutes of circuit training followed by ten miles on the stationary bike. One day she might give in to Leslie and Jo's encouragement to try yoga, but for now, she preferred the high-octane endorphin rush of her current routine. When she couldn't handle rigorous workouts anymore, yoga might be something to consider.

She didn't believe Leslie's insistence that yoga was, in fact, a strenuous workout. Leslie constantly shared articles and fitness advice for *women our age*, courtesy of Leslie's sister Heather.

"She's an occupational therapist, so she knows how the body works." Leslie would say. "Plus, she's been married to a doctor for almost thirty years, so it's almost like she's a doctor too. You should listen to her."

Moirin had scoffed at that. Heather seemed to constantly add to the rules about what they should or shouldn't be doing to live longer. When did fifty-three become old anyway? She objected to changing her diet and said so. She had so few vices, so food shouldn't matter. Leslie had snapped at that. "What's the problem? Less sugar and salt. Less red meat. More stretching. Walk to keep your bones healthy." Leslie seemed adamant that somehow, more rules would equal a better life.

She kept listing items long after Moirin stopped listening. Resigned that neither Leslie nor Heather would ever stop sharing information, Moirin accepted the magazines, blog posts, email articles, and social media links that discussed every aspect of aging, sometimes in painful detail. Some she read, most she deleted or moved to a folder labeled 'Look at Later,' prioritized slightly above the junk folder.

For now, her diet and exercise routine are working just fine, thank you very much. Moirin chuckled at what she could imagine would be Leslie's response to that sentiment. It would probably generate another flurry of emails with links to podcasts and the latest medical discoveries about aging. Or some new hypothesis about how being close-minded would cut thirty-four minutes from her lifespan.

Once home, she was refreshed by a shower, but a few muscles ached, and her back felt stiff. She considered reaching for the bottle of all-purpose anti-inflammatory pain relievers, but that seemed like giving in to the weakness of an aging body. Instead, she opened a bottle of wine, poured a glass, and went into the living room. Turning on the stereo, her tension eased as the soft jazz swirled around her.

Before she could sit down, a competing tune emanated from her phone, increasing in volume until it drowned out the soothing jazz.

Frank Sinatra's *My Way*.

The ringtone she'd downloaded expressly for one person. She muted the stereo and answered the call.

"Hi, Mom."

"Hello, dear. Well, I just had to call with the most exciting news." Her mother's voice sounded breathless and almost giddy.

"Really? What's going on?"

"Evelyn from the Ladies' Club notified me today that the Woman of the Year nominations were out, and I am one of the finalists this year," Iris said.

"Congratulations," Moirin said. "That is such a prestigious award. You've never said anything, but I know you've coveted one of those." She raised her wineglass in a silent toast before taking a sip. Even though her mother couldn't see it, the salute was given.

Iris scoffed. "I suppose you know me, don't you, dear? Yes, I've always wanted one. It signifies the best of both worlds. It's recognition of professional accomplishment, but as we all know, it's quite the popularity contest."

"Oh, mom, you're my hero, you know that?" Moirin chuckled. "You've never been one to pander to others, so I think winning this particular popularity contest makes it that much sweeter for you."

"I'm glad I can set a standard for you, sweetheart." Iris sighed, and her tone changed. "But Ian called in the middle of the commotion. I thought it was about the nominations, but wouldn't you know, Felicity put him up to calling about golf. So, we've got a tee time for seven o'clock on Saturday." She moaned, sounding so pitiful that Moirin almost felt sorry for her.

"Oh, you'll enjoy yourself. You should do that more often," Moirin said. "You need to start working less and having more fun."

"Now you sound like your father. He thinks just because he's retired, I should be as well."

"Well, it wouldn't be the worst idea, Mom."

"Humph. Well, yes, something to think about. So, Ian tells me you're working hard yourself."

"No more than usual, I suppose. Maybe a few extra details to ensure the Board's vote."

"Yes, of course. You must ensure that. I'd like to see your name on the Woman of the Year nominations in the next round. Your father and I were talking about what you and Colin are focused on. Moving toward renewable energy sources is socially conscious. That's the type of thing that will get you noticed at a national level, especially with the environmental group study."

"I'm probably already known on a national level, but any good press is good for the company." Moirin raised her wineglass to take another sip, only to find it empty. How had that happened so quickly? Deciding one glass was enough for tonight, she set the empty goblet on the table.

"How is Dad doing?" Her mother often brushed off the health questions, despite Moirin's repeated efforts for details. Everything was fine, she insisted; they were both simply getting older with the minor inconveniences, aches, and pains that were to be expected. Moirin conceded after a few attempts, but not before admonishing her mother that should there ever be any serious health issues, she expected to be alerted immediately. She wasn't entirely convinced by her mother's assurances but had no choice but to trust.

Now that her father was retiring, Moirin hoped that her mother would slow down as well. That hope was equal parts concern that her mother would be present to help her father and that she would relax and enjoy life. Life beyond work. Exactly what her friends often pestered her about.

Jo and Leslie seemed to have found balance, sure, but their jobs weren't nearly as demanding as hers. Heather's career required more commitment, but she was divorcing now, so how well had that worked out? Moirin's mother was the only one she knew who had a fulfilling career and a family, but for years, the two were hardly balanced. Would her mom ever try to relax more to enjoy retirement with her husband? Who knew how that would work out?

If Iris ever came to a balanced compromise, there might be hope that Moirin could as well. She just needed to make time to meet someone. She scoffed. *Add that to the list.*

8

The following Tuesday, her workday started with a staff meeting, interrupted by an irate overseas supplier demanding to speak with her. Before transferring the call, the finance manager briefed her about several discrepancies between a project manager's budget and the finance office's purchase order approvals. The result was the supplier being partially paid on several invoices. It wouldn't normally require action from Moirin's level, but the supplier was crucial and threatening to cut off further deliveries. Not something she would want the Board to get wind of, so she gave it her full attention. When that issue was settled, two more followed, of course, requiring immediate resolution. It seemed it was going to be one of those days.

After resolving the third issue, she enjoyed a cup of coffee and read through the messages in her crammed email inbox. One midway down the screen caught her attention. It was from Seth. She set her cup down, leaning forward to focus on the screen.

The subject read: *Not much, but a start.* Her interest piqued, she clicked to print the attachment when a muffled knock sounded from her door. She looked up to see a pair of khaki pants topped by a huge bouquet of flowers.

"Hello? Can I help you?"

"Ms. Garrett? I have a delivery here for you," the bouquet said, bobbing.

Moirin looked closer and saw that the large glass vase was gripped by two thin arms wrapped around the base. The arrangement was almost a foot wide and was bound to be heavy.

"Here, let me help you before it pulls you over," she said, rushing to the door. "How did you ever get up here without tripping over something?"

A giggle floated through the blooms. "It wasn't easy, Ms. Garrett. But I got it here in one piece."

There was an audible sigh from the petite mail clerk as she was relieved of the burden. Moirin set it down on the coffee table and stepped back to admire the arrangement. The vase was overflowing with two dozen large tulips in half a dozen brilliant colors. The large floral display changed the entire atmosphere of the room. She looked from the flowers to the clerk and back again. It wasn't her birthday, and the flowers had a more personal feel than that of a professional appreciation gift.

"There's a card in there," the clerk said, pointing.

Moirin blinked. "Yes, of course. Thank you for bringing these up."

She dug the card out from the blossoms and tore open the sealed envelope. She looked down at the flowers again, the playful, riotous colors bringing a smile to her face as she read the message.

Sorry for interrupting your meeting. A busy day isn't an excuse for being rude to a pretty lady. May I take you to dinner to apologize? -Jace

On the last line was a telephone number.

She stared at it, reading the words several times. A chuckle escaped as she thought of the moment in the elevator. She felt a flutter of emotion, something reminiscent of the giddy feeling from high school days when she developed a crush on a cute boy. She laughed outright at the fanciful thought.

Still smiling and clutching the card in her hand, she returned to her desk. She tucked the card in the drawer and pulled the page she'd printed from Seth's email.

Her smile faded, replaced with a frown as she read through the short note. Emotion coursed through her, pulsing out as toe-tapping nervous energy. A knot of tension formed in her chest as she re-read the message. A second time, then a third.

Reaching over, she picked up the office phone and dialed Seth's number. "Moirin, what a pleasant surprise," he said, answering on the first ring.

"Hi. I know. I haven't talked to you in months, and here I am bothering you two days in a row."

"No bother," he said. "I guess you saw my email."

"Yes, just now. Am I reading this right?" She desperately wished for an error, but knew Seth wouldn't make a mistake like this.

"Your mystery got my curiosity going, so I stayed late last night and poked around a bit. Turns out, it didn't take too long. I looked up a few of the addresses. None were flagged for any issues, but that would be expected for the project. Since there wasn't much in our system, I checked the state property database as well. Most of the addresses were industrial or commercial properties, all owned by businesses involved in the PEP project. All except this one. I thought maybe you got one of your personal properties on the list by mistake," Seth said.

"I don't understand. Somehow, only four of the Garrett properties are on the PEP list, and I'm guessing our fifth one has been replaced by something you're telling me has *my* name as the property owner. Which is odd because my condo is the only property I own."

"Well, it seems like you were right to be worried about this list of yours. I'd recommend a little more digging into what your friend might be up to."

Moirin tapped her finger on the desk as she frowned at the email. Fingers of uncertainty crawled up her neck as a sense of dread grew in the pit of her stomach. This wasn't about Steffie. Gregorian was launching an attack against Garrett Industries, or against Moirin personally. This could be the start of a plan to besmirch the reputation of both. Now that she was aware, she had the upper hand and at least an opportunity to figure out his plan and stop it.

"Thanks, Seth. I appreciate it."

"Glad I could help," Seth said.

Moirin glanced at the massive flower arrangement hulking on the table. She pushed aside the disturbing thoughts of Gregorian. "So, while I've got you on the phone, let me ask you something else."

"Okay, shoot." She could hear the squeak of his chair as he adjusted in the seat.

She hesitated. "Ah, well, I'd like your opinion on something. Some*one* actually."

"Really?"

"In your office yesterday, the man who interrupted us. Jace. I didn't get his last name. I got the impression he worked there."

"Oh, yes. You mean Jace Caradova."

"So, you know him then? Is he an okay guy?" Moirin asked, cringing at how the question sounded. Shades of high school.

"Yeah, yeah. Solid. Brand inspector for the State. Has a cattle ranch in the area. I was sort of expecting your call." His voice carried a chuckle.

"You were? And why is that?"

"He stopped by after you left and asked about you. Said you talked briefly. He overheard you tell one of the ladies up front you were here to see me," Seth said.

"What did you tell him?" Maybe she was turning into an adolescent girl again after all. Next, she'd be asking Seth if he would pass Jace a note in study hall.

"Oh, less than he could get from a business card. Just your name and where you worked. Why?"

"He sent me flowers with a written invitation to dinner. Before I proceed, I wanted to get your take on him." The adolescent girl was gone, and now she sounded like she was considering him for a job. Moirin rolled her eyes.

"Well, well. You musta made quite an impression on him." Seth's tone changed from teasing to thoughtful. "He's a good man, Moirin. No worries there."

"Thanks, Seth. I appreciate that," she said, hanging up.

She sifted the pending stack at the front of her desk. She found the page she had given Seth the day before and compared it with the email attachment she'd just printed.

She rummaged through her desk and pulled out a third list, the one Ian had brought to her office the day of the PEP meeting. She smoothed the page, running the palm of her hand from top to bottom. She placed the first two pages on either side.

She opened the corporate asset tracking program and typed in the first address. *No records found.*

The list from Riggs contained all the addresses that were approved for the project. Garrett Industries had offered five for testing. Seth had noted the corporate ownership of each address on this list. Moirin recognized most from the kickoff meeting. Delvin-Smoothers, LGK, Fester & Foss, and one in the name of Moirin Garrett. She looked at the property record attachment that Seth had included, which showed her name. Her stomach twisted again.

She needed to figure out what Gregorian had done, and fast. This was the last thing she needed with the extra attention on her every move. She entered the address in her phone's GPS app to check the location. It was only ninety minutes south. She could easily make the drive and investigate the property. On the way, she could make a few phone calls and have more records research completed.

First thing tomorrow, she would get records from the clerk's office. She needed to know when it was purchased, who filed the property deed, and who had been paying the taxes. How had someone set up such a complicated ruse? Resolved to get ahead of whatever game Gregorian was playing, having a plan eased her panic, although it was going to be a long night of worry waiting for the county offices to open tomorrow. Still, she had beaten him once before, and she'd do it again. She had to. The stakes were much higher this time.

Her cell phone dinged a meeting reminder. *Girls night dinner.* Her first thought was that she couldn't possibly. Too much was going on right now, and she needed to focus on work. Just as quickly, she realized it couldn't have come at a better time. She could use the distraction so she wouldn't drive herself crazy all night.

Before she had time to change her mind again, Moirin threw files and notes in her briefcase and hurried out the door. She had skipped too many of these nights recently, and the support of friends might be the perfect antidote for the stress building up and threatening to suffocate her.

Moirin looked at the unoccupied chair, piled with purses, then back at the faces of her friends. "Heather's not coming tonight?"

Leslie shook her head.

"I talked to her yesterday. It was a bad weekend." Jo's lips pressed together into a thin line.

"What happened?" She looked first to Jo, then to Leslie. The three were at one of their favorite restaurants that offered great food and a casual ambiance. They aimed to have dinner together every Tuesday but managed only two or three times a month. Tonight was one of those nights. She had been wrapped up in her special projects, but she needed a break and wasn't about to miss this opportunity. Last week, she remembered a day late to text an apology for standing them up.

"Such a shame." Jo clucked her tongue.

"What's a shame?" Moirin asked.

"This divorce has been so hard on her," Leslie said, shaking her head in disgust. "Heather wanted to do a mother-daughter spa day with Camila for her birthday, but Camila had dinner with her dad instead. Then, she said she was too busy to spare any other time the whole weekend. She actually texted a thank-you when Heather left a voicemail wishing her a happy birthday."

"Oh, that's terrible. How could her own daughter do that?" Moirin asked.

"It's Tabor's influence, I think. He's her father, so she wants to be like him. She'd do anything for his approval. I know it's been a tough couple of years for Camila, but she's getting ready to move out of state for medical school now. Heather's been so supportive, but c'mon, she needs to insist on respect." Leslie's lips twisted into a bitter smile, "I was there when Camila told her straight up she couldn't understand because she wasn't an MD. She said "Dad's a *doctor*, so he knows. Mom, you're just an Occupational Therapist, so you've never had the same coursework pressure.""

"She didn't," Moirin gasped. "That little snot did not say that to her own mother, did she? Heather has a Master's Degree for heaven's sake."

Leslie leaned forward and fairly hissed. "She said all that and then some. Totally oblivious to how hurtful it was. I can't believe my own niece could be so mean. Heather's been a great mom, and you know I'm not saying that because she's my sister."

"Poor thing. No wonder Heather wasn't up for dinner tonight. I hate to hear this, though. She's only had a few months to adjust to being in that big house by herself." Moirin took a sip of her water.

"Well, that's only going to be a matter of time, too. Tabor's moving pretty fast with the divorce. Once they settle things, the house will be sold, and Heather will be looking for a new place to live," Leslie said.

"Separated on May Day, divorced by Columbus Day. Thirty years gone — just like that." Jo snapped her fingers with a flick of her wrist.

"I feel awful that I haven't tried to connect with her more. It's been a few weeks since she came to one of these Tuesday dinners, but I've been so busy since then...." Moirin's apology trailed off.

"It's fine," Leslie said, "but don't think we didn't see you sneak your phone out of your purse to check it." She looked at Jo, who nodded in agreement. "You know the rules — no work during girls' dinner. You owe the table a round."

"Fine, fine, I'm sorry. I'm putting it away." Moirin stuffed the phone back into her bag and turned to Jo. "I'm sorry, so Heather, then." She motioned for Jo to continue.

"Yeah, I think other than this setback with Camila, she's actually okay. She did that yoga retreat with us, and I'm trying to get her to go out on a date."

"Dating? You've got to be kidding," Moirin worked to keep her mouth from gaping open. "She's barely separated."

"She needs this," Leslie said. "I'm not pushing her to date, really. Just start considering the idea of spending time with someone. Maybe meet some new people. I sort of told her she needed to do it for me. That I was ready to start dating again and wanted moral support. I told her we'd sign up for a dating service together, you know, something easy online."

It was hard to imagine Leslie using a dating service. Men usually fell over themselves to talk with her. Moirin was envious that, despite the difficult decades Leslie had endured as an adult, her skin was nearly perfect and devoid of crow's feet and scowl lines. She swore she'd never had Botox, but Moirin wondered. It already wasn't fair that Leslie's tawny-blond hair had just the right amount of pale gold that grey hairs became silver and blended in naturally in the wavy locks cascading below her shoulders.

Moirin couldn't think of a worse idea than Leslie getting involved in online dating. So much could go wrong. Leslie's ex-husband would certainly see that as a poor role model for their pre-teen boys. She had a troubled history but finally turned her life around in the past few years. Her boys had only recently agreed to spend time with her, but she still had a long way to go to rebuild their trust. Why would Leslie risk a man interfering with that? But, looking at her now, Leslie seemed unconcerned about the potential consequences.

"Maybe just put a profile up, to make Heather feel better. Doesn't mean I have to go out with anyone," Leslie shrugged. "But I can take a look and see what's out there, right?"

Jo laughed. "I told you almost the same thing the other night, Moirin. Except you've already seen the man and he's interested."

Leslie's head swiveled in Moirin's direction. "What? There's a new man?" Leslie said, drawing her words out slowly. "Oh, do tell."

"No, I'm too busy with work. I'm left with my unpleasant interactions with Gregorian Plankett and a professional association with Mr. Riggs Robinson. Neither of whom is dateable."

"Well, I see." Leslie blinked a few times, then sat back in her chair. "I see." She was granted a few extra minutes to process the information because two servers appeared loaded with plates and drink refills.

"Psst," Jo leaned toward Leslie and stage-whispered, "Is it just me, or do you feel like she's leaving something out?"

Moirin took the opportunity to check her email discreetly. She had felt her phone vibrate several times and was again compelled to violate the no-work-at-girls'-dinner policy.

"Ah-hem," Leslie cleared her throat loudly enough for occupants at a neighboring table to look over. "We see you, Moirin. You don't have the gift for clandestine activities. Put it back, and let's listen to Jo tell us all about her dating prospects." She motioned to the waitress. "That's two rounds on you now."

"Oh, good, I need more wine. I, unfortunately, have no dating prospects." Jo said mournfully. "I work with a bunch of youngsters, and the only age-appropriate men in my life are the contractors bidding for my roof project. And all of them seem to have plumber's fashion sense if you get my drift."

"Oh, you're awful." Leslie giggled. "Surely there are better options. I don't know where to find them, but maybe after dinner we can cruise around like we're eighteen and on the prowl again."

"Ah, tempting but no." Jo shook her head emphatically. "At our age, what can we expect, really? I'm too young to be done living but too old to be looking for passion and romance. Let's face it, we'll never be eighteen again."

"That's a depressing thought," Moirin said.

"No way. I don't accept that. I've had too much crap in my life to think that *all* the good days are behind me." Leslie waved her hands. "Wait, wait...I know. Most of the crap was my own fault, I'll admit it. But now, I'm finally getting it together. I want to find friendship and love. What if Heather's right with all her wellness stuff, and we live another forty years or more? I don't want to be alone that long."

"Exactly my point. Imagine celebrating a twenty-fifth wedding anniversary," Jo said with a sigh.

Moirin felt a wave of emotion she couldn't quite put a name to. "Technically, yes, it's possible. Get married in the next year or two, then, sure, you could celebrate a twenty-fifth before you're eighty. And there's no reason to think we couldn't all live to be in our eighties."

"Would you want to risk it, though?" Leslie said.

"What risk? Look at me," Jo said. "Between my parents, Erik, the miscarriages…my whole life has been surrounded by death, but I'm still here. I'm still living."

"You're right. Life is a risk. And love is a risk. Look at Heather. After thirty years, Tabor walks out. No warning. You don't have any guarantee," Leslie said.

"But she's not giving up," Moirin said, pointing her fork in Jo's direction. "She'll get out there again, I'd bet."

"Yeah, well, it's not the same," Jo sighed deeply.

Moirin and Leslie were silent, watching as Jo fiddled with the straw in her iced tea. "What's all this really about, then, Jo?" Moirin asked.

"Everything I've said is true." Jo looked up and flexed her jaw before continuing. "But it's about money too. It's been tough being alone, and now I'm afraid of running out of money when I'm too old to do anything about it."

"Honey, why would you be worried about that? You own your house, you still work, and you invested Erik's life insurance money, didn't you?" Moirin knew Jo wasn't wealthy ,but never thought she had financial difficulties.

Jo looked from Moirin to Leslie. "I feel like my savings are getting drained with constant house repairs, and health insurance keeps going up every year. Since I turned fifty, there are more discounts on stuff, but it's not enough. Doctor visits and medication are getting more expensive. Medicare doesn't kick in for another eleven years. *Eleven years*. And by then, who knows what things will look like? Maybe Medicare or Social Security won't even exist. So, I need to keep working. I just *have* to. But what if I can't? What would I do?" Jo's voice had risen to a shrill level by her last question.

"Whoa, Nellie, slow down. You're making a big pile of stress there." Leslie's tone was low and soothing as she tried to halt Jo's tirade. She patted Jo's hand. "Breathe. One thing at a time, honey."

Jo's eyes welled with tears. She blinked rapidly to push them back as she cleared her throat.

Moirin reached out and grasped her other hand. "It's all going to be okay. We'll make sure of it. If you want to date or marry someone, you do that, or you stay single, it's your choice. But do not, I repeat, do not think marriage is a solution because you're worried about money. We will help you figure this out. You know we're here for you, right?"

Jo drew in a shaky breath as she pulled her hands back, patting Leslie and Moirin's hands after she let go. She brought her hands together at her mouth and blew into them as if she were warming up cold fingers. "What would I do without you guys? I didn't mean to throw everything out there like that. I'm sorry. I guess I'd been holding it in too long."

"What are friends for?" Leslie smiled gently as if afraid a bigger expression would break Jo's fragile composure.

"Yes, well, of course, you're both right. I'm fine for now. Everything's going to be great. I'm sure I'm worried for nothing." Jo sat up straight and shook her head emphatically, then abruptly changed the topic of conversation. "So, after all this talk, I think I need to check in on Heather more often. She's not tough enough for the dating pool right now."

"I'd have to agree. Let her find herself first, get seasoned a little as a single." Moirin followed Jo's lead and let the lighthearted tone take over.

"Oh, really? You're well-seasoned. When's the last time *you* were out on a date?" Leslie said.

"Well, okay, yes, it's been a while."

"See? It would be good for you to meet someone." Leslie said.

"I don't have any trouble meeting someone. I got flowers today from someone I just met." As soon as the words left her mouth, Moirin could have bitten her own tongue. She hadn't intended to share that tidbit. She swore silently.

For a moment, Jo and Leslie stared at her, and then Jo started laughing. Leslie joined in, shaking her finger at Moirin.

"I knew it." Jo's voice was triumphant.

"Oh, aren't you the coy one." Leslie grinned as she reached out and gathered the empty plates and dirty dishes from the table, making a show of clearing the space between them. She stacked everything in the empty place setting. After using her napkin with exaggerated care to wipe the crumbs from the table, she placed her palms on the edge of the table and leaned in. "Details. Now."

Moirin joined Leslie and Jo's laughter. She could see the stress evaporate from Jo's face and realized her own anxiety was temporarily gone as well. It was the magical power of a good friendship. Even without sharing every detail, they all felt better knowing they could count on each other.

The thought flashed through her mind as she considered how much to share with her friends. Moirin looked from Jo to Leslie. She couldn't hold back the smile. "All right, all right. So, I had a meeting at the Ag Department yesterday. There was a man I rode the elevator with; we exchanged basic pleasantries, spent a few moments together in the waiting room. Later, he walked in on my meeting with Seth. After I left, he went back and asked Seth for my card so he could send me flowers." She shrugged. "His name is Jace. He's a brand inspector for the State and was there to meet with his boss."

When she told them what he had written on the card, Jo and Leslie sighed together. "Aawwwww..."

"And what did you say when you called him? Are you going out with him?" Jo asked.

"No, um, I don't know. I haven't called him yet."

"Why not?" Leslie demanded. "You have to, Moirin. A chance meeting like that with a guy who's age-appropriate, gainfully employed, and handsome? You just can't not."

"Ugh, grammar, Leslie, please!" Moirin said. "But you're right. I was thinking about calling him. The flowers were a nice touch. I only met him for a moment, but there was something about him I liked. I'm busy at work. I don't know, maybe I can find time for a date or two, I think. I might call him."

Leslie and Jo groaned simultaneously.

"Okay, I'll *probably* call him."

"You should definitely call him." Leslie nodded emphatically before saluting Moirin with her wineglass.

9

"Great, that takes care of the first three items. What's next?" Moirin looked up from the sheaf of papers to find Wanda's attention fixed on a spot behind her shoulder.

She didn't need to turn around. A light scent of crisp green grass with a hint of apples emanated from the vase of Jace's tulips, which commanded nearly a foot of space on the surface behind her. Moirin had placed them there because they were too distracting sitting in front of her on her desk. She found her own attention had been drawn to the blooms countless times since they had arrived. She had reluctantly moved them to a less distracting spot behind her chair.

Instead of distracting Moirin, they now distracted Wanda, who kept frowning when her eyes shifted in that direction. Moirin thought she knew why. As her trusted assistant, Wanda was a confidant, privy to many aspects of Moirin's activities that others were not. Wanda knew she hadn't been on a date in quite some time. No doubt the woman's curiosity was in overdrive, especially since the small envelope that came with the flowers was safely stowed in Moirin's purse, thwarting any attempt she might make to identify the sender.

"Wanda?"

A slight red crept up her assistant's neck, coloring the curved edges of her chins before flushing her rounded cheeks. "Sorry. It's just that, well, wow. Those are really something. You make an impression on someone at that gala last week?" She clucked her tongue and nodded at the arrangement.

Moirin couldn't suppress a smile. "They're beautiful, aren't they? But no, no one you could find on any of the invitee lists. You'll have to wonder." She hadn't called Jace yet, as she told Leslie the night before, she'd probably call. Likely. At the very least, to thank him for the flowers. And dinner might be nice.

Wanda sighed heavily. At forty-two, she was a self-proclaimed old maid and lived vicariously through others. The romantic dalliances and escapades of fellow employees made for excellent gossip, and Wanda was at the center of the office rumor mill.

"Well, then. I suppose we'll move on," Wanda said with a slight grin, then schooled her features into a more serious expression as she consulted the papers on her lap. "The quarterly reports are being assembled for the board meeting at the end of the month." Moirin nodded as Wanda continued. "The departmental finance reports have all been submitted, and I've saved them on the secure server for you. Oh, and Colin apologized for the delay, but he's printing a copy of something or other report to your meeting in," Wanda stopped to consult her watch, "fifteen minutes."

"Something or other report?" Moirin raised an eyebrow. Wanda was rarely imprecise.

Her assistant shrugged. "He was talking fast, mumbling, I don't know. Frankly, I'm pretty proud I picked up on the word *report*."

"Moirin. Hey. Are you ready for us?" Colin walked into the office without waiting for an answer. He settled himself on the couch and dropped a pile of papers on the coffee table. He seemed relaxed.

"Or, now, I guess." Wanda laughed and stood up.

"Yes, I can't wait to hear about your progress, Colin." Moirin grabbed a notepad as she stood up from the desk and moved toward the seating area. "Thank you, Wanda."

"Dad was just coming down the hall. He should be here in a minute."

"That's okay. It will give us a minute to chat." Moirin sat down in one of the chairs adjacent to the couch. She clipped her pen to the notepad before she tucked it in her lap, folding her hands on top of it. She was pleased with the unexpected opportunity for the two of them to speak privately. "What's the update on the Oklahoma project? Did the vendor resolve the transport issue?"

"Yes, thank you for your advice on that one. It's amazing how quickly a problem can get solved when the threat of financial penalty is dangling."

"Excellent. Glad I could help out," Moirin said. "And everything else is going well? On the home front? I was talking with Aunt Aggie the other day, and she asked about Brittany. I realized it has been a while since we've gotten together."

"She's doing well. She doesn't want to do much that doesn't involve the kids right now. This fall, Ryan will go off to college, and Megan will head to Florence for her semester abroad. Brittany will have a few months with a temporary empty nest, she says."

"A temporary empty nest?"

"Yes. It will be just the two of us until Christmas, when Megan comes back. She'll finish up her senior year here in Colorado, and then we'll see what she decides for college."

"She's just finished her junior year, right? Isn't she working on applications now?"

"She is, yes. I think making that list would be easier if she'd settle on a field of study." Colin growled.

"A bit undecided, is she?" Moirin stood up and motioned to the water pitcher on the credenza. "You want something?" Colin nodded, and she poured two glasses of water, then put them both on the table before she sat back down.

"Do you know which way she's leaning?" Moirin asked. "Has she said anything about what she wants to do?"

"I'm not sure Megan knows what she wants to do with her life. But I *am* sure Brittany will push her to pick a college close to home. At least then, she'd have one of the kids nearby. When Ryan got into Stanford, he was so excited. He never saw how much it upset his mom to think of him going off to California." Colin shook his head with a rueful smile.

Moirin knew he was proud of his son, and the distance to California didn't bother him. In a few years, Ryan would be back and take his proper place working at the family company. Garrett Diversified would benefit from the superior education the boy would get. Like Colin, Moirin was less emotional about the separation than Brittany.

"I suppose most mothers feel that way." Moirin shrugged. "Well, not mine, of course, but most."

Colin smiled. "Aunt Iris has always been more career-oriented. It hasn't done you any harm, it seems. My wife is more concerned with the happiness of her children than their success. It would likely suit her fine if they were smiling every day, even if they were penniless and had to live with us the rest of their lives."

"Well, that would avoid her empty nest then, wouldn't it? How do you feel about them moving out and moving on? Looking forward to it being the two of you alone again?"

"I'm hoping she'll pick up some new hobbies, maybe find some new friends." Colin reached down and took a long drink from one of the glasses. "I'm like you, Moirin. I work long hours and won't apologize for loving the job. That's not going to change for me any time soon."

She nodded. She agreed but constantly felt like she *should* apologize. It was unfortunate that society seemed to approve of that attitude when it came from a man, but not so much when it was a woman.

Colin waved his hand as he continued. "And, honestly, I would imagine over the next ten years, this place will take up even more of my time. You and Dad will both be retired, and I'll take charge. Ryan will work with me. In twenty years, it'll be me preparing for him to take over, but that's a long time from now." He scowled and shrugged again. "Brittany's going to have to find something else to do with her time until then."

Moirin felt a sharp pang. Ten years? Her own retirement was many years away, certainly not something she'd even begun to consider. Right now, she was looking forward to Ian's retirement and taking over as CEO in mere months. She hadn't thought about the time when she'd be put out to pasture or even pushed out to make way for Colin and Ryan. Apparently, Colin had thought about it. If she were to think about it, her estimate would be fifteen to twenty years. It seemed that in his mind, that day might be far sooner than she was planning.

"Ah, I see you two have started without me." Ian's voice boomed as he stomped into the office with the force of a hurricane wind. He threw himself on the sofa next to Colin, the breath wheezing out of him as he dropped his hands between his knees. "What'd I miss?" A tuft of silver-gray hair swayed at the top of his head as if uncertain whether it should fall to the right or left. Undecided, it stood straight up.

"Nothing yet. You're right on time." She launched into her prepared list of topics, leading the discussion. She knew how rare it was to work with family and not have power struggles or disagreements, and she valued their work harmony. Occasionally, Moirin had spirited debates with Uncle Ian, usually over mitigation of environmental impacts, but they had never truly been at odds.

Today, they had little dispute as they reviewed topics from income statements, the departmental budgets, and the quarterly report being readied for the upcoming Board of Directors meeting.

"These are all ready to assemble and create the annual report?" Ian flipped through the printed pages. "I heard you had a problem with the quarterly reports, and the annual was running behind."

"No, a minor issue, but it was resolved." Moirin was relieved that the IT department had finally resolved the data issue, and Ted sent a corrected report. She had hoped to keep it under wraps, but apparently enough people knew that it had worked its way back to Ian. She gave as little information as possible. "The first drafts in the alternative energy sector, specifically hydro, showed troubling results, but we were able to find the error and correct it."

"Hrumph." Ian cleared his throat and gave her a hard look. "You did now, yes? We're solid on these numbers? You're sure?"

Moirin studied his face, looking for clues to his agitation. It was unusual for him to question her work, and his disbelieving tone was out of character. "Yes, absolutely. I verified them myself. We can move on and look at the forecast for next year in these areas."

Ian sighed, dropping one stack on the table and picking up the other. He rubbed his eyebrow, and Moirin noticed the circles under his eyes. She decided to cut some of the details she'd planned to share so they could end the meeting sooner. There was no need to bring Ian in on any more minor details.

Thirty minutes later, she checked the last item off the agenda. Ian paced the room as Moirin and Colin exchanged final notes. He stood at her desk, turning pages and flipping open file folders stacked there.

"That's it then. Great job, Colin," she said, turning her head to stretch her neck. "What's on your mind, Ian? I can tell the way you're prowling around there's something else we need to talk about."

"Well, on that note, I'm out of here." Colin laughed as he gathered his belongings and darted into the hallway.

"It's a big deal, what we're talking about doing with the corporate structure," he said without preamble. "Any time a business changes its CEO, there's an impact on the business. Charles has been pushing it, and I agreed, but I'm not sure it's the right time." He paced back and forth in front of the window.

Defying all logic, her heart simultaneously sank as her stomach rose, expanding to block her throat. She coughed and stood up. "We're on a solid path, stable, in a manageable growth phase. I think the time *is* right." She spouted all the right buzzwords and key phrases.

"I don't know. Are you ready?"

Moirin chuckled. "Absolutely. I've prepared my entire life for the job. I've worked every hour of my professional career for this company, never held a job anywhere else."

"You know, I never have either." He stopped and stared out at the mountain, arms crossed and a pensive look on his face. "What will I do now? I'm only sixty-nine."

The knot in her chest eased. She wanted to hug him to ease his worries, like soothing a forlorn child. It was retirement jitters, not second thoughts.

"You are going to enjoy time with your wife. Love your grandchildren and spoil the new great-grandbaby when he or she arrives. Enjoy the time. There's a reason why they call it the golden years."

"Gold, huh," he snorted. "Well, yes, enough of this now." He struck his hands together as if brushing off dust and left her office.

She knew her time was coming, but not for many years yet. Retirement would follow a successful tenure as CEO. This was her season to enjoy her career success. Or would be when the Board voted its seal of approval. To that end, she reached across the desk and used her fingertips to drag the manila envelope closer. She untwisted the twine and dumped the contents on the desk.

A summary document topped the stack. She skimmed the items. The process was less than what an external candidate would be subjected to. None was unreasonable; it was simply unnecessarily complicated. A silly exercise in wasted time. Verification of credentials and educational records, professional organizations, supervisor and subordinate interviews, and a background check, including criminal, credit, and social media. Fortunately, the last item was nearly nonexistent. Who had time for social media?

She had been doing the job for years now; having Ian step aside would essentially only change her business card. The vetting process seemed intrusive, but as her father had said, she had nothing to hide. That she knew of anyway. To be certain, there were a few tasks she needed to finish. Namely, chase down the shenanigans being perpetrated by Gregorian and the mysterious property. She tossed the papers onto her desk. There was no time like the present to take decisive action.

It was one of those rare afternoons with no meetings scheduled, so she took full advantage of the opportunity. It was only two-thirty, which meant she could be at the mystery property by four, with plenty of daylight hours left.

She straightened the diminished piles of work and packed up her briefcase. She turned to grab her jacket from the back of her chair and caught sight of the flowers. She hadn't realized she was frowning until she felt the tension leave her temples. The flowers would brighten up the condo, and she would enjoy them more at home than here at the office.

She shifted her briefcase's shoulder strap and picked up the vase, carrying it to the car. A smile was still playing around her lips when she merged onto the interstate.

10

Ninety minutes later, Moirin checked the map against her notes. Her early start allowed her to avoid the evening commuter traffic through Denver. This far southeast of the city, she was in unfamiliar territory. Uninhabited, barren territory. Anticipation fueled her interest in what would otherwise be a dull and uneventful drive.

She had called in a favor with a contact at a local title company to run a records search. She wanted to keep this under the radar for now, in case Gregorian had a few more unpleasant surprises. She wasn't sure how an unknown property ended up with her name on it, but there weren't many positive possibilities. She hoped she'd be able to reverse or resolve the issue before it came to light. It was irritating that she needed to be clandestine about it, though; she prided herself on honesty and transparency.

Before anything else, she needed to see things first-hand. She was accustomed to assessing data and reports, but that's when she trusted the source. Somehow, Gregorian had changed the PEP list, but she wasn't sure of his intent. It was worth the drive to see what was there. To survey it firsthand. She hoped for evidence of buildings, an employee to interview, or some evidence of, well, *something*. Generally, keep an eye out for anything suspicious. She hated being away from the office, but if there was anything to see here, it was better to visit during business hours than on the weekend.

The car's tires crunched on the gravel drive as she turned in slowly. Less than fifty feet from the county road, a rusted chain blocked the drive.

A yellowed, rusted sign was attached to the chain. NO TRESPASSING. Similar notices were posted on trees lining the roadway. The undergrowth was dense enough that she couldn't see onto the property itself, but hints of tire tracks disappeared into the vegetation. She got out and surveyed the area. There were no signs of current inhabitants. She hesitated, but the need to know won out over the trespassing sign. If she were caught, she hoped the penalty would be minor. As she pulled the chain from the post where it was hooked, she prayed she would not be caught. For as rusty as it was, the chain moved with surprising ease. Leaving it lying on the ground, she returned to the car and drove in.

At first glance, it had the elements of some commercial operation. A large concrete pad lay to the left. She recognized the layout and equipment, though they were outdated. It was a hydraulic fracturing well pad, obviously not in operation for quite some time, based on the stands of weeds and vegetation growing unchecked.

She parked the car and plucked several plastic storage bags, two pairs of disposable nitrile gloves, and an ink pen from the center console. The car door echoed like a cannon in the silence. Dressed in jeans, a plain tee-shirt, and sneakers, she felt uncomfortably casual. Her attire only lent to the surreal sensation of this moment. The air was odd here. Deserted by humans but still teeming with life. At first, it was quiet — the unique quiet of an abandoned property, but within minutes, sounds of nature took over.

Crickets chirped, birds sang, and leaves rustled in the light breeze. The air was clean and smelled of fresh growing things, but the ground around her was ugly. The concrete and steel, unrecognizable rusted metal scraps, and piles of rock rubble blighted the area. She had seen many sites like this when she first started at Garrett. It was the stark reality of drilling and the thing that drove her to practice environmentally-responsible energy production. It wasn't supposed to be like this.

She turned in a circle, taking in the details around her. What a waste. She could rationalize the need for equipment with concrete and steel supports for drilling sites, but this was depressing and sad. There didn't seem to be much going on. She took a step and then paused, unsure of her objective. She was at the edge of her comfort zone, attempting this bizarre on-site investigation. She had no idea what she hoped to find here, but taking action felt good.

After putting on a nitrile glove, she pulled one of the bags from her pocket. Bending down, she grabbed a handful of dirt, dumped it in the envelope, and sealed it. On the exterior, she noted the location where she'd acquired the sample. She repeated the process, taking another soil sample from near the concrete pad, and a third from the area where the underbrush was thick. It wasn't exactly optimum testing procedure, but it felt good to take steps to confirm or disprove contamination. She put the samples in the car and considered her next step. Since she was here, she might as well take a look around.

She took a deep breath and assessed her surroundings. Something here had to provide a clue. She walked toward a dilapidated building. One was an abandoned construction trailer, leaning at a precarious angle, its frame on one side sunk deep into the earth. One section of rusted metal skirting was puckered, as if bent when a strong force shifted the structure. Another piece of skirting had pulled away and moved in the slight breeze, squeaking like an unoiled hinge. The sound was almost mournful and eerie.

Someone was using the place, coming and going, at least infrequently. She could see tracks where tires had left deep ruts in the ground from a time when the ground had been wet. From the narrow wheel lines and the fact the trail disappeared into the shrubs, she guessed it was from a four-wheeler.

Moirin walked toward the second structure, which, at first glance, seemed to be much safer. It was a metal building, small, she thought. It looked to be about twenty by forty. At one point, it was red with a white roof. Now, the sides were a muddy brown; the roof yellowed and rust-streaked. On the left side, there was one grimy-looking window next to an equally grimy-looking man-sized door. To the right, a rolling equipment door was pulled down, secured by a heavy chain and padlock.

Moirin pulled on the man-sized door and found it unlocked, but it took all her strength to push open. The door's metal bottom scratched against the concrete floor, screeching and groaning in complaint. Dirt and dust motes swarmed her eyes. The stench inside was initially overwhelming. She left the door open, mostly for clean air but also to allow more light into the dim interior. It would undoubtedly take a lot of effort to close it again, anyway.

It smelled like old vegetation, as if leaves had gotten inside and left to mildew. There was an undertone of something dead, mixed with the unpleasant odor of oil and engine fuel, all covered in a layer of dirt. Moirin put her hand over her nose, trying to breathe from her mouth while she adjusted to the stench.

She removed the cell phone from her back pocket and fumbled to find the flashlight app. The weak beam did little to pierce the darkness, but she was able to identify items when she shone the light on them directly. The hulking shadow of a four-wheeler sat in the back corner. In the center of the room, a worktable was set up, strewn with hand tools and trash. Sandwich wrappers, empty half-crushed soda cans, empty automotive parts boxes, and other unrecognizable garbage littered the surface. She shook her head in disgust. Whoever had been using this building was a pig.

A desk with a decrepit-looking chair stood under the grimy window in the front corner, the surface of the desk piled with crumpled and yellowed papers. She gingerly picked up a semi-clean screwdriver from the table and walked to the desk. The air was more tolerable here, near the open door. The light was better, too. She used the pilfered tool to sift through the papers on the desk, looking for anything identifiable. Something that would answer her two most pressing questions. Who had been using this place, and how had they known it was abandoned?

It hadn't been abandoned for decades, that was for certain. The buildings were old, probably dating back thirty or forty years, but the growth would have been worse if they had been abandoned for that long.

She sneezed from the dust that swirled up as she parsed through the pile. Parts receipts, diagrams, user manuals, and nothing with a name. So far, the search revealed nothing of interest. There had to be something here. Using two fingers, she pushed back the chair and opened the center desk drawer.

A pizza menu, coupons from the chain whose burger wrappers littered the table, more small receipts, pencils, paperclips, and the typical assemblage of useless trinkets. A folded lined page from a spiral notebook caught her attention. She fished it out and unfolded it. It was filled with scribbled notes. Several phone numbers, dollar amounts, and a couple of addresses. Finally, a clue. Or, a potential clue. She stuffed the page into her jeans pocket. Revitalized, she continued searching.

She came up with four business cards, a couple of oversized postcards addressed to *Resident,* and a business-size check stub for the amount of twelve hundred and three dollars before she was finished. It might be unrelated garbage, but she couldn't overlook the possibility they could lead her to answers.

She took the dusty items to her car and stowed them in the glovebox, then grabbed the gym bag in the back seat. Inside, she had packed black linen slacks, a short-sleeve silk blouse, and black kitten heel dress shoes. She used the filthy building to change, being careful not to touch any surface with bare skin.

The high expectations she had started the day with disappeared. She was disgusted that the trip had been a waste. There weren't any definitive answers. She couldn't afford to spend any more time away from the office. Her phone held three voicemails and a backlog of emails, so the drive north was occupied with returning calls and mental engagement on other topics. The clues gained from her afternoon's search remained tucked securely in the car's glovebox, effectively out of sight and mind until she could determine the next step.

She left the property and reset the chain at the entrance. Legally, it was her property and she had every right to be there, but she didn't want anyone to know she'd visited. Not until she knew more. Questions swirled as she traversed the interstate north, but no clear answers presented themselves.

The sun was starting to set when she arrived home. She took a hot shower and changed into crop pants and a short-sleeved linen shirt, leaving her feet bare. Orson purred as he circled her legs, coming dangerously close to tripping her several times as she moved about the condo, once even tripping himself.

"Yes, buddy, I see you. You're obviously quite neglected, I know. Well, let's get you taken care of, then. It's not like I have anything else to do, right? No problems at work, nothing going on with Jo or Heather, and no dark-eyed man that keeps popping into my thoughts. It's all about you, Orson." But, the certain handsome dark-eyed man did pop into her thoughts with disturbing regularity.

In the kitchen, she opened a tin of food for him, putting it on a plate and setting it on the floor, then dumped the ingredients from a pre-made Caesar salad into a bowl for herself. Grabbing a bottle of vitamin-infused lemon-flavored water from the refrigerator to go with the salad, she sat down at the dining room table. Arranging her laptop next to the plate, she wondered if this was a typical dining experience of single women everywhere. Perhaps men were more likely to eat sitting on the couch watching television, but Moirin preferred to read or catch up on social media while sitting at a table.

Tonight, she clicked through the backlog of emails in her personal account. She opened one from Heather with a subject line of 'check this out.' Moirin opened it and chuckled at the title of the article she had pasted in the body of the email. *The Impact of Loneliness on Health of Women over Fifty.*

She looked at the date, certain that Leslie had encouraged Heather to send this after their conversation last night. The email was a week old, but the article was published last month. She started to read about the increased risk for heart attack, dementia, stroke, even greater inflammation, and overall achiness identified in the study. She was intrigued by the author's explanation that loneliness was connected to relationship quality rather than quantity. She wondered if Heather had thought of her ships in port analogy after reading the article.

She ate mechanically, becoming so engrossed that she was surprised when her fork clanked against the bottom of the empty bowl. The study examined the difference between a person's desired relationships and their actual social interaction. It concluded that while social isolation is easy to measure, the subject's emotional response to that isolation was what determined their loneliness, and that was much more difficult to quantify.

She tapped a finger against her lips in contemplation—the difference between one's desired and actual social relationships. So, single life in and of itself couldn't be considered lonely, assuming she didn't want more. She had her work, friends, and Orson. The family business provided plenty of stimulation, social contact, and challenge. Her work with the Foundation filled the need for a positive impact on the world. All in all, her life was exactly the way she wanted it.

Orson sauntered into the room and settled at her feet to perform his after-dinner grooming. "Orson, check this out." Moirin read aloud from one paragraph. "That's really something, huh? This is basically saying that dating could be good for my health. Do you think there's any truth to that? I'm at less risk of a heart attack if I'm not lonely. Well, I have you, don't I? I think you're enough to make sure I'm not lonely." She glanced down at him. His raspy breathing and wet licking seemed loud in the otherwise quiet condo.

She looked at the large arrangement of flowers, now sitting at the center of the table. Well, perhaps her life wasn't *exactly* the way she wanted it. The empty plastic holder where the card containing Jace's phone number was visible amongst the blooms. She had tucked the card away for safekeeping. That said a lot about her subconscious thought of the matter.

Orson meowed encouragingly.

She chuckled. "Okay, okay, I'll call him. For the sake of my health, of course."

She dug the card out from her purse and dialed the number.

"Hello," Jace said. Her mind had replayed the words from their first meeting often enough to make his voice familiar.

"Jace, hello, this is Moirin Garrett. We met at the Ag office?"

"Of course. Hello. I was hoping you'd call."

"How could I not? I wanted to thank you for the flowers. They're beautiful. It was quite a surprise."

"I don't often meet such beautiful ladies in my line of work. I regretted later not spending every moment in that waiting room chatting with you." She could hear the humor in his voice.

"Well, that is laying it on pretty thick," she said, laughing. "I might have to get my hip waders out."

"Oh, do you fish?" His voice seemed to take on an edge of excitement.

"Uh, no, not for a very long time. I had an uncle who used to take me fishing when I was a little girl."

"Now I can't get past the image of you in those hip waders."

The flirty banter continued easily, and they ended the call making plans to meet the following night for dinner. She disconnected the call and was startled to realize they had talked for nearly twenty minutes. She hadn't flirted that easily in years, and never with someone she barely knew.

She found herself looking forward to their dinner more than she would have expected.

11

The Italian Steakhouse was a good choice for a first date — not too casual, not too formal. The Thursday night dinner crowd was light. As soon as she walked in, she spotted him, looking even better than she remembered. He must have been watching the door and saw when she entered because he walked toward her.

It had been almost a decade since her last first date. More than four years since her last relationship ended. She should be at home right now, focused on work, not gallivanting around having dinner with strangers. As if in agreement, her cell phone vibrated, clamoring for her attention. She stuffed her hand into her purse, feeling for the smooth device out of habit. The vibration of the phone again vied for her attention, but it didn't win out over the man. For once, she was willing to put work on hold for a few hours. She pressed the key to silence it and pulled her hand out of her purse.

She smoothed her knee-length moss-green sheath dress, a hue that brought out the green in her eyes. Her auburn hair brushed her shoulders, styled tonight in soft curls. She hoped the light foundation with eyeshadow and lip gloss in a cinnamon-toned palette she had chosen gave her the shimmery, golden look it promised on the makeup packaging. She thought she read both approval and appreciation in his eyes. Oddly, her nerves calmed, but the butterfly sensation in her stomach increased. *What am I doing here?*

He reached out and caught her right hand between both of his own. She relished the warmth and strength in his grasp. The moment was as familiar as their connection in the elevator. With her three-inch heels, she was nearly as tall as he was. His eyes met hers with confidence. His dark hair showed some salt and pepper color, but his well-trimmed goatee was dark, almost black, and his leathery complexion reflected an outdoor lifestyle.

"Moirin. So nice to see you again." His smile softened what would have been a formal greeting.

"Hi. I'm glad we could do this. Thank you again for the flowers." Tongue-tied, any flirty response eluded her.

"My pleasure. They have our table ready. Shall we?" He motioned with a broad sweep of his arm. Stepping back a fraction, he waited for her to walk ahead and then placed his hand lightly at the small of her back. He guided her the few steps to the hostess stand, where a girl led them to a table. He stepped closer, reaching around to pull out the chair for Moirin before rounding the table and seating himself.

Settling in, Jace leaned back comfortably. "I wasn't sure how you would react to me sending you flowers like that. I'm happy you called."

"I wasn't sure I would. Honestly, a couple of friends convinced me. And, it didn't hurt that Seth vouched for your character."

Jace laughed. "I'll have to thank Seth for that."

They fell into conversation like old friends. They talked of their childhoods, hobbies, and places they'd each traveled. He was witty and entertaining, like those first moments in the elevator. It was like they'd known each other for years. Conversation was effortless, flowing easily until their meal was served.

Jace had a thoughtful look on his face as he leaned back, allowing the waiter room to serve dinner. They began eating, and between bites, he asked more questions. "So, tell me about your work. I take it Garrett is a family company. What is it you do there?"

"Yes, it's an energy company founded by my great-grandfather. I run the operations side. How about you?"

"I work for the State of Colorado, under the Department of Agriculture. I'm a brand inspector."

"What is that exactly?" Moirin said, intrigued. She had a fleeting thought to look it up after Seth mentioned the term, but she hadn't made the time.

"Brands as in identifying marks on horses and cattle, not a marketing image or company product." He explained. "I'm going to assume you haven't had much experience with the livestock industry. That's what brand inspection primarily supports."

"I see. So, what would a typical day entail for you?"

"A lot of it is what the name implies; I inspect the brands on the animals. Whenever livestock is transported — locally or out of state — or the ownership changes, the brand must be inspected to certify ownership. There are about seventy of us around the state. We go inspect and certify the brands before they're moved or sold."

"All the cattle in the state?" she asked, surprised. She didn't have much experience with the animals directly, but she drove enough of the state to know there were thousands throughout Colorado.

"Not just cattle, horses too, and some more exotic breeds. Most of it is routine, but there's some variety to the job. Even a bit of law enforcement and investigation sometimes. The Brand Inspection Division keeps a record of all brands so we can verify ownership. Sometimes stock wanders off, leaves its home property, and we go out, check the brands, and get it back to where it belongs. Other times, when stock is stolen, we handle the investigation."

"I wasn't aware there was enough of that to warrant a full-time job, let alone a whole department of the state." The idea that Jace had investigative skills intrigued her. She leaned in, intent on hearing more details.

She had called the county tax office the previous day and had made little progress. The title search revealed it had been in Moirin's name for over two years. It didn't make sense that Gregorian had arranged this before they'd even met. Something else was going on. Moirin inquired who had been paying the annual taxes, but the confused tax clerk kept insisting she should call her bank if she had a question about the payment.

Her next step would be to obtain a copy of the deed. She expected the signature to be a forgery, but wasn't sure where to go from there. Once she involved her attorney, she might lose control of the secrecy necessary to fix the situation before it imploded her life. For now, what was the next logical step in the investigation?

If she could inconspicuously pepper the conversation with questions about investigative processes, she'd write notes down later. It was an unbelievable stroke of luck to have access to a professional investigator, and Moirin took full advantage of it. Jace seemed amused as he answered all her questions.

"We inspected over three and a half million head of livestock last year and ID's brands on over forty-thousand head that were lost or stolen. Cattle and horses are constantly being moved around and through the state. Transport, sale, slaughter, it's a business with a lot of moving parts."

"I see that. It seems unusual. How did you get into that line of work?"

Jace carried the remainder of the dinner conversation with talk of his family's ranch, his college years, an internship with the state, and eventual employment at his current job. Moirin was surprised at how quickly the time passed.

"Have you ever been married?"

"Yes. I was married for twelve years. Divorced." He shrugged but didn't offer additional details. "How about you?"

"No. My work keeps me pretty busy."

"Ever been close?"

The question took her by surprise, and she considered it for a moment. "Well, no, not really. I've had a few long-term relationships but ..." She mimicked his earlier shrug as if further explanation wasn't necessary.

"Okay, that can be a deeper conversation we'll save." His fingers tapped the table lightly. "How about your favorite movie?"

"I don't watch many and can't remember the last time I went to a theatre, but I enjoyed Dead Poets Society on video," Moirin offered.

Jace chuckled. "Okay, fair enough. That's an old one. I guess movies aren't your thing."

"How about you? What's your favorite movie? Of all time, not just recent."

"Well, I don't think many can beat Casablanca."

Moirin laughed outright. "You're giving me a hard time about an old movie? Casablanca has to be forty-five or fifty years older!"

"You can't argue with the classics, though." He smiled. "Maybe we can take in a more current movie together sometime and discuss the strengths."

They finished dinner, and after declining dessert, Moirin checked her watch. "I had no idea it was so late. This evening has flown by. I think this is the most enjoyable first date I've ever had." She surprised herself with that honesty.

"I've enjoyed myself too, Moirin. Thank you for having dinner with me."

"It's been my pleasure."

"I'd like to see you again. Are you free next weekend?" He trailed off, for the first time that evening, seeming unsure.

"I'd love to." The words were out of her mouth almost instantly. She wanted to see him again, and the scheduling challenges around work priorities didn't even cross her mind.

After he paid the check and they left the restaurant, he walked her to her car. "Thank you for a wonderful evening, Moirin," he said. He stepped closer and hugged her.

He smelled of outdoors and leather, with a hint of spicy cologne. The warmth of his body flowed through her, and when he stepped back, the warmth stayed, as if his arms were still wrapped around her.

"Good night, Jace." A smile spread across her face.

"Good night, beautiful," he said. "I'm going to call you tomorrow." The statement held a promise deeper than the words.

12

Moirin's finger tapped the top of the steering wheel as she sat at the light, waiting for it to turn green. She felt a smile pull at her lips when, at the same time, knots tightened in her stomach. It had been like this all morning, bouts of energetic anticipation offset by unsettling distress sweeping through her. She normally compartmentalized better than this. It was thoroughly unpleasant, and her own lack of focus was irritating.

She had forgotten what it was like to be in the early days of a new romance. If this thing with Jace could be considered a romance. It was a bit soon for that.

He called again last night. The conversation drifted from one topic to another, and they talked for almost an hour. He was intelligent, funny, and engaging. They compared vacation experiences and bucket-list locations. They had both been to Barcelona and Lisbon, but neither had been anywhere in France.

They had talked of pets – her cat and his dog – dreams for the future and even fears of old age being foreshadowed by the ever-increasing aches and pains. They joked about whose physical barometer was more accurate in rain and snow predictions. Moirin didn't question his insistence they'd settle the bet at the first snowfall, months away. The combination of his life experience and education made him well-versed in many topics, and his easy-going personality made him a great conversationalist.

The stoplight turned green, and she pressed the accelerator, feeling the car surge forward. The motion eased her pent-up anxiety a bit. She was anxious to get to her parents' house.

She intended to discuss the Board's assessment with her father today. The conversation with Ian worried her, and she wanted to ensure there would be no delays in the transition of power. The change in location for brunch, however troubling the reason, would provide a better environment for the sensitive conversation she wanted to address.

When her mother called this morning, her tone was almost casual as she said Charles wasn't feeling well and asked if they could have brunch at the house instead of the restaurant. He had bouts of poor health over the years, but she couldn't remember the last time they canceled brunch.

Although, to be honest, this wasn't a cancellation; it was a relocation. Moirin couldn't keep her mind from visualizing the worst-case scenario. Her father, tucked in bed, with his face pale, his breathing labored. Or in his pajamas, lounging on the couch because he was too weak to get up. If his condition was as bad as she feared, she had it firmly in mind that she would call an ambulance.

The drive seemed to take hours, but in less than thirty minutes, she swung the sedan into the circular drive of her parents' house. She parked in front of the rambling two-story, five-thousand-square-foot mini-estate. She was a freshman in high school when she first realized not everyone lived in homes like this one. It had a heated entry driveway, so no one ever had to shovel snow or spread salt to eliminate ice during the brutal Colorado winters. The technology also ran under the sidewalks, creating clear pathways to the custom-cut glass entry doors year-round.

The entry opened to an elegantly tiled foyer, the spatial gatekeeper protecting the home's privacy. A large round table holding a massive flower arrangement sat squat in the center of the room, like a sentry challenging all comers. Few uninvited visitors managed to make it past this space. Those privileged to be granted entry were impressed by the open floor plan and opulent furnishings. The formal dining room flowed into the expansive great room, where a stone fireplace dominated one wall, and another's wide plate glass offered an unencumbered view of the mountains.

Moirin crossed the foyer and heard voices wafting down from the upper level. She started to climb the stairs but stopped as the words became clear.

"Now quit your hovering, Iris. I'm not a blasted invalid. I can put my own pants on."

"Don't snap at me. I'm only trying to help."

"If you want to help, leave me be."

Her mother's response became muffled as if she had walked further away. Moirin heard faint thumps of footsteps and shuffling.

"Socks." Her father's voice suddenly bellowed.

Moirin chuckled out loud, the knot of worry easing in her chest. Her mother may have exaggerated his condition, or he was feeling better. Either way, there was no way she was going upstairs and getting in the middle of whatever that was. She reversed her course and ducked into the combination library and her father's office, and her favorite room of the house.

Some of her earliest childhood memories were of being in this room, curled up on one of the plush leather sofas, reading a book while her father scribbled intently on piles of paperwork. Like her own office at Garrett's corporate headquarters, this room was filled with bookshelves where the volumes were interspersed with photographs and countless awards. His years of service further cataloged through the framed certificates and accolades lining the walls.

Honored with awards and frequently quoted in industry publications, he was recognized on a national level for his expertise in the field. Even in retirement, he still received invitations to national events, and his opinion was sought on major topics. Despite her own accomplishments, Moirin felt insignificant next to his success.

"Oh, good, you're here."

Iris' voice from the doorway broke Moirin from her reverie. She closed the gap between them and hugged her mother. "How are you? How's Dad?"

"He seemed to have some trouble catching his breath earlier, and he got overly tired getting dressed." Iris frowned. "But he insists he's fine. Doesn't want me hovering, he says."

"I heard a bit when I came in." Moirin hesitated to say more. Iris had never been a nurturing mother, and Moirin had rarely seen any evidence that she was a pampering spouse. The exchange she overheard between her parents had initially relieved her worry, but now she was uncertain. The fact that her father accused her mother of hovering was disturbing, particularly if Iris had truly been hovering.

"Oh, posh," Iris huffed, "He seems fine now; should be down shortly. Dorthea offered to make a light brunch for us here today. That woman is a godsend," Iris said.

Dorthea was the house manager — a combination housekeeper, personal assistant, and all-around right-hand in the Garrett household for the past twenty years. She had come to them from an agency, initially part-time, to help with house cleaning, but her position had grown over time into a full-time live-in manager. Nothing seemed to get done in the household if Dorthea wasn't commanding it. She lived in the in-law suite above the garage, but rarely worked the weekends unless there was a large party or social event. The fact that Dorthea was making brunch ticked her concern up a notch.

"Is there something you're not telling me, Mom? Should we try to call a doctor to the house or get Dad to the hospital?"

"No, no. Just tired, he says. As it turns out, Dorthea wanted to take the next couple of days off anyway. She was in her office doing next week's work in advance when I started banging around the kitchen. I didn't even know she was there until she demanded to know what sort of mischief I was up to with Edna's pots and pans. She offered to cook, I swear." Iris threw her hands up in surrender as she laughed.

Moirin joined in her mom's mirth, relieved. "I'd imagine self-preservation had something to do with it. If you had ruined Edna's pans, she'd have quit for sure. Dorthea would hate to fill in while she searched for another cook."

Iris pursed her lips and gave a solemn nod. "That's the truth."

"Dad working here or just going through old papers?" Moirin waved at the boxes piled on the floor.

"I think he wanted to talk to you about a few things before he shreds all this. Or, he promised he'd start shredding soon. I'm not sure he's fully committed to retirement the way he keeps finding *just one more thing.*"

"Hmmm, sounds like someone else I know. I thought I heard something about you cutting down your hours after your next case, but that was almost two years ago." Moirin laughed and wagged her finger. "There's always going to be just one more thing to keep you going when you're doing what you love."

"Touché. But then, I've never *wanted* to retire," Iris said. "Besides, we're talking about your father, not me."

"I can assure you, Dad has no formal responsibilities with the company beyond Chairman of the Board. He's just finding ways to stay busy."

"I'm not sure it's enough. He seems bored. He's been asked to join several other Boards and advise on a non-profit panel for one charity or another. I'm not sure which." Iris let her shoulders rise slightly, then fall delicately as if apologetic she'd forgotten the details. "Maybe that's what some of this paperwork relates to."

"Hm. Perhaps."

"Enough of this stuffy office. It's a beautiful day. Let's go to the patio and have a drink while we wait for your father. I've asked Dorthea to open champagne for mimosas."

Moirin allowed herself to be led through the foyer toward the kitchen. As they passed the stairs, they could hear the muffled voice of Charles, apparently on the phone.

"We've talked about this, and this is how it's going to be." A pause. "Well, that now is a different story entirely."

Iris rolled her eyes. "We might have time for *two* drinks."

She listened, but it sounded like her father wasn't anywhere close to finishing his phone call. She sighed and followed her mother through the house. They stopped in the kitchen, where Moirin filled two glasses with orange juice and champagne, adding a splash of Grand Marnier to her mother's and a fresh, fat strawberry to the rim of her own. She saw that Dorthea had set out dishes for lunch, so she motioned for her mother to carry the drinks while she picked up plates, silverware, and napkins and walked to the patio table. She made a second trip for the Sunny-Side-Up Herbed tarts, one of the few dishes Dorthea had mastered, and yogurt parfaits.

They sat in the shade, enjoying the near-perfect Colorado early summer day. It was sunny and warm, but a light breeze made it comfortable. The flagstone patio looked over a tree-filled lawn where rabbits bounded in the shadows of the trees. The sound of birdsong and the occasional chatter of squirrels was pleasant, and Moirin relaxed into the chair.

She and her mother sat in companionable silence until Charles joined them.

"Let's just have a quick bite here, then. We have some things to discuss, Moirin."

No greeting, no small talk. And he called her Moirin. Not honey, not gingersnap. She resisted the urge to sigh outright. What now?

They ate with minimal conversation, and soon Charles pushed back his chair, the metal foot cap scraping unpleasantly across the flagstones. He dabbed his napkin across his lips, then tossed it on the half-eaten tart. "Let's head in."

Without waiting for an answer, he walked toward his office, arms stiff and hands clenched. Any signs of weakness and fatigue had disappeared.

Moirin followed him to the office. The décor reflected a powerful and influential man. The dark green walls and heavy wood paneling of the room were masculine and understated. Large, thick oriental rugs covered the hardwood flooring, one under the desk and another twice its size, dominating the seating area. A plush leather sofa faced the fireplace, flanked by two captain's chairs. Squat brass lamps with dark brown shades sat on heavy end tables next to each chair. This was the site of father-daughter talks when questions were answered, advice dispensed, lectures delivered, and the occasional punishment doled out.

He took one of the captain's chairs and, without looking at her, motioned towards the other. She sat.

He sighed and folded his hands across his chest. "Why do you need to be so independent?"

"Excuse me?"

"We had a clear plan. A clear path. Keep your head down, nose to the grindstone. The Board is literally performing an evaluation of your actions. Past and present."

"Yes, of course. I know this."

"Then why the shenanigans?"

"Dad, I have no idea what you're talking about. Everything is under control."

"Is that what you'd call it? I got a call from Peter that the quarterly reports were delayed, and he's sweating getting the annual report to print on time."

"Peter called you? I'm sorry, Dad, he shouldn't have."

"Of course, he should have. He's the CFO. If those reports aren't on time, it's his butt. And the last thing we need is for federal regulators to come in fussing about our bookkeeping."

"There was a data issue. I knew about it, and I put IT on it. It's resolved, and Peter has the reports. Beyond that, I can't explain why it happened, but sometimes computer software simply glitches. I've been assured it's fixed."

"It doesn't make it look any better. Then, I'm hearing whispers about you and that environmentalist getting cozy in the corner at lunch a few days ago. What are you thinking there? You're creating gossip fodder. Is there something that you think you need to shmooze or bribe your way out of?"

"How could you ask me that? There's nothing." Moirin felt her face flush, and she worked to keep anger out of her voice. "Since when is having lunch with someone bribery?"

"It's appearances, Moirin. I told you not to do anything out of character. Getting involved with that project was enough."

"The PEP was already in process, and I know it was really Mom's insistence that I get involved instead of Ian. That was the right call. Regardless, the company had already committed to the testing. That was all the PR department, cleared by Legal."

"Never mind that, you're in it, and we need to be aboveboard on this. Now, do we have a problem here?" The stern edge to his voice took her back to childhood.

"No." She shook her head slowly, her eyes locked with his. "Let's be honest here, Dad. Your position as Chairman ensures you have visibility into every part of the company. The past, what, four or five years? I've been performing many of the duties of CEO, picking up the slack for Ian. It doesn't bother me that Ian doesn't do the full job. It's provided valuable experience and will make the transition easier. In all that time, I have never done anything counter to the company's goals. Why are you questioning me now?"

"I'm not, honey." His tone softened, and his face fell as if the sheer effort of anger had exhausted him. "I know how hard you've worked, but you know Ian has received all the credit. He's the one who was at the helm, leading you and Colin, approving and directing our inroads into less earth-impacting energy solutions."

She smiled at this. Her father disliked the term environmentally-friendly or, worse yet, green, when it came to energy production. There wasn't an idea or effort yet, he expounded, that wasn't harmful to something somewhere along the way. He supported Moirin and Colin's efforts to reduce or eliminate the most detrimental. They went to great lengths to avoid taking a position or creating controversy on some popular endeavors that they knew from in-depth research had harmful effects.

"I know this also, Dad. Ian has never been fully on board with some of the initiatives, but he's limited his negative comments to our closed-door meetings. Honestly, he's done a great job not voicing any strong opinions publicly."

"But for all intents and purposes, the Board, and everyone else, credits him with those advancements. You can't rely on your reputation and good decision-making or leadership history. All of the success for the past five years belongs to Ian. Which is why, right now, the snafu with the financials and questionable liaison with that Riggs fellow is such a problem. You have to be perfect. Better than perfect."

"The lunch with Riggs was about Gregorian. I'm concerned about his influence on the Foundation and what he might be up to."

"Don't get close to anything that man is doing, Moirin. Gregorian is toxic, and anything he's mixed up in will taint you. Keep your distance there."

"I will, Dad. I just need to make sure that." Her words were cut off when her father slammed his hand on the table between them. The brass lamp shook.

"You just nothing. Leave it alone, whatever it is." His eyes bored into her.

"Yes, sir. I understand." She had learned over the years when to argue and when to acquiesce. She had never lied to him and wouldn't start now. She understood his directive, but knew she couldn't ignore the fact Gregorian had altered that property list. She needed to know why. She would, however, be more careful about investigating. She didn't promise to leave it alone; she only confirmed she understood his demand. A fine line, but one she could live with.

"Fine, then. Anything else?" Charles asked.

"Yes, actually, there is something we need to discuss."

He raised his eyebrow, his silence asking the question, as if too annoyed with her to form words.

"Something is going on with Uncle Ian. He's been odd. I talked with Colin and he seemed a little cagey about it, frankly."

Charles visibly relaxed, his shoulders dropping as he leaned back in his chair. "Ian, huh? Well, that could be anything. What has you worried?"

Moirin took a deep breath. "A few times in the past couple of weeks, he's seemed distracted or worried about something. Other times, he's acted fidgety, making comments about not wanting to retire. He was in my office the other day and seemed to be getting cold feet about stepping down."

"Really? I hadn't gotten that impression at all. We started talking about this six months ago, and the past couple of months, he seemed to be looking forward to the change." Charles frowned, tucking his chin, surprised and contemplative.

"I can't put my finger on it, but he seems off. I'd like to make sure we're all on the same page."

"You talked to Colin? What did he say?"

"He would only tell me his relationship with his father was strained lately. That much has been obvious at the office," Moirin scoffed. "He would only say that Ian had *some things* he was dealing with and that he and Brittany were trying to help."

"It doesn't sound like it's work-related. I'll ask Aggie if she's talked to him. Might be a health issue or money." Charles shrugged.

Moirin nodded. "It could be personal, but it's impacting the workplace. Could you talk to him?"

"Of course, gingersnap. I'm sure it's nothing, but if it will make you feel better, I'll have lunch with him this week and we'll see what's what."

"Great, Dad. I appreciate it."

13

After brunch, Moirin planned to spend the afternoon at the condo, curled up on a chaise lounge on the patio to read. A new book she'd ordered had arrived in yesterday's mail. She had plenty of titles in her electronic reader, but the tactile sensation of turning pages, running her finger across the lines of text, or strumming her fingers across the page's edge during tense sections made the physical book experience far superior.

She sighed happily as she settled in and began reading. Midway through the first page, Orson mewed plaintively. Absently, Moirin shifted her knee and patted the cushion beside her. Orson jumped up and settled in, purring softly. Spoiled feline.

Orson napped as Moirin read contentedly for over an hour before her phone rang. She glanced at the name on the caller ID. *Jace*. Her stomach flipped, sending an odd sensation coursing up to the base of her throat. It might have been excitement, anticipation, dread, or a combination of the three. Or, it was just annoyance at being interrupted from her book. *Ha*. She put the book down. Clearing her throat, she answered the call.

"Jace. What a pleasant surprise."

"Hi. I know I told you I had a full weekend, but I lucked out. Everything went smoothly today, and I finished what I needed to get done. If you're free, I'd love to see you today."

He spoke slowly and deliberately, his voice full of confidence, delivering the words in that deep male baritone and easy cowboy drawl she was starting to find quite sexy.

"Yes, I'd like that." She didn't hesitate to accept his offer, and didn't stop to analyze her own excitement.

He arrived an hour later while she was in the garage, stowing dry-cleaning in her trunk to drop off the next day. At the sound of a vehicle engine, she turned, looking out past the open garage door to the driveway.

He parked his extended-cab Dooley, rolling down the window as she walked over.

"Hey there. I'm not quite ready yet; you got here faster than I expected," she said. "Do you want to come inside?"

"Oh, am I being too eager? I can leave and come back," he said with a grin.

She chuckled. "Since you've already lost any sense of mysterious reserve, you might as well stay."

"Actually, I need to return a call," he said, holding up his phone. "It won't take long."

"You don't have to stay out here. Come on inside. You can use the patio if you need privacy."

Jace nodded and cut the engine of the truck. He got out and walked over to kiss her on the cheek. It felt like a part of an ingrained habit. As first kisses went, it wasn't passionate, but it felt right.

He kicked off his boots at the door, then followed Moirin through the condo in his stocking feet on a brief tour that ended at the patio. She glanced at his feet and frowned. She looked up, but he had turned away, already engaged in conversation on the phone.

She shook her head and went back inside, closing the door behind her for his privacy. She finished her make-up, then put her few dishes in the dishwasher, refilled Orson's water dish, and fluffed the couch pillows, waiting for him to finish his phone call. Orson circled her feet, following as she moved from room to room.

When Jace hung up, he stepped into the living room, looking apologetic. "I need to make one quick stop on the way to dinner. It shouldn't take long."

Orson jumped from Moirin's side to the back of the chair next to Jace.

"Oh," Jace said, stepping back.

"Sorry. This is Orson. He's a bit territorial. Just letting you know who's in charge, I suppose."

Jace evaluated the cat, taking in evidence of past injury. "He's quite the survivor, huh?" He reached out and scratched behind Orson's partial ear.

"I suppose he is. Whatever he went through in life, it hasn't dimmed his spirit." Moirin was pleased to see Orson lean to the ministrations, his loud purr audible from several feet away.

"Well, we can all take a lesson from the resilience of our animal betters, right? I'm more experienced with dogs and horses, but Orson here is one cool cat."

Moirin laughed. "Let's get going before he gets a big head."

When they pulled into the ranch, she lowered her window as they slowed down, enjoying the view of a peaceful pasture dotted with cattle. Jace had parked and indicated he would only be a minute. Moirin chose to remain in the vehicle, intending to peruse her email, but quickly discovered her signal strength was limited. Instead, she watched Jace as he performed his work, disconnecting her seatbelt so she could shift and better observe the process.

Sitting in the front passenger seat of his pickup truck with the window down, the cool breeze blew in. Despite the herd of cattle nearby, the air didn't carry the expected manure odor; in fact, it was almost crisp and fresh. The scent of the grass and sunshine filled her nostrils. She never realized sunshine had a scent.

She watched as he stood in the pen by the gate, his back to the sun. The rancher had walked Jace to a group of horses, where Jace seemed to inspect them, then make notes on several pages. The rancher stood nearby, waiting for the signed paperwork that would allow horses to be transported out of state.

"Here you go." The voices carried in the stillness to the truck. Jace scrawled something at the bottom of the forms. He handed the papers to the rancher's waiting hand.

"Thanks, Jace." Jace had told her that Ned Mitchell was one of the first ranchers he had ever done inspections for, and the two were on a first-name basis. As she listened, it was obvious the two had formed a friendship over the years.

"No problem. Just call when you're ready to move those cattle. You should get a good price next week if the market holds." Jace nodded, slipped on his sunglasses, adjusted his hat, and said, "You heading over to Benally's Saturday? They got a jackpot." Moirin wasn't familiar with a casino by that name. She hoped Jace wasn't a gambler. She couldn't imagine that would reflect well on her with the Board.

"Yeah, I was thinking of going for the ten and eleven. You?" Ned inquired. They exchanged what sounded like a shorthand code, and she had no idea what any of it meant.

"Prob'ly so. I got one run set, but looking for a five heeler." Jace pulled his hat off and ran his fingers through his jet-black hair to cool his scalp before replacing the tan Stetson. "Be nice if it cooled off a bit by then."

"It would at that." Ned folded his certification and stuffed it in his shirt pocket, patting it firmly. "All righty, we're all set. Likely see you next week, buddy."

"Yup." Jace nodded, then turned and walked the short distance to his truck and opened the rear door. He placed copies of the paperwork in folders, using the travel desk in the back seat. He looked over and winked at Moirin.

The unusual setup had caught her attention when she first entered the truck. "You could probably avoid the office altogether with that portable workplace," she commented.

"I usually do. My territory is pretty large, so it is a time-saver," he said, waving at the travel desk. "I carry most of the paperwork I need. Forms, regulatory, completed inspection certificates, brand record update reports, and, of course, the past six months' reports for missing and stolen."

"That's the stock you told me about before," she said.

"Yup." He secured the copies of the forms he'd created into files and closed the door. Climbing into the front seat, he secured his seatbelt, then winked at her before shifting the truck into gear and heading down the driveway.

"Many times, a rancher will report missing stock; they never know if the stock has wandered off or if it's actually been stolen," Jace said. "It's not unusual for a calf to end up on the wrong side of a fence or for a cow to walk over downed barbed wire. The loss of a single animal or a small group is often stray, but we have to investigate every report."

All this for a bunch of animals. She had always assumed that life outside the big city was slow and dull. Clearly, there was far more complexity to this life than she had realized. She was vaguely familiar with the concept of chores and could imagine the work involved in caring for animals. The physical labor she had expected, but never realized how much more complicated things were. At least the fresh air was nice, notwithstanding the occasional shift in the breeze that brought a pungent odor of manure. *That* she could do without.

They reached the end of the rancher's driveway, and he glanced over at her. "I'm sorry for the detour, but now that it's done, I'm all yours. I know of a great casual steakhouse close by with live music on Sunday nights. I can guarantee you the best prime rib you've ever tasted."

He wasn't wrong. They enjoyed the house special — prime rib — and a surprisingly talented local band. The lively mix of bluegrass and country encouraged toe-tapping and a Texas two-step over conversation. Much to her surprise, she appreciated the tunes. She had never been a country music fan; late-night clubs blaring top forty hits had been her preference in her younger days, and now she enjoyed jazz or classical. She never thought she would enjoy the country genre she had often poked fun at. But, this was hardly the twangy old-time crying-in-your-beer stuff — it was good music.

When the band took a break, Jace reached over to grasp her hand. "You enjoying yourself?"

"Yes, very much." She said, enjoying the warmth of his hand on hers, his callused palm rough on her fingers. She shifted her fingers to lock them into his.

"I think I must be growing on you," he chuckled.

"You think? Why's that?"

"You seem a lot more relaxed than on our first date. You're smiling more."

"Oh. Well, yes, I suppose I am."

"Definitely. You have a beautiful smile, and I like that you're enjoying this evening. I'd hate to be the only one." His warm brown eyes captured her own.

She looked around the room. "It's a little outside the norm for me, I'll admit. I like it, though," she said. "Is this a typical night out for you?"

"I'll be honest. I have far more nights staying at home than going out. But, yes, when I do go out, it's usually something of this sort. How about you? What is a typical night out for you?"

"Many of my social events revolve around work. When not at the office, I'm usually at a business or charity event. Any real time to myself, I spend at home or having dinner with friends. I can't tell you the last time I had dinner like this, an actual date." She realized the truth in the statement, surprised at how much she had missed it.

He leaned back, putting his right palm flat over his heart in a gesture of appreciation. "I'm honored," he said. "But I'll have to make sure you enjoy it enough to make a habit of it."

The band returned from their break and started playing the first few notes of a slow romantic song. Jace smiled and extended his hand. "Dance with me."

"To this?" she laughed.

"Yes, Miss Moirin, to this." He said with a slow smile. "You're a multi-talented lady. I know you can dance, don't try to sandbag me."

"You are, of course, correct about that," she said. "There isn't much I can't do."

The dancing was natural, like so many moments they'd had together. They moved together with a perfect rhythm. Talking, dancing, and flirting, they laughed often, each making small excuses to touch the hand or arm of the other. They returned to their table, taking seats side by side to continue talking until their waitress politely asked if they would like to close out their check as the restaurant was closing soon.

"Time flies in such pleasant company."

"Indeed, it does. I'd wish I could rewind this night and enjoy it all over again," Jace said, kissing her lightly, full on the lips.

He drove her home. When they arrived, he got out, first walking around to her side of the vehicle to open her door, then walking her to the door of the condo.

"I'm glad I met you, Moirin Garrett," he said, leaning in for a kiss. It started tentative, then deepened, becoming more passionate. Definitely not a simple peck on the cheek.

She pulled closer, overcome with the sensations of the moment. The cool night air fluttered across her heated skin. The scent of Jace, the warmth of his skin, the softness of his lips, and the heat of his kiss. The entire world existed only in that moment.

The moment ended, and they drew apart.

"Sweet dreams, beautiful," he whispered.

"Good night, cowboy," she said.

After she unlocked the door and stepped inside, she closed it and leaned against it, smiling. Maybe there was something to this dating stuff after all.

14

Tuesday morning, Moirin sent a group text reminder for dinner with Leslie, Heather, and Jo. The confirmation made it less likely she'd allow work to distract her, as too often she'd allowed herself to beg off at the last minute; in truth it was more just laziness and workaholic indulgence.

> *6:30. Anastasio's. Tiramisu's on me, but I swear I won't be buying any rounds. My phone will be off!*

Too many projects had been demanding her time. She'd always managed to make time for her friends despite a hectic schedule, but lately, she felt like she was losing touch at a critical time. Heather's divorce and her daughter's moving away to college were major life upheavals, and Jo's stress breakdown at their last dinner had Moirin worried. With Leslie, life was a continual string of challenges and misadventures. She'd been too quiet, so there was undoubtedly some trauma or difficulty on the horizon or currently afoot.

Moirin hoped they hadn't followed through on their threat of launching online dating profiles. She couldn't see much good coming from that. Although her own recent foray into the field of dating had worked out fairly well so far. She was looking forward to sharing the details of her recent dates with Jace.

It had been too long since she'd had a boyfriend and was feeling giddy about it. If only there were a different word. *Boyfriend.* She wasn't a teenager

131

anymore, but a term like *beau* was a little too southern belle to feel natural. What would be the proper moniker with which a mature person would introduce an exclusive dating partner? She'd pose that question to the girls tonight. They might each need that word at some point. She grinned at the absurdity and turned to focus on the work in front of her.

The standard workday routine of scheduled meetings, reviewing reports, and handling problems quickly took over her focus. With concerted effort, the stubborn work pile that had taken up residence on the corner of her desk gradually diminished. Quarterly reports were behind her, and the draft of the annual report was complete.

She reviewed several emails from departments expressing concern about instances where the inventory database returned errors. It was troubling to think that Ted's experience may not have been an isolated incident. She wrote a task request for the IT supervisor, directing a full systems audit be performed. This was a potentially serious issue she'd need to keep close tabs on, and added several calendar entries as reminders to follow up.

She leaned back in her chair, took a deep cleansing breath, and cleared her mind. She closed her eyes, tapping her thumb and middle finger as she allowed her thoughts to flow. Focusing on dropping her shoulders and releasing tension, the stress melted away. *Breathe in through the nose. One Two Three Four. Exhale through the mouth. One Two Three Four.* The box breathing technique she'd learned from Leslie was one of her favorites. She'd been doubtful at first, but it was surprisingly effective for focusing and relieving anxiety.

She filled a glass of water and sipped it before settling back at her desk. She reached for the phone and dialed the PEP office.

"Steffie speaking." The intern's tone was peppy and upbeat, the voice bouncing through the receiver before the first ring. Moirin choked slightly as she attempted to swallow, covering her surprise with a light cough.

"Ahem. Good morning, Steffie. Just the person I needed to speak with. This is Moirin Garrett."

"Ms. Garrett, good morning. How can I help you?" Her tone changed to efficiently professional.

"I need your assistance." Moirin paused and took a deep breath.

"I'll do my best." Her reply was chipper.

"I need to ask for your discretion and utmost confidentiality in the matter."

"I'm not sure.." Her voice trailed off, hesitancy outweighing any inclination for helpfulness.

"Steffie, I assure you, it is neither illegal nor unethical. It's entirely likely the action I'm requesting will be in your own best interest as well."

"I don't understand, Ms. Garrett."

"When we had the PEP kickoff meeting, I overheard part of a telephone conversation Gregorian Plankett had. He was in the hallway, and while I only heard a small part, it was enough to cause concern. He spoke of making changes to a list."

"Oh." The word was scarcely a squeak.

"I took steps to investigate, and I've determined that someone, indeed, did make a change to the list of locations identified for the PEP project."

"I'm sorry, Ms. Garrett, that's not possible." Steffie found her voice, and it came across strong and defensive.

"I'm glad to hear you say that. So, if I were to compare the list Garrett Industries provided to PEP and the official project testing list, I would find they would match."

"Of course, anything else is impossible."

"So, if those lists did not match, one would be wrong, and we would need to correct it."

"You're saying there was a mistake?" Steffie gasped. "The whole project would be in jeopardy. Keeping the integrity of the testing and confidentiality was part of everyone's agreement to proceed. That would be horrible. I'll have to tell Riggs."

"But we wouldn't want to do that over a silly oversight or typographical error. If we did, then everyone's integrity would be called into question.

Reputations, resume experience, future reference letters, so many things would be called into question."

"Yeah, that would be so bad. I wouldn't want that." Moirin could hear the clink of an earring hitting the telephone receiver as Steffie was apparently shaking her head adamantly.

"Excellent. I believe between you and me, we can correct what I will refer to as a simple typographical error. We will fix it without any fanfare or notification. We agree that an actual error is impossible, so a minor mistake being corrected does not need documentation."

"Yes, that's much better." Steffie's words rushed out, eager to agree with the proposed solution.

"Do you have the original lists that were provided at the project kickoff?" Moirin was relieved to move into the problem-solving stage. Once she had talked Steffie through identifying the incorrect location and substituting the correct original one, she again emphasized confidentiality.

"Do I need to be worried about Mr. Plankett? I was in charge of the list and keeping the records. I don't know how he changed it, but he's going to know I changed it back. Will I get in trouble?" Steffie's voice wavered again.

"If you can, try to avoid him. You've done nothing wrong. You corrected something that never should have happened. I believe he was trying to create a problem, but you helped me stop him. If anything, you just need to maintain innocence. This list is back to how it was originally, and there should be no indication it was ever different."

"You're sure, Ms. Garrett?"

"Absolutely. Thank you for your help on this, Steffie."

"Okay, then." The girl sounded doubtful, but there was nothing more that could be done to ease her mind. Moirin hung up the phone, expecting to feel a weight lift, but it simply transformed into an uneasy knot beneath her breastbone. Like a burning spot of indigestion, she tried to rub it away but couldn't. She had only treated the symptom. The uneasy weight would stay with her until the larger problem was fixed. The address on the list had been corrected, but a questionable property still existed in her name, and Gregorian's endgame was unclear.

That would be the next hurdle to overcome. Wanda stood at her office door, waving and tapping her wrist. Moirin had ignored two meeting notifications, and if she didn't go to the conference room immediately, the entire team here and on the video chat would be left to awkward small talk waiting for her arrival. She nodded, grabbed a notebook and her tablet with the agenda notes, and hurried down the hall.

Moirin slid into the chair with a groan, dropping her purse on the floor by her feet. Heather, Jo, and Leslie had the table cluttered with wineglasses, an appetizer tray of stuffed mushrooms, and a half-empty basket of breadsticks.

Heather laughed and slid a glass of wine across the table. "Only fifteen minutes late. For you, that's practically on time."

Moirin rolled her eyes, then nodded and picked up the wineglass and took a long drink. "Work has been crazy."

"Your work is always crazy," Heather said dryly.

Jo snorted in agreement.

"Ok, even crazier than normal. But I don't want to talk about it yet," Moirin said, waving her hand. "Tell me what's going on with you."

"Heather was just telling us about a fun new work project she's started," Leslie said.

Heather dropped her head in her hands and moaned. "It's not funny."

"Who said anything about funny? I think it's fantastic." Jo said.

"Give me details," Moirin demanded. "I'm sorry I'm late, but catch me up."

"Heather's clinic is expanding their service offering. One of her physical therapists pitched an idea for a new program. The owners loved the idea, and as the managing therapist, Heather's been put in charge of designing and implementing the program."

"That's great," Moirin said. She bobbed her head and raised her wineglass in salute. "Congratulations."

"Ugh, thanks." Heather halfheartedly waved her glass in Moirin's direction before taking a gulp.

Moirin leaned over to Jo and put her hand in front of their faces, her fingers splayed in a pantomime wall. She hissed in a loud stage whisper. "Why is she not happy about this?"

Jo laughed. "She's repressed. The program is Physical Fitness for Sex After 50."

"I am not repressed," Heather protested. "I'm just traditional. And private," she mumbled.

"Fuddy-duddy," Leslie said.

Moirin laughed. "Heather, it will be good for you to get out of your comfort zone. The physical fitness part is easy for you. You know all the mechanics of exercise, stretching, and everything else. It's not like you're going to be teaching, ah, the other specifics or suggesting positions, right?"

Jo and Leslie exchanged a look and burst out laughing.

"Oh, you're not, are you?" Moirin wrinkled her nose, then gave Heather a frozen, toothy smile, with her eyes open wide and eyebrows raised high. "Yikes. Okay, well, have fun with that."

Jo and Leslie howled, and Moirin collapsed into giggles. Heather joined in, laughing until tears streamed down her face.

Their waitress gave them a tolerant smile as she approached. "You ready to order?"

Moirin composed herself enough to convey her order, as did Heather and Leslie. Only Jo continually snickered as she requested the poached fish and pureed sweet potatoes. "And another bottle of wine, please," she said sweetly.

"We'd better give her a bit of a tip for putting up with us tonight." Heather shook her head. "Changing the subject, how's the work on the house going, Jo?"

Jo sighed. "It's progressing. I hope this is all I need to do for a while. A roof is a major expense, not to mention a huge mess. I didn't realize, I guess. Plus, replacing the hot water heater at the same time. These service guys are making a ton off of me."

"Are you okay with it? Home repairs can be pretty stressful. The process, but the money too. That's one part of owning a home I won't miss." Heather said.

"Yeah, it would be easier if I didn't have the problems. Or if I had someone a little more knowledgeable to ask about stuff, but it's okay. The money is tight, but as long as I'm still bringing in a good paycheck, it's fine," Jo shrugged and reached across the table, grabbed the wine bottle, and refilled her glass.

"You know you can ask for help any time," Moirin said. "I don't know much about fixing stuff, but I know people who do. Believe it or not, Colin is a pretty good handyman. You can't do everything yourself, and life gets easier when you don't *try* to."

"Oh, and this comes from your wealth of experience leaning on others for help?" Leslie snorted.

"That's not fair. I have lots of people who help me," Moirin said.

"No, you have employees. People you pay to do specific jobs that you literally could not survive without. That's different." Heather said, leaning back to allow the waitress to refill her water.

"Speaking of your job, how is that going? Are they still going to make you prove you're worthy of your job?" Jo asked, swirling the liquid in her wineglass before taking a sip.

"What's that?" Heather said, frowning.

Moirin sighed, draining the last of her wine. She held up the empty glass, and Jo grinned as she refilled it. "That bad, huh?" Jo tsk'd her tongue sympathetically.

Moirin looked at Heather. "They're vetting me as a CEO candidate."

"Vetting you like they don't know you basically already do the job amazingly well?" Heather raised one eyebrow, pursing her lips like a high school English teacher whose star pupil misspelled a basic vocabulary word.

The Board wants to keep things above reproach. It makes sense, we're an international company, and I'll be the first female CEO in its history. It's shocking how few female CEOs there are worldwide. It's only around ten percent. And that makes it even more important for my promotion to be based on merit, not nepotism."

"That's actually kind of a compliment. For them to go through the process to make sure no one can say you didn't earn it. It's like they're protecting you." Jo said.

"Yes, I'll appreciate that part, but they gave me the plan for the vetting process. I'd say it's more for the benefit of the Board covering their own backsides. It seems intrusive and frankly, almost humiliating."

"Really? Wouldn't it be the same thing if you were applying for the same job at a different company?" Heather said thoughtfully, scratching her fingernail absently on the table.

"Honestly, it would be even more so, but somehow, because it is my family's company, it just feels more intrusive."

"Excuse me, ladies." A young man balanced three plates on a large tray as he shifted his weight from one foot to the other. Moirin leaned back, allowing him more room to serve.

"I have the Cobb salad," he said, looking at Moirin.

"Yup, that's me," Heather said.

"I had the fish, and she's the burger," Leslie said, first holding up one finger, then pointing at Jo.

"So, you had the steak and shrimp." He slid the plate across the table in the vicinity of Moirin, then turned and disappeared toward the kitchen.

The conversation stalled as they rearranged water, wineglasses, and cutlery. They passed the salt and pepper, then ate in silence for a few minutes.

Jo swallowed hard, then took a drink of water before clearing her throat. "So, what are they doing exactly that's so intrusive?" Jo asked.

"The basics first, then a deep dive into my life. They sent me a whole package. They'll verify my education, transcripts from college, and resume, which I must update first. That's a weird thought." Moirin scoffed and shook her head. "Then, professional references, interviews, industry organizations, and contacts. There can't be anything that someone would dig up later to make me, or the company look bad. Probably because it's a family company and, no matter what, someone will assume it's favoritism, there will be those who will look harder for skeletons in my closet. Some deep, dark, secret, horrible things I've said or done in the past thirty years."

"I'm glad no one is looking into my background that close." Leslie shuddered. "I'd be unemployable forever." She chewed on a forkful of fish.

"This year, I had made that New Year's resolution not to be at the office quite so much. I was doing better before all this."

"Yes, you were. Not great, but better." Leslie nodded, but held one hand up with her fingers splayed, and tipped it in a see-saw motion. "You missed our yoga retreat."

Moirin shrugged. "I'm a work in progress."

"I think this vetting thing is stressing you out more than you're admitting," Jo said, leaning back and assessing Moirin critically. She swirled one finger in the air in a figure-eight gesture. "Are you sleeping okay? I thought you looked tired, but it's more than that. You're looking done-in."

"I have to agree with Jo, honey," Heather said, patting the table in the vicinity of Moirin's hand, which was just out of reach. "You do look like you're under too much stress."

"I've got it handled." Moirin picked up her knife and cut into her steak, pressing the blade down into the porcelain, creating a spine-tingling screech.

Jo jumped, jarring the table and choking on a bite of her burger.

"I don't think you really have it handled," Leslie said, grabbing Moirin's wineglass as it wobbled, dangerously close to tipping over.

"Fine. I'm starting to feel it. Is that what you wanted to hear?" Moirin tossed her knife down on the plate. "The gala and the Pep project were enough, but this vetting scares me." Her voice softened to a whisper. "I feel like crazy things are happening. Things that are out of my hands. I've always had everything under control, so I don't know what to do with this. And I really don't know what to do with being scared." She leaned back and crossed her arms, her jaw clenched and lips pursed, as if sheer physical will could hold back the emotion.

"I'm sorry," she mumbled, tossing her napkin over her half-eaten steak.

"Don't apologize," Jo admonished her. "You don't have to be superwoman. C'mon, girlfriend, we already know you're human." She drew her finger around in a circle of the four women, "This here is a safe space where you *can* be scared. You can be confused, or weak, or just plain tired, but this is the place you can draw strength and recharge. We got you."

"All day, every day," Leslie said. "Lay it all out, be honest about the craziness, and we'll help you straighten it. You did that for me at my worst."

"We can all be superwoman out there in the world because we have each other here," Heather said. "And I, for one, would love to focus on fixing somebody else's crazy right now. Can I please help you?"

Moirin's eyes moistened, but she blinked to clear them. A lump burned at the base of her throat as the knot in her chest loosened. It was crazy to feel like crying from relief, because nothing had been fixed, but it felt like it could be. "I don't deserve such good friends."

Jo waved to the waitress, who came and cleared their plates, refilled the water glasses, then brought coffee and Moirin's promised tiramisu.

While they savored the dessert, Moirin shared the details on her run-ins with Gregorian Plankett and the mysterious property in her name. Once she started, the worries poured out. She told them about the sudden, random system glitches in her multi-million-dollar database that had worked flawlessly before this point, and her tense moments waiting to see if the quarterly reports would be delayed.

The supportive but blank looks around that table urged Moirin to explain. "You may not realize, but the consequences of a corporate quarterly report, or worse, an annual report being late, can be significant. It can affect credit ratings, shareholders' confidence, contracts, negotiations, and so much more. The Board could certainly blame me. I feel like it was a minor miracle getting that ironed out." She cut a slice of tiramisu with the edge of her fork. Taking the bite, the silky, smooth texture and flavor of the sweet cocoa filled her mouth. She savored it before taking a sip of coffee, allowing the warm brew to replace the cool creaminess. Things didn't feel quite as hopeless as they had before.

"I'm just thankful no one has found out about this property. Can you believe I even went down there to take a look? I've never done something so silly. I'm not even sure what I hoped to accomplish from that. It just shows how twisted up my thinking is, I suppose."

"Did you figure anything out since going down there?" Heather scraped the last remnants of the tiramisu from her plate and licked her fork clean.

"Not really. I called my attorney, and I'm having them pull all the property records, do a title search, uncover as much information as they can. I tried picking Jace's brain on investigations. Without telling him why, of course. I have a few ideas."

"I'll come over one night, and we can go through everything together. Two heads are better, you know," Heather said.

"I think you should ask for Jace's help directly. He's probably better at things like that. But, if you think three heads would be even better than two, you can count me in." Leslie pushed back her plate, a full third of her dessert left untouched. She took the napkin from her lap and laid it on the table, smoothing out the wrinkles before folding her hands on top.

"Thank you, truly." Moirin cleared her throat and sniffed. Ironic how, after thirty-plus years of being tough and strong, the idea that weakness was acceptable could move her to tears of relief.

"Enough of all that. I agree with Leslie, you need to ask Jace for help. And while we're on that subject, I want to hear more about this honest-to-goodness, horse-riding, took you to a ranch with cattle everywhere, dancing the two-step with you, cowboy."

Moirin laughed. "Happy to."

15

Moirin reached for the carafe on the credenza in her office to refill her coffee mug for the third time. Wanda brought it in fresh and hot each morning, but by this time of the morning, it was stale and tepid at best. Moirin tipped the pitcher, and a small stream gurgled out, splashing into the mug. She tipped it further, ending with the pitcher completely upside down, cap flapping open, secured only by one small hinge. Three small drops fell into the mug. She sighed and downed the liquid in one gulp.

Leaving the mug and empty carafe, she circled her office at a brisk pace, swinging her arms. She stretched and took a few deep breaths before returning to her desk. She really should get a standing desk with a treadmill underneath. She spent far too many hours sitting. One of Leslie's special reports for those-over-50 claimed sitting was the new smoking. Initially, she'd been concerned, but since the article advised sitting for no more than thirty minutes without a break, she'd determined that was an unreasonable goal.

Leslie had chastised her many times about her coffee consumption until Moirin read a few articles on the benefits of coffee. She'd vowed to embrace that stance and ignore any other articles on the topic of coffee that found otherwise.

Still, the standing desk seemed like a good idea, and she made a mental note to mention it to Wanda. For now, she settled in the wide, cushioned chair her father had once occupied and pulled open the PEP project status report. This break between her early morning staff meeting and an upcoming video conference with the European management team was enough time to dig into the report.

Riggs summarized the progress and presented clear bullet points of next steps, without any mention of errors or updates to the study site locations. Either Steffie had kept the confidence, or Riggs determined it didn't need to be shared. Either way, it was a relief that the issue seemed to be resolved. She sat at the desk, elbows planted, and hands folded under her chin, feeling a moment of peace.

She looked up when Ian rapped on the door frame of her office. He waved a sheaf of paper. She smiled wanly and motioned him in.

"I have the European team shortly, but I have a couple of minutes. What's up?"

He walked across the room and settled himself in a chair in front of her desk. "I know you worked through a problem for Ted's team. Seems like your database wasn't living up to the promise." He slid a page from his hand across the desk. "I'm seeing some more problems coming up. I think we might want to consider shelving this thing."

Her good mood evaporated. "That seems like a knee-jerk reaction. I haven't heard of any other problems. IT said it was a corrupted subroutine that was pulling an incorrect subset." She gave a short bark of laughter at Ian's glazed look. "I know. Sounds like some gobblie-gook techie-speak, but the problem was fixed. I'm fully confident." She grabbed the page, glanced at it, then slid it back across the desk to him.

"You'd better look again." Ian raised his eyebrow, nodded, and pointed at the page. "I'd think you'd want to keep any of your mistakes maybe under the carpet for now. Wouldn't it be better for the Board not to know your pricey toy doesn't work?"

"Uncle, Ian. It's fine. There is absolutely nothing for you, or the Board, to be worried about." She flicked her wrist, glanced at her watch, then stood. "I need to log onto the video portal. I'll grab the door on your way out."

Ian frowned and grabbed the pages, crushing them in his hand. "We'll come back to this later."

Moirin followed him to the door, closed it firmly, then leaned against it, sighing. The last thing she needed right now was Ian chasing phantom problems. She had enough real-life issues to address. She pushed aside her uncle's baseless concerns and shifted her attention to the company's European interests. For the next hour, that was all that mattered.

After the video conference, she called her attorney. Jo and Heather's encouragement the night before had convinced her to meet the property ownership issue head-on. After a lengthy discussion, they settled on a plan. Regardless of what the title search revealed, it was best to distance herself from the property and spin the ownership to a positive end.

"We've got at least two different issues to address, Moirin. I'm going to say getting rid of this thing is the highest priority. If the Board comes across it in the vetting process, you'd have a lot of explaining to do, especially since we don't know who put this in your name or why. There could be some really nasty surprises we're not prepared to handle." Adrianna Marcum had been her personal attorney for over ten years, but in all that time, Moirin's issues had been relatively minor. Adrianna had handled the purchase of the condo, created a will, established an endowment for a charitable foundation, defended Moirin against a nuisance lawsuit, and advised on estate planning. Her firm covered all the disciplines, and Adrianna pulled in other attorneys when their expertise was needed. Moirin had come to trust her instincts implicitly.

"Shouldn't we focus on the who and why first? So I can be prepared to defend myself?" Moirin felt a flash of anger, and she mentally ran through the reasons she should argue the point with Adrianna.

"No, I think positive impact should be first, then transparency as a defense. If this comes up, showing it's a past, resolved issue will be your strength. We can position it as old news and mitigate the possibility of having you or Garrett Industries pulled into a PR nightmare."

"All right." Moirin was reluctant but saw the advantages of the approach. "What's your plan?"

"We create a conservation center with the land, create a cash endowment for the necessary demolition of buildings, removal of the infrastructure, and any cleanup. Return it to its natural condition and let them encourage grasslands, trees, owls, grasshoppers, whatever." Adrianna's voice became muffled, lost on the speakerphone beneath a crackling sound of shuffling papers and the light *plop* of folders dropping on the desk. "Ah, yes, I had one of the paralegals prepare some options: grasslands, owl habitat, eagles. I'll email it over. The point is, it doesn't matter what they're trying to save or protect; it's about you supporting it and being concerned about reverting blighted land. That will be the story."

"I like it. It's a good move. An old abandoned industrial property converted back to nature." Moirin sat back in her chair, rocking slightly as she studied the ceiling, considering the angles. "I see the value. No matter what despicable history we find, it's already a redemption story."

"Great. Choose something and we'll get moving on it right away."

"Thanks, Adrianna."

"My pleasure. We'll talk soon."

Moirin pressed the intercom button, connecting her phone with Wanda's.

"Yes, ma'am?" The clicking of computer keyboard keys continued nonstop in the background. Wanda never used the speakerphone, treating all Moirin's communication with absolute confidentiality. How she answered the phone and typed simultaneously was a mystery and testament to Wanda's impressive efficiency.

"I'm not going to have time to leave today. Would you bring me a salad from the café?"

"Sure, boss. I'll head down there now." The keyboard clacking stopped and was replaced with a metallic-sounding glide and thump. Wanda had already taken her purse from the desk drawer, ready to scurry down the stairs the moment the conversation was terminated.

Moirin hung up, filled with appreciation for her conscientious assistant. The annual bonus and pay bump were a given, but she made a note to order a nice gift for secretary's day this year. She hefted the printout of the annual report draft, dug a red pen from her desk drawer, and settled on the couch to read and make notes. She barely finished page one when Ian trudged into the room, dropping into one of the club chairs opposite the sofa.

"Uncle Ian," Moirin said dryly, dropping the report to her lap. She folded her arms.

"That," he said abruptly, pointing at her. "That's what I was afraid of."

"What?" Moirin exhaled deeply in an exasperated sigh. "What are you talking about?"

"You're irritated. Annoyed with me. That wasn't my intent." He leaned forward, elbows on his thighs, and clasped his hands together. "I'm only looking out for you."

"Coming in here earlier, getting worked up is looking out for me?" Moirin cringed as she heard the sarcasm in her tone.

"You may not realize it, but making the move up to CEO is a major step. When I took over from your dad, it took a while to adjust. For me and everyone else here. I'm worried you're not ready." He cocked his head and pursed his lips in an apologetic half-smile, the same one he used when he told his granddaughter he loved her, but she needed a lot more practice before trying out for the neighborhood t-ball team.

Moirin scoffed. "You don't think I'm ready to do the job I've essentially already been doing for several years now? Doing my own job plus yours, but ensuring you get all the glory and credit? That's what you're worried about?"

"Don't be snide, Moirin. I've allowed you the opportunity to learn. I'm perfectly capable of handling my job, and I'm starting to think now may not be the best time for me to retire."

"Are you kidding?" Moirin grabbed the report from her lap and tossed it on the couch, scooting forward and leaning toward Ian.

Ian sat back and folded his arms. "I'm completely serious. You're juggling a lot right now, and I'm not sure you're handling it all. There have been some mistakes. Your database isn't working, the quarterly reports were almost late, you had a hiccup with the PEP project, and you're constantly running from one meeting to another. I'm not sure you're keeping it together."

"I haven't dropped the ball on anything. Haven't missed a deadline, a meeting, and there is nothing wrong with the database." Moirin raised her voice, feeling a flush run up her neck and flooding her cheeks as anger washed over her.

"Calm down. An emotional hissy fit isn't going to change things." Ian's expression changed to a disapproving frown. "I think it might be in the company's best interest if I stay on as CEO."

Moirin stood, clenching her fists to stop her hands from shaking. "I am not being emotional and have never in my life had a hissy-fit," she shouted. "I am a competent professional and I have earned my place here."

"We just need to stay the course and make sure we're in a stable place before making any changes." Ian stood and crossed his arms. "Be reasonable."

"What this company needs is vision and experienced leadership with an understanding of the significant changes facing this industry. It is not a time to wallow in the complacent rut of outdated strategies. I refuse to sit behind you and allow you to keep a stranglehold on our future. Your era's done, accept it." Moirin hissed.

"Ah-hem." An uncomfortable and overly loud throat-clearing came from the doorway.

Moirin whirled toward the sound. Wanda stood awkwardly, holding a plastic container, her glance shifting from Ian to Moirin. Ian pushed past Wanda and stomped down the hallway. Without a word, she walked over and accepted the salad from Wanda, then gently but firmly closed the door. There would be no conversation about what Wanda had just witnessed. Moirin was irritated that she'd let emotion overwhelm her professionalism and blamed the weepy admission at the restaurant the night before. She'd admitted her weakness from fear, and when Ian hit that wound, she'd had a complete emotional meltdown. A humiliating moment compounded by a witness who seemed as shocked at the behavior as Moirin was herself.

She stood with her eyes closed and focused on box breathing. In through the nose. *One two three four.* The air in the office was thick, too thick to breathe. Out through the mouth. *One two three four.* The fibers of the carpet beneath her shoes were bristly and uneven, making it difficult for her to maintain her balance. She put her hand on the wall to steady herself, and the texture was sticky and hot. The entire office was oppressive and unbearable. Her stomach soured from the stench of the salad clutched in her hand. She threw it in the trash and escaped to the hallway.

Moirin ducked past the elevators to the stairwell, tripping down the ground level. Once outside, she headed for the reflection garden, a small oasis between the three concrete columns that made up the U-shaped building of Garrett's corporate headquarters. A designer had insisted it was a necessary addition to the ground, for the mental health and well-being of employees, they'd said. This was the first time Moirin had been drawn to the space.

Four flagstone walkways intersected from the corners to a central fountain surrounded by lush green grass. Wooden benches were tucked in amongst flower plantings, creating secluded areas of privacy. She walked through the garden, drawing in the sweet and spicy floral scents until she had calmed down. She felt emotionally wrung out and physically exhausted.

She sat down and stared at a cluster of bright yellow snapdragons. They were like the ones that had grown by the gas grill on the back patio of her parents' house. Dad would pluck the flowers and delight Moirin years before with animated dragon conversations, pinching the blooms to make them open and close like mouths. Iris would chastise them for ruining her favorite flowers, but she always fussed at them with an indulgent smile.

Moirin sighed. She had many good memories of the three of them together. Her core family unit, the two people who inspired and shaped all the actions of her life. Charles, who instilled business principles and a fierce desire to be the next successful generation of leadership for Garrett Enterprises, and Iris, who encouraged her to be a strong, independent woman, neither beholden nor dependent on anyone. She was the product of her parents' successful tutelage.

How had that brought her to this moment? The anger had dissipated, that emotion replaced by regret and embarrassment. Her uncle was funny, generous, kind-hearted, and nearly seventy years old. He had been strict but fair with his children and was proving to be an indulgent and often silly grandfather. He didn't deserve the tongue-lashing she'd given him. He'd hit a sore point – something she hadn't even shared with her friends.

As much as she worked tirelessly, pushing the company to higher success, solving problems, mentoring, and cultivating business relationships, all of her achievements felt hollow. She needed the compliments and acknowledgements to justify her choices. The idea of a no-confidence vote from the Board, of failing their vetting process, would be admitting her entire life's work was a failure.

She'd never be like Ian, who went home at night to a wife who loved him, children who worried about him, and grandchildren who adored him. She never set out to shun those connections but honestly thought there would be time later for a husband and children. It never seemed the time growing short until the opportunity was long past. Sitting here now, in the middle of bumblebees and snapdragons, the loss was poignant. Even the thought of success was unsatisfying.

Ian will retire. I will become CEO. The final career aspiration achieved, my life's goals complete. Won't Orson be so proud of me?

Jace's slow smile came to mind, and a peaceful warmth enveloped her like the embrace of his arms. After only two dates and a handful of telephone conversations, she trusted him more than she had anyone else in years. Except for Jo, Leslie, and Heather, of course. No man in her life had ever been a closer friend than the three of them. She marveled at how quickly Jace had become important to her. She wondered what counsel he would offer in this situation.

Words from ex-boyfriends came to mind. *Talk to me, trust me, I'll understand.* But each one assumed that since she worked for her family's company, nepotism ruled, and she would always end up on top. That her path was smooth and all obstacles magically removed. But it wasn't an easier path; it was harder. She had spent years proving to her father and uncle, not to mention the board of directors, that she could one day run the company, especially since she was a woman. They had never had a female executive before, and her last name wouldn't ensure that if she failed, anyone would be forgiving. She couldn't afford mistakes.

Especially since you're a woman. That was almost the worst part. Not because she was married with responsibilities at home, not because she was a parent, and her priorities were questioned. Either could be true of Charles or Ian. But no one ever questions that. She never had either of those things to question her on. They questioned her solely based on her anatomy. Not intelligence, education, work ethic, or performance. *Especially since you're a woman.* But Iris had known and prepared her. Moirin had learned to smile and ignore the remark.

She didn't rely on her last name because her father and uncle Ian made sure she wouldn't. The other men in her life had never understood that. She rarely spoke of challenges at work because she often felt patronized. *You'll figure it out, Moirin, you're smart as a whip.* Like some encouragement you'd give a teenager. Or, the advice that really drove her crazy — *Just ask your dad for help.*

Jace seemed different. They hadn't come to a point where she had tested that theory and wondered if he would be different. Aunt Aggie and Jo made it look so easy to blend work and relationships. Aggie had Silas when they started the vineyard together. Jo and Erik had a small video store. They lived together, worked together, and talked about everything, it seemed. Moirin wasn't sure if her challenges were more complicated or if she simply hadn't found the right partner.

"Hey, what are you doing out here?"

Moirin looked up at Colin. "This is our space for mental health and well-being. I thought I'd spend some time here and soak up some zen."

Colin laughed and sat down next to her. "I don't think that's the right use of the word, but good for you. It's a great space." He plucked a single snapdragon and squeezed, making the monster's mouth open and close.

Moirin smiled. "Dad used to do that to entertain me."

"Who do you think taught me?" Colin rolled the flower in his fingers, then tossed it aside, slapping his hands together to brush off the pollen.

"He always finds time for little moments of play, doesn't he?"

"Uncle Charles and Dad both do that. Grandpa taught them there was more to life than just work. The whole point of life is the stuff outside of work. There can be a reason for work, but work can't be the reason for life."

"Grandpa said that?" Moirin turned to face him.

"Yeah. Dad used to say it all the time." He picked at the tiny flecks of yellow pollen that littered his slacks. He tried to brush them away, but they stubbornly held on. "So, the office is buzzing. There's a rumor going around that you lost your cool with dad."

Moirin closed her eyes and sighed, running her index finger across her forehead from the bridge of her nose to her hairline and back. "Not my proudest moment."

"You want to tell me what's going on?"

"I don't know what's going on with him. He said something a few days ago about being afraid to retire, and today he said it was in the best interest of the company if he stays on as CEO."

Colin cocked his head at Moirin, his eyes squinting in a quizzical expression. "That doesn't sound right. That's literally the opposite of the plan we've talked about for the past year."

"He hasn't said anything about that to you?"

"Nothing. I always thought he was jealous of Uncle Charles, the way he'd go play golf, sit on the Board of different companies, and pursue whatever project came up. I thought he was excited to be leaving the day-to-day in the office."

"I know. I can't understand what changed." Moirin shrugged and shook her head. "The things he was saying today didn't make sense. I should have seen it and realized something was off, but I went straight to anger and defensiveness. I'm sorry. I'll apologize to him later as well."

"I'll stop by the house tonight and talk to him. Maybe I can talk to mom privately and see if she knows. Maybe he's just afraid of retiring. That happens to some people, you know. They see their friends retire and get bored, then they die in a year. Maybe it's getting real and starting to freak him out."

Moirin scoffed. "That doesn't sound like your dad, but I suppose anything's possible. Let me know what you find out." She glanced at her watch, then stood up and brushed her pants. "Great. Now I'm covered in pollen, too. Anyway, I need to get back upstairs."

Colin nodded.

"Thank you for this. I appreciate it." She patted his shoulder before heading into the building.

~

The seemingly endless emails and 'just one more thing' kept her in the office until nearly seven o'clock, and only the incessant growling of her stomach finally forced her to call it a day.

On the drive home, her emotions began swirling, the highs and lows of the day replaying on an endless loop without the focus of work to keep them at bay. Without thinking, she hit the audio dial and made a request.

Calling Cowboy Jace Caradova.

She chuckled. What had possessed her to enter his name in such a ridiculous way? The sexy habit he had of lifting his hat and running his fingers through his hair. The memory of it brought a smile to her face.

"Hello, beautiful." The slow words, delivered in his warm baritone, curled around her like a caress. She felt instantly more relaxed.

"Hi there. How was your day?"

"Pretty typical. Horses, cattle, and paperwork. And yours?"

"Pretty typical. Meetings, emails, and paperwork," she said with a laugh. "I'm heading home now and wanted to hear your voice."

"I'm glad you called. I have another stop to make before my day's done, but I've been thinking about you."

A giddy teenage-era tingly warmth spread through her. A hundred replies flew through her mind, but none conveyed her current emotion. At least nothing she wanted to share.

"Hmm, me too," she said.

"I'd like to see you again. Are you free for dinner Friday night?"

"I can't on Friday. It's my nephew's high school graduation. I'd like to see you, though."

"I have a roping on Saturday. You should come watch."

"I wish I could. There's just so much going on, I really should spend extra time in the office. It sounds like fun, though. I'll let you know if something changes." Moirin had no idea what a roping would entail, or indeed if it would be fun, but she was interested in learning about all the aspects of Jace's life - his hobbies and interests, food he liked, and the books he enjoyed. She craved every detail, even if she had to steal bits of time in between her interminable workload.

"I'll text you the address just in case. No matter what, I'll see you soon, beautiful."

16

Thursday afternoon, her cell phone, sitting face-down on the desk, buzzed insistently as the ringtone gradually increased in volume. Moirin grabbed it, intending to silence the device when she caught sight of Jo's smiling face on the caller ID. She had ducked more than a few of her calls this week. Feeling guilty, she pressed connect.

"Ah! She lives!" Jo's exuberant voice reverberated through the phone.

Moirin cringed. "I deserve that. I'm sorry." After the emotional outburst at dinner and snapping at Uncle Ian, she had to compartmentalize better. Trying to regain an analytical approach, she had avoided emotional conversations with Jo.

"After the other night, I've been worried about you. You don't return my calls, you don't answer Leslie." Jo clucked her tongue. Moirin could imagine she was shaking her head in disappointment as well.

"What can I say? I'm a terrible friend."

"Of course not. Just neglectful sometimes. But we need to go out tonight," Jo said.

"I can't tonight, Jo."

"I'm sorry, that's an incorrect answer. I will only accept a yes."

"Really..."

"Okay, fine, then. I'm not above using guilt. We can make it all about you still. I won't tell you I was fired, the contractors at the house trampled my garden, hot flashes and night sweats are my new normal, and the headhunter I'm working with is super pessimistic, so I might have to move to Timbuktu for a new job."

"Oh, Jo, why didn't you say something?"

"Nope, nope, not doing this over the phone. Tonight. No excuses. There are things we both need to talk about. Plus, you need some time off work. And I'm going crazy being unemployed and stuck in the house. We'll talk, but we're having fun too, so dress like it. I'm picking you up at seven o'clock." Jo's voice was firm.

"I'll see you then," Moirin said sedately. So much of what Jo had just said was troubling. Had she been so focused on her own problems, that she'd missed major issues in her best friend's life? Or had everything fallen apart in two days?

When Jo rang the doorbell a few hours later, Moirin wrenched open the door before the sound faded.

Jo shrieked and took a step back. "For goodness sake, Moirin. You nearly gave me a heart attack."

"You're ten minutes late." Moirin grabbed her purse as she held up her opposite arm, brandishing her watch in Jo's face. "I've been pacing by the door, and even Orson was getting stressed out waiting."

"Hmph. You sound snippy, but I forgive you because you look good," Jo said. Moirin's peasant skirt, sleeveless V-neck silk tank, tortoise-shell belt, and matching sandals earned an approving thumbs-up gesture from Jo, who wore a wide-legged ivory-colored Palazzo jumpsuit with her favorite cork platform wedges. "I'm driving."

Moirin locked the door and followed obediently to Jo's Forerunner idling in the parking lot. She knew the air conditioning was on high. Jo often complained about the summer temperatures, but Moirin suspected that hot flashes were the true culprit. There were times lately that she herself appreciated the ability to turn the frigid air on herself when she became suddenly flushed. Not that she was ready to admit that hot flashes were to blame.

Jo hummed happily as she navigated the vehicle into traffic, weaving between slower-moving cars. "I'm so glad you agreed to come out tonight," Jo said. "I talked to Heather earlier, and she was telling me all about her online dating."

"Really? She's actually doing that now?"

"Well, not really. She set up an account, but she hasn't put a profile up. She's just reading through men's profiles right now." Jo grinned. "But it's a start, right?"

"That sounds more like Heather." Moirin chuckled.

Jo laughed. "We'll see what happens, right? Maybe she can find someone like Jace, huh?"

Moirin felt the warmth of a blush creep up her neck. *What was that?* Just thinking about Jace made her insides flutter like a love-struck teenager. Snippets of conversations and text messages flashed through her mind, and she could feel the smile pulling at her lips.

Moirin laughed. "Once I told him I took the flowers home, he said I should have something at the office that would remind me of him. So, he sent a basket of fruit. He said that should be a dull enough gift no one would question it, right? He said it was quiet, unassuming fruit, and no one would think it was from a flirty new boyfriend."

"He said that?" Jo chuckled. "So, of course, all you can think of is a flirty new boyfriend."

"Exactly," Moirin said. "He said, '*I don't care if you're looking at a beautiful rose or a shiny red apple. Either way, I want you to know it's a gift from me and that I'm thinking of you. Knowing that it's our secret makes it a little forbidden and fun.*'"

"Oh, I like that so much."

"I'm not sure yet if he's trying hard because this is new, or if it's just his style, but he keeps surprising me," Moirin said. "Just this morning, our office "won" three dozen donuts that were delivered by special courier. I didn't think much about it until I received a text from Jace wishing me a 'sweet day with sprinkles on top'. That wording was so incongruous with his rough cowboy image that I started laughing. I know Wanda must have thought I was crazy."

Jo laughed as she pulled into one of her favorite neighborhood bars and parked near the front. They found a small table and sat down as the deejay announced that karaoke night was starting.

"Thank you so much for letting me drag you out here tonight. We haven't had a night like this in forever," Jo said.

Moirin smiled. She really should be working, but her toe was already tapping to the music, her to-do list getting more distant. A waitress delivered their drinks, and Jo took off in search of the karaoke binder full of songs. Moirin wasn't going to escape tonight without a turn or two on stage with Jo. Thankfully, they had been friends long enough that they had a repertoire of songs—favorites they belted out on car trips, sang along to on the radio at home, or on nights like this when karaoke was on the agenda.

Jo reappeared, the thick binder thudding heavily on the table as she plopped down. "This will be so fun. You can't imagine how hard it is to be at home every day. I'm going a little stir-crazy without work. Can't wait to have a job again," she mumbled as she flipped through the pages.

Moirin couldn't imagine what Jo was going through. Career insecurity or unemployment were concepts she'd never considered.

"Oh, yeah," Jo exclaimed, slamming the book shut.

"What? Which one did you find?" Moirin ran through their go-to songs and tried to figure out which one would get Jo so excited. "*Baby Baby*" by Amy Grant? Or maybe *Me And Bobby Mcgee*" by Janis Joplin? Jo loved that one. Moirin hoped it was "*Man! I Feel Like A Woman*," which was her favorite, but Jo rarely chose. As much as they both leaned more towards eighties rock than country, Moirin loved Shania Twain.

Jo came back to the table, a Cheshire-cat grin on her face.

"So, which one are we doing?" Moirin asked.

"You'll see," Jo said with an enigmatic shrug.

"C'mon. How am I supposed to prepare mentally? You know I like to run through the words. I hate looking stupid when I stumble on the words."

"Oh, you never look stupid. You never forget the words, and besides, it's karaoke. The words are on the screen. And I can guarantee you know every word of the song without even thinking about it."

Despite her insistent queries, Jo refused to name the selection but instead pretended to be engrossed by each singer, twisting in her seat, barely containing her excitement until their names were called. As they headed toward the stage, Jo bounced with a dance in her step, and Moirin started to worry in earnest. What had Jo done?

They stood on stage, waiting for the first notes. Moirin's eyes were fixed on the screen, holding her breath until she saw the song title, a split second before the music started.

Jo grinned and winked at her.

No way. Moirin froze for a moment before forcing her legs to move out of the spotlight into the safety and anonymity of the shadows.

Jo dance-stepped to her, hooked elbows, then pranced, pulling Moirin back to center stage.

The first notes were as familiar to Moirin as her own name. The music, the words, and, heaven help her, every dance move. Feeling perilously close to ridiculous, she couldn't help but chuckle as Jo led her through the dance moves. It only took a few minutes before Moirin gave herself up to the song.

Sisters, Sisters. A Rosemary Clooney classic from *White Christmas.*

She had listened to the tune hundreds of times, part of an annual holiday ritual she and Jo had started thirty years before. They loved Christmas movies and watched all their favorites as part of a month-long holiday binge - *It's a Wonderful Life, Holiday Inn, Miracle on 34th Street.* And of course, *White Christmas.*

Jo had the moves down perfectly. Moirin was mortified. It was like getting caught dancing around the living room in your pajamas, singing into a hairbrush. They both knew every move of the Haynes sister act. Each time they watched the movie, she and Jo would get up and dance around the living room during each musical scene, singing the lyrics along with Rosemary Clooney and Vera-Ellen, copying their moves exactly. She felt the flush creep up her neck, and she tried to pull away. Who does Christmas karaoke in the middle of June?

Until Jo turned toward her. Her friend's face was beaming, and the words she sang were touched with laughter. When was the last time she'd seen Jo look so happy? Moirin couldn't walk away from the performance now.

With the lyrics about keeping any eye on her, Jo leaned in, knocking her head against Moirin's as she tried to share the microphone. That was not part of the choreography. Moirin laughed and shook her head, encouraging Jo to perform the dance steps properly. If they were going to do this, they might as well do it right.

Look left, head-bob, look right, head-bob. Step, lead with the shoulder. Pantomime the oversized feather fans. Hoots and catcalls were coming from the audience scattered around the bar. They hammed it up even more.

They'd better not let any man come between their friendship.

Jo was nearly breathless, and her eyes sparkled. The big finish - sashay the hips and sweep off the stage as they both collapsed in laughter. The audience erupted in applause.

This was precisely the reason Jo's friendship was so important to her. Who else would bring such silliness and unabashed joy into something as simple as a karaoke night? The sister of her heart.

17

Moirin stared at the property title search results on the screen. Her stomach twisted, curling as she tried to think logically. The email from Adrianna had been one of many in her inbox, but the subject line drew her attention, and she skipped on the list ahead to click on it. The unease built as she read the message, then opened the attachment. The anxiety quickly morphed into surprise, then anger, and finally, a measure of relief. A rapid progression of realization, questions, and nauseating comprehension of the situation left her staring at the screen in shock.

It was proof that Gregorian Plankett was connected to the property fraudulently transferred to her name. His name wasn't listed as a former owner, nothing so obvious, but Adrianna's paralegals had done a deep dive into every former owner for the previous hundred years. Admittedly, that was overkill, but Adrianna's team was nothing if not thorough. The property had changed hands a dozen times, but the last four were the most interesting. The paralegal had provided copious notes detailing the connections of prior owners, business names, and shell companies they'd uncovered.

It was exhilarating to have identified the culprit. It shouldn't surprise her. Gregorian Plankett made no secret of the fact that he hated her. Now that her attorney had begun the process of transferring the property to the conservatorship, Moirin was far less concerned about the consequences. She had won. If anything came to light with the property, her hands would be clean; more importantly, her reputation would be safe. Gregorian Plankett's plan had failed.

There was small satisfaction in closing the email and sedately moving the message to a secure folder. She wished for a file or, better yet, a thick book she could decisively slam shut. Worse, she couldn't crow about her vindication, not yet. Nor could she risk printing any of the information or leaving it lying around.

The PEP organization was certainly compromised, either simply because Gregorian Plankett was on their board or because others in the association had nefarious goals. She was confident the staff at Garrett was trustworthy, at least where Gregorian Plankett was concerned. She doubted he'd maintained contact with anyone at Garrett after he failed to get on their board. He had been heavy-handed and obnoxious with too many people, and nearly everyone was relieved the association ended.

Invigorated by the private victory, she was ready to tear into the next task that needed taming. A quick review of her calendar confirmed she had no afternoon meeting schedule, and it was too early to leave for the day. Ryan's graduation wasn't until six o'clock, so she still had plenty of time to put effort into another project.

She opened the file containing the past five years of corporate annual reports. If necessary, she intended to demonstrate to the Board the complete reliability of the system database. It had only been the last few weeks that any issues had arisen, but none had led her to question the system. To ensure the board agreed, she planned to run thorough integrity reports on the annual report data, spanning a timeframe before and after the new system was installed.

She switched to a different secure folder and retrieved the data for the oldest report. She could have easily delegated the tedious task, but analytical work made her brain feel sharper. The reliable way numbers added up and converted to profit and expense was satisfying.

She made her way steadily through three years of data, energized by her victory over Gregorian and obsessed with proving her multi-million-dollar system was above reproach. Clicking save on the file, she stretched, leaning back in her chair and catching sight of the huge walnut-framed clock on the wall.

Seven twenty.

Her heart jumped as adrenaline shot through her.

No, no, no. Grabbing her cell phone, she punched the screen, pulling up her driver's cell number. He answered on the second ring.

"Edgar, thank goodness. I'm terribly late for a crucial family event. Can you be at the office in ten minutes?"

"Of course, Ms. Garrett. I'll be waiting." His words were calm and efficient, easing her panic to a state of distressed agitation.

Rushing to her executive washroom, she slid open the door to the small closet and grabbed a sundress appropriate for the party. Shedding her business suit, she slung it across the vanity and wriggled into the dress. Dropping to her knees, she snatched a pair of buff-colored sandals from the shoe rack in the closet.

Four minutes had already passed. Facing the mirror, she touched up her makeup, then ran a brush through her hair before securing it with a colorful clip that matched the tropical turquoise, orange, and peach flowers on her dress.

After a final check in the mirror, she returned to the desk to log out of the computer. She grabbed her purse and glanced at the photo of her dad and grandfather on the shelf. A wave of nostalgia and sense of purpose swept over her, stopping her short. Taking a deep breath, she nodded at the photo. "Thank you for having faith in me. This family is everything to me, and I won't fail either of you now."

When she exited the building, Edgar was waiting, as promised. She gave him Uncle Ian's address, which Edgar had driven to countless times, taking Ian home, and urged him to hurry.

"Not speed or be reckless, of course, but as quickly as possible. I was caught up and am late to Ryan's graduation."

"Do you want me to try and catch them at the school?"

Guilt pricked at Moirin. Her tardiness was inexcusable. "No, I'll join them at the party."

The graduation ceremony had ended a while ago, and by the time they traveled to the northern suburbs of the city, the party would be in full swing. Her absence would be noticed and condemned, surely by her mother, but likely by Uncle Ian and Aunt Felicity as well. Ryan was bound to be upset.

Edgar drove the town car expertly, weaving efficiently through traffic, making excellent time. Moirin breathed a sigh of relief as they pulled up to Ian's mini-mansion, ablaze with lights. Fabric swags in the school's colors of blue and yellow were draped artfully around the entryway. Huge flowerpots overflowed with blue and yellow irises, hyacinths, and lilies.

"Would you like me to wait, ma'am?"

"No, thank you, Edgar. Please enjoy the rest of your night."

"Yes, ma'am. Have a pleasant night."

One of three valets, clad in black uniforms with blue and yellow lapel squares, approached the car, and, with a signal from Edgar, opened the back door and offered his hand to Moirin.

She stepped out, smiled wanly at the valet, then squared her shoulders and entered the house. Three women in matching crisp black uniforms with blue and yellow accents stood poised to serve from positions across the broad foyer.

One logged gifts and cards as they were offered, carefully noting names in a gilded notebook. A second would usually have manned a coat check, but on this warm summer night, accepted shawls, purses, and bulky items that partygoers chose not to carry. The third directed guests toward food, offered drinks, and provided older guests discreet answers to inquiries about the powder room or location where cigar smoking wouldn't offend the lady of the house. Despite the fact it was a high school graduation party, Felicity would insist on nothing short of elegance.

Moirin chuckled. She could already see enough teenagers crowding the room to realize that maintaining any sense of decorum would be unlikely. The older guests were likely already congregated in the sitting room or formal garden, leaving the main living room and media room to the guest of honor and his friends.

Making her way to the bar, she surveyed the offerings of imported flavored and sparkling water, energy drinks, soda, and tea. She looked at the bartender, raising an eyebrow. With a grin, he stepped back and waved his hand toward the shelf of adult-only libations. *Perfect.*

"Chardonnay, please."

Bolstered by her drink, Moirin swallowed her guilt and scanned the room for her nephew. His favorite aunt missing the ceremony, then half the party, must be disappointing for him. She liked to believe she was closer to Ryan than Aunt Aggie or Gillian, close enough to count as an aunt. She was relieved she hadn't seen him in the foyer. Excuses still ran through her mind as she mentally drafted the perfect apology. It was almost finished when she saw his dark head in the corner of the room near a line of tables loaded with food.

He looked up, and she waved, catching his attention. Flashing a smile, he slapped a high-five with another boy, then bounded in her direction. He worked his way through the crowd, grinning and stopping briefly a few times until he reached her.

"Aunt Moirin. Thanks for being here. Did you enjoy the graduation? Wasn't Cal a hoot? He practiced that valedictorian speech on me, so I knew what was coming. It was epic, right? Hey, did you get enough to eat? Where's your plate? If you didn't have any, you've got to try those little German chocolate cupcakes. They're awesome."

Ryan rose on his toes, craned his neck, then shouted. "Dooley, dude, you made it!" He gripped Moirin's shoulder, giving her a quick, affectionate squeeze before pushing off, propelling himself towards his friend.

Moirin's stomach churned. Her carefully crafted apology was no longer necessary. He didn't realize she had just arrived. He hadn't missed her at the graduation.

She was torn between relief that he wasn't upset and hurt that he hadn't seemed to notice her absence. But then, he was a teenager. That alone earned him some leeway. She remembered being self-absorbed during those years herself.

Sipping her wine, she strolled through the room, then down the hallway, looking for Uncle Ian and Aunt Felicity. She certainly owed Felicity at least an apology. Uncle Ian would understand she'd been held up at the office. She stopped several times to greet and chat with people she knew, surprised at how many of the party attendees were well past Ryan's age.

She found Ian and Felicity with her parents on the back patio.

"Hello, sweetheart. Don't you look beautiful in that dress!" Felicity stood and air-kissed in the vicinity of her cheek. "I fairly melted in that stifling auditorium, but you look fresh as a cool morning."

"Thank you, Felicity," Moirin murmured, glancing at her mother, then Uncle Ian. Neither seemed annoyed. Either they hadn't noticed her absence, or it hadn't bothered either of them. Charles patted the seat of an empty chair, and Moirin sank into it.

"Come here straight from the office, did you?" Charles said softly, with the hint of a chuckle.

Her head swiveled in his direction.

"You think I didn't see? There were plenty of times when I snuck into a party late, hoping your mother hadn't noticed. I recognize the guilt-relief mix, but don't worry, there were so many people milling around at the graduation and here at the house, you're safe." He winked.

She knew he was right. Not even her mother had shot her a look of irritation. She should be relieved, but she was suddenly tired, more than tired. *Bone weary.* The expression Aunt Aggie occasionally used came to mind.

"You know, Dad, Orson has been alone all day. I spoke to Ryan already, and since he was the guest of honor, I think I'll call it a night."

"You do look tired. Is everything all right?"

"Better than all right," she said, nodding. "I had a major victory today, actually a couple. I'll tell you all about it on Sunday." She stood and smoothed her dress.

"Okay, sweetheart. We'll see you then." Charles rose and kissed her cheek.

"Goodnight, Uncle Ian, Felicity. It was a lovely party." She turned. "Mom, I'll see you on Sunday."

She made her way back to the front door and stepped out, breathing deeply. The night echoed with the chirps of crickets and the buzzing song of the mountain cicada, along with fragments of hushed human conversation. The scent of the hyacinths by the door blended with the freshly cut grass. A bird chirped and another answered the call.

The outdoors vibrated with life and activity, far more stimulating than the well-attended party inside. A calm spread from her head, across her shoulders, and down her spine, relaxing each muscle where it flowed. Her shoulders dropped, no longer tense from the stress of corporate worries and strategizing solutions for the next big problem or seeking life balance.

No one had missed her earlier in the evening, true, but once she was here, she was comfortably part of the family, welcomed and included. That alone should be evidence of a good work-life balance. It wasn't unusual for her to leave work and attend a family event. Despite Leslie and Jo's frequent insistence to the contrary, she wasn't a workaholic. Moirin hummed as she tapped in a request to the car service app on her phone.

Your driver will arrive in seven minutes. Please watch for a blue Prius.

The sounds of the party were distant, a slight tinkling, murmured conversation, a laugh carried on the breeze. There were so many people here tonight that it was easy enough for one person to be overlooked. She was relieved there hadn't been backlash for missing the graduation ceremony.

Overall, it had been such a good day. But now, the sense of satisfaction and triumph she'd felt at the office had faded somewhat. Why did it always seem that when you had bad news, sharing it with someone helped lessen the pain or disappointment, but sharing good news somehow seemed to recharge the original good feeling?

Impulsively, she slipped off her sandals and stepped off the path, allowing her toes to sink in the luxurious grass. When was the last time she'd walked barefoot outside? It felt decadent and freeing, just like Jo had described after her yoga retreat. She really should have joined her friends that weekend. Why had she convinced herself she couldn't take the time? Work would have waited. She scoffed, then tapped on her phone.

"Well, hello there, beautiful." Jace answered on the second ring, his warm baritone voice, as much as his words, brought a smile to her lips.

"Hi. Have I caught you at a bad time?" Moirin asked.

"Not at all. Did your family event go well?"

"Yes, it was wonderful." Last week, she'd told Jace about the graduation party, describing the family members who'd be attending, and some of the more colorful dynamics. Jace didn't have a large extended family in the area and enjoyed hearing about hers. Tonight, she didn't feel like sharing the details of someone else's life. She craved only the personal connection with Jace, even mundane life details. Something that was theirs. "How was your day?"

"There's always a lot of paperwork on Fridays, so I spend the afternoon trapped inside. I had a few guys over to practice and just finished a bit ago. Having a beer, looking at the stars, thinking about a beautiful redhead I met not too long ago. Wishing she were here."

She felt a smile lift her lips. "That sounds perfect."

"I think so." His words were slow and deliberate. She smiled again, knowing already the many layers of meaning he was communicating through those three words.

"Do you still have the roping event tomorrow?"

"At Benally's? You bet. You change your mind about coming?"

"I did." A flamboyantly neon blue Prius pulled into the drive. "Actually, my car is here. Can I call you back in about an hour?"

"Of course, darlin'. I look forward to it."

With a breathless goodbye, Moirin swept up her shoes and dashed to the car, grinning like a toddler clutching a cookie. Life was becoming balanced. It was time to have fun. Jace was definitely that.

18

The following day, after picking Jo up at her house, Moirin followed a combination of Jace's directions and the insistent orders from her GPS to find the arena. As it turned out, the conversation she'd overheard the previous Sunday between Jace and the rancher hadn't been about a new casino.

Benally's was an equine arena where cowboys like Jace came to play. *Compete*, she corrected herself. Jace had wanted her to watch a team roping he had entered, assuring her she'd enjoy it. Doubtful how enjoyable a day at a dirt arena would be, Moirin convinced Jo to come along. At least if she sat under a hot sun choking on dirt, she'd have good company.

Moirin was surprised at how crowded the parking lot was and the variety of trailers and rigs parked there, but quickly realized it made sense. This was an event on horseback, so each competitor brought their horse and equipment. She maneuvered her Lexus between two truck-horse trailer combinations, each at least twenty feet long. Next to them, her vehicle seemed downright tiny.

The parking lot was just a dusty field separated from the meager grandstands by a stretch of green grass. There was a distinct lack of sidewalk, and Moirin was thankful she had the foresight to wear flats. She chuckled at her friend's dark-brown cowboy-style footwear, embellished with stitched roses and trailing ivy across the toe and disappearing up the ankle under her blue jeans. "Nice boots, cowgirl."

Jo flashed a bright smile. "Aren't they the cutest?" The words gushed out as Jo hop-stepped with enthusiasm. "I saw them at the western wear store and knew I just *had* to have them. I feel like I fit right in around here."

"Well, you're certainly excited about this event today."

"Are you kidding? I've wanted to see more real-live cowboy action after I went to the rodeo a couple of years ago."

Moirin linked arms with Jo and pulled her close. They walked toward the arena, rubbernecking like a couple of country bumpkin tourists in reverse: two big-city girls awed by the sight of cattle right there in front of them. There were several large pens of horned steers where riders milled around on horseback. Some horses were tied at hitching posts, patiently waiting for their riders, while others chomped on hay or pranced at the trailers.

The air was filled with the creak of leather saddles and the occasional whinny of a horse. Dust swirled through the air, kicked up by the hundreds of hooves in the immediate area. Moirin choked on the dust but more so on the pungent odor of manure. She and Jo both sidestepped several fly-encrusted piles on the short walk to the grassy strip. As they neared the small grandstand, another unfamiliar sight met them. Cowboys of every size and description rode horses of an even wider variety, some slowly walking and conversing in small groups, while others were riding hard, focused on some single-minded pursuit. They stood for a moment, overwhelmed by the scene.

Moirin elbowed Jo, then raised her arm to wave. "There. That's Jace. Do you see that black horse? Jace is the one with the dark hair in the red-checked shirt."

Jo craned her neck, searching through the dusty crowd of horses and riders. Jace had seen Moirin, and he mounted, then rode over to where they stood at the metal fence.

He tipped his hat. "Ladies." He gave Moirin a knowing smile as he raised two fingers to his lips, kissed them, then extended them toward her. "Beautiful."

"Hey there." She had intended to perform a perfunctory introduction, but his sensual greeting drove all thought from her mind. "Uh, Jace, oh, sorry. This is my friend Jo Sandersen. Jo, this is Jace Caradova." Moirin motioned from one to the other, completing the introductions. She tried to recover her composure as her heart thumped in her chest like a teenager with a first crush.

"It's nice to meet you, Jace. I'm so glad Moirin invited me to join her today. This is something." Jo said, looking around.

"Just wait until we get started." He shifted in the saddle, the leather creaking at the movement.

"I was watching the horses as we walked up. They're beautiful." Jo reached her hand out through the fence to Jace's mount, her palm up for the horse to sniff. "What's this guy's name?"

"Panther's Pride. I call him Pan."

"Pan. I like that. It suits him." Moirin said. "So, what do we do here? Just take a seat? Is there a program or anything?" She tried to be nonchalant.

Jace pointed to an area behind her. "There's a board over there — in front of that small building. There's a paper posted with a list that will show you everyone entered. It's alphabetical by last name and shows the assigned team numbers. They'll have us rope in that order, starting with team one."

"Oh, okay," Jo said.

"They'll change the list for each roping. The first one will be a number twelve, then an eleven, and a ten. I'm entered in all three. Find yourself a seat, and I'll come find you between runs." He brushed two fingers over the rim of his hat as he dipped his head, winked at Moirin, then rode off.

She looked at Jo, who seemed to mirror her blank look, then they both chuckled. "I understood the list being posted, but after that, he pretty much lost me."

"Hm. Something about a ten, eleven, twelve." Jo shook her head and reached out to link arms with Moirin, pulling her toward the building Jace had indicated. "Let's head over to that-there board and do us some investigatin.'"

"That was the worst cowboy impression ever. Or was that supposed to be an old prospector?" Moirin asked.

"Not a good impression? Should I have added 'pilgrim' at the end?" Jo pursed her lips thoughtfully.

Moirin snorted. "Absolutely not."

"Fine. Let's take a look at this list and find a good place to sit."

Several sheets of paper were held precariously in place on the board by a single staple each. Moirin used her cell phone to snap a photo of the page with Jace's name. After they sat down, she would decipher it. Less than two dozen spectators were seated in the stands.

A scratchy recording started, blaring a haunting version of the national anthem, the notes echoing over the small arena. A hush fell over the attendees as hats and hands were clasped respectfully against chests while the familiar tune played. The crowd's silence continued as a brief prayer was offered, followed by the jarring exuberance of the fast-talking announcer, shouting out a complicated series of numbers with the finesse of a seasoned auctioneer.

"Okay, ropers, this is your number ten. Watch your flagger on the heel; crossfire rule is in effect. This is a three-steer roping; top twenty will make it to the short round. We're gonna get this one started now. Remember, this will be followed by the eleven, enter twice, pick or draw. Books open until the start of the second round."

It was incomprehensible to Moirin but seemed the contestants found it to be crucial information because there was suddenly a flurry of activity and noise coming from every direction. Horses pranced, and cattle knocked against the gate as tinny country-western music piped through the speaker at a volume too low to make any lyrics recognizable.

"Let's see if we can get someone to explain this," Moirin said, pointing to a cluster of people seated.

"Perfect." Jo walked up a few steps and introduced herself.

"This is the first time we've been to one of these. Do you mind if we sit next to you and ask some questions?"

"You betcha." A young blond woman responded, shifting in her seat to smile at them. "I'm Savannah, and this is Tina. That's Galen over there."

They were an odd-looking trio. Moirin gauged Savannah to be about fifteen — a wholesome, fresh-faced teenager in a plain yellow tee-shirt and unadorned jeans. Her long hair was secured in a single braid down her back, hanging from under a black baseball cap. Tina looked about fifteen years older, maybe early thirties; her coal-black, frizzy curls barely visible under a cowboy hat. She wore rhinestone-embellished jeans and a tank top with lots of heavy silver jewelry. Galen was an older man of indiscriminate age with a yellow-white beard, wearing boots worn down at the heels and a threadbare two-tone plaid shirt tucked into stained blue jeans. A huge gold-tone buckle connected the ends of an ornately carved leather belt.

Moirin tried to act nonchalant as she sat down next to Jo, directly behind their new acquaintances. She leaned forward between two women to offer her hand. "I'm Moirin."

"Nicetameecha," Savannah said. "I'll give you the low-down real quick. So, the gates are over there to the right. When the header nods, they open the gate. The steer runs out, and there's a roper on each side. The one on the left side of the steer is the header; he is supposed to rope it by the horns or the head. The other one, on the right, that's the heeler. He will rope the steer's back legs after the header gets the horns and gets it turned in the right direction. That's about it."

"Okay, seems easy enough to follow," Moirin said.

"How is it yall're at a roping and don't know what's going on?"

"We came here to watch a friend. Jace Caradova."

"Wonderful! Yeah, we've known Jace for years," Savannah said.

A swooshing and thump caught their attention as a short-horned steer ran out from the gates, flanked and chased by two cowboys, barreling down the arena at full gallop, ropes swinging wildly above their heads. The one closest to them suddenly flung his rope with a wide loop, which settled neatly below the horns. The steer and horse turned in unison, like a couple of figure skaters in a choreographed dance. The second mounted rider threw his rope, neatly catching the hind legs for a second. Moirin gasped at the speed of it.

The steer flicked one leg and knocked the rope away. The horses stopped, and for a second, the steer stood, tail swishing, looking expectantly at the first cowboy. They all took off at a run, headed for the exit gate at the opposite end of the area, as the announcer's voice blared over the speakers. *Nine-oh-six with a penalty in the field puts them at 14.06. Team two ride in.*

"Yup. Jace's a good guy," Galen nodded, more intent on the action in the arena than in conversation.

Moirin looked at Savannah. "So, what just happened there?"

"Oh, yeah, okay, so, the goal is to rope the steer, the header around the horn, then the heeler around the legs. If the heeler only ropes one hind leg instead of two, that's a five-second penalty like that team there. Their time of nine point six seconds went to fourteen-six. The only other thing is that they have to give the steer a head start. There's an electronic eye set up to make sure. If they leave the box too soon, it's called *breaking the barrier.* A single buzz means the header broke it, and two buzzes if the heeler did. That's a ten-second penalty."

Moirin listened to Savannah's explanation as she watched the next team's efforts. She heard the swishing whine of the rope cutting through the air. A quick snap of the header's wrist sent the loop toward the steer, but the animal made a split-second sidestep, and the lasso landed on its back. Moirin realized that the animals in the sport were smart enough to duck and weave, making the catch a challenge.

The announcer kept up the running monologue. *Point three four off the line. No time.*

"Hey, there's Jace now," Savannah said, pointing.

Jace entered the arena riding his horse. They watched as his horse pranced into position in the header box. A second rider was in the heeler box, on the other side of the chute where the steer stood. Jace pulled gently on the reins, backing his horse up against the rear of the box, then held still.

He gave a quick nod. The gate opened, and the steer charged out, headed for the opposite end of the arena. Jace flew from the box, his sleek black horse thundering after the steer, the heeler riding up on the other side. Both ropes flew in circles in the air, for a moment, the loops in perfect unison. Jace's rope settled over the horns, and the steer turned in concert with Jace's horse, the front feet of the bovine matching pace with the equine. A split second later, the heeler threw his rope and caught the back legs of the steer.

Both horses stopped momentarily with the steer between them. Then, all three began trotting calmly towards the exit, making a small herd of three animals.

Clean run. Six-point-four-one.

Moirin clapped. It was the lowest time she had heard so far. Jace looked up at her, tipping his hat. He urged his mount toward the exit, clearing the arena for the next team.

Moirin's nostrils were assaulted by the pungent stench of horse droppings being created at an alarming frequency from the sixty or so horses milling around. Their riders seemed to be unconcerned about the mess or the smell. The clouds of dust swirled around the horses' hooves and seemed to choke the air, then were blissfully cleared by a cleansing breeze.

She looked around this unfamiliar world. This was so natural. It was dusty, dirty, and fragrant. And beautifully real. It was a stark contrast to the ugly remains of human concrete and rusting metal she saw at the abandoned site she'd visited. She looked at Jo, who was smiling and chatting with their new friends. It was just another Saturday afternoon to them, but Moirin knew this experience would be added to her collection of favorite life moments. How had she gotten so far away from gritty real-life moments like this?

"Known that boy for years. Good header," Galen said, looking back over his shoulder.

"So, Jo, how did you meet Jace?" Tina turned and asked.

"Oh, I just met him today," Jo said. "Moirin's been dating him for a couple of weeks, I guess. Where did you guys meet again?" Jo turned to Moirin.

"The Ag Agency office. I had a meeting in the building where he works. We met in the elevator, actually."

"Really? What is it you do, Moirin?" Tina said.

"I work for Garrett Diversified."

"The power company?" Tina asked. Moirin nodded as Galen turned around to gawk.

"Darned prissy environmentalists over there gonna ruin everything," he mumbled and turned back to the action in the arena.

Forty-two Evan Stoddard and Glenn Gravens, forty-three Kyle Alexander and Kristen Swiss, forty-four Jace Caradova and Shawn Saunders. Forty-five, forty-six, and forty-seven, be ready. Forty-two, Evan and Dodd, you're up.

She couldn't resist. She leaned over to Tina. "What was that all about?" she said, pointing to Galen.

"Aw, it ain't nothing. Galen's just opinionated when it comes to land stewardship. He gets riled up, but you can't blame him. I doubt those office-bound executives over there have any clue how to really protect the environment. No offense, honey."

Moirin felt Jo's hand on her arm. She looked over and saw Jo working to suppress a smile. She managed a garbled, "Is that so?"

Galen nodded vigorously. "Take wind energy, right? The federal government has put in, what, like thirty billion dollars in the past thirty-five years, subsidies and grants, right? What's it got us? We get less than three percent of our energy from it. Plus, there's all the extra cost where it's like three times what they say to produce, because of storage and all. You know, when the wind doesn't blow all the time."

"Yes, I know." Moirin managed to squeak out the words.

"Yeah, Galen knows a lot about all that. Nothing is ever what they say, and it's so easy to twist stuff around," Tina said and turned suddenly, shifting her focus. "So what do you do, Jo?"

Jo exhaled noisily and laughed. "Me? Oh, I uh, I do marketing stuff."

"Oh, that's cool," Tina said. "I've got a pet grooming business. Mobile van. Y'all got pets? Oh, wait, my husband's up." Tina twisted around to watch the action.

It went on, team after team. Sound blended in a comfortable rhythm, a murmur of incessant numbers, names, and the dull metallic clang of the gate. An occasional long baritone buzzer. Contemporary country music played low in the background, barely discernible except in those rare moments when all other sounds fell silent.

Jace came to sit with them in the stands a few times when he had enough of a break between his turns, once bringing them bottles of water from the concession stand.

Moirin was so focused on the action that she never saw it coming. A sudden cold, wet attack yanked her attention. She squealed and jumped, nearly knocking Jo off the bench beside her, whirling to confront her attacker. Jace stood with a wicked grin on his face and scoffed, punching his arm.

"You're pretty stealthy for a big guy, you know?"

He shrugged. "You looked hot."

She couldn't tell if he intended it as a double entendre. She narrowed her eyes, assessing him. His expression was unreadable for a minute, then he winked and turned to someone calling his name. He waved, then sat next to her. He slid his arm around her and massaged the back of her neck briefly before dropping his hand.

The other spectators seemed to know each other, and they each greeted Jace. Jace included her in each conversation, and she felt a flush of pleasure when he introduced her as "my special lady, Moirin." In his slow cowboy drawl, the words sounded intimate, as if speaking a relationship into existence. Moirin smiled a bit more each time he repeated it, imagining how she might introduce him to people she knew.

Jo caught her eye and winked before turning back to one of their new friends. In addition to Savannah, Tina, and Galen, Jace introduced Moirin to a retired couple, Pat and Patty, who occasionally roped but, more often than not, just watched. Jenn and Alicia, wives of two ropers whose names Moirin didn't catch, and one roper's girlfriend, who was overseeing several young children. The spectators seemed to come and go, not staying in the stands long. Many seemed to watch their specific teams, then rush off to other duties.

Savannah had explained that every team took a turn in the first round. If a team had missed the first steer, they were out. Round two progressed the same as round one, but with fewer teams. After the first two rounds, teams were ranked fastest to slowest based on the sum of their times. Only the fastest twenty teams would compete in the third round, called 'the short round'. From those, the top five would win money.

Jace clapped and cheered the teams that did well. Everyone seemed to encourage each other without any of the jeers, boos, or catcalls common in other sports. It was refreshing.

"I'm up in a few minutes. I need to get my horse over there. After this, they'll drag the arena before the short round, so it will take a little while. Come over to my rig. The black truck and silver trailer over there." He put his arm around Moirin, drawing her head close to his as he pointed.

She nodded, and he jumped down from the stands. Moirin watched as he walked to Pan.

"I like him for you," Jo said. "Seems nice, smart, and easy-going. And pretty sexy."

Moirin laughed. "I have to agree. On *all* counts. He's easy to be with."

Jo grinned and poked Moirin in the ribs with her elbow. "Aw, look at that. Our tough Moirin has a soft marshmallow heart after all."

Moirin scoffed and focused on the action in the area, but not before she felt a blush creep up her neck and warm her face.

"He's a good guy," Savannah said. "He's pretty particular about who he dates, so you must be okay. Lots of people respect him around here. Solid, honest, you know?" She twisted around to face Moirin, leaning in close. "He's got a real good heart, too. Helps Tori with her work rehoming animals - dogs and horses and stuff. He hates to see animals abused or neglected. And he's always working with the younger guys on their roping. Just a good all-around guy. You're pretty lucky." Savannah narrowed her eyes as if assessing Moirin's worth before flashing a grin and turning towards the action again.

They watched several more teams, then Jace and his partner entered the boxes. Jace nodded for the steer to be released. His horse moved powerfully, in sync with Jace's motion as they paced the steer. Jace threw his rope, capturing both horns, making the process look easy. His partner followed suit, capturing the back legs, and they grinned at each other.

That's high call now. We're gonna drag the arena and start the short round. Five minutes and we close the books on the nine, ropers. Get in there.

She looked at Jo. "It looks like we get a break in the action. You want something to drink? I'll stop at the concession stand then find Jace's, ah, rig." The word felt odd in her mouth.

"Yes, I'd love a water. I'm going to walk down with you. I think that's a restroom in that building over there." Jo motioned with her head.

"Sounds good." Moirin checked her watch. "I can't believe that took two hours. It seemed faster, didn't it?"

"It did, but I think after this one, I'm pretty much roped out. I heard the announcer say there's another one after this. We don't have to stay for that, do we?" Jo said, her expression hopeful.

"I'm going to say no. I think this was enough for our first time out." She laughed when Jo let out a noisy sigh of relief.

They crossed the dirt-packed walkway, the thunderous engine drowning out all sound, making further conversation temporarily impossible. Moirin stopped and watched as a large tractor dragged an oversized rake around the arena, tilling the soil smooth like a dirt version of a Zamboni.

Jo headed for the bathroom. After a quick stop at the concession, Moirin walked to Jace's truck and trailer.

"Hey." Jace greeted her as he tied his horse to one of the metal rings attached to the side of the trailer before leaning in for a kiss.

"Hi." She worked to keep her voice level, but the kiss had sent a shiver down her spine. What was wrong with her?

Reaching into his front pocket, he pulled out a pair of sunglasses and slipped them on. His demeanor shifted back to the casual cowboy as he turned to her. "So, are you enjoying the roping?"

"We are, yes. I'm pretty impressed with your skills."

"I've been at it for years, and some days it's more luck than skill, but thank you all the same."

Jace shifted his eyes to a spot behind her head, and she heard the scuffle of footsteps. He nodded a greeting at two men who had approached them. Moirin turned and recognized them from the past few hours of watching the event.

"Moirin, this is Kyle King and Graham Douglass. Graham, Kyle, this is Moirin Garrett."

"Nice to meet you both. Kyle, congratulations. It's my first roping, but three catches all under ten seconds is a good day's work, I'd say."

"Whoa-ho," Graham exclaimed, slapping Jace on the back as Kyle grinned. "This is a sharp one, and pretty too. You better try to hold on to her, Caradova."

"I'll do my best, buddy."

Jace turned to Moirin. "You pick up fast."

"Well, I like baseball, so keeping track of the stats here was pretty easy. It's been like two innings of a game, except that there weren't any averages set coming into the game. I just had to pay attention once it started."

"You're right. That pretty much sums it up. Well, except for the number. It's your ranking based on overall performance. The higher your number, the higher your skills are expected to be. They range from two through ten."

"I see. And what's your number?"

"I'm a six."

Moirin laughed. "I asked that question as if I knew what it meant."

"It's about in the middle, a little better than some but not as good as others." She suspected he was being modest again.

"Well, I better get back over there," he said, checking the saddle and arranging Pan's bridle and headpiece. He leaned in and gave Moirin a deep kiss before mounting.

"Good luck," she said. Two simple words were all she could form. The impact of the kiss sent a wave of excitement and longing through her. She suddenly wished she were alone with him somewhere romantic, not watching him ride away into the crowded, dusty practice arena.

She strolled by toward the concession area, her eyes frequently drawn back to the areas, where she watched Jace as he cantered and galloped, warming Pan up to compete. Nearing the building, Moirin spotted Jo walking toward her, an odd mixture of excitement and embarrassment on her face. Moirin thought she saw Jo look behind her furtively as if someone might be following her.

"Are you okay?" she said.

"Yes, um, just something that took me off guard. You're not going to believe it." Jo said. "I think I might have just found a new job."

19

Moirin set the coffee to brew, humming a country song she'd heard over the speakers the day before. It was the same song that had been playing at the steakhouse the night Jace had taken her dancing. She two-stepped around the kitchen, with Orson as her unlikely partner, high-stepping and mewing playfully. She danced over to the cabinet and pulled out a can of seafood medley as Orson swatted at her hand, mewing more intently.

"There you go," she said, reaching down to scratch his ear.

The coffeemaker hissed and popped, gurgling at the end of the brew cycle until it heaved a final long sigh, indicating its efforts had been successful. Moirin poured a cup, added a generous dollop of vanilla toffee cream, then headed out to the patio to enjoy the cool morning.

The melodious tunes of *My Way* wafted from her phone, growing louder until she grabbed it from the living room table as she walked by and stopped to punch the answer button.

"Good morning, honey. I'm not calling too early, am I?" Iris sounded happy and chipper, easing Moirin's concern over the early morning call.

"No, mom. What's up?" She sipped on the steaming coffee, relishing the indulgent addition of the flavored creamer.

"We thought we'd have brunch again at the house this week. Your father wants to talk to you about the Board's status in the vetting. Strategy for what's next. He thought the privacy of the office here would be better than the restaurant."

"I appreciate that, Mom. Thank you." Charles may have requested the change, but it was Iris's decision to cancel the reservation. Moirin knew if Iris had preferred it, they would have been having their standard brunch at the restaurant.

"You're welcome, dear. We'll see you here then at ten. Please don't be late. Dorthea already spoke to Márcio, and he'll have the eggs Benedict and lemon poppyseed crepes ready for her to pick up. I would have hated to impose on her again to cook."

"That's so thoughtful, Mother," Moirin said, stifling sarcasm. "I will be on time." She tossed the phone back on the table and continued to the patio. She settled into the lounge chair and closed her eyes. She breathed deeply of the crisp morning air, the scent of freshly cut grass with a hint of floral, creating a light summer perfume. The cup was empty too soon, leaving her with the choice of the morning communion with nature sans coffee, or tearing herself away to trudge inside and refill her cup.

She absently held the empty cup to her breast, like a child would clutch a beloved stuffed animal. The tranquility of the small space filled her with peace until the pitiful yowling of Orson, trapped on the other side of the French door, shattered the calm.

Much to Orson's delight, Moirin returned indoors, and he shadowed her for the next hour as she puttered around the condo and prepared for the day.

Moirin parked her Lexus in the driveway fifteen minutes early. Mother would be pleased. She entered the house and stopped in the foyer, cocking her head to listen. Muffled voices echoed from both the right, the direction of her father's office, and the left, from the vicinity of the kitchen. She opted for the kitchen.

"Good morning, Dorthea." She said, hugging the house manager before grabbing a cup and filling it from the coffee on the counter.

"Good morning, Moirin. It's nice to see you again." Dorthea smiled and continued arranging the morning's brunch on warming platters. "This will be ready whenever your parents want it. Iris said you'll be in the breakfast room this morning. The gardener was spraying yesterday, and she said there's still an unpleasant scent that needs to clear. At least you'll have a pleasant view."

"It's perfect. I've always loved it in there." Moirin assured her as she settled on one of the stools at the island, watching as Dorthea bustled from one task to another. "Is there anything I can help with?"

"Oh, heavens no," Iris said as she breezed into the room. "Come now, Moirin, leave her alone now so she can finish and get back to her day off."

Iris pulled on Moirin's elbow, drawing her up from the stool. Moirin looked at Dorthea for confirmation. The older woman waved and shook her head. Moirin shrugged and turned, mouthing silently to Dorthea behind her mother's back. *Sorry.*

She grabbed her coffee and followed Iris to the breakfast room. A fresh carafe of water, another of coffee, and a small decanter of orange juice were already set on the table, along with a bowl of sliced fruit, nestled in a larger bowl of ice, and a basket of croissants. Three place settings, complete with cloth napkins and heavy, polished silver cutlery, were arranged for optimal viewing of the garden.

"Good morning, gingersnap." Charles strode in, his booming voice echoing in the small space.

"Good morning, Dad. You're chipper today." Moirin hugged him before they each sat at the table.

Dorthea brought in the hot dishes, slipping them quietly to the center of the table, then leaving silently. Charles reached over and dished onto his plate, taking a croissant before passing the basket to Moirin.

"So, how is everything going, dear? We haven't chatted in a while." She allowed Moirin to spoon fruit from the serving dish onto her plate, then pointed delicately to the platter of eggs. "I noticed you came late to Ian's. Your father said you didn't make it to the graduation."

"Yes, I'm busy right now, but all is well. Life balance and all that. The office, PEP Project, the girls, Orson." Moirin ticked off the pillars of her life as she passed the eggs, then refilled her coffee cup. She deliberately withheld her new dating status. She wasn't prepared yet to share any details about Jace.

"Wonderful." Iris beamed at her.

"I do feel bad I missed Ryan's graduation ceremony. I got caught up at the office." Moirin shrugged, wishing she had a better excuse. "I popped in at the party to offer congratulations. At that point, I think he was eager to be off with his friends." Moirin took a sip of coffee, then reached for the sugar. It wasn't the normal smooth brew she stocked at home. Her mother usually served a more mellow blend.

"Oh, I wouldn't worry about it. He's a teenager, and who even knows who's crammed in those seats for the ceremonies? You came to the party, dear. Making an appearance is really all that matters, anyway." Iris nibbled on a small bit of croissant she'd broken off. "You are focused on your responsibilities in the office, as you should be. Keep your priorities straight, especially now." She nodded at Charles.

"There's plenty of time for family events when you're past the Board vote." Charles cleared his throat and jabbed the edge of his fork into the eggs.

There always seemed to be one more project, or one more task to get past before she could relax and focus on other things. Years of those priorities had brought her to this point. Never finding a work-life balance that led to a wedding, children of her own, and the life milestones she might have celebrated with them. Ryan and his sister Megan, first cousins once removed, were the closest children in Moirin's life. Ryan's high school graduation was a once-in-a-lifetime experience. She'd missed it, but Iris and Charles seemed completely unbothered.

After brunch, Iris announced the light breeze outside had sufficiently cleared the chemicals that she could enjoy sitting in the garden to read her newest legal journal.

Moirin followed her father to his office and settled on the leather sofa. Charles chose to sit in his favorite captain's chair. Her phone was within reach, sitting next to her on the couch, ready to record notes and tasks, a to-do list as an outcome to their conversation.

"I hear it's been a busy week for you." Charles crossed his legs, folded one arm across his stomach, and used the other to prop up his chin. His casual, thoughtful pose was one she'd seen countless times during their father-daughter talks over the years in this room.

She couldn't help but recall those times when she was young, and he would read bedtime stories to her while Iris toiled studying for the bar exam. In her teenage years, these same two seats were the site of all their most meaningful conversations. Moirin would seek her father's help with homework or advice on navigating high school challenges while Iris worked late downtown at her law office.

"I suppose no more than most. But, yes, there's a lot going on right now." Moirin nodded, waiting to see which topic he wanted to discuss first.

"Last week, you said you understood keeping a low profile, and I appreciate you taking that to heart. I haven't heard anything else about that Riggs fellow, and I trust now you've left Plankett alone."

She nodded again, unsure how to respond. It was true she'd had no further interaction with Riggs, and *technically* she'd left Plankett alone. At least directly. Indirectly, was another story. Her attorney was well on the path to donating the 'unexpected' property to a conservation group. That's how Moirin thought of it now, an 'unexpected' property.

One of Plankett's buried shell companies had spent a significant amount to purchase that property and later fraudulently transfer it to Moirin's name. He had to consider it a write-off at that point. Still, she donated a valuable asset she hadn't purchased. It felt underhanded at the very least. Whatever Plankett had planned, she'd successfully thwarted, but who knew how long she would feel anxious, awaiting his retaliation.

"Ian and I had lunch on Thursday," he continued.

"Oh? How did that go?" Moirin smoothed the unwrinkled fabric of her linen slacks with long, quick flicks of her thumb. Uncle Ian seemed fine at Ryan's party Friday night, brushing off her apology, but he might have expressed a different attitude to her father privately.

"He's fine. Seemed normal to me. Yesterday, we did a quick nine holes, and he said he's looking forward to spending more time on the links to get rid of that slice of his."

"Really?" Moirin felt her shoulders sag in relief. She hadn't realized she'd tensed up, expecting consequences from her outburst on Wednesday.

"He wasn't pleased about some set-to you had last week, though. He said you were stubborn about a timeline change and got aggressive in the conversation." His voice went up a few octaves at the end, and he cocked his head quizzically. She wasn't sure if it was a statement or question.

"That's true. I had been dealing with a few tough things that day, and he surprised me by suggesting the change. I did come on a little strong in my opinion." She stopped short of fully explaining her anger. Why had Ian even mentioned the argument if he hadn't shared why they argued – his suggestion to *not* step down as CEO?

"Moirin," Charles tsk'ed his tongue, a disappointed frown pulling at his face. "You know better. You can't lose your temper like that. If it had been anyone but Ian…"

"I know, I'm sorry. I don't think the Board will hear about it." Moirin recalled Wanda's shocked look but had confidence her assistance wouldn't spread gossip. Not about her boss' emotional meltdown, anyway. "I can talk to Ian again. I'll make sure we're on the same page about the timeline."

"Well, it seems your worries were unfounded." Her father seemed satisfied the matter was settled, but Moirin was even more concerned about Ian's state of mind. "So, let's go through this vetting."

Moirin took copious notes as her father issued advice for the Board presentation. They were pursuing their own course of vetting, but someone pulled it from a standard playbook. He waved his hand as if clearing the air of a bad smell. "No one cares about your college scores from thirty years ago, and recommendation letters are a dime a dozen. I know they asked for three or four from professional contacts, but they'll be meaningless, right? Of course, they'll be glowing support. Who is stupid enough to ask for or turn in a recommendation letter that's not flattering? PPffft, waste of time." He waved his hand, brushing off the idea.

Moirin had to agree. "I'm doing what they've asked, including an updated resume, which also seems ridiculous. But, I have to respect their process."

"Of course. I support that. You need to hit hard on what matters, though. Your five- and ten-year plans. I know you refresh them every year or two but update them now if you haven't already. That will be important. Give them the meat of what you bring to the role – your greatest accomplishment so far and a clear vision for the future. Be honest, too. Put some of your shortcomings in there and how you mitigate them. Wouldn't hurt to have a report on the company's current problems and how you're solving them."

Moirin tapped notes into the memo page on her phone. "Most of this has been on my mind. I can have it put together in a few weeks. Do you know the timeline they'll have everything done? Do we know when they've set the vote?"

"Shorten your timeline. I'm guessing they will take three to four weeks, so you need to have your data ready sooner. They'll likely set the vote for the July Board meeting. Gives them time to look for any skeletons they think might be out there."

Moirin swallowed to dislodge the lump of butterflies that ascended from her stomach to her throat. "Should be fine," she mumbled.

"I'm proud of you, gingersnap. Your grandfather would be proud of you, too."

"Thanks, Dad. I'm going to head into the office for the afternoon to get a jump on next week. Maybe get one of these papers written." Moirin held the phone up. "Tell mom I'll see her next week."

Charles grunted. Moirin left, her mind drafting a list of report updates as she drove to the office.

~

She sat back in her chair, satisfaction surging through her as she smirked at the perfectly clear, shining surface of the desk. Not only was the full backlog of work cleared, but her email inbox was up-to-date, and she had reviewed the final draft of the Annual Report. All that was accomplished after she outlined a document with her father's recommended items. It was only four o'clock, so she'd put in another hour on the historical financial review, then take hard copies of her five- and ten-year plans to read and edit at home tonight.

As she double-clicked the computer file, Moirin heard the elevator chime. Surprised that anyone else was working on the weekend, she got up from her desk and cautiously went into the hallway. She heard a muffled voice and strained to determine the direction. It got louder for a moment, and she turned, trying to keep her steps as quiet as possible until she knew the source. There. Ian's office.

As she drew closer to the office, she heard Colin's voice, a one-sided conversation with someone over the phone. She heard him laugh sharply.

"Again with this? What is it with you? Ok, fine, tell me," Colin said. She heard shuffling as Colin moved around, then she heard another voice, distorted. She realized he had put the phone on speaker. How convenient. Moirin walked closer to the open door, then leaned against the wall with her arms crossed, blatantly eavesdropping.

"I got this in my email. It was from *National Geographic,* so it's the real deal, okay."

"Uh-huh"

"So, yeah, in Norway a couple of years ago, the glaciers are melting, right. They found an old Viking highway. Like right over the mountain pass. They're finding horseshoes, sleds, tools, and all kinds of stuff."

"Okay," Colin sounded distracted. The sound of shuffling papers and movement told Moirin that he wasn't paying much attention to his caller.

"They've found tons of bones and arrows that are thousands of years old. And I read another article from the *Smithsonian* where they found tons of artifacts and evidence there were villages there like a thousand years ago. There was like a Viking sword, man, that was found on a beach in Iceland a few years ago. A couple of days later, a skeleton turned up. Turns out a whole village was uncovered when the ice melted. Stuff was just washing down from the mountains and landing on the beach."

"You've got to stop reading this stuff. Yes, there's all kinds of history buried under dirt and rocks and ice. All over the world. We're careful when we dig. We're not going to destroy anything historically significant."

Moirin relaxed. Colin seemed to be arguing on Garrett's behalf that they were a responsible organization. She wondered who the agitated man was on the other end of the conversation. Colin seemed to know him well. There was something about the voice that sounded familiar.

"That's not what I'm saying, man. You're missing the point."

"What's the point, then?" Colin sighed, as if this role of long-suffering sounding board was familiar.

"If all this stuff is under the ice, don't you get it? There was a day when the ice wasn't there."

"So?"

"So? Are you kidding? A thousand years ago, the waters were higher. There was less ice, and people had roads and villages all over the place. *Then* the ice came. It took their homes, and it made their roads impassable. It changed everything."

"What?"

"What if they had the power back then to keep that ice from forming? We'd never have the glaciers we're trying to save now. Can you imagine what the last thousand years would have been like without those glaciers, man?"

"I don't know. Higher water levels, less snow, or something. I'm not a climatologist."

"Okay, me neither, but I don't think it would have been good. But you're right, how can we know? How can anyone know?" The man's tone was almost manic.

"So, you think we should just let nature decide," Colin said.

"Exactly." The caller seemed triumphant, as if a major victory had been achieved.

"That's a little simplistic. If ice growing and shrinking is a natural cycle, that's one thing. But if humans are impacting the process, that's not okay.

We need to keep our impact as minimal as possible and let nature do its thing."

"But are you sure you know the difference?"

She waited to see how Colin would respond.

"You know what, I'll give it some thought. But right now, I'm in the office on a Sunday afternoon, and Brittany's irritated with me, but I gotta get these reports squared for the board meeting. My dad's been breathing down my neck, and I can't deal with you on top of all that."

Moirin heard a shuffling and scraping, and then the distorted voice went silent. Colin must have picked up the phone and turned off the speaker.

The last comment echoed in her mind. *Dad's been breathing down my neck.* It was out of character for Ian, but she'd seen odd behavior from him lately. Rather than confront him now, and add to his stress, she decided to talk to Colin the next day. It would give her more time tonight to consider an approach.

She walked back to her office, toying with the idea that she should reach out and invite Brittany to lunch one Saturday. No one knew more about a husband's stress than his wife, right?

20

Tuesday afternoon, Moirin tapped out a brief group text to Jo, Leslie, and Heather, knowing she'd be forgiven for the late cancellation, but would have to make up for it with details later. She couldn't suppress the smile as she sent the message.

Won't make it tonight. Dinner with Jace at his place.

"A couple of guys are coming over to rope," he'd said when they made the arrangements. "I have a practice arena, and we get together once or twice a week. We'll throw some steaks on the grill afterward." He gave her the address and detailed directions. After dating for a few weeks now, she was looking forward to seeing his home. She wondered idly how he would feel about joining a Sunday brunch with her parents. He had a way of connecting with people. He would probably charm her mother and impress her father. She'd like to find out.

Within minutes, she had a return flurry of text messages

Jo: Have fun! Call me tomorrow

Heather: Can't wait to hear all the details

Leslie: Go girl!

She left the office obscenely early, before five o'clock, to feed Orson and change from her business suit into a pale green loose linen shirt with three-quarter length sleeves, crop jeans, and ballerina flats. She gave Orson an extra scratch behind the ears, promising she'd only be gone a few hours.

Arriving at the address, she hesitated as she read the ranch name emblazoned across a large wooden sign supported on either side by massive posts. *Rancho de los Caradova.* A traditional ranch entry, but the size and quality of the sign announced wealth, which took her by surprise. Jace never acted like someone who came from money; he was much too down-to-earth.

The two-lane driveway was a long, packed-gravel road, bordered on either side by a white railing fence, partially obscured from the public road by trees. The railing fence extended out from the driveway at least a quarter-mile in each direction, creating large pastures. She drove the tree-lined route to the house. Or, rather, the ranch complex.

At the end of the road, she saw the main house, a large barn, a shed, and several outbuildings arranged in a U-shape. The heavily-packed gravel area resembled a business parking lot, except that vehicles were pulled in without rhyme or reason. Moirin saw Jace's truck, along with three unfamiliar trucks near the barn, all with horse trailers attached. A tan late-model mid-sized sedan sat near the house. Looking around, she also saw a four-wheeler and two small tractors.

Leaving her car near the sedan, she walked toward the barn, drawn by the sounds of activity. The now-familiar sounds of pounding hoof beats, clanging gates, and men's shouts led her around the building to an outdoor practice arena. She walked to the fence, stepping up to watch over the top.

An energetic brown and white dog came bounding up to her, wagging his tail enthusiastically. She couldn't help but reach down to scratch the ears of the happy-looking dog with a foxlike face, pointed ears, and a bushy, curling tail. He was only as tall as her knee. The full, thick coat was multi-toned brown on the back and pure white on the stomach, chest, and legs. His face was the same multi-toned brown as his back, with black ears and snout, and two slashes above his eyes, just like eyebrows, giving him human-like expressions. He sniffed her approvingly and took off running toward the arena center.

The arena was set up in much the same way as Benally's but seemed much smaller. The header and heeler box were at one end, with the chute for the cattle between them. Neither of the men positioned in the boxes looked familiar. Jace and two other men mounted on horses lined up just past the starting line and watched casually, leaning forward, arms crossed on their saddle horns. A sixth man chased an errant steer through the exit gate at the far end of the arena.

The gate opened, and both header and heeler found their mark, quickly roping the steer. She applauded. The three mounted riders turned as Jace urged his horse forward.

"Moirin. You look beautiful today." He leaned down for a kiss.

"Thank you. This place you have here is what's beautiful," she said.

"It's been in the family for a few generations, and everybody adds their piece. The arena's my contribution," he replied with a grin. "Come meet everyone. We'll have you work the gate for us."

She recognized one of the men from the roping she and Jo had attended and stepped forward.

"Graham. Hi, nice to see you again."

He nodded, "You too."

Jace nodded to the man next to him. "This is Shawn." He waved at the other three riders. "That there is Travis, Rooster, and Carson. Guys, this is Moirin."

"Shawn. Travis. Rooster. Carson," Moirin repeated, nodding to each.

"Yup," Travis nodded in acknowledgment.

"Nicetameetcha," Rooster mumbled, immediately turning and riding off.

"Ma'am," Carson tipped his hat.

"And I think you met Gaski," Jace said, slapping his leg to call the dog over.

"I did. Gaski, huh? That's an unusual name. He looks like a border collie mix?"

"Nope, he's actually an Icie — Icelandic Sheepdog. The Vikings bred them to herd and protect livestock. Gaski means Cheerful."

"I've never heard of that breed, but he seems to be named accurately. You know I'm more of a cat person, but I think I like him." Moirin laughed at the dog's antics, running along the fence barking at the cattle, before speeding back to Jace.

"He's pretty friendly. He's a great herder and a pretty good retriever, too." He leaned down to pat the dog.

"Sounds like he has some important jobs." Moirin laughed. "Speaking of jobs, you said that I'm to work the gate. What does that mean?"

Jace dismounted and walked alongside her, leading his horse to the fence next to the header's box. He explained the header's nod was the signal to press the button and release the gate. The header would be watching the steer the entire time, so she would need to watch their gestures. She assured Jace she was up to the task and climbed up on the fence, settling herself on the top rung.

She marveled that balancing on a fence, surrounded by dust and smelly livestock, was starting to be in her comfort zone. A month ago, it would have been unthinkable. She understood why boots were so popular as she found her ballerina flats continually slipping off one foot or the other, falling to the dirt. She finally kicked them off and left them beneath the fence. Having her feet and bare toes already filthy by her standards was disconcerting. If she continued to frequent this environment, she would need to invest in jeans and cowboy boots.

She watched for the head motions of the ropers and released the cattle right on cue. The practice field was filled with conversation and good-natured ribbing that she would expect from a group of friends. What surprised her was the level of support and coaching she witnessed.

"Rooster, keep that tip down before you throw."

"Watch that left hand, you're pulling."

"Nice one, Carson."

When Jace rode over, she asked him about it.

"Yeah, we help each other out," he said. "Team roping isn't a cut-throat competitive sport. It's a pursuit of personal achievement. It's not about beating someone else; it's about improving your own skill."

"That's a nice idea, but, in the end, competition is still about beating everyone else to get first place," Moirin said, watching for Rooster's nod from the header's box. Shawn's horse stomped lightly in the heeler's box, anxiously awaiting his rider's signal to surge forward. Rooster's chin ducked slightly, indicating his readiness. Moirin pushed the remote in her hand and released the steer.

Jace cocked his head, watching the action as he considered her words before shaking his head. "You never know in a roping. You go out and do your best every run. You might break out, your heeler might leg, but as long as you catch, you're still in it. Every go-round, someone misses. It's part of the sport. You just have to stay focused and mind your own loop, trust your partner to do his part."

"So, who's your partner? You've roped with several I've seen." Moirin turned toward him, unsure how that part of the sport was determined.

"There aren't any fixed partners. It changes every roping. At some events, you choose a partner and enter together. Others, your partners are drawn like a lottery."

"Then how do you work as a team?" she asked.

"That's what makes this both a competitive and collaborative sport. I need to be the best header I can be — clean off the line, catch quick, and turn the steer to the optimal position for my heeler. I have to trust my heeler is going to catch, and he needs to trust I'll catch and turn for him." Jace explained.

"Doesn't it get contentious when one of you misses? How many times do you rope with the same heeler if he always misses? Or a heeler who never gets to throw because the header doesn't catch? I think I would get annoyed if I were doing my job but never winning because of someone else's failure."

"It would depend. If they never caught, or just never caught for me. If the heeler was winning with other headers, I might start thinking I was doing something wrong." He grinned suddenly and winked as he tightened the reins in his hands, then clucked to Pan, nudging the horse to the box.

"Carson, let's run a few," he shouted. He pointed for Gaski to stay with Moirin, and she was impressed with the dog's instant obedience.

What she'd seen of team roping was entertaining to watch, but the philosophy behind it was fascinating to her. It wasn't just a sport; it was an extension of a lifestyle. The Cowboy way of life. She loved the idea of collaborative teamwork with individual responsibility. It was similar to other team sports, like football or baseball, but she wondered how the team spirit would fare when the players got all mixed up in each subsequent game.

As Jace explained it, in team roping events, a person could often enter the same event multiple times with different partners. Everyone tried their best on each run, and everyone seemed to encourage each other, even cheering when someone did better than you. She noted at the event the previous weekend, there'd been no jeers or booing from the spectators, and mostly good-natured trash talk between competitors.

She wondered how she could get her teams at the office to adopt the philosophy. If she stayed around Jace long enough, perhaps she could adopt the philosophy herself.

As Moirin watched their practice, she tried to catch the odd terms they threw at each other as they gave each other pointers. She began to see the distinct skill areas that had to be mastered to excel in this sport. One element was the cattle — some fast, some slow, others showing a sneaky intelligence to duck the loop at the last minute. The second piece was horsemanship. Travis confirmed the mounts were typically trained as either a head horse or heel horse, and few were skilled enough to be both.

The final skill was handling the rope, a combination of core athletic ability and superior hand-eye coordination. Smooth motions from shoulder-wrist combinations culminated in the quick snap of the throw. The roper's hands flashed as they wrapped the rope around their saddle horns to "dally" or secure the rope. Sometimes they weren't fast enough, and the steer ran, snatching the rope from their hands.

Moirin remembered once, as a child, when a kite had been ripped from her hand in a similar way, a painful burn when the twine string yanked across her palm. The zipping sound made it clear this strand was far heavier and more dangerous. A sharply inhaled breath, a quick rub of the palm across the thigh, and shaking fingers were all the evidence she needed that it hurt as much as it looked like it would. She thought Jace had been joking when he told her it wasn't unusual to lose a finger or thumb during roping.

She respected the sport and the necessary skill even more as she watched their dedication to practice. They each took turns at the box, alternating from watching to shoo'ing the cattle toward the exit gate.

After an hour, they turned the steers out to pasture and unsaddled the horses. Gaski joyfully took off after his master, eager to help.

"Let's get those steaks on the grill." Jace slapped his hands, rubbing them together. "Who's hungry?"

Shawn begged off, saying his wife had dinner waiting for him and he'd be sleeping in the doghouse if he didn't get home to it. He loaded his horse in the trailer, offering a nod and brief wave as he pulled out.

Travis and Rooster declined. Rooster had brought his and Travis' horse in his trailer, and even if Travis wanted to stay, Rooster had business to attend to and couldn't wait.

Graham didn't have any time constraints and nodded. "All right if I put my horse in a stall there?" he asked Jace.

"Sure. We can throw him a flake of hay if you want. I'm going to get the grill started. If Moirin watches it for me, I'll go feed the horses then." Jace looked at Moirin, eyebrows raised. She nodded in agreement.

"I'll take care of it, boss," Carson said, leading his horse toward the outdoor stalls. "I'll be up to the house in a while, then."

"Boss?" Moirin gave Jace a sidelong look.

He shrugged. "Yeah, Carson stays in the bunkhouse, helps out with the chores. He usually comes up to the house to eat with me."

"This is quite a place you have here. It's a lot more than I expected." Moirin said.

"Well, we'll save the property tour for another time. Let me show you up to the house, and we'll get dinner started."

He led her across the graveled area to the stone pathway leading to the house. Gaski ran ahead, darting after birds, clearing the path for the trailing humans, before bouncing off toward the yard. Jace veered off to the right, heading for the back deck instead of the front door. He stopped to snap on the gas grill, warming it up while they retrieved the steaks.

Moirin stopped as they stepped inside. The space was large, the size of her condo's living room and kitchen combined. The room design would make a gourmet chef weak in the knees. A deep farmhouse sink had a companion prep sink adjacent, both situated in front of a window that provided a breathtaking view of the grounds and distant mountains. Across from the sinks was an oversized French-door refrigerator with three drawers in the lower half, which Moirin assumed was freezer space. The third wall seemed to be mostly pantry and storage space, except for a space carved out for double wall ovens. The last side opened to a table with seating for six. A six-burner cooktop and indoor grill took up half the island in the center of the room, with prep areas on either side. Next to the refrigerator, Moirin could see a floor-to-ceiling bookshelf that housed a collection of cookbooks.

"This kitchen is gorgeous. Who's the gourmet cook?"

"My mom. She redesigned this about ten years ago when they lived here. It's my house now, but they stay occasionally. They retired and spend half the year in Arizona now, but like to travel in the summer. Mom loves the RV, and Dad loves to make Mom happy. I enjoy when they swing by and stay for a couple of weeks now and then."

"That's so sweet," Moirin said.

"Yeah." He continued, "They like the travel, but they'll always call this home. It's been the family home for five generations now. I can't imagine living anywhere else."

Moirin nodded, looking around the room. The house reflected that same feeling of family. The fact that his family's business continued through five generations spoke volumes about the close family ties and support that sustained it.

The warm brick and dull silver of the stainless steel appliances complemented the brown and red decor. She could feel the warmth, the welcoming environment designed to put friends and family at ease. The decor of casual elegance was the perfect mix of comfort and convenience. She reached over, taking the tray of spices, dinnerware, and a bowl of pasta salad Jace had set out while he picked up the platter of steaks.

She leaned past him, kissing him on the cheek.

"What was that for? Not that I'm complaining," he said, winking

She felt a smile spread over her face. "Just to say thank you for the invitation. I've enjoyed this. I like seeing you in your home environment."

"I'm glad you came out. It's nice having you here. Let's get these out there before those guys come in mobbing us for food," he said, chuckling.

Moirin followed him to the deck and went about arranging the table as Jace busied himself at the grill. She sat down, watching as he cooked until Carson and Graham walked in from the path leading up from the barn.

"Perfect timing, guys." Jace directed Graham to help with the steaks and sent Carson inside for a jug of iced tea.

They savored the meal as they sat on the deck, taking in the beautiful sunset and the balmy evening air. Birds chirping and insects buzzing, blending with the occasional nicker of a horse and low of cattle. Moirin could hear Gaski's excitement as he ran through the trees, stirring up birds again with sharp barks. Soon after finishing their plates, Carson and Graham excused themselves, leaving Jace and Moirin alone.

For a while, they chatted about Jace's work, then Moirin's, but eventually the conversation tapered. They sat in companionable silence, side by side on a rollback wood glider, Jace's foot rocking them gently back and forth. The sun slid lower. The vibrant colors of the sky muted as stars appeared above them, the sinking sun giving its last glow of warm color on the horizon.

21

It was barely seven-thirty, but Wanda was already at her desk. Moirin smiled in greeting and accepted the pile of handwritten messages. She knew her voicemail would be full as well. On any given day, the most critical issue could come in from either source. Those with her private number called her line directly, while the rest were forced to go through the corporate red tape, ending up at her efficient gatekeeper, Wanda.

Up and down the hallway, the offices were still relatively quiet, the staff just starting to arrive and gear up for the day. She heard the distant whirring of a mechanical device, the ringing of a phone, and the hum of the air conditioning. Wanda turned back to her computer.

Moirin entered her office and closed the door behind her. She dropped her briefcase and the messages on her desktop and walked to the bank of windows. Usually, the view of the mountains and lush green trees in the distance gave her a sense of peace and contentment. They seemed so far away this morning. Beautiful but distant and unattainable. As she stood, the muscles in her shoulders tensed, and her stomach twisted uncomfortably. She closed her eyes and took a deep breath. The cold metallic taste of artificially cooled air filled her mouth.

She wondered what Jace was doing at this moment. She imagined being at his ranch, breathing in the natural, warm scent of horses, tasting the gritty air, and basking in warm yellow sunshine. Last night, the air was filled with birdsong, insects chirping, and intermittent chuffing from Gaski as he sniffed around the trees. Horses neighing and cattle lowing had been faint in the distance. The patio where they had sat melded from flagstone to thick grass, then blended in the distance with the trees on the horizon.

It was all so natural, so balanced.

But not so here in her world.

Her universe was waking up around her in a cacophony of racket: a ringing phone, the ding of the elevator, and a gradually increasing rumble, the mumbling of fifty people engaged in casual one-on-one chit-chat or conversing on the phone. The office jungle was coming alive as the inhabitants began their daily prowl.

Moirin shook her head and stepped into her proper role, walking briskly to her desk to confirm the day's calendar schedule. She was hoping to find time for a meeting with Colin, or, at the very least, a private lunch. He had been booked solid yesterday, and her day on Monday only allowed a brief exchange, which had been unsettling.

She had determined a direct approach would be best, admitting she'd overheard part of his telephone conversation the day before.

"You were here on a Sunday? I didn't see you." He seemed surprised, but Moirin was relieved that she didn't detect any nervousness or deception.

"I have a few extra things on my plate between the PEP project and the Board's vetting. I left shortly after you arrived. I didn't want to interrupt you," she said.

"I appreciate that. I wanted to get in and out of here as fast as possible. Brittany hates it when I work weekends."

"I'm concerned about your dad. I heard you say he's been pushing you about something. I know that's unusual. He's normally so laid back, but lately he seems stressed."

"You're not wrong. I think we need to do something." Colin sighed, rubbing the back of his neck. "I've been worried."

"*There* you are." Wanda's voice carried from down the hall. Moirin turned to see her assistant rushing toward her. "Dixon called. He's got an emergency and needs to talk to you right away. He was headed up to your office."

Moirin nodded to Wanda, then turned and pointed. "Colin, let's talk later about this."

"Definitely," he said, nodding.

The head of IT, Dixon Ferguson, was cool-headed and methodical. He was generally the one to calm others during emotional meltdowns over a computer crisis. If he was coming to speak to her directly, it had to be serious.

When she arrived back in her office, Dixon was already seated.

"I'm almost afraid to ask." Moirin sighed as she settled behind the desk. She folded her hands and waited.

"I don't know what set off your suspicions about the database, but you were right. We found a virus in the system," he said.

"Don't we have firewalls and email quarantine protocols in place to ensure that sort of thing doesn't happen?" Moirin tried to keep her anger and frustration from her voice. It was never effective to get emotional, particularly when facts were still unknown.

"We do. This was deliberately uploaded into our network. From an internal computer in this building." He shook his head, as if incredulous himself at how something like that could happen.

"What's our exposure?" Moirin tapped her finger on the desk.

"I still have them running tests, but right now, none. It doesn't seem that anyone was able to access any information, no data was lost, and we've not been locked out of any systems. I think we lucked out, and it was a poorly designed virus. Or it was just a prank that wasn't intended to do real harm. Maybe a dare between programmers. You never know with some of these kids."

"But you feel confident it's been removed and there is no lasting damage?" Moirin's chest tightened, and her stomach twisted at the potential implications. "Will you be able to track which computer it was uploaded from?"

"Moirin, I'll do my best, but we might not be able to trace it. I've got a few guys working on it, and I'll let you know."

"All right. Thank you for the personal update. For now, I'd like you to report any progress directly to me. Let's not have an electronic trail just in case."

"Of course. But just in case of what?" he asked.

"That's the problem, Dixon." She tapped a pen on the desk, a cascade of possibilities running through her mind. "I simply don't know."

He opened his mouth, then closed it without speaking. He nodded and pushed the chair back. "Understood."

"Thank you." Years of working together had facilitated trust. She was counting on it now. She watched him exit the office and considered the hundreds of people who worked in the building. How many of them could she truly trust? At her level, although she was acquainted with many, she worked directly with few. It made that certainty impossible.

Shaking her head, she turned to the computer. It was best to focus on those things she could control. She pulled up Colin's electronic calendar, studying to find a vacancy.

It was nearly as full as her own, but he had an open hour at one o'clock. *Perfect.* She tapped out a meeting request, then asked Wanda to reserve a table at the bistro down the street. They'd be more likely to have a productive private conversation away from the office.

Before then, she should check on her uncle. Moirin pivoted around her desk and headed for Ian's suite down the hall. He sat behind his desk, furiously scribbling on a ledger page, pausing as he flipped pages back and forth in a bound report.

"Got a minute?" she said, knocking on the open door before crossing the room and sitting down in front of the desk. It hadn't been a question.

"What? Oh, uh, sure, Moirin, sit. Sit." He leaned back in the large chair, hinges squeaking and leather crunching as his weight shifted.

"I wanted to check in on you," she said. "Apologize again for my outburst last week and make sure we are on the same page."

"I appreciate that." Ian sat forward, the mechanism on the base of his chair slamming into its wood frame with a clunk. "Charles and I talked, and he seems confident of everything. The Board's vetting, your readiness, and that it's a good time for the business to make a change."

"I'd hope that you would be confident in all that as well. I have to admit, I was shocked you thought otherwise. I want to ensure your full support in this. If there is anything that you think we need to discuss, please let me know."

He nodded slowly.

Moirin continued, "I've gone back through the initial testing and projections from the database. Everything is as it should be. I'm in the process of re-running all the annual report numbers since the inception to verify the data."

Ian sat forward and frowned. "You what?"

"I know that was one of the topics that most concerned you, and I wanted to address it. Uncle Ian, I can promise you the company is in good hands. I'll devote my time to securing its future success. This company will continue to thrive and will remain strong for Colin, for Ryan one day, and even the next generation Avery's working on."

Ian chuckled suddenly. "I admire your commitment. We're fine, sweetheart." His office line rang, and he leaned forward, squinting at the caller ID display. "I have to take this call," he said, lifting the receiver, but covering it with his hand. "It's okay," he whispered, then removed his hand and turned his attention to the incoming call.

Moirin stood and raised her hand with two fingers, like a frozen farewell wave. *Okay,* she mouthed silently and left the office.

One meeting and a conference call later, she dashed out of her office, ignoring the ringing phone, anxious to meet Colin for their lunch.

Breathless, she entered the bistro and spotted Colin sitting at a small table. There was a basket of bread in the center, and two water glasses sat dripping condensation. She was either late or he had arrived early. She glanced at her watch and sighed.

Hooking her purse over the back of the empty chair, she sat down across from Colin. "Thank you for meeting me. Sorry, I'm late."

"Of course. I went ahead and ordered for us both," Colin said.

Moirin smiled gratefully.

"You know, I was sitting here thinking we should do this more often," Colin said.

"We should. Every time I see you, it seems we have a set agenda and don't have the time to stray from bullet points." Moirin laughed and took a long drink from her water glass.

"I hate being directed by bullet points," Colin said. "We're the bosses. We should be allowed to stray as far off topic as we please."

Moirin snorted. "We'd never get anything done."

"True. We'll plan more lunches, then." He laid his menu down, ran his finger down the spine, then tapped the surface. Moirin sensed his hesitation but couldn't tell if he was trying to avoid talking about his father or was unsure how to begin.

She saved him from the uncertainty. "I know this might be difficult, Colin. I don't want you to feel like you're betraying his confidence, but we both care about your dad. If he's struggling with something, we can find a way to help him together."

"He has some things going on, I won't deny it." He took a long swig of water while Moirin waited for him to continue. Colin sighed. "I only found out the past few months, but Dad's living on a house of cards. A few years ago, he worked himself into a major financial bind, and he added a lot of debt to get out of it. That's just made his problems worse now."

"I never would have suspected that. Are you certain?"

Colin raised an eyebrow, twisting his mouth into a wry smile.

"Of course you're certain. I'm sorry. How bad is it?"

"He won't tell me exactly. He approached me a few months ago about tapping the family trust."

Moirin gasped. "Oh, Colin, I'm so sorry. I don't know what to say. Well, what did *you* say?"

"I reacted about like you would. Grandfather set up those trusts for each of us. Dad already spent everything he had access to, and he wanted to take mine and Gillian's as well. Borrow, he said. But that's *my* children's inheritance. I can't let him squander it." Colin's voice took on a bitter tone. "After I refused, a few days later Mom said that he brought home paperwork for a reverse mortgage."

"Well, that's a ridiculous idea. I don't disagree with you on the trust, though. He borrowed his way into a bigger hole, and if he used the trust, it would be gone forever."

A server arrived silently, efficiently serving each of them a pan-seared maple-glazed salmon with arugula salad. Moirin smiled. "Thanks for remembering my favorite."

Colin nodded. "It's mine too."

Moirin waited for the young man to leave before continuing. "We both know his salary and bonuses. Do you know how things got so desperate?" She took a bite of the salad.

"I guess a big investment went south a few years back, and it hasn't helped that he can't say no to Mom about anything. They've been living beyond their means for years. You know, they take extravagant weekend trips and throw those lavish parties. Mom spends money indiscriminately on shopping sprees, lunches, and treats her friends to spa days. She renovated to install a gourmet kitchen, bought a cabin in Aspen, and a beach house in Maui. Dad indulges her. He gets overextended, pays off little bits here and there, but the hole they're in just gets bigger."

Moirin wasn't surprised. Aunt Felicity was far worse than Iris when it came to both personal shopping and striving for a perfect public image. Their Denver home was considered a mansion by many, professionally redecorated every three years, constantly renovated, and known for lavish parties. A socialite and generous philanthropist without her own family money, Felicity was never compelled to earn an income. No, it wasn't surprising that her spending habits created financial hardship for Ian.

"This does explain some of his distraction and odd behavior," Moirin said.

"I think he's working on a post-retirement plan," Colin said, talking between bites of salmon. "He's looking at old reports, reading all the newest studies, and reviews of groundbreaking technology. The past few months, he's called me at odd hours on the weekend, insisting I go to the office to find some report or download a file on a thumb drive for him. Some things make sense, like the Scandinavian wind turbines or carbon capture. Other things are just rabbit holes, I think. He had Ryan help him install a secure VPN at the house so he could work more from home."

"How worried do we need to be?" Moirin savored the fish, which was perfectly prepared and delicious. If only she could cook like this at home.

"For now, I think their finances are stable enough to cover the minimums. He still seems stressed, though. I'm not sure he's telling me the full story, but maybe he will open up to your dad if you suggest it."

"That's a good idea. He won't resent his brother as much as his son or niece. I'll try to talk with dad tonight."

Both relieved to have a plan, the conversation moved to a more pleasant topic of summer plans, now that Colin's children were both out of school. Moirin didn't mind. It was another opportunity to live vicariously through those with children and grandchildren.

She breezed into the office the next day, feeling lighter than she had in weeks. The conversation with Colin was productive. Although they were both worried about Uncle Ian, the honesty about their concern and their agreement to address it was encouraging. Working with relatives came with challenges, but it was best for both business and family that everyone had their goals aligned. The company ran smoother when they weren't at odds.

Wanda tapped her watch as Moirin approached her office. She was late for another meeting. She pushed her personal thoughts aside and focused on her business. It would probably be another one of those days where she didn't have time to catch her breath from one task to the next.

That afternoon, during her fourth meeting of the day in a conference room packed with twenty-five other attendees, a nervous junior analyst fumbled as he set up his presentation. He jabbed a thumb drive at the side of his laptop, searching for the drive port. The young man reminded her of Steffie, the perky intern from the PEP project. Finally, the analyst picked up the laptop, squinted, then lined up the thumb drive with the port and successfully snapped it in place.

The thumb drive. During lunch the day before, Colin said Ian had sent him to the office to download files to an external drive. She tapped out an email to Dixon Ferguson, asking him about the security of USB drives and whether one used for downloads could, in fact, inadvertently upload. She was also curious to know what files may have been saved to an external hard drive from Ian's computer recently, particularly during non-business hours.

When she returned from the meeting, there was a reply in her email inbox. Dixon was still taking the matter quite seriously. In the past three months, numerous files had been saved, but most had been financial data, including the past five years' annual reports. Moirin stopped reading the message to ponder for a moment. Why would anyone be interested in a file that was part of a printed report sent to shareholders?

Wanda knocked on the office doorframe. "Hey, boss. Need anything else before I take off?"

Moirin looked up. "No, thanks. Have a good night."

"Okay. I'll see you tomorrow."

Moirin walked to the bookshelf and thumbed through the volumes, pulling out the prior years' printed reports, the ones distributed to shareholders. She took the five books to her desk and flipped through the newest. Dixon had said the downloaded reports had focused on financials. She logged onto the internal company secure server and accessed the financial reports for the same year, and the report she had lying open. Line by line, she compared the data.

It was late when she finished. The sky outside was inky black. The mountains were invisible past the chunks and glittering dots of light scattered throughout the city. On another night, it might seem festive.

Tonight, they represented failure — a feeble attempt to pierce the darkness of night.

A sickening dread, overpowered by anger, caused her hands to shake. She had expected this research project to be a quick exercise in futility. An hour before, she realized her mistake. The financials had been altered on the annual report four years ago. It had taken longer than she anticipated, but she traced it back, despite someone having worked hard to bury it.

A project had been funded, then terminated a year later. It wasn't unusual. Projects that didn't work out, or were unprofitable, were shuttered. The Fairwind project. The name was vaguely familiar. She remembered only the barest details but was certain the numbers in the financials were far higher than the actual budget.

It made little sense. Why had these reports been accessed from Ian's computer? Had Ian suspected something, or had he been a party to it? Was Colin involved? Or were they both innocent and unwittingly led her to this discovery? *Doubtful.* Every part of this wasn't just doubtful; it was unthinkable.

Swallowing hard, she typed an email to Wanda. By routing it through her assistant and requesting a few unrelated details, perhaps it wouldn't raise suspicions, should anyone be looking. She requested details on three projects, but was only interested in the details of one: a deep dive into partners, vendors, who were paid, and whose contracts were cancelled. Anything with financial impact.

It was years in the past, and a minor anomaly in the larger scheme of things, but another troublesome thorn in her side at a time when she needed everything to be smooth. The property, the program bugs, and now financial inconsistencies? Maybe the Board had been right to insist on vetting. Had she overlooked crucial details, or was someone working against her? *Sure, a nefarious evil villain out to ruin you. Get a grip, Moirin. Just coincidence.*

She sighed, anger fading into exhaustion. She logged off the computer, pulled her purse from the desk drawer, and flipped off the lights as she left the office.

22

By noon on Friday, Moirin was eager for the weekend to begin. Not for a break from work, but the opportunity to accomplish more when others weren't also working and demanding her attention. When the thought crossed her mind, she cringed. Already, she had abandoned her commitment to a better work-life balance. Wanda was collecting the data she needed, but it would take time. Until she could take the next step in research, she refused to be held captive by the stress of worrying. Shaking her head, she grabbed her phone and tapped out a group text message.

> *Sorry for bailing on Tuesday. How about meeting at my place for dinner? We can catch up on what I missed and I'll tell you all about my date.*

> *Done. I'll bring dessert.* The response from Leslie was almost immediate. *I'll make sure Heather comes too.*

Jo texted an hour later.

> *I'm working late, but I'll come over after.*

Before leaving the office, Moirin logged on to her favorite Korean barbecue restaurant and ordered a feast for takeout. She vowed to do extra time at the gym to make up for the indulgence. Arriving home, she slid the car into a spot by the front door, opting not to use the garage. Juggling three bulging bags, body angled like a listing ship to keep her briefcase and purse from sliding off one shoulder, she fumbled with her keys to unlock the door. Pushing it open, Orson appeared, meowing as he stuck his nose out, nearly tripping her as she tried to enter.

"Hello, handsome. Lovely to see you as well." Kicking off her shoes and dumping the briefcase and purse over them, she lugged the food to the kitchen. It would keep nicely in the warming oven after she transferred it to ceramic dishes.

"I know, I know. You've been terribly ignored." Moirin bent down to scratch Orson's ear before filling his dinner bowl. She laughed as he feasted, still managing to generate a rumbling purr.

Turning on the sound system, she selected a CD of the Dave Brubeck Quartet. The snazzy tones of *Take Five* filled the condo. She danced to the front hall, properly putting away the items she'd tossed when she arrived home, adding an extra flourish and a spin where the music demanded.

When Heather and Leslie arrived an hour later, Moirin had showered, changed, and was relaxing with a glass of wine, curled up on the couch, flipping through the old annual reports again as Orson swiped playfully at the pages. He darted into the bedroom when the door slamming kicked off a pandemonium of thumps, laughter, and overlapping chatter. Stashing the pile of work under the coffee table, Moirin grabbed her wineglass and rose to greet them.

"Something smells good," Leslie said. "Did you cook?"

Moirin chuckled. "No, if I had attempted it, I doubt it would smell this good."

Heather finagled her arm around Moirin in an awkward hug, working to avoid a collision with the wineglass. "Thank you for the invitation."

"My pleasure. Come in, sit down. Can I get you something to drink?" She turned to Leslie, "What I lack in cooking skills, you know I make up for in mixology. What's your mocktail pleasure?"

"Ooohh, how about one of those berry sparklers?"

"Coming right up." Moirin turned to Heather. "Water, wine, or sparkler?"

"I'll have what you're having," she said.

"Great. I'll get your drinks, and you guys can set the table," Moirin said. "Jo will be another hour or more, so she said not to wait."

"Oh, I can't wait to hear all about her new job," Leslie said, dropping her purse on a chair in the living room before walking toward the kitchen.

"And I can't wait to hear all about your date Tuesday night," Heather said, locking elbows with Moirin as they followed Leslie.

"Looking for pointers? Jo told me Leslie's talked you into online dating."

"Oh, for heaven's sake, I don't even want to talk about that silliness." Heather pulled her arm back, snorting in a forced laugh. Moirin thought she caught a shadow cross Heather's face. Sadness, perhaps?

Moirin followed them into the kitchen. They jostled around each other as Moirin made drinks, Leslie retrieved plates and silverware, and Heather pulled the food from the warmer. After several trips to and from the dining room, the meal was arranged, and each took a seat around the table.

They passed the serving dishes and filled their plates. Moirin reached to the center of the table and pulled napkins from the decorative holder, passing one each to Heather and Leslie, and keeping one for herself.

"This was a great idea, Moirin," Heather said. "I am so sick of sorting and packing. I'm happy to be away from the house. Plus, I can't get barbecue like this out there."

"That worked out well for all of us. It's been a few weeks since I last saw you. I missed girls' dinner this week; you missed the week before." She trailed off. The breakup of her marriage had taken them all by surprise. Moirin wasn't sure that Heather was really holding up as well as she was trying to show. "How are you, really?" She speared the barbecue with her fork and dragged it through excess sauce before taking a bite.

"It's the oddest thing, really. I remember a few years ago, when Camilla moved into the dorms her sophomore year. Back then, I thought that Tabor and I were starting a new chapter as empty nesters. I didn't expect either one of us to work less, but I really thought we'd start having date nights or dinners at home, just the two of us. Remember that weekend at that lake house, where we talked about starting new hobbies? I think I was a little excited about a new chapter in life." Heather chuckled, her mouth twisting into a wistful smile.

Moirin nodded. "I remember. Jo was going to give you cooking lessons, and you were determined to find something you and Tabor could do together."

"You know, I never did." Heather shook her head. "Neither one, actually. I tried to pull Tabor into a few hobbies I thought he'd like - buying the bikes, signing up for those French lessons we never took, that pottery class fiasco. I don't want to say it's all his fault. I didn't do nearly enough, I'll admit."

"Oh, hun," Leslie said, clucking her tongue. "You did, though."

"No, it's okay. I've had weeks now to mull this over, and I realize we've been emotionally separated for a very long time. We were together out of habit. We never had any common interests. We had a life, of course, but nothing common that was *fun*. You know, I can't remember the last time we laughed together. Like that cliché, just two ships passing in the night." She sighed. "No, worse than that. We were two ships docked side by side in port. Parallel lives, constantly in sight of each other but not really interacting."

"You never told me any of that." Leslie held her hand flat against her chest, staring at Heather.

"Sometimes you don't see a thing until you're forced to look at it." Heather shrugged and took a long drink of her wine.

"I don't know what to say about all of this? How can I help?" Moirin pushed her plate aside and reached for Heather's hand.

She shook her head. "Let me be a cautionary tale to you both. Family is important. Work is important. But those things aren't *you*. I see that now. I thought I was defined by being a wife and mother, having purpose in life by being a physical therapist, and helping people. I thought all of that was *who I was*. But I'm not a full-time mother anymore, I'm almost not a wife. And Jo's taught us that a career can disappear just as fast. Without any of that, who am I? What am I?"

Moirin's heart wrenched. Heather was steadfast as the motherly influence of their group. Hearing her so pensive was difficult.

"I don't think we can answer that for you, honey," Leslie said.

"No, I'm not asking you to. I know this is on me now to find out who I want to be now. This is what I'm telling both of you: don't put off making a life. Especially you, Moirin. I've been thinking a lot about you the past few weeks. We took different paths, but ended up in a similar place. If you suddenly found yourself without your parents or your work at Garrett, would you be as adrift as I am? For all your tenacity in creating a career, have you really created a life?"

Moirin pushed down the irritation that flashed in her chest. She had a life people envied, didn't she? "I'm happy. I have interests beyond work and family. There are charities I work with, Orson, you two, and Jo. And maybe Jace. I think he qualifies as an interest now." She laughed and reached over to the closest serving bowl, adding another helping to her plate.

"Oh, speaking of, let's talk about Jace. You went to his house on Tuesday? What was it like?"

"He has a beautiful ranch about a half hour north of here. They were doing steer roping practice when I arrived, so I had the opportunity to meet a few of his friends, his horse, and his dog." She laughed at Heather's grimace. She had a cautious acceptance of Orson, but regarded any other animals, particularly those as large as cattle and horses, as dirty and undoubtedly dangerous.

"They were all very nice. I enjoyed the night, "Moirin said. "And, he grilled steaks like a pro." Her cell phone buzzed. She shifted in her chair to wrench it free from her back pocket. Glancing at the caller's name, she scoffed, then hit the ignore button, sending the call to voicemail.

She looked up to find Leslie staring at her. "What?" Moirin said. "I thought it might be Jo. It was nothing." She stuck the phone under her thigh and raised her hands, turning them to show they were empty, like a blackjack dealer between shuffles.

"Ha," Leslie mumbled a few unintelligible words under her breath before shoving a large forkful of barbecue into her mouth.

"Well, he sounds wonderful," Heather said. "I hope we get to meet him soon. You know he's going to have to pass the friend test."

Moirin laughed as her cell phone buzzed again from under her leg. The vibration against the chair somehow made it even louder than it had been when it was on the table. She glanced at Leslie, trying to suppress a laugh at Leslie's exasperated expression as she deliberately stared at the ceiling.

"I don't suppose he'd want to join one of our Tuesday dinners sometime. I can't imagine he'd be comfortable getting the third degree from a tableful of women. Maybe an event with less pressure. A garden party at your parents' house, maybe." Heather prattled on, moving piles of food around on her plate, oblivious to the interaction around her.

"Oh, no. I haven't told them yet. I don't think either of them wants me to lose focus at this particular point. It's best not to tell them anything until there's really something to tell." Moirin said as she slid the phone out, keeping it below the table's surface before surreptitiously checking the screen.

"Oh, that's too bad. I would think they'd be happy you're finally dating someone again." Heather furrowed her brow and sipped on her wine.

"I'm going to say this counts as a girl's dinner, so I'm enforcing the no-cell phone rule," Leslie said. "Since it's your house, you can't buy the table a round, so I'm confiscating the phone." Leslie put out her hand, palm up. When Moirin hesitated, Leslie stood to add toe-tapping to her rigid pose.

Moirin laughed and handed Leslie the phone. "Fine, fair enough. What could go wrong on a Friday night?" If an urgent situation arose, anyone would know to call the residential landline. After all, it was printed on all the after-hours emergency cards.

Leslie walked to the buffet, set the phone screen-side down on the surface, then returned to the table, dusting off her hands. "That's better. Let's clear some of these dishes and break out the dessert."

Two hours later, Leslie and Heather left after Moirin gave each a warm, heartfelt hug. It had been too long since they'd had a leisurely evening like this, filled with honest sharing and laughter. So much laughter that Moirin's ribs ached as she leaned back on the sofa. Orson stalked out of the bedroom, jumping up and settling himself comfortably against the sofa's arm.

"Sorry that having guests disturbed your night, Orson, but I enjoyed myself tremendously. I keep thinking of Heather's comment about having a life. I think she's right." She leaned over and scooped Orson into her arms, turning him so that they stared eye-to-eye. "I know I planned to work this weekend, but I think a break is in order. Everything is going pretty well overall. How about you and I go see Aunt Aggie this weekend?"

Orson mewed, and she interpreted that as acceptance. "Perfect. Let's call Aunt Aggie then." She walked to the dining room to retrieve her phone. Turning it over, the screen lit up and displayed a long list of missed calls, voice messages, and text indicators. Typical.

Grabbing a notepad and pen from her briefcase, she settled back on the couch to review. She addressed the work issues first. An overwrought middle manager with a storm outage escalated the matter of repair times, sending three messages through the company server to her email. Customer-impacting certainly, and perhaps a PR issue, depending on the duration, but not something to be escalated to the Chief Operations Officer at corporate. She made a note to follow up in the morning and sent an email to the regional director and VP of client service.

There were two text messages from Jo, the first that she would be later than expected, and the second that she wouldn't make it over after all.

Lastly, she listened to the voicemails. Jace left a message saying he was thinking about her and would love for her to call if she had time later that night. *Definitely. Right after I finish listening to the other voicemails.*

The second was from the overwrought manager apologizing profusely for bothering her with his messages. This issue was resolved. Apparently, his boss, the regional VP, gave him quite a dressing down for prematurely looping in the executive level on his message distribution. Moirin could hear the tremble in the man's voice as he expressed regret for his overzealous notifications. Clearly, he feared for his job, but she didn't think his actions warranted termination. She admired his tenacity in serving their customers. She saved the message nonetheless in case it was needed later.

The last message was from Uncle Ian. She pressed the option for play, and his voice boomed through her phone's speaker. "Moirin, what in tarnation is going on? We have an outage covering two counties in California. Ops is going nuts. Why aren't you all over this? This is incompetence, dereliction, selfish disregard, and I don't know what. You can bet the Board will hear about it, and that's going to be it. You hear me?" There were muffled thumps and scrapes before the recording stopped.

Moirin sat back, stunned. Ian sounded deranged, and for what? Unfortunately, outages were a regular occurrence in their business. It was unfortunate that two highly populated counties in California were impacted, but, by her calculations, the entire event was over in less than four hours. Certainly, far better than many storm-related outages. Under any normal circumstance, neither she nor Ian would have been aware of the situation until much later.

What had triggered the rage she heard in his voice? It was out of character, and the threat of the Board's notification was unreasonable. As irritated as she was at his micromanagement, his mental stability was an even greater concern. She rubbed the phone between her fingers, flipping it as she pondered his words, wrestling with a response as much as the device in her hands. No, she wouldn't reply at all, not tonight anyway. This might be one issue best left until Monday in the office.

She cleaned up the remaining dishes from dinner and started the dishwasher. After wiping the countertops, she refilled her wineglass and returned to the couch. Those simple domestic tasks cleared her thoughts. She smiled and called Jace.

"Hello, beautiful." She could hear the smile in his words.

"Hi. I'm not calling too late, am I?" Orson cuddled up beside her, purring his contentment. She stroked his head.

"Not at all. I was hoping you'd call. How was your day?

"It was good. I made such good progress I've decided to take the weekend off."

"Good for you, darlin. Want to come watch a team roping? We could have dinner out on the patio and watch the stars afterward." He drew out his words, teasing her with the temptation of an evening in his arms.

"I've already made plans but will definitely hold you to a raincheck on that," she said. "I'm going to drive up to my aunt's winery in Wyoming. It's been a while since I've visited, and I think a getaway will be good." She took a sip of the wine, one of Aggie's blends.

"That sounds great. It seems like you've been under a lot of stress with your Board evaluation and property business. It's good to get away and find a fresh perspective. Clears away the cobwebs."

Moirin smiled. She made the right decision in confiding some of her office-related challenges to him. She hadn't given much detail, but enough to seek his opinion. She valued his input, and, despite the short time they'd been acquainted, she trusted him. They had discussed a wide variety of topics, and his knowledge was extensive. His viewpoint was completely different than her own, making his insight fresh and often intriguing. Their relationship was progressing, and she shared more of herself all the time. She wasn't ready to confess the depth of her feelings yet, but she couldn't deny them.

"I think that is exactly what I need. I've been stretched so thin working on anything that could impact the Board's assessment. I've probably added more stress than necessary. I shared with you that Uncle Ian seemed to be on edge lately." She scratched Orson's ear.

"I think maybe you both have, yes."

"I know. I snapped at him once and regretted it. Tonight, he left me a voicemail, very upset about something that turned out to be a minor issue. He escalated it to an unreasonable level, and right now, I'm resisting the urge to respond. I need to consider how to handle it."

"When you reach the end of your rope, you dally off and turn left," Jace said, matter-of-fact.

Moirin laughed. "I've heard of 'tie a knot and hang on' but never dally and turn left. Does it mean the same thing?"

"Well, instead of just sticking it out and staying in the fight, take more deliberate action and control the situation. Be proactive, not just resilient," he said.

"Ah, sage advice indeed. I think I'll go ahead and take the weekend to consider how to apply that." Most of Jace's quotes seemed to center on the ideas of self-reliance, strength, and a laid-back enjoyment of life. His relaxed approach was somehow both comforting and peaceful. It was an appealing change from her high-pressure work environment.

"That's also wise. A well-thought-out response will be better than a heated exchange every time. So, your aunt's winery is a nice place to relax?"

"It absolutely is. I'd love to take you there sometime," Moirin gushed for several minutes on the beauty and peace of the spot just over the border into Wyoming, her love of the wines, and what an outstanding person Aunt Aggie was.

"Well, I can't wait to visit there myself and meet your aunt," Jace said when she finished her detailed descriptions.

"We'll plan on it," Moirin said. Her heart fluttered at the idea of showing him a piece of her world she held dear. A trip like that would take their relationship to the next level. "In the meantime, how about dinner on Sunday night? I'll probably be back by late afternoon."

"I would love that, darlin'," he said.

"I can't wait to see you then. Sweet dreams." The last two words slipped out before she could censor them. It was sappy and romantic.

"Sweet dreams, beautiful."

She disconnected the call, unable to stop the sappy smile she knew spread across her face. Every conversation with Jace left her feeling treasured.

She finished the last of her wine before making the last call of the night.

"Don't yell at me, I'm sorry I didn't make it over," Jo said, without preamble of a greeting.

Moirin chuckled. "I wasn't going to yell. How was work?"

"Ugh, not my finest hour. I don't want to talk about it." She groaned, and the sound grew muffled.

"Hey, take the pillow off your face. How bad could it be?"

"I fumbled, I mumbled, I messed up names. Clay told me to come back next weekend only if I promise to watch videos on their social media and listen to the announcers."

"Great, so you're not busy this weekend. We both need a break. I'm going to Aunt Aggie's. You should come. Actually, I insist you come."

The last part was unnecessary as Jo was already shrieking, "Yes, yes, yes."

23

Moirin maneuvered the car onto the ramp to the Interstate heading north. The drive to the winery would take several hours, and Moirin intended to make full use of that time to discuss several topics Jo had been avoiding. Being captive in the car might help Jo finally open up.

"So, what's going on with the job hunt?" Moirin said. "It's been, what, a week or two now that you've been looking?"

"Well," Jo seemed hesitant. "A little more than that. I didn't tell you right away when it happened."

"Hm. I get that. So, tell me more about this headhunter," Moirin said. "If it's been a few weeks, why hasn't he found something? How can someone with your education and experience not have multiple interviews, if not offers, in that time? Maybe it's time to find a new search firm."

"It's been frustrating," Jo said, picking invisible lint from her sleeve. "He's young and not overly impressed by my resume. He suggested I take a couple of online certification classes, refresh my dates, as he put it. I'm doing it, but it seems like a waste of time. I've been on a few interviews, but they've been mid-level jobs at best. Essentially just a paycheck, you know?"

"Have you asked him to aim higher? Been specific about the type of job you want?" Moirin took her eyes off the road for a sidelong look at Jo, squinting with her eyebrows raised.

"Don't give me that look," Jo wagged her finger.

"What look?" Moirin turned her attention back to the traffic. "You and I both know you like to keep people happy, and that usually means you don't stand up for yourself. You hired this guy, and he's going to make a commission if you get a job. It should be the job you want, not the easiest one for him to get for you."

"Well, I have tried. He says I haven't been back in the workforce long enough to land a director-level job. I can't stand the idea of writing ad copy or setting up email marketing campaigns for the next ten years. I keep thinking, I want something I can sink my teeth into. Something with purpose and, preferably, a decent paycheck."

"I don't understand. You have degrees in both Business Marketing and Communications. That's obviously enough education. You were with Malveen Media for over three years, and more than ten years as an entrepreneur before that, running all your own marketing. That's plenty of experience."

"First off, entrepreneur is a little inflated. Erik and I had a corner video store. Local retail businesses are easy to market. It was fun. And so was the firm, in the beginning. Being part of a team and creating content for various clients was great. Unfortunately, I can't use that as a reference. I didn't just get laid off, Moirin —not even downsized. I got fired. Everything nowadays is social media, hashtags, influencers, and viral marketing. I tried to keep up, but it kept changing so fast. I worked with a bunch of young kids, and they were constantly reminding me I was older than most of their parents. In the end, it wasn't even fun anymore. Face it, I was fired because I'm obsolete."

"I'm sure that's not true," Moirin said, her certainty wavering as soon as the words left her mouth. She had occasionally overheard younger staff members making flippant comments or ageist jokes about older employees. Not at Garrett, but that didn't mean it hadn't happened.

"If I argued for an idea," Jo continued, "they would say I was being feisty and asked if I doubled up on my vitamins. They always wanted me to work on the retirement community accounts and the old-age medical supply companies because they said I understood that target market." She scoffed. "One of them kept calling me bones, saying I was like one of those diagnostician doctors because I always knew just what a failing account needed. Humph. One of the girls finally told me they call anyone over forty *bones* because they think we're all fossils."

Moirin broke into laughter, partly at Jo's indignation and partly at the idea that her fifty-three-year-old friend was a fossil. "I'm sorry, Jo, I didn't mean to laugh. It's just ludicrous. I wish you had shared all this when it happened. Don't let it bother you. It sounds like a hostile work environment, and those kids were just plain wrong. You are talented and creative and a long way away from being a fossil."

"Maybe, but still, no one is going to hire someone my age to be in marketing when they can have someone younger with their pulse on the newest trends. Face it. I need to make a change."

"Do you think giving up entirely is the right option? Why not work for a paycheck and volunteer in an area you're passionate about?" Moirin asked. It seemed like a clear and simple solution.

"I don't know what it's like. What you do is way more fulfilling than most people's jobs. You're fourth generation of a family-owned international corporation, for Pete's sake. That's major. You'll probably work there longer than even your dad or uncle has. You'll be eighty and still going to the office," Jo scoffed.

While probably true, the image was disturbing. Moirin shook her head. "We're not talking about me. We're talking about you."

"I don't know if I can explain it," Jo said, lacing her fingers together and tapping her fist on her chin, her eyes closed. "I love marketing. But I want to represent quality products or services. I don't want to help shysters sell junk. I want to feel like, on some level, I'm doing good. It's not that I don't want to do any volunteer work, but I don't want it to be like penance because I'm ashamed of what I do for a living. Does that make sense?"

"It makes a lot of sense, especially for you and your big old heart," Moirin flashed Jo a grin. "Hold out for something that feels right. In the meantime, is everything else okay? I don't mean to sound like Leslie, but I read an article that losing your job is one of the most stressful things you can experience."

Jo chuckled. "Leslie and her articles. Yeah, I'm okay. Like I said, I wasn't happy with the work. The way the company was shifting, it wasn't fun anymore. It wasn't a good fit. I just felt like the people there were my friends, you know? I thought maybe one or two would miss me and reach out or something, but no one has."

"They weren't your friends. They were just co-workers. And, from the sound of it, not very nice ones. They took advantage of you and didn't treat you with much respect. Shake that negativity off, girlfriend. Good riddance."

"Easy for you to say. *You're* employed."

"You'll find something. If your headhunter doesn't come up with a few good opportunities soon, let me know, and I'll introduce you to the firm Garrett works with. They're excellent."

"Thank you so much. I'll keep that in mind. Hopefully I won't need it, but just in case, right?" Jo shrugged.

"So, now, I've been dying to ask. What's going on with that rodeo announcing?" Moirin tried to suppress a grin. She exited the interstate and turned onto a two-lane road that would take them to the winery. She was always happy to leave the flat plains of northern Colorado behind in favor of the lush green area that surrounded the winery. The mountains were visible in the distance, and trees lining the road became more plentiful.

"Oh, man, that was almost embarrassing last night." Jo slapped her forehead with her hand, keeping her eyes covered as she shook her head. "Everyone was so cool about it when I made a mistake. The other announcer with me covered for me so well. Clay noticed, though."

"Is this really something you want to do, though? How does it tie into marketing?

"It doesn't," Jo said. "It's a little extra money while I'm looking, and I think it will be fun. I remember that radio show I did in college was a blast. And I love the whole cowboy vibe. From the time we went to watch Jace rope, to now, hanging out at the area learning to announce, it's just been a different world. I don't know how to describe it."

"You don't have to," Moirin said. "I understand. Since I met Jace, I've seen this whole new world I never knew existed. There's something very appealing about it."

"Yeah. And I love the way you light up when you talk about him. I think you might be getting serious about this guy."

"What? You mean Jace? It's too soon to think about that. I'm not sure what it is, but I know I enjoy his company. He challenges me, makes me think, but he also makes me laugh. He's someone I would want as a friend. I'm happy to start there."

"I love that for you."

"I wish you could find it again, too." Moirin glanced over at Jo, smiling.

"For now, I'd be thrilled to start with a job, and just hope for the best after that."

"It seems like you're not sure," Moirin said.

"There's no manual for getting old. I don't know what I'm supposed to be doing with my life right now. Am I too old to start a new career? Is working as an announcer at a roping arena even a new career? Do I try to hold on to marketing? Work any job I can until Social Security kicks in? I don't have the answers yet."

There had been too many changes lately. It just underscored how uncertain life had become. Maybe it was to be expected for *women their age*. Leslie was helping Heather downsize her house today. Once the divorce was final, she'd be moving to a smaller place. She said she'd rather go through their belongings now, divide up their life, and move on. It was sad that the physical reminders of their years together ended up in piles marked 'yours or mine' and 'keep or discard.'

"Heather said something to me last night about creating a life. It keeps circling in the back of my brain."

"I feel so bad for her now. She was already freaked about Camilla leaving and having empty nest syndrome, but now she's starting over with nothing. Thank goodness she still has a good job."

"That's along the lines of what she said. She lost her sense of purpose as a mother and a wife. You have your home and memories with Erik, but lost your job. She asked what it would be like for me if I lost my parents or my job."

"I don't really see that happening," Jo said.

"Well, no, but it started me thinking. She's right. A well-rounded life needs more than one or two points. We need work for purpose, hobbies for fun, friends, love. All of that. A chair needs four legs to be stable. Even a stool needs at least three legs, so it doesn't fall over."

"Are you saying we each only have three legs, so if we lose one, we fall over?"

"Something like that."

"Hmm," Jo said, her brow furrowed in concentration. "I guess that makes sense. I'm happy we have our friendship, or I would have fallen over already, I guess."

Moirin laughed. "I think I would have as well." She turned onto a narrow lane, passing under a large wooden sign. *Hillson Winery.* "We're here."

24

S he followed the tree-lined lane, which ended at a gravel parking lot surrounded by a small complex of buildings. Driving to the end, furthest from the main entrance, she parked next to the grass by a large utility building. After that drive, she and Jo would both welcome the extra steps. Up here, she usually avoided the prime parking spots. Aunt Aggie said those should always be reserved for paying customers. Today, it seemed that Aggie had plenty of those. Moirin estimated there were over two dozen cars in the parking lot.

She exited the car and stretched, inhaling the scent of the pine trees as she admired the distant mountains. She leaned in and unlatched the carrier to release Orson, who bounded happily onto the grass. She reached down to the floorboard and retrieved his leash, attaching it before he wandered too far. On the other side of the car, Jo exited and started high-stepping, jogging in place.

Moirin turned when she heard voices coming from the closest building. She motioned to Jo, and they walked in that direction, slow enough for Orson's awkward stalking.

"Wow," Jo said. "I always forget how beautiful it is here. How can you not love this? Do you think Aggie would adopt me so I can move here?"

She scoffed, throwing her a look of exasperation. "I've been in love with this land since Aunt Aggie and Uncle Silas taught me about growing grapevines. When I was little, I sometimes dreamt about being a park ranger or something, but I always knew I'd be running the Garrett empire. I guess it was fortunate that I fell in love with business, too. I always wanted to make Garrett as successful and profitable as possible, but I try to find ways to create energy more responsibly." Moirin shook her head. "I never lost my love for the land." Despite refusing Aunt Aggie's continual requests to join the business, this place held good memories.

She had spent much of her childhood here, witnessing each phase of the winery expansion. Aunt Aggie had managed every step of the winery's growth carefully, gradually adding buildings and amenities. It was situated just south of a major interstate, so it was easily accessible.

The property itself consisted of over fifty acres, with pastures and tree shelters extending far beyond the section dedicated to plantings. To the south, the stunning panorama of Medicine Bow-Routt National Forest provided a picturesque backdrop, almost surreal in its beauty. The tall rocky peaks were visible above the forest tree line; the tallest summit sprinkled with vivid white patches. Lower, in a valley, the edge of a lake sparked in the sunlight, surrounded by scruffy bushes and colorful wildflowers that grew from the sparse soil between boulders covered in bright green moss. She couldn't see all those details from the winery, but she knew they were there. It was one of her favorite spots to hike.

Hillson Wines boasted fifteen acres of mature grapevine that Aggie had cultivated for over thirty-five years. They started the enterprise as a dream when they were newlyweds. Moirin had heard Aggie's plans and dreams for the property for as long as she could remember and loved seeing each come to life. Aggie had installed a drip irrigation system for the vines. She built a two-thousand-square-foot utility building for dry storage and a winery building twice that size, which housed a state-of-the-art lab, wine presses, fermenting vats, and chillers. Hillson had the latest bottling and labeling equipment, as well as storage for over five hundred cases of wine, which always impressed visitors when they toured the facility.

They approached a wide roller door that stood open. Moirin stuck her head inside and shouted a greeting. Orson trotted next to her.

"Wow. This place is so cool. How have I not seen this before?" Jo was in awe.

"Ha-loo," Moirin shouted.

"Gingersnap." Her aunt's beaming face appeared from behind a shelf. A second form emerged, her aunt's vineyard manager, Edgar.

"Hi there, Moirin." He nodded and ducked back behind the shelf, intent on his work. Aunt Aggie seemed to have no such dedication and hurried to the door, wiping her hands on the backside of her jeans as she moved forward.

"Did you bring that new man of yours up here for me to meet?" She huffed, blinking as she stepped into the sunshine, craning to look behind Moirin's back.

"No, it's just me and Jo." Moirin stepped in for a hug. "And my man, Orson. Sorry for just popping in on you like this. Jo and I both needed a break from ... well, from *things*. You know how it goes."

"Pfftt." Aggie waved her hand. "Anytime, sweetheart, anytime." She nudged Moirin with her shoulder before wrapping an arm around her waist. "If it were up to me, you'd be here all the time."

Moirin laughed, looking down at her aunt fondly. Aggie was the smallest of the family, barely five feet tall and unlikely to ever tip the scales past a hundred and five pounds, despite an appetite Moirin thought rivaled that of a teenage boy in a growth spurt. Aggie's activity level burned through any number of calories she could consume in a day. She kept her long silver hair in a braid, often caught up under a wide-brimmed hat. Moirin admired her aunt's commitment to limiting sun exposure, although her deeply lined olive complexion attested to many afternoons spent basking in the sun.

"Jo, my darling girl, come here and give me a hug," Aggie shouted.

Jo popped out from behind the equipment. "Sorry, I was following Edgar. Aggie, this place is ah-maze-ing." She scurried outside and wrapped her arms around Aggie in a bear hug. "It's great to see you, Auntie."

"Oh, it's good to see you, too, Josie-girl. It's been too long. So, are you hungry? Do you want to eat?" Aggie looked from Jo to Moirin, nodding. For someone who never had children of her own, she was an indulgent aunt and always ready to feed, offer cookies, or encourage the most outrageous adventures.

Moirin laughed. "That sounds great. I'm starved."

"You girls can take your bags to the house later. We'll get the guest rooms fixed up for you."

"May I take Orson to the manager's room for now while we have lunch? He's been in the car carrier for a few hours, and I'm not sure I could coax him back in there without a battle." Despite her claim, she picked up the squirming cat and held him while Jo ran to get the carrier.

"Oh, of course. Edgar's got things handled in there, what with two or three helpers he's got. I was just sticking my nose in his job, making a nuisance of myself, you know. He'll likely thank you later for getting me out of his hair." Aggie replied, arms flapping in a wide shrug, her trademark gesturing speech. Charles always said if you wanted to keep his sister quiet, just tie her hands.

"Perfect. It looks like the bistro is popular." Moirin nodded at the parking lot with the rows of cars. She waited for Jo to catch up, swinging the lightweight carrier as she jogged up behind them.

Aggie grinned. "Things have been busy; that's a fact. But I've got plenty of room, so we'll have a nice lunch where we can chat. Tandy's managing today, and she's got a good waitress helping out, so don't you worry."

They headed toward the bistro in the main building, the crowning jewel of the winery that served the retail and entertainment aspect of the business. The natural fieldstone and raw timber structure was two stories tall in the center, with a single-story wing on either side. It housed the retail showroom, tasting room, and small gift shop. Aggie had added a manager's living quarters in the second story, a fully furnished one-bedroom open floor plan with a private office.

As soon as Moirin entered and closed the door, she unclasped Orson's leash. He bounded off, scrambling to the couch and settling on the back for an unobstructed view out the window.

Moirin set out water, poured food into a bowl, and placed the car carrier nearby. She left the door to the carrier open in case Orson decided to curl up in a familiar space. Leaving the cat basking in the sunshine, they headed back downstairs, Jo ooh-ing and ah-ing over every change and improvement made since her last visit.

On the left of the main entrance downstairs, a high-ceiling banquet room provided a backdrop of rustic elegance for private parties and weddings. A separate outdoor area had a concrete patio complete with a fire pit and lounge seating, which kept the venue in high demand and booked months in advance.

The north wing, located to the right of the retail area, housed the restaurant, which had seating for fifty. It had grown from the small space Aggie had first opened, but she liked to call it a bistro. It sounded more European and cultured, Aggie said. The dining room had an entire wall of glass panels facing west, allowing an unimpeded view of southern Wyoming's spectacular sunsets. An outdoor pavilion provided additional seating, enticing guests with a gas-powered stone fireplace. On warm summer nights, Aggie would open the panels, blending the indoor area with the outdoor pavilion. A path led to an open arbor in front of the pavilion where local musicians would entertain.

Moirin led the way into the dining room, waving a greeting to the hostess as she walked by to join Aggie at a table. Beside her, Jo exhaled deeply in awe at the expansive view of the grounds.

They chose seats on either side of Aggie, who reached out and grasped hands with each of them as they sat.

"I am so pleased to have you girls here," she said, shaking their hands for emphasis.

"It is truly a delight to be here," Jo said. "When Moirin suggested it, I was just thrilled. I love seeing you, but I have to say, Aggie, you have done amazing things since I visited last."

"Ha-ha. Well, that's what happens when you let a few years slip by."

Jo looked stricken. Moirin frowned, searching her memory. She couldn't remember the last time Jo had come to visit here. She knew her own trips to the winery had become more infrequent, much to her regret.

"I'm sorry, Jo, we should have done this ages ago."

"Pish-posh, you're both here now. So, Gingersnap, what's going on?" Aunt Aggie used the nickname with affection, one that she insisted she had bestowed on Moirin because of her spicy sweetness and not her red hair.

"Honestly, I needed a couple of days away from everything, and Jo's been going through a lot. I thought it would be good for both of us to soak in the tranquility," Moirin said. She stared out at the expanse of vines, the trellis framework, and supporting posts laid out in the familiar design. The vineyard. A small tour was being guided along the perimeter, led by a girl with a long blond ponytail trailing from under a baseball cap with the vineyard's logo.

Moirin smiled at Aunt Aggie. "It's peaceful here, you know."

"I do." She nodded, waiting for her niece to continue. She looked at Jo, who had left the table and stepped out onto the patio. She stood, leaning on the wood railing, gazing across the landscape, captivated by the vines.

Moirin breathed in the warm air and relaxed, sinking into the chair. She looked over at a young family dining several tables away. A mother, father, and two small children were eating, talking, and laughing. An ordinary scene that shouldn't have drawn any emotion from her, but it did. A loving, longing emotion she couldn't quite define.

"So, what's bothering you?" Aggie narrowed her eyes.

"Some things are just complicated. You know, the office, life balance, dad, Ian..."

"Moirin, honey, things are only as complicated as we make them. It took me years, but I've figured out that just about everything in life is simple." She drummed her fingers on the table, her eyes intent on Moirin's, a slight smile playing around her mouth.

Moirin chuckled when Aunt Aggie leaned back, crossing her arms, surrounded by an air of smugness. "You're right, of course. Life is simple.

Choose a path, find passion, and ensure life balance. It's all very zen, isn't it? I just feel like I can only do one thing at a time really well. Focusing on one thing means everything else falls to the wayside."

"You are showing great wisdom by seeking me out. We'll talk it all out and get you fixed up. But first, let's order some food. Later, we'll walk the rows, and then you can give me your opinion on the new blends this year. Then, when your mind is clear, you can tell me all about it."

Aggie was her rock. "Sounds good." She waved Jo back to the table so they could order. Suddenly, she was starving.

After lunch, Jo went to the manager's suite to send resume queries, with Orson keeping her company. Moirin appreciated the time to speak with Aggie privately. They went to Aggie's office, adjacent to the tasting room in the main building.

Moirin began by playing Uncle Ian's strange voicemail message. "He's never this worked up over anything. He sounds livid, doesn't he?"

"He does. I don't think I've ever heard him that angry," Aggie said. "What did you do?"

Moirin scoffed. "Nothing that should have elicited that reaction. I had my phone off last night because Leslie and Heather were over for dinner. Someone called him when they couldn't reach me, with what *they* felt was an emergency situation."

"Oh, for goodness sake, Moirin." Aunt Aggie's lips were pursed, her eyebrows raised, and her hand clutched at her throat, waiting in breathless anticipation for the next piece of the story.

"Everything is fine," she assured her aunt. "The situation has been handled, and it didn't rise to the level I would have defined as an emergency in any case. There were four different levels they should have gone through before contacting me anyway, and they *never* should have contacted Ian. The worst part, honestly, was Ian's reaction and the message he left me."

"If I hadn't heard it myself, I wouldn't have believed it." Aggie narrowed her eyes, sticking out her chin, staring at Moirin like a detective studying a crime scene. "I know for certain this didn't come out of the blue. I'd say there's a lot more to this story, like something's been building for a while."

Moirin sank back in her chair and closed her eyes. She could feel the weight of Aunt Aggie's continued stare. She groaned and sat up, rubbing away the tension at the bridge of her nose. "It's likely my fault. I've been preoccupied with my own concerns, and I didn't realize until recently that Ian has been dealing with tremendous pressure as well."

"Well, let's deal with Ian first, then you can tell me what's been going on with you. What do you say?" She crossed her legs and folded her hands over her knee, looking like a newly minted therapist on her first day.

Moirin sighed, then managed a chuckle. "Sure. I can tell you what I know, but I'm certain it's not the full story."

Aggie raised her eyebrows.

"I had some concerns about Uncle Ian lately. He's been short-tempered occasionally the past few weeks and vacillating about retirement. When I talked to Colin, he shared that Ian is in financial jeopardy. As in mortgaged to the hilt and trying to borrow from the family trust to make ends meet."

"What?" Aggie's voice squeaked.

Moirin shook her head. "I know, I was shocked as well. I think he's worried he can't afford to retire. And from what I understand, Felicity doesn't know anything about it. I tried to talk to Dad about it, but I'm not sure he's approached Ian yet."

"Well, I'm certain Charles could help Ian find a way out of whatever mess he's gotten into. This wouldn't be the first time. Your father has been bailing him out for years."

"What?" It was Moirin's turn to be surprised.

"It's not something any of us talk about, really, but Ian's the youngest and he's always been a little spoiled. He glides through life like he's entitled to the best of everything but never learned to earn it. I don't think our father, and later your dad, did him any favors by fixing everything for him."

The knot in her chest loosened. Moirin exhaled a sigh of relief. "I was so worried this was going to be a major ordeal. Of course, I'm not thrilled to learn that the company CEO is a wastrel, but I can be thankful if it's limited to his personal life."

"Well, I can't say I'm not disappointed. I thought he had grown more responsible. I don't think I've heard Charles mention any issues in, oh, quite a number of years." She tsk'ed her tongue. "I hope it's not too much for Charles to fix this time."

"I hate that this is happening. I don't like the idea of pushing this off onto Dad, but I suppose it's the right thing to do. "I've always respected Ian, and I don't think Colin was comfortable trying to straighten out his financial issues, and frankly, neither was I," Moirin said. "Thank you, Aunt Aggie. I feel like a weight has been lifted."

"Well, then, we'll see what happens. Talk to your father about it again, and I'll ask him the next time we talk as well. It will work out one way or another."

"I hope you're right." Moirin got up and walked to the mini-sized refrigerator. She pulled out a bottle of water, holding it up in offering to Aggie. She shook her head.

"So, what sort of things have had you so wrapped up?" Aggie asked.

Moirin took a long drink of the water and circled the small room before settling back into the chair. She heaved a long, dramatic sigh and rolled her eyes.

Aggie laughed.

"Where to begin?" Moirin said, tapping her finger on the bottle. "Normal work routine aside, the Board of Directors decided for appearances that I needed to be vetted before being promoted to CEO when Ian retires. There's been a lot of paperwork, and everything I've done is being evaluated. One of our software systems, a program I spearheaded, picked up a virus that very nearly delayed our quarterly reporting. I was actually sweating that one for a while, but it was resolved. I'm still working with IT to see how it happened."

"Uh-huh," Aunt Aggie nodded, encouraging her to continue.

"Then, as I was digging down into the first problem, I came across some financial inconsistencies from four years ago. I'm a bit concerned but hope it will come to nothing. My largest concern has been the PEP project. It's an environmental study that Garrett agreed to participate in. You knew that, right?"

Aggie nodded.

"The project seemed straightforward. We allowed a few corporate sites we selected to be assessed for any environmental impact caused by commercial or industrial activity. To make a long story short, someone altered the list to add a property."

"That's odd. Why would someone do that?" Aggie frowned.

"I have to believe it was a personal attack. The property in question was contaminated, and it would have been a major PR problem for Garrett, not to mention me personally. The property was fraudulently put in my name, I assume, to destroy my credibility.

"You can't be serious." Aggie sat back and crossed her arms. "Who would do such a thing? What are you going to do about it?"

"You're the first person outside my legal team that I've told. My attorney has been working on it, and the exposure has been mitigated, thank goodness. She was able to take steps to handle it very quickly and quietly. I still don't know why, but at least I know who."

"Who?"

"A business associate named Gregorian Plankett. He tried to get a seat on the Board at Garrett a few years ago. He seemed friendly with Ian, but Dad and I had both dealt with Gregorian prior to that, and neither of us wanted him on the Board. He has a reputation for being unscrupulous, and he's obnoxious. He asked me out once, and when I declined, he became quite unpleasant. When I found out he was on the PEP Board, I wanted to assign someone else from Garrett to represent us in the project."

"That sounds perfectly awful." Aggie cocked her head. "Wait, what did you say his name was?"

"Gregorian Plankett. I doubt he had dealings up here," Moirin said.

"No, I don't think so. But that name is familiar. Plankett." Her brow furrowed in concentration, then her eyes narrowed, and she grimaced like she tasted something sour. "I *do* know that name.

"Really? Is he a member of your wine club here?"

"No, not him. Much further back. There was a woman named Plankett a long time ago. I'd bet dollars to donuts that Gregorian is her son. She was also unscrupulous and thoroughly unpleasant."

"Do you think there's a connection?" Moirin was intrigued.

"It's not a common name. And she was pretty hard to forget. Ooff," Aggie seemed to shrink in her chair. "Oh, yes. Bit of a disturbed situation there."

"It was a long time ago? What do you remember?" Anything that Aunt Aggie could recall might help Moirin's current situation.

"I don't think any of us could forget the details. It was a mess for a while. Charles had just proposed to your mom when all that business started." Aggie nodded, wriggling in her chair, getting comfortable to tell her story. "Now, before Charles met Iris, he had been dating a girl, Janet. No, that's not right. Jana. Yes, he was dating Jana casually for a couple of months. That's Jana Plankett, of course. When Charles saw Iris in Chemistry class, he was smitten."

Moirin nodded with a smile. She had often heard the story of her parents' meeting. Their mutual 'chemistry' in Chemistry class.

"Well, Charles immediately broke things off with Jana and pursued Iris. She played hard to get, but they started dating pretty quick afterward. Now, about seven months later, Charles proposes. Our parents threw a huge engagement party and put an announcement in the paper. They were thrilled." Aggie paused, swallowing, then opened and closed her mouth a few times.

"Let me get you a water." Moirin retrieved a bottle from the refrigerator and walked back to her aunt. She twisted the cap off and handed it to her.

"Thank you, sweetheart," Aggie said, taking a dainty sip. "Ah, that's better."

Moirin settled back into her chair, leaning forward, anxious to hear the rest of the story.

"So, it was only a few days before Jana came to the house. We all lived with our parents at that time, even Charles, although he had started his junior year of college by then. So, Jana came around, very pregnant, claiming the child was his. Said she saw the wedding announcement and wanted Charles to do the right thing and marry her instead."

"Why wouldn't she have come to Charles when she first found out about the baby?"

"I wondered that, too. I knew right away that something was fishy in her story. Especially the timing," Aggie said, nodding slowly.

Moirin caught the hint. "You thought that based on how far along Jana was, that Dad would have had to cheat on Mom for the timing to work."

"Exactly. Charles was too smitten. Never would have happened," Aggie said firmly.

"So, what happened?"

"It didn't matter what Charles said; the girl was pregnant. And there was no disputing she was a former girlfriend. Dad wasn't about to have the family name besmirched in any way, and at first, insisted Charles break his engagement. Mother wasn't happy because they'd hosted that big party announcing it. Oh, my, it was a mess. Both my parents were sticklers for traditional values. I think they were torn for a while."

"I can't imagine how difficult that was for everyone involved."

"And this was back in the '60s before DNA and parental testing were available." Aggie shook her head. "They went around and around. It's the only time Charles ever really stood up to our father. He insisted he couldn't be the father. He had taken Iris to the opening night of the ballet on their second date. I remember him marching into the living room, slapping the ticket stubs on the table, dates printed right on there. To him, it was irrefutable proof. He said he'd broken up with Jana more than three weeks prior, before even asking Iris out on their first date. Of course, he would; he was a gentleman like that."

"And Grandfather relented."

"Eventually, but not then. He hinted maybe they'd had a clandestine meeting. Well, Charles became furious at that insinuation. I don't think they spoke for an entire week after that."

"So, how did they resolve it? Obviously, Mom and Dad got married as planned," Moirin said.

"Eventually, Dad got the lawyers involved. They hired a private detective who determined Jana was with someone after she and Charles broke up. They found a friend of Jana's who claimed she'd told them about the baby, crying that the father took off when she told him. I felt bad for her then. But, she shouldn't have tried to hoodwink Charles," Aggie scoffed. "Father made her sign a non-disclosure and paid her a settlement. I think he pitied her, that man running off like that, but he wasn't going to allow her to sully the Garrett name."

"So, that was that, then?" Moirin said. "You never heard from her again?"

"No. Today is the first time since then that I've heard that last name." She took a long drink from the water bottle, the plastic crinkling as it collapsed.

25

Moirin strolled across the property, soaking in the summer sun. Her thoughts spun as she tried to make sense of the details. If anyone else told her that crazy story, she never would have believed it. But Aunt Aggie was the one person in the world she trusted more than all others.

"Are you okay?" Jo walked next to her, glancing over after an extended silence. Moirin has retold the story Aggie had shared. Jo didn't feel the emotional punch Moirin did, but was empathetic to the shock.

"What? Oh, yes, I'm fine," Moirin said. "One never sees their parents as part of a love triangle or having a colorful past, I suppose. I'm just shifting my thoughts, I suppose."

Jo laughed. "I'll bet. So, what is it you wanted to show me out here?"

Moirin smiled as they walked toward the canopy of green. The leaves were interspersed with tiny green and yellow flowers. "You're going to love this."

She always felt a sense of peace among the vines. She walked, bending here and there to examine the fruit, just as her aunt had taught her, explaining to Jo how they cultivated the vines. The midafternoon sun was warm on her back. It was like healing energy to her bruised spirit.

She was still working through an emotional stew but had a nervous energy that demanded activity. Ian's financial irresponsibility, Plankett's sordid parental history, and her father's long-past romantic ties to Jana Plankett. Sorting out her emotional confusion, disappointment, and general disillusionment could wait until she had more time to process it. At this point, she couldn't think of a better place to be to find peace than in the rows of grapes.

The vines were trimmed to an optimum height of eight inches above the ground, allowing for proper ventilation. Aunt Aggie employed a dedicated crew to manage the vineyard, but Moirin still looked for evidence of pests and disease, showing Jo what to look for. Shriveled leaves, discoloration, or a moldy coating on the leaves signified issues that could be devastating to the crop.

"I've been reading where they've had success in training dogs to sniff out insects and certain diseases in the vines," Aggie said, joining them. She crouched near Moirin, examining a neighboring plant.

"You're kidding."

"No, I'm thinking about getting a Border collie or beagle, you know? Something that would be friendly around the guests here."

"How would you even train one to do that kind of thing?" Jo shaded her eyes with her hand, looking at Aggie.

"We had someone in the tasting room a few weeks ago who trained detection dogs. He talked to me about it, and I've done some research since. I'm intrigued. If the dog is trained to sniff out one thing, I guess it's pretty easy to change their focus and have them sniff out something else."

"That's interesting. There are so many things to worry about with these vines. That might be worth looking into a bit more," Moirin said.

"You never know what off-the-wall idea can turn out to be one of the best things," Aggie reached over, leaning on Moirin's shoulder to push herself up. She brushed the soil from her palms, then offered a hand to Moirin. "I think I like this Jace fellow in your life. It seems like he's been good for you. Considering how you're handling all this, and aside from the unexpected family history, you seem calmer, happier even. Much more relaxed than I've seen you in a long time, gingersnap."

Jo laughed, throwing an arm across Aggie's shoulder. "I completely agree."

Moirin grabbed Aggie's outstretched hand, pulling herself up. "You know, I do feel relaxed. It's not just because of this place," she said, sweeping her hand across the field. "The past few weeks, my perspective has changed. Jace has been a big part of introducing me to a world I hadn't seen before. His ranch, the horses, the team roping."

"It's funny how when you're open to new things, you discover all sorts of things you enjoy. And sometimes an entirely new view of the world."

"Touché, Aunty, Touché," Moirin said.

"Let's head up to the lab, and I'll have you try the new blends." Aggie turned to Jo, "I can show you where all the magic happens."

"I'd love that," Jo said.

They made their way from the fields back to the cluster of buildings, following the walkway toward the winery building where they had left Edgar earlier. The winery building also housed the blending lab, a room dedicated to the science and art of winemaking. Hillson Wine's first recipes were developed by Aggie and Silas together before he passed away. Aggie had experimented with various flavors and grapes since then, creating a desirable line. Moirin appreciated the wines and was somewhat of a connoisseur of tasting, making her visits to Aggie even more enjoyable. It was easy to forget the demands of her life, at least for a while, when she was here.

Stepping from the bright sunshine into the building, Moirin stopped, allowing her eyes to adjust for a moment. Aggie was already several feet ahead, hurrying toward two men standing by one of the large vats. She walked between them, locking elbows, then turned them around.

"Edgar, you remember Moirin," Aggie said. "John, this is my niece. I'm not sure you two have met."

Edgar turned, flashing a wide grin. "Of course. Good to see you again."

John stuck his hand out. "No, we haven't. Good to meet you, Moirin."

"And this is her friend, Jo. I'm going to be taking the two of them around today," Aggie said. "Jo, this is Edgar, my manager, and John, his right-hand man."

They exchanged mumbled greetings and handshakes before Aggie resumed walking, leaving the two men to their conversation. Moirin and Jo trailed behind Aggie.

"She loves giving the grand tour," Moirin whispered to Jo. "I'm sure you've seen some of this before, but it's always interesting to see what she's up to each time I visit."

"We've added a new fermenting vat over that way," Aggie flapped her arm to the left. "But, I want you to show you something over here." She ducked behind a hulking piece of stainless-steel equipment, winding her way to a door tucked out of sight from the main walkway. "This is our development tasting room. It's connected to the lab," she said, pulling a keyring from her pocket and flipping through to find the correct one. She opened the door with a flourish. "Ta-da!"

She bustled around the room, pulling out tasting glasses, bottles marked with number and letter codes, some crackers, and a carafe of water. "I want you to try a few things."

Moirin selected a stool at the table, and Jo slid onto the neighboring one. They spent several hours tasting blends, then discussing the harvest and the winery's business challenges.

"Let me ask your opinion," Aggie said at one point. "I have numerous awards, one just recently for this newest blend. What's the best way to leverage that? A press release is always good; it can get you a mention in a magazine or newspaper. I know other wineries have added the award to their label, but I'm not sure. Would someone be more likely to buy if there's a ribbon or special seal, do you think?" She looked at Moirin, shrugging as she grimaced.

Moirin chuckled. "I know you dislike self-promotion, Aunt Aggie. I don't know myself, but if you remember, Jo is a marketing expert."

"Oh, my yes. I'm sorry I had forgotten, dear. Well, then, what say you? What should I do?" Aggie grabbed a stool and pulled it, scraping across the floor, to the table opposite Jo. She planted her elbows on the table and rested her chin on her hands, expectantly waiting for wisdom.

"Oh, well, okay." Jo blinked a few times, frowned, then looked around the room, taking in the details. Her eyes settled on the wine bottle in front of her. She picked it up, hefted it, and studied it for several minutes. "This is just off the top of my head. I'd want to take some time to do market research and drill down on this industry specifically. I would make a few recommendations for your marketing overall. On the labeling, yes, add a secondary sticker or a sleeve of some sort to slide over the neck. I wouldn't redesign the entire label because if a wine garners a higher award, you'd want to change it. No sense in printing too much of something that won't get used."

"Uh-huh," Aggie nodded. "That's a good idea."

"Brand awareness is vital in a business like this," Jo said.

Moirin shifted on the stool, arching her back to relieve a muscle cramp. She stifled a yawn she felt building. Aunt Aggie sat in rapt attention as Jo explained key connections between marketing and building customer loyalty.

"I have some other ideas based on the brochure I saw in your tasting room, and some questions about your overall goals," Jo said.

Moirin stood up and stepped to the other side of the table. "Aggie," she said, putting her arm around her aunt's shoulder. "If it's all right with you, I'd like to head to the house and rest a bit."

"Oh, of course, honey. I'm sorry; here I am, yammering away, and I didn't even think about the long day you girls were having. Jo, dear, I should let you rest as well."

"Oh, no," Jo said, "This has been fun. If you don't mind, I'd love to continue this conversation." She looked up at Moirin. "Is it okay with you if I stay here with Aggie and join you later?"

"Of course. I'll stop by the office and pick up Orson. We'll see you down at the house later." A few quiet hours of solitude sounded perfect. Perhaps sitting quietly on the patio, or even finally finishing the novel she'd started several weeks previously. Once Orson was secured in his carrier and stowed in the back seat, she drove down to Aggie's house, a half mile from the winery's main complex.

The house was a three-bedroom stone structure set on four and a half acres, separated from the public areas by a privacy tree line. A small stream ran near the garden, and Aggie had incorporated the water into the landscape. A private fire pit with a seating area overlooked BLM lands that were accessible from the house property. The Bureau of Land Management oversaw thousands of acres of public land used for wild horse herd management, forestry, campground facilities, and numerous other purposes. The area was crisscrossed by well-developed trails used for hiking, horseback riding, ATVs, and snowmobiling in the winter.

A heated, four-car garage provided ample space for the car, a work truck, three ATVs, and two snowmobiles. Since Moirin was young, she and Aggie had ridden ATVs across the expanse of BLM land during the summer and raced snowmobiles there after the snow started. The rest of Aggie's deeded acreage lay on the opposite side of the winery. She leased some of the additional lands for cultivating alfalfa and grass hayfields but kept ten acres surrounding the winery in a natural state. She said it lent to the feel of the untamed Wyoming wilderness she wanted the guests to experience.

Moirin had doubted that anyone would feel like they were in the wilderness with the amenities and the proximity of an interstate, but often heard guests exclaim that the winery was a hidden gem. Something Aunt Aggie was doing had been working. Moirin didn't doubt that Aggie's planned expansion to bed and breakfast facilities in the next few years would be successful.

Moirin pulled into the driveway, parking next to the garage. Releasing Orson from the carrier, she grabbed both hers and Jo's overnight bags from the trunk, leaving her briefcase behind. She had no intention of shifting into work mode again until Monday. Entering the house through the unlocked side door, she wrenched off her shoes, leaving them on the throw rug at the entry. Orson shuffled in, and she closed the door behind him.

The interior was a modern cabin with massive timbers and high ceilings. Moirin usually loved the wide-open space, but today trudged through the space, lugging the bags. She tossed Jo's on a chair in one guest room and took her own to the room across the hall. She dug into the side pocket, pulling out a cell phone charger and the half-read paperback.

Shortly, she settled on the patio in a plush lounge chair, her feet up on a hassock, with a glass of lemonade on the small table at her side. The pergola above her filtered the harsh rays of the sun, bathing the area in a muted yellow glow. The adjustable shade she'd pulled down ensured the setting sun wouldn't intrude on her relaxing oasis.

Orson jumped on the hassock, draping himself across her feet. "Too hot for that, buddy," she said, reaching down and pulling him up, relocating him to the chair beside her. He groaned and kneaded the cushion as he watched her, his eyes narrowed to slits. Moirin laughed and picked up her book. Three pages in, her cell phone rang.

Why didn't I leave that thing charging in the bedroom? Out of habit, she'd carried it outside, plugging the charger into an outlet behind the table. She sighed and glanced at the screen, her hand already moving to the *deny* button. She stopped when she saw the photo on the screen.

Jace.

She sat up, laying the book in her lap, and grabbed the phone. "Hi, there," she said, feeling a smile spread across her face.

"Hey, beautiful. Am I interrupting anything?" His voice sounded tired.

"Not at all. I'm relaxing on the patio. Just started reading a book."

He grunted. "Sorry, that's the second book I've intruded on."

She laughed. "Actually, it's the same one I was reading a couple of weeks ago when you called. I still haven't had time to finish it. But it's fine, it's kept this long. How was your day? Did your roping go well?"

"Eh, not bad. I placed second and fourth in the first roping, didn't make the short round in the second one."

"Congratulations. Sounds like you did well."

"Thanks. I planned on entering in three of them today, but I had to cut out early. A situation came up at work, and I'm going to have to leave in the morning for Grand Junction. I'll probably be out there for a few days. I don't know yet for sure. I'm sorry, I'll have to cancel our date tomorrow."

"Oh, that's too bad. I was looking forward to it. I understand, though."

"How are things going up there with your aunt?"

"Wonderful. I do love it here. I also had an interesting and unexpected conversation." She shared the details of her father's history with Gregorian's mother, choosing not to mention anything about Uncle Ian. The Plankett connection was surprising enough.

When she was finished, he whistled. "That is interesting. It makes you wonder if his mother told him anything. Whether he feels thankful or indebted to your family in some way, and that's why he tried to join your company's board."

"All afternoon I've been wondering variations of the same thing. It's entirely possible he doesn't know. He's successful and prominent in the Denver business community. It makes sense he would be interested in connecting with other influential businesses. If he felt a connection, wouldn't he have said something? I'm wondering why my father didn't."

"Are you going to ask him?" His voice was thoughtful.

"I think it might be wise. For now, I'm happy to put the thoughts of work and strategy on the back burner. You sound tired. Is everything all right with you?"

He chuckled. "It's a work thing. You know how it is – sometimes the mental gyrations of work wear you out more than the physical ones. It'll be fine. I'll turn in early tonight and have a fresh mind for it tomorrow."

"Sounds like you need to plan a getaway soon yourself."

"Ah, darlin, I just need a night with you, sitting back looking at the stars and holding your hand. Maybe a sweet kiss or two."

A flutter in her chest spread, sending a shiver down her arms, despite the warm afternoon. "I would love that. Especially the kiss or two."

"It's a date." His voice lowered to a whisper. "Sweet dreams, beautiful."

"Sweet dreams." She disconnected the call and laid the phone on her chest, smiling. It was a few minutes longer before she picked up her novel and resumed reading.

By the time Aunt Aggie and Jo arrived at the house, Moirin had finished the book, made up both guest beds, showered, and changed clothes. She was putting the final touches on her makeup when she heard the door shut and the sound of voices murmuring from the kitchen.

When she joined them, Aggie was pulling steak from the refrigerator as Jo chopped vegetables for a salad.

"Hey, you look refreshed," Aggie said. "Are you hungry?"

"Absolutely. How can I help?"

Aggie commanded the kitchen like a drill instructor, directing Moirin and Jo through the meal preparation. They worked together, rubbing spices into steaks, mixing salads, and having a good-natured argument about the best wine pairing for the meal.

They sat down to eat, and Jo bowed her head, offering a simple blessing over the meal. Aggie smiled and patted her hand.

"I'm so happy you brought Jo with you this weekend, gingersnap. She has so many good ideas. She's a little marketing genius, I think," Aggie said, beaming at Jo.

"That doesn't surprise me a bit. I've always thought so." Moirin nodded as she cut into her steak.

"It's nothing, really." A red blush crept up Jo's neck and colored her cheeks. She dabbed at her mouth with her napkin.

"Of course, she's modest. She's agreed to put together a whole new marketing campaign for the winery. Brochures, mailing, print ads, the works."

"Are you comfortable taking on all that? Do you have the time with everything else?" Moirin looked at Jo, raising her eyebrow. During their drive up, Jo had talked so much about the headhunter, online classes, and the part-time arena job, adding more to that might be overwhelming.

"I think it's just the inspiration I need. Everything else right now seems like drudgery. Except for the announcing, but who knows if I'll keep that up? Designing a complete national marketing plan is something I can really sink my teeth into."

Jo's bubbly enthusiasm was contagious, and Moirin couldn't help but smile and nod. "All right then, I'm all for it. Let me know how I can help."

"Well, I was wondering if you thought it would be okay for me to put this on my resume. Once I'm done, of course. List it as a consulting project or something." Jo's voice was hesitant but hopeful as she looked from Aggie to Moirin.

"I don't see why not," Moirin said. "It's actually a very good idea. Maybe you could find other companies and do more consulting."

"Oh, that would be heavenly," Jo said, lifting her glass to sip the wine.

"You girls are a pretty good team, you know?" Aggie jabbed her finger in the air, pointing back and forth between them. "Imagine what you could do teamed up together, hmm?"

Moirin laughed. "You can have Jo, but my plate is full. Relatively speaking, of course. Literally, at this moment, my plate seems to be empty. Could you pass me the salad?"

The night air was still and seemed to magnify the sounds of the insects chirping and buzzing. Fireflies blinked their nightlights as they flew around on their insect errands. Moirin stared into the crackling fire, dully watching the flames swirl from yellow to red as they twisted and danced in the twilight. She sat between Jo and Aunt Aggie, while Orson investigated the shrubbery nearby. After cleaning up from dinner, they settled into chairs around the fire pit just as night was settling in.

To Moirin, it was the most relaxing time of day, between evening's twilight and the full darkness of night. The day's activities were over, the tasks had been completed, and no errands left to be done. It should be the hour of pure indulgent relaxation, but Moirin was unsettled.

"I can feel you fidgeting from over here. Let go of that stress, sweetheart. Nothing good comes of it." Aggie said. She began humming under her breath.

"I can't help turning it all over in my mind. The secrets, so many things swept under the rug."

"It's some pretty old baggage. It was years and years ago." Aggie leaned over and refilled Moirin's wineglass before topping off her own. "It can't matter much now."

Moirin chuckled. "I'll feel more settled after I speak with Dad. You know what else I was thinking about?" Orson shuffled out of the underbrush, his curiosity satisfied, and jumped up on Moirin's lap to stretch out.

"What's that gingersnap?"

"Jace. In less than a month, I've grown closer to him than any man I've ever dated. I feel comfortable confiding in him. He knows nearly everything going on in my life. Of course, not about Uncle Ian, but most other things. This afternoon, when we talked, I told him about Gregorian. Do you think I'm trusting him too much? It has been fast."

"Trust is an overused word sometimes, and it can mean different things in different situations, I think." Aunt Aggie paused, studying the fire before continuing. "Trusting someone close to you, having faith in them, is something that takes time to build. It's not the same thing as just the expectation of integrity in someone you don't know. Generally, general trust in a person's honesty and wholly trusting someone with your heart or life secrets is as different as saying *I love a hamburger* is from *I love you*."

"That's an interesting comparison."

"Here's a story."

Jo snickered softly. Aunt Aggie was famous for her parable-style stories, and she always prefaced them with *here's a story*, just like a fairy tale's *once upon a time*. Moirin smiled, waiting for her aunt to enlighten her.

"A man went to the farmer's market one day and wanted to buy a cantaloupe. He chose a nice one and took it to the vendor. He held out a dollar. The lady at the table told him it cost a dollar and ten cents. He said he had a dime in his car and would run to get it. She said she trusted him, and he could take the cantaloupe and return with the dime. He put the dollar back in his pocket, then picked up the cantaloupe. The girl objected, saying she needed the dollar before he could leave. He was surprised, saying if she trusted him for the dime, she should trust him for the whole dollar too."

Jo put a hand to her mouth, but a giggle escaped. She cleared her throat and sipped her wine, suppressing any further nonverbal noises.

"Is this a big trust or small trust parable?" Moirin eyed Aggie.

"Don't act like you missed the point I was making. I'm talking about Jace. You trusted him enough yesterday and the day before, right?"

"Yes." Moirin picked up her wineglass and ran her finger along the edge before lifting it to her lips and taking a drink. "But it seems that the point of your story is that the girl didn't trust the man at all. She was willing to risk the dime in the interest of being nice, but when he took back the dollar, her reaction showed she didn't actually trust him."

"So, what's changed? You've gained surprising knowledge about your Uncle, and you found out a perfect stranger was sneaky decades ago. Nothing about either Plankett really reflects on your parents, or on you. That whole thing wasn't something that either of them did; it's something that happened *to* them. Neither of those instances has anything to do with your trust in Jace. You have to deal with each thing separately, sweetheart."

"You make everything sound so simple."

"Sometimes it is," Aggie said. "Isn't that where we started today?"

"I hate when you do that." Moirin narrowed her eyes, attempting to glower at her aunt, but unable to keep the grin from pulling at her lips.

"What? Make you focus on what's important?" She laughed, poking at Moirin's shoe with the tip of her boot. "Moirin -girl, that's why you come to talk to me. Now, stop all this second-guessing. Just let yourself be happy with him. Don't make problems where none exist. You've got enough in other parts of your life."

"Is that why you and Uncle Silas were so happy?"

"I think so. He taught me to treasure my happiness every day. I'm so thankful we did — right up until the day he was taken from me. You lose out on so much when you focus on the negatives instead of the positives."

Moirin leaned back, looking at the stars, thinking about Aunt Aggie's words. In the vastness of the black sky, tiny stars sprinkled everywhere; here on Earth, she was a speck. Her lifetime was but a moment, and all of her problems were insignificant. At that moment, the benefit of hindsight provided clarity. Aunt Aggie was right, just as Jace had been right all along. Moirin groaned aloud, and Aggie looked over with a questioning glance.

"I think I've had too much wine, Aunty. My mind's getting philosophical."

"All of this will work out," Aggie said as she stood. "I'm glad we had this time tonight, but there's a full day coming tomorrow. Your room's ready for you, so I'll see you in the morning for coffee, okay?" She paused next to Moirin's chair, leaning down to rub her shoulder. "I think you're on the right track, honey."

"Thank you, Auntie. I'll see you in the morning." Moirin stood, giving Aggie a hug and kiss before turning away to bank the fire.

Minutes later, as she followed her aunt into the house, with Orson trailing after.

26

The next morning, they stayed at Aunt Aggie's only long enough for one cup of coffee. Aggie apologized for rushing off, but the winery was hosting a wedding in the afternoon, and she needed everything to be perfect. She invited them to stay at the house as long as they'd like, but after a brief discussion, they opted to drive back to the city.

"You said you needed to talk to your dad about that stuff Aggie told you. Why don't we go to their house for a while? I haven't seen your mom in ages."

Maneuvering around a semi-trailer truck, Moirin flipped on her blinker and eased into the right lane before glancing at Jo. "Really? Don't you have a lot to do at home?"

She rolled her eyes. "Yes, but nothing fun. Those online classes that the headhunter suggested, YouTube videos Clay said to watch, and a couple of hours searching job boards for places to send my resume. Places that don't want to hire someone my age anyway."

"You think going to my parents' house will be more fun? Oh, you're desperate to avoid your adult responsibilities today."

"Please," Jo said, her hands clasped in supplication.

Moirin shook her head. "Sure. I do want to talk to dad and get some of this off my mind before starting another work week."

A few hours later, in the kitchen of her parents' home, Moirin poured a mug of coffee and selected a fruit-filled pastry from a tray in the kitchen. She placed a paper towel across the mugs and balanced the pastry on top.

Jo was nearly head-to-head with Dorthea as they peered at a 100-year-old recipe for Ramequins à la Parisienne.

"Some ground pepper and an atom of nutmeg," Jo read aloud. "Huh. I'd love to make this with you if you're up for it."

"Of course. I'd love the company. I found this little gem at an estate auction, and I'd like to make everything in here at least once. A helper and taste-tester would be welcome," Dorthea said, chuckling.

Moirin left them to their fascination and went to the garden, joining her mother at the table as Orson sunned himself nearby.

"You missed brunch this morning," Iris said without looking up from her magazine.

"Yes, Mother, I texted yesterday that I wouldn't make it. I went to visit Aunt Aggie." She took a bite of the pastry, hoping her mother couldn't hear the inelegant sound of her stomach growling.

"With everything going on right now, did you really think it was a good time for a getaway?"

"Honestly, yes, *because* of everything going on right now." Moirin started to take a sip of coffee, but thought better of it as the heat rose to her face. She pulled back and blew on it delicately. "I needed a break from it all. There comes a time when you realize micromanaging and compulsion have turned into a mania that does no good. Having a little fun, being at the winery with Aggie and Jo was relaxing and restorative."

"Distracting," Iris scoffed, slapping the magazine on the tabletop and looking her daughter in the eye.

"Are you upset that I took time away from the office or that I enjoyed myself?" A flash of anger overtook her senses.

"I just don't want you to lose focus, dear. You're close to achieving your goals, and it would be a shame to start slacking now."

"I've been a successful and respected businesswoman for a long time, Mother. I doubt anyone else would consider a weekend off to be slacking. In my opinion, a life dedicated solely to work is no life." She bit viciously into the pastry, washing it down with a gulp of coffee.

Iris grimaced and looked away.

"Yes, well, I would hate for you to become sidetracked by Aggie's little projects or drawn into the drama all your friends seem to have. It would be a shame if all your life's sacrifices up to this point were for naught." She sniffed and picked up her magazine, snapping the pages in the air, the cracking jarring Orson out of a sound sleep.

She pushed the remaining pastry aside. "Mother, I respect you and Dad, but your constant discouragement to have a life outside of work is frustrating. How can you not see that?"

"Don't raise your voice, dear. It's not dignified." Iris flipped the pages of the magazine. "It's not that I discourage a life outside of work, it's how and with whom you choose to spend your time."

"Exactly. I was listening to a podcast. The guest recently shared Jim Rohn's concept that a person's mindset, behavior, and attitudes are an average of the five people closest to them. It made me stop to consider who those five people are in my life." She leaned back, crossing her arms. "Not just who those five people are, but who I want those five people to be."

"Obviously, me, your father, Ian, Colin, and perhaps your friend, Jo, in there, although I'm not certain she is one you should emulate."

"How could you say that? We've been friends for thirty years. She is one of the most honest, kindhearted, and loyal people I know. I would love to be perceived like that."

"She's also a pushover and is currently unemployed. Do you want that as well? I must say, though, she's a bit better than those other women you're friends with - the one getting a divorce and the other too flighty for anything substantial."

"How can you stand being so judgmental? Those women are my closest friends. Of course, they have their challenges, as does every other person in the world. So what? I'm an old maid, Ian apparently is terrible with money, and you care more for your standing in the community than the welfare of your own daughter." Her voice grew louder, sounding shrill to her own ears.

Iris dropped the magazine on the table. "Don't you dare question my commitment to my family. Everything I've ever done is to help your father, yes, improve our standing in the community, but all to give you every advantage in business." Moirin saw her mother's eyes narrow and her jaw tighten, a sure sign that her anger was building. "You have no idea what I've sacrificed."

Her temper snapped. "What *you've* sacrificed? What about what Dad's sacrificed? Or me? Don't you feel any guilt at all?"

"What could I possibly have to feel guilty about?" Iris looked shocked at Moirin's accusation.

"I have spent my entire life trying to earn your approval, and nothing I have ever done has been good enough. I trusted you, Mom, and you put your own selfish motivation first. Over me. Over dad. How can you sit there and say that you care?"

"Don't be dramatic," Iris scoffed. She dabbed at the perspiration on her temple with a paper napkin.

"Dramatic? You have taught me, by word and by example, to prioritize work above all else. You've said that my reputation is the most important thing I could have. I look around now and realize how much of life I've missed. It's likely too late for me now, for love or family, but disparaging my friends is low, even for you."

Iris narrowed her eyes to mere slits. She pushed her coffee cup to the center of the table and leaned forward, resting her elbows on the table as she stared at Moirin. "You are being utterly ridiculous."

"I feel sorry for you, actually. I don't think you know what it's like to have friends. You've spent your whole life focused on work. Even though you had a family, a child, that was secondary to your career."

"No." Iris shook her head. "You're wrong."

"You can't see the truth, even now, can you? *Still.*" Moirin hissed the last word.

"I." Iris started to form a response, then fell silent. Her shoulders drooped in fatigue.

"It's selfish, Mom. You don't take responsibility for your choices and those you thrust on me."

"I'm sorry you feel that way," Iris said, rubbing her arm.

She looked diminished, uncharacteristically slumped in the chair. A twinge of guilt overtook the anger. What was wrong with her? This tirade was far worse than the emotional outburst she'd had with Ian.

Moirin pushed back from the table, and dragged her chair closer to Iris. She placed a hand on her mother's knee. "Mom, I don't want to fight with you."

Iris looked up but didn't speak.

Moirin wanted to tell her mother all about Jace and their growing relationship, but she knew her mother's response would drive a deeper wedge between them. She sighed. "Maybe we can have lunch one day this week. I need to talk to Dad."

Moirin walked away, leaving her mother sitting in the bright sunshine, staring into her empty cup.

Her body vibrated with conflicting emotions. Anger, regret, disappointment, sadness. She wanted to scream or break down and cry until she was spent. Neither was an appropriate response. Instead, she drew in a deep, cleansing breath and exhaled slowly. Her steps slowed, and her heartbeat gradually returned to normal. Feeling pressure against her leg, she reached down and picked up Orson. "Thank you, buddy. You always know when I need a hug."

She flashed a smile and a two-finger wave at Jo as she passed through the kitchen, headed for her father's study. Jo looked up briefly, then ducked her head back toward the open cookbook. Pulling her emotions in check, Moirin thought of her next conversation. Anger and frustration solved nothing. Only concise dialogue and clear exchange of ideas led to a positive outcome. Nodding her head to her internal pep talk, she released Orson and knocked at her father's study door.

"Hey, Dad."

Charles was seated behind the desk, reading from a stack of papers. He looked up, dragging his glasses to the end of his nose. "Good, good. Come on in. Sit, let's talk."

She sat in the guest chair on the other side of the desk. Charles took his glasses off and set them on the stack of papers. He leaned back and laced his fingers behind his neck.

"I hear the Board is about done with their vetting," he said, looking pleased.

"I'm relieved. I didn't expect much to come of it, but it's surprising how nerve-wracking it is to know someone is going through your work history with a fine-tooth comb."

"Well, you're almost through it. I can't imagine what you were worried about." Charles said.

"To be honest, there have been several things lately that have been a thorn in my side. We talked about Gregorian Plankett,"

"Now, I told you to leave that one alone," Charles interrupted her. "Why are you bringing that up again?" His face turned red.

"You become irritated so quickly when that name is brought up." Moirin shook her head. "Why haven't I noticed that before? It happened to come up in a conversation with Aunt Aggie yesterday, and she told me the story about Jana Plankett."

"She had no right." Charles glared at Moirin.

"It doesn't matter. It was a long time ago, but Gregorian is a part of the Denver business community. I've had dealings with him. You and Ian have as well. He tried to get a seat on our board for pity's sake. You didn't think I had a right to know?"

"No. I did not. Ancient history that has no relevance today. I'm sure Gregorian doesn't know anything about that business. He's never made the slightest hint to me." Charles raised his eyebrows.

"No, he hasn't with me either." Moirin shook her head. "When Aggie told me, I was shocked."

"So, we'll leave it in the past as well. Anyway, in a few weeks, we'll be starting a new chapter at Garrett. I'll be happy to give up my seat and let

Ian be Chairman for a few years now. I have some new things of my own planned. He actually should be here shortly to discuss a few transition matters."

Moirin sighed. "Oh, Dad. About that."

"What now?"

"Aggie also told me about Ian's past financial troubles."

"That meddling sister of mine, why would she, what?" Charles sputtered, searching for words.

"Don't blame her. It was something else I brought up first. I'm concerned, Dad, and so is Colin. I think Ian might be in real trouble, and he needs help."

Charles calmed down enough for Moirin to relay the details Colin had shared, adding a few observations of her own.

"I did not need this right now, honey, I really didn't." Charles got up and poured himself two fingers of whiskey from the glass decanter on the credenza. He faced the wall, muttering, before tipping his head back and downing the alcohol in a gulp. He poured a second and brought it back to the desk. He sat down and leaned toward Moirin, resting on his forearms. "Don't worry. I've bailed Ian out of things like this before. It's nothing."

"How can I help?"

"You can't. Besides, you have enough to worry about already. So, besides finding time to gossip about her brothers, what is Aggie up to? How is the winery?"

Moirin smiled, relieved to move on to more pleasant topics. She told him of the new awards, shared her opinions on the new blends, and Jo's proposed involvement in a new marketing plan.

"Good for her. I thought her branding was getting a bit stale."

The doorbell's notes of the "Bell Song" from Lakmé echoed through the hallway.

"She has the most beautiful vision of starting a bed and breakfast next year. I think it would be a good addition to her wedding packages. It's truly a beautiful spot."

"Huh," Charles grunted. "That's not a bad idea."

"What's not a bad idea?" Ian said from the doorway. "You know I'm still in charge right now. She needs to be talking to me about anything new, not you."

"Ian, please, you know I wouldn't do that." She tried to keep the defensive tone out of her voice.

"Ian, I think you and I need to talk." Charles looked sharply at Moirin. "Privately."

"Fine." Moirin whirled and marched toward the hallway.

"Close the door behind you."

Moirin pulled the door shut as she left and returned to the kitchen to find Jo. She was comfortably ensconced at the window seat, curled up with a cookbook on her lap and three more at her side. She looked up as Moirin entered. "Hey, are you ready to go home?"

"Sure." She glanced at her watch. "Since Jace cancelled our date tonight, I have plenty of time to go to the gym and stop by the grocery store."

"I'm anxious to get home now and start writing notes. I've been looking through appetizers, and an idea's percolating for a recipe-and-wine-pairing newsletter and a few other things. I can't wait to get started researching deeper for the winery's marketing plan."

"I'll drop you off first, then take Orson home before." She stopped short, whirling around towards the hallway. "Oh, no."

"What?" Jo asked.

"Orson is in Dad's office, where he's in a closed-door meeting with Uncle Ian." She rolled her eyes. "We'll have to wait until they're done."

They stared at each other for a moment. "Let's go for a walk," Moirin said. "I need to get out of here for a while, and I could use the fresh air. You can tell me all about your ideas."

"Sure," Jo said agreeably. She closed the cookbook and neatly stacked it with the others on the window seat.

Moirin led the way to the front entrance, avoiding the closer side door that would have taken them through the garden. She wasn't ready to face her mother again yet. They headed down the driveway to the sidewalk. Jo put up her hands, raising one then the other like an animated scale of justice as she looked at Moirin.

She shrugged, then turned to her right and started walking. There was something almost magical about strolling on the century-old pathway under the canopy of trees past the stately houses that lined the road. The old brick sidewalk was a source of pride in the historical area. It showed years of wear, but was well-maintained, still smooth, and each brick perfectly aligned.

"Thank you for coming with me this weekend, Jo." Moirin hugged herself, chilled in the shade, despite the warm day.

"I should be the one thanking you. It's been great. Just the time away I needed to refresh my brain and reset."

"I'm glad. That's what I had been hoping for as well," Moirin said.

"It hasn't turned out the way you hoped?"

Moirin considered the question. They walked in silence for several minutes before she answered. "Yes and no. Discovering that my father had a history with Gregorian's mother was shocking, and raised a whole new set of questions in my mind. Something about Uncle Ian that Aggie told me has me concerned, but I don't think either of those things relates to corporate issues with Garrett. In a way, I suppose that provided a mental break from the focus on work, doesn't it?"

Jo laughed. "Sure, buried family secrets and mysterious revelations would be a shift from work. Yup, those count. So, did you tell your mom about Jace?"

Moirin shook her head. "No. I started to, but she was being so, well, *Iris*, that I got irritated instead and lost my temper. It was awful, but we'll work it out. I want to tell her soon, because I plan on inviting him to the company picnic next month."

"Oh, wow, that's a big step. All public and everything," Jo said. "But Heather will never forgive you if you don't introduce him to us first."

"I know. Maybe in a few weeks, when things settle down a bit, we'll plan something. I'd like to get past this next board meeting and get a few things off my mind, you know?"

"I do. I should probably get started on a few of my own things, too. Let's circle back to the house and see if you can get Orson yet. I'm feeling motivated."

They turned back, retracing their steps to the house. A block away, Moirin saw several cars parked on the street. That was unusual. A knot formed in her stomach. Hairs on the back of her neck stood up — an unconscious, primitive reaction to danger. She started jogging. Red lights from an emergency vehicle reflected off the brick facade of the house, sweeping over the neighboring homes in a pulsating pattern.

27

The front door was standing open.

Moirin's limbs felt wooden. She couldn't draw a full breath, fighting against the blanket of dread that threatened to suffocate her. She gripped Jo's hand. Time slowed as she crossed the threshold.

Dorthea stood in the foyer, her face ashen. Tears flowed down her cheeks, and her lip quivered. She saw Moirin and held out her arms.

The distinctive squeak of rubber shoes on marble floors accosted her ears. Two distinct patterns of squeaking, individual yet overlapping, grew louder. Rubber wheels groaning and metallic grinding added to the horrific cacophony of sound. The source came into view. A man in a blue uniform pulled a yellow stretcher from the kitchen, while a second man in a matching uniform guided it gently from behind.

Moirin felt panic rise as she recognized the pale face against the white sheets. "Mom?" She whispered.

"Oh, Moirin, no," Jo's voice shook, and she cleared her throat.

Moirin felt a hand rub across her back. An eerie sensation crawled up her spine like terror brought on by a horror movie. She yanked herself away, taking a step back.

"We didn't know, honey. We couldn't have known." Dorthea wrung her hands. "She was just sitting. The tea."

No one seemed to be able to finish a thought.

Moirin grabbed the sleeve of the EMT as he passed. "What is it? Is she okay?"

"It looks like a heart attack. We're going to get her to the ER. They'll take care of her there."

~

The waiting room was ugly. The television was silent, but the overhead fluorescent light buzzed with the ferocity of a swarm of approaching bees. She fought the instinct to run for safety. They had said she could see her mom, just for a minute. She certainly didn't want to, but she needed to. Her father remained quiet, sitting in the hospital waiting room, stoically grasping a bible he'd taken from the chapel.

She sat in a different room, alone, waiting for an orderly to come escort her to the morgue. She had left her mother sitting in the garden, bathed in sunshine, and now she was lying in the morgue. Moirin almost hoped they would forget she was waiting here. She could simply stay here, in this ugly room, and rewind the past few weeks.

None of it would be real. Mom couldn't be gone. Their last words wouldn't be in anger. Moirin wished she had never come across the file or never thought to question the records. Everything would have been fine. Now, nothing was ever going to be fine again. She would never be able to see her mother again, to apologize, to make things right.

She had used such ugly words. Maybe she deserved to be here now, stuck in this ugly room.

But a nurse did come to escort Moirin on the grisly errand. Moirin kissed her mother, leaning down and drawing in the scent of death. It still didn't make it real. There was no closure. Only regrets and a surreal sense that this day was a nightmare that wouldn't end. How much more was she expected to endure?

Too soon, Moirin was back in the ugly room. She didn't have the energy to find her way anywhere else. Where would she go? She paced, ranted at the walls, sobbed, and lost track of time. She had no idea how long she'd been there when Leslie walked in.

"Oh, Moirin, I am so sorry," Leslie said as she pulled Moirin to her feet and hugged her.

Conversation swirled around her, bits and pieces of life continuing on, the world moving past this moment. Heather had left, after a hug and a murmured, "I'm so sorry, I have to work tomorrow."

Jo's hug came next. "Leslie is taking me to get a change of clothes. I'll come to your place later."

Numb, Moirin returned each embrace.

One of them, she was honestly unsure which, had walked her back to the waiting room where the family was assembled. Aggie, Ian, Felicity, Colin, and Brittany had joined her father. Why had they all gathered here? Mom was gone.

Aunt Aggie spoke in low tones to Ian in one corner. Felicity approached, tears in her eyes.

Moirin put her hands out as if making a barrier. "I need to be with Dad."

She walked to her father's side. She wrapped her arms around him, and they wept.

28

It felt like hours later that they returned to the house. The sun had set, and twilight pulled shadows over the neighborhood as Leslie pulled Moirin's car into the driveway. The twenty minutes from the hospital had been mostly silent. Moirin stared sightlessly out the window, the knot in her chest growing as she listened to Aunt Aggie sigh deeply time and again from the back seat.

They exited the vehicle, the three doors slamming in unison with a crack, like the first volley in a twenty-one-gun salute. Moirin ascended the stairs and entered the foyer. Orson was waiting. He mewed, rubbing against her leg. She shuffled away from the door, allowing Aunt Aggie and Leslie to enter.

When she and Orson arrived that morning, skittering around the foyer as he did now, Mom was alive. She coughed and cleared her throat to push back the tears. Orson took a step back, then launched into her arms. Orson seemed to sense her fragile emotions and allowed himself to be hugged without complaint.

As Moirin stood, gripping Orson, Aggie took charge.

"Let's congregate in the kitchen, girls," she said. "Dorthea will make us a nice pot of tea, and we can plan what's to be done."

Aunt Aggie led the way through the house with Moirin and Leslie obediently trailing behind her.

Moirin heard hushed voices mumbling as she entered the kitchen. Edna held Aunt Aggie in an embrace, both women visibly crying while Dorthea stood, rubbing her hand across Aggie's back. Moirin released Orson and joined the group, drawing strength and comfort from the older women. Her cheeks moistened with tears she allowed to flow.

She pulled back, drawing in a shuddering breath. "Thank you so much for being here, Edna, Dorthea." She rubbed each woman's upper arms before turning and sitting at the table, where Leslie was already seated.

A three-tier platter of small sandwiches and cookies already stood at the center of the table. Aggie and Edna brought cups and saucers, and Dorthea followed with a silver teapot. Iris herself would have approved of the full and proper tea service that followed, adhering to every element of etiquette.

"The wake will be Tuesday night, and the service on Wednesday, likely in the morning, but I'll have to check with the parish," Aggie said.

"I'll do that," Moirin's voice was flat as she stared into her tea.

"We will be prepared for Mr. Charles to receive family and guests here from lunch throughout the afternoon on Tuesday, and a noon meal on Wednesday, then," Edna looked at Dorthea, and they nodded to each other.

"I'll work on the menu with you," Moirin said, looking up.

"Honey, you don't have to do that," Edna said, patting Moirin's hand.

"I do. It's my responsibility," Moirin said. She shifted her focus to Aggie. "Who do I need to speak to at the parish? Is that for the wake and the funeral mass?"

"Just the mass. The wake will be held at the funeral home. We'll have to select one so the hospital will know where to send her." Aggie's voice was soft, her words coming slowly as if each syllable were an effort to create.

"All right. That's, ah," Moirin stopped and shook her head. "Yes, we'll need to do that first."

Leslie took her hand. "Moirin, honey, you don't have to take charge of this. We're all here to help. Jo and Heather, too."

"Yes, of course. I don't want to ask Jo for any help," Moirin looked from Aunt Aggie to Leslie. "She's had too many funerals in her life. No. I'll make a list now. Promise me you won't involve her." Jo had too much experience in this area. She'd planned five funerals, and that was enough to ask of anyone for a lifetime. Moirin looked sharply at Leslie before walking to the kitchen desk and retrieving a notebook and pen.

"Contact the parish and the priest," Moirin said, scribbling. Iris and Charles were members of the Catholic church, as was the entire Garrett family. Although few had attended mass in years, they would all expect services to be held within three days. She looked up and sighed, "Aunt Aggie, you don't mind doing that with me?"

"Of course not, dear. I'm honored to help."

The next few hours were filled with the practical, morbid details of transitioning a life into a memory. There was a proper order to things, and Moirin's page was soon scribbled, crossed out, and rewritten several times. Selecting the funeral home, then the casket, and arranging a time for the wake, followed by notifications to additional family, friends, and to Iris's office to address the business of closing her law practice. After selecting pallbearers, they could write and submit the obituary for the newspaper.

They heard the front door and men's unintelligible voices growing faint as the sound of footsteps on the stairs grew louder.

Moirin started to rise, but Aunt Aggie stopped her. "Let him be tonight. Ian will make sure he's settled." Moirin stared at the ceiling for a moment, then returned to the grim task at hand.

Edna got up several times to refill the tea kettle. She and Dorthea talked quietly, planning the food for the next few days, arranging tents in the backyard, and hiring parking attendants.

"There are decisions to be made about the services: the rosary for the wake, songs for the wake and the funeral Mass, readings, the Funeral Liturgy, and the Rite of Committal," Aunt Aggie said, dictating the list. "Charles will want to make most of those decisions tomorrow."

Moirin nodded and continued scribbling. "Death certificate and legal documents," she mumbled, her eyes welling with tears for the umpteenth time in the past hour.

"Sweetheart, that's enough now." Aunt Aggie reached over and removed the pen from her hand. "It's nearly nine o'clock. We're all exhausted."

Moirin nodded, folding the written pages three times and tucking them into her pocket, as if they were precious treasure.

"I'll drive you back to your condo," Leslie said. "I'll stay in your guestroom."

"You don't have to," Moirin protested.

Leslie waved her hand. "I went to the hospital with Heather. My car's back at my place, so this is more convenient for me anyway. And I'd like to be there in case you need anything."

Moirin smiled, hoping it conveyed appreciation rather than the exhaustion she felt. She scooped up Orson, who had remained sleeping directly on top of her feet, and followed Leslie to the car.

Finally, this awful day was over.

Monday morning, when Moirin awoke, nothing felt right. Orson's weight was on her foot, the warmth of his body penetrating through the lightweight bedspread. Sunlight streamed in through the sheer curtains. She heard sounds of someone moving about, a clattering of dishes, and a gentle *thump* of a cabinet closing.

Her eyes felt gritty and puffy. Her throat hurt. The fog of sleep cleared, and the events of the previous day rushed back.

Mom was gone.

She leaned over and picked up her phone, scanning for text messages and voicemail notifications. She had the volume turned to the highest setting, just in case. A few notifications from her work email, but no voicemail messages.

She smiled at a text from Jace. A heart and hug emoji followed by *thinking of you, sweetheart. I'll bring dinner to your place tonight when I get back.* She had slept through the notification when the message arrived at five-thirty this morning. Last night, when she'd spoken to him before falling into bed, he'd still been in Western Colorado. He had been so upset, frustrated that he hadn't been there for her, but relieved her friends had rallied.

He insisted he would come over as soon as he returned. Moirin pressed the phone to her chest, reliving the memory of his presence, the warmth of his arms around her. It would be good to see him tonight.

She got out of bed, showered, and dressed in linen slacks and a sleeveless button-down shirt. It was forecast to be brutally hot today. She walked through the condo barefoot. The noise increased as she neared the kitchen, and the scent of coffee and freshly baked muffins intensified. Her stomach growled, reminding her she hadn't eaten in over eighteen hours.

"Good morning. You didn't have to do all this," she said, walking into the kitchen.

Jo spun around. "I'm sorry. I didn't mean to wake you."

"It's okay. I don't think you did," Moirin said.

"Sit, sit. Here," Jo said, pushing a cup of coffee into her hand and motioning to a chair at the small breakfast table. "You hungry? I made blueberry muffins. Want one?"

"Yes."

Jo beamed at her, looking like a proud parent whose child had just accomplished a monumental task. Moirin tried to return the smile, feeling like it *was* a monumental task.

"Where's Leslie?" The typical whirlwind of activity and noise that accompanied their friend was missing.

"I sent her to the store. Your refrigerator was pitifully empty."

"Huh. And you sent Leslie? You know she'll probably come back with flax seeds, couscous, and vegan cheese, right? I think my take-out menus would be better."

"Stop complaining. We're here to take care of you." Jo wiped down the countertop and bustled around the kitchen, tidying.

"Sit with me," Moirin said, patting the table.

Jo tossed a few utensils into the sink that was already brimming with unwashed bowls, measuring cups, and a muffin tin. She poured a second cup of coffee and sat down.

They held hands across the table.

"Are you okay?"

"I have to be. There's no other choice, is there?" Moirin slid her hand back across the table and curled it around the coffee cup. She stared at it for a moment before lifting it and taking a drink.

"We fought. I was so angry at her, but in the end, I didn't want to listen to anything she had to say. I just got up and walked away." Her voice broke as she tried to keep the tears at bay. "What if that was the final stress? What caused her heart attack?"

"Honey, you can't think that way. It was just her time. You guys had words, and nothing's going to change the last memory you have. It's rotten, no doubt about it. But your mom was a lawyer. She argued for a living, and we all know she loved it. One minor round with you didn't do her in." Jo said.

"I'm never going to get to talk to her about it now. I'll never know what she was thinking." Moirin wrapped her hands around the coffee cup, trying to absorb the liquid's warmth into her icy fingers. "I'll never be able to apologize."

"Honey, you don't have anything to apologize for. You have been running yourself in circles for years, trying to be the best, putting work ahead of everything to be successful. You've avoided relationships, pushed men away when they got too close, convinced they would distract you from some lofty life goal. She let you sacrifice any chance of happiness for her own idea of success. You have to forgive yourself for being upset. And you have to forgive *her* for being selfish."

"Selfish?" Moirin froze, the coffee mug halfway to her mouth. The word slipped out and hung in the air like an angry accusation. The same word she had used in the last conversation.

"Yes," Jo said firmly. "She pushed you your whole life to be like her. Professional, successful. That would have been fine, but she never wanted you to date too much, even told you not to get serious or consider marriage. You told me, *and* I heard her say it myself. You never told her about Jace, did you?"

Moirin glared at Jo, refusing to answer.

"Of course not. She would have discouraged it, and you like him too much. You didn't want to go against your mom's demands, so you didn't tell her. If you think about it, you were trying to be nice by not telling her. You knew it would only upset her."

"I wasn't nice to her. That's what I'm always going to remember."

"No. And you know what? She wasn't always nice to you, either, but you still loved her. Not being nice to each other every now and then is an unfortunate product of being family. That doesn't take away from the fact that you loved her fiercely and always wanted her approval. You're going to remember that. The way you always wanted to please her made you work harder and be better."

Moirin nodded.

Jo patted her hand. "It's okay. You can grieve. But you know what? You can keep the good stuff and let yourself off the hook for the rest of it. You can be with Jace and not feel guilty. You can take time off and relax without worrying about her disapproval."

"I don't know if I'm ready for all that right now, Jo." Moirin sighed and sipped her coffee. "I'm just tired right now, but I know there's so much I need to do."

"There's no right or wrong way to get through grief," Jo said. "I went through it with Erik, and with every one of the babies, so I'll help you with some of the details."

"Of course, yes." Moirin nodded. It was an odd relief to know she had a long list of tasks that would require action: practical things to check off a list, not emotional baggage to assess and process.

It was Monday. Sunday's paper was still on the stoop, unread. The relaxing flow of the weekend was shattered. Right now, she should be preparing for the upcoming workday. Instead, she was planning her mother's funeral.

Jo got up and retrieved a yellow legal pad from the counter. When she sat back down, Moirin could see at least a dozen lines filled in, each line with a word or short phrase. Moirin got up and retrieved the list they'd worked on the night before.

An hour later, Leslie and Heather sat with them at the large dining room table, finalizing the details. They decided on a funeral home and time for the wake.

Jo was on the phone with Aunt Aggie, working on writing the obituary and making notifications, when the doorbell rang.

Moirin walked to the door, her movements feeling disconnected and foggy as if she were occupying someone else's body. Her first attempt to open the door failed, and her grasp missed the doorknob. An older man stood holding a large basket. She accepted it numbly, then belatedly realized she had failed to offer a tip. She turned, but the parking lot was empty. How had the man disappeared so fast? Nothing made much sense today.

"Moirin, honey? Are you okay?" Jo appeared behind her, concern etched on her face.

"What?" Moirin turned around.

"You're just standing here. Can I take this for you?" Jo eased the basket from her hands, pulling her gently back to the dining room, where she settled Moirin into a chair and positioned the basket in front of her.

"You read this card and see who it's from. I'll get you a warm-up on your coffee." From the corner of her eye, Moirin saw the long looks exchanged between Jo, Leslie, and Heather, but ignored them. She worked to extract the card and pulled the cellophane wrapping from the delivery.

> *Dear Moirin:*
> *We are so sorry to hear of your loss. Jace asked for my*
> *assistance in preparing this as a small xgesture of support*
> *until he can be with you. This is a difficult time, but we*
> *hope you can find comfort in your memories and the love*
> *of those around you. May thxese small items help you find*
> *some personal stress relief and moments of relaxation.*
>
> *With our thoughts and prayers,*
> *Jace (Jr) Caradova, Jace Sr & Nina Caradova*

The kindness of the gesture brought fresh tears to Moirin's eyes. Her hands touched the items in the basket, almost reverently. Jo came and stood next to the chair, reading the card over her shoulder.

"That is the sweetest thing I've ever seen. For Jace, but his mom, wow, what a great lady." Jo looked through the collection of lotions, essential oils, packages of teas, a scented candle, a book on grief, an assortment of cookies, and a pair of thick, indulgently soft socks.

"This was so thoughtful." Moirin shook her head as a tear slipped down her cheek. "I haven't even met her yet, and she's done all this for me. And that Jace thought to ask her. He's really something, isn't he?"

Jo hugged her. "He is."

Leslie and Heather crowded in, reading the card and ooh'ing and aah'ing over the basket contents. A small moment of happiness in an otherwise difficult day. All too soon, they had to turn their attention back to the dismal tasks at hand. Heather made an order from the florist, then took the spare keys and drove to the Garrett residence to pick out several outfits from Iris's closet. Heather had a practical style, and Moirin trusted her capable, diplomatic approach to every task.

Leslie went through Moirin's computer and put together a photo presentation that brought them both to tears.

Through it all, Moirin remained numb. When she wasn't actively focused on a task, she was randomly overwhelmed by various emotions: anger, regret, and guilt. Her thoughts knotted in a tangle, and the only relief was through focusing on the decisions at hand. She worked through Jo's checklist, item by item.

When it was time to go to the funeral home, she faced the task alone, sending her friends back to their own lives for a few hours. She knew they wouldn't stay away long, but this was something she wanted to do alone. The utter solemn presence of the mortuary was oddly peaceful.

Halfway through the details, she wished Jace were with her. She imagined this moment being easier with his strength and encouraging smile. A comforting arm around her shoulder. She closed her eyes and, for a brief moment, she felt his presence. With renewed strength, she dealt with the necessary items at the funeral home, then drove to her father's house.

Aunt Aggie was there, sitting next to Charles in the formal living room. Moirin couldn't remember the last time she'd been in the small room. Moirin hugged each of them.

"I've taken care of everything, Dad," Moirin said, rubbing his shoulder.

His red-rimmed eyes were dry as he looked from his sister to his daughter. "Yes, Aggie told me. Thank you, honey."

They all nodded, a grim, soundless dipping of heads that conveyed what no words could express.

Aggie shifted in her chair, the creaking of the antique wood breaking the silence. She cleared her throat. "I've arranged for a car to take us to the wake tomorrow afternoon."

"Thank you, Aunt Aggie," Moirin said.

"I'll call Edgar and come to the office in the morning," Charles said, his face pinched. "My wife just died. I can't be having a cloud of these other things hanging over us."

"I understand how you feel, Dad, but it's not necessary. This is a stressful time, please take it easy."

"Aggie, can you give us a minute?" Charles asked.

"Of course. I'll go make us some coffee." Aggie rubbed Moirin's shoulder as she left the room. She knew her brother's we-need-to-talk face all too well.

"Yes. I don't even know where to start," Charles said, his voice edged with disappointment and anger. "Between this thing with Plankett and then Ian's mess. Why didn't you talk to me about it?"

"Dad, I'm sorry, but I was handling it. I didn't need help."

"No, maybe you didn't need help, but you could have confided in me. Now we've got to fix this. Especially now." Charles said, his voice breaking on the last word. He cleared his throat. "Any family tragedy, and people will be looking for weakness, cracks in the foundation. We cannot allow that."

"I will protect Garrett Diversified, first and foremost. My second priority is the family, the future for Colin and Ryan. I have a legacy at stake here, too. I'll do what needs to be done," Moirin said.

"I will go talk to Ian tomorrow. We were in the middle of the discussion when, ahem, when Dorthea came in yesterday."

Yesterday. It was only yesterday.

Her father cleared his throat again and finished his thought. "It's been in the back of my mind throughout all of this, and I have a plan. Is there anything else you're handling that you'd like to share?"

She filled him in on all the details of the fraudulent property, the legal team's research, and Adrianna's steps for the conservation center. He asked several questions, sat in thoughtful silence, then grunted approval. His rapid acquiescence was uncharacteristic, but given the events of the last twenty-four hours, it wasn't surprising. She stood up, walked over to him, and gave him a hug.

"I'll see you at the office tomorrow, then. Call me in the meantime if you need anything."

She had lost track of time. It was late afternoon or early evening, on what could have been any ordinary Sunday. It felt normal and comfortable to be working on the computer, notepad at her arm, and Orson curled up on the chair next to her. His endearing half-winking eye and permanently amused expression made her smile whenever she looked at him. Occasionally, she reached over to stroke his head. His gentle purring would ratchet up each time.

Nothing in front of her was urgent. It was busy work to keep her mind occupied, creating answers to potential questions, business strategies with contingency plans for projects next year and beyond. A few related to the near future and the questions the Board might pose. With unanswered questions about Gregorian's master plan, Moirin needed to pivot her responses quickly. Preparing for uncertain circumstances with various possible outcomes and what-if scenarios. The skills learned from her mother would be put to good use.

She pulled the notepad from under her leg, comparing earlier scribbling to her more concise computer outline. The doorbell rang, breaking the silence of the condo. She suppressed a flash of irritation. She hated being interrupted in the middle of a productive work session. Who would be disturbing her at home?

Home. Working on a weekday.

Reality flowed over her.

She saved the computer document and stowed the computer on the bookshelf. The doorbell rang again. Orson skipped under her feet as she went to the foyer. She flipped on the porch light and, realizing that dusk had settled, turned on the hallway light as well.

She peered out the window, then flung the door open.

Jace gave her a slight smile that further reminded her of the gravity of today. He held a large bag emblazoned with the logo of a local barbecue restaurant. Shifting it to one hand, he reached out with the other and hugged her. Some of her annoyance evaporated with his embrace.

"Honey, I am so sorry," he said.

Moirin had heard that so many times already that it had almost lost meaning. The look in his eyes held such empathy that she knew he would take her pain away if he had been capable.

"Thank you," she said, stepping back. "Come on in. Thank you for being here. And, for feeding me."

He stepped inside, closed the door behind him, and put the bag on the floor. "It was literally the least I could do," he said. He kissed her, then wrapped her in a long, comforting bear hug. She held his hand on the short walk to the kitchen, where they moved around the room, working in harmony like an old married couple. At least, an old married couple where one person had no idea where anything was kept.

Together, they assembled the food at the dining room table. Throughout their meal, Moirin tried to keep her attention on the conversation, but her mind wandered.

"Tinsley, the other inspector I was working with, identified the brand, and we put that with the other information, which led us to the stolen horses," Jace said, trying again to engage her attention, this time with an interesting work story. He had already told her about the misadventures during his trip home, how happy Gasky was to see him, and again how shocked he was to hear about her mother, and how much he regretted they hadn't met. She nodded and *um-hum'd* her way through most of the topics.

Several times, her eyes drifted to the bookshelf and the laptop lying just a few feet away. Never had she desired to split herself into two parts until that moment. She loved that Jace was here and wanted to stay with him for hours. Equally, though, she couldn't wait for him to leave so she could get back to work. The computer called to her like a siren's song.

"Are you okay, Moirin?" It was the third time he had asked. "I know you're dealing with a lot. I'm here for you and trying to talk, but I don't feel like you're with me."

"I'm sorry. You're right." She pushed the plate away and rested her elbows on the table, rubbing at her eyes with the palms of her hands. She sat upright and took his hand. "My thoughts are spinning right now. My go-to move when my mind is in chaos is work. It's a structure and process I can rely on. I can only do one thing at a time. When that one's checked off, I move on to the next. I don't know how to be relaxed and emotionally vulnerable. I don't know how to do this." She used both hands, pointing back and forth between them.

Jace chuckled. "It's okay, darlin." He stood up and took her hand, leaving the dirty dishes on the table and walking to the living room. They settled on the couch where he put his arm around her and pulled her close. "Now, you just relax and talk like you're hanging out with your girlfriends. I'm going to stay right here and listen to anything you want to say. I won't try anymore to distract you or tell silly stories."

Moirin smiled up at him. "I liked your silly stories."

He smoothed back her hair and kissed her forehead. She burrowed into his warmth, feeling a sense of safety.

"Mom was a brilliant attorney. She was a conscientious mother and was my biggest cheerleader when I was young. I remember once she took two days off from work to go on a debate trip with me. She sat in the front row, looking so proud." Moirin listened to the sound of Jace's heart as she lay her head against his chest. *Mom's heart would not beat like that again.*

"I'd bet she was always proud of you."

"Yes, I'm sure of it. There are some things I have to do now for my dad, for Garrett. The details are unimportant, but I promised him I'd do it in my mom's honor. As much as I would love to lie here another hour next to you, I can't feel settled until I take care of this."

"I understand," he said, standing up. "Call me or text anytime. I'll be here to pick you up for the wake tomorrow, but reach out for anything else you need."

"I will," she said, accepting his outstretched hand to help her up.

She walked him to the door, and they shared a lingering kiss. His warm embrace was so comforting and filled with promise that she hated to end it. But it needed to end. She pulled away, knowing she must shift her attention to a different direction.

After he left, the condo was cold and empty. Orson mewed plaintively, as if he felt it too. It might have been equal parts gnawing grief over mom and regret over Jace.

29

On Tuesday, Moirin, dressed in a navy suit and ivory silk shirt, arrived at the office before seven o'clock in the morning. She hadn't slept much the night before, and now simply wanted to be in her office, barricaded behind a closed door, before the inevitable parade of condolences came.

Moirin needed her full attention to every matter that crossed her desk. She would not allow a family tragedy to affect the company's future through oversight or inattention. She gave Wanda strict instructions to cancel all meetings for the day and only put through the most urgent calls and messages. Of course, everyone would know that Iris had passed away, and Moirin couldn't ignore the flood of influential friends and acquaintances who would reach out today.

Wanda vowed to deflect as many as possible, providing callers with information about this evening's wake and funeral on Wednesday, or where they could offer condolences in person. Only the most persistent would be put through to her office.

She had to get through today, and then she could grieve. She couldn't escape the reality of the wake and funeral, but, at that moment, the machine of the company's business didn't care. Part of her relished the normalcy of it all.

Moirin was reading an email when Wanda opened the door and tiptoed to the credenza to leave a fresh carafe of coffee. She looked up but didn't speak. Moirin worked up a wan smile of thanks before Wanda turned and left the office. Moirin waited until the door latch clicked closed before getting up and refreshing her mug with the hot brew.

She stood at the window, the Rocky Mountains crisp and clear against the brilliant blue sky. A few fat, pillowy white clouds lazed high above, casting large sections of shade over the land below. Nature followed its established course. Life moved on. She shivered and turned away.

The door opened again, and Charles entered, looking gaunt and tired, although it was barely ten a.m.

"Hey, Dad. Would you like some coffee?"

"That would be nice, thank you." He heaved a heavy sigh as he sat on the leather sofa.

Moirin set her mug on the coffee table, then prepared a cup for her father. Light cream, one sugar, just the way he liked it. She brought it to him, then settled in the chair across from him.

"How are things with Ian?" she asked.

"He's worked himself into quite a hole, but we'll work it out," Charles said. "You may have been unaware of his financial circumstances, but you've always had a good idea of ours. Your mother and I did well on our own, not to mention the trust I inherited."

Moirin nodded. Her parents had always been reasonably transparent about their assets, sharing the details of their respective wills and estate planning.

"I know you've also been responsible, and far more frugal than your mother and I have been. You're my only heir, honey," he said, shrugging.

She understood what he didn't want to say aloud. "It's fine, Dad. You're right, I don't need the money. Even if you were to liquidate your entire net worth to help Ian, I understand. I wouldn't be upset."

Charles snorted, sputtering on the sip of coffee he'd taken. "Hardly that. I doubt even I would reward that level of squandering. There's helping, then there's enabling. This situation falls under helping, and he'll be taking on a significant amount of responsibility as part of this plan. It's not a handout."

"No, No." A shout bled through the door from the hallway. "You can't go in there."

A thump, followed by a crash and the sound of glass breaking.

"What the?" Charles placed his coffee on the table and stood, his eyes wide and expression puzzled.

Moirin rushed toward the door. As she was crossing the room, the door flung open, slamming against the wall, Wanda still hanging onto the doorknob. Gregorian Plankett stood at the threshold, chest heaving, his face flushed red, fists clenched at his side.

"Good heavens!" Moirin bolted to Wanda. "Are you hurt?"

It seemed as though Wanda started to shake her head no, but then her hands began shaking, and tremors overtook her entire body.

People started pouring into her office. Stan, the assistant to the CFO, and Katrin, who abandoned the mail cart in the hallway to rush in, followed by Colin, and by two burly security guards.

Katrin and Moirin helped Wanda to her desk.

Charles began shouting, clearing everyone out of the office, including the security guards.

"Gregorian, sit down and be civil," Charles barked the order.

Moirin came back to the office, closing the door behind her. Turning, she stood in front of the men, hands on her hips. "Mr. Plankett, I don't know what kind of melee you allow in your companies, but here at Garrett, I simply will not tolerate brawling or physical abuse. Now, state your business before I call the authorities and press charges for assault and trespassing."

His face contorted with malevolence and hatred that was palpable. Moirin took a step back.

"You think you can do anything to me? You can't touch me. You are here and you exist because I've allowed it. Don't test me. I can end you like that." He leaned forward, his features twisted as he extended his arm, snapping his fingers with a crack.

Moirin took another step backward, her legs hit a chair, and she collapsed into the seat. Gregorian turned toward Charles.

"And you, old man. You and I should have settled things years ago. You think you're going to try and come after me now?" His face turned a darker shade of red, and spittle flew from his lips as he snarled the words.

"I have no interest in you," Charles responded with contempt. "I never have. Years ago, I helped you get a start in business, only out of respect for your mother. That was a mistake. I thought that once upon a time, she was a scared and desperate young woman, but I see now that she was a despicable, conniving opportunist, and she seems to have passed those traits on to you. In spades."

"You have tried and failed for years to ruin me," Gregorian said. "I lost millions in that Fairwind project, you tried to humiliate me, blocking my appointment to your board, and now you pressured PEP to remove me from their Board. Do you think I care?" Gregorian spat on the carpet between them. "That stupid environmental baloney. But the public humiliation of getting removed from that two-bit Board? Nah, I won't take it. The recompense is coming, old man."

He stood up, shaking his fist. "You both better watch your backs." He stomped to the door, yanking it open before stopping and looking back with a sneer. "Oh, and condolences on your *loss*."

After Gregorian's unsettling visit, Moirin called Edgar to take Charles home. Over his objections, she then called Aunt Aggie and gave her the abbreviated highlights of their visitor's words. "I'm having the car bring Dad back home. Just watch out for him, would you? If he's not there within the hour, let me know. I don't want him taking any detours to who-knows-where."

"Of course, dear," Aggie said. "And, take a breath yourself. That sounds like a terrible ordeal on top of everything else. You should leave soon yourself."

Moirin dropped her shoulders. "Yes. I will soon. I promise."

She hung up, ushered her father to the elevator, then walked the corridors for several minutes before realizing she had no destination. She reversed her direction and went to Uncle Ian's office. It was dark, and the door was closed.

His assistant said he had left, using a tone that conveyed surprise, as if the woman disapproved of Moirin being in the office herself. Moirin applauded herself for resisting the urge to snarl.

She walked into Colin's office, knocking on the doorframe, and stepped through, closing the door behind her.

"Moirin." Colin looked up from his desk, surprise and concern washing over his face. He started to stand, but she motioned him to stay, taking a seat in the chair, facing him across the desk.

"Let's talk about a few things. You have time." It was a statement with the barest hint of a question. A question that demanded an affirmative answer.

"Yes, of course," he said. "I expected you'd be taking the week off. I'm so sorry about Aunt Iris."

"Thank you." A sharp pain pierced her chest. For a moment, *that one thing* hadn't been at the forefront of her mind. Grief tried to take over, but she pushed it away for another time. She blinked. "I'll be out for the next couple of days, but I needed to be here today. As it turns out, a more unexpected and unsettling reason than I planned."

Colin's face crinkled in confusion.

"A few things. First, Dad came in this morning to talk with Ian. They worked the financials out between them, which lets both of us off the hook in that situation."

Colin grinned, breathing an audible sigh of relief. "Oh, thank you. That is good news. It's a huge weight lifted."

"I'm happy that worked out. I was quite worried for a while about how we'd handle that, but family rallied."

Colin cocked his head. "How's that?"

"I talked to Aunt Aggie and to Dad, and they rallied around their baby brother. It seems it's always been that way. I think of them as my elders, and forget sometimes they're siblings."

"It is odd to think of them like that, but I'm happy. So, what was the unpleasant thing?"

Moirin rubbed her hand over her forehead. "Gregorian Plankett."

"Ok," Colin said. "I don't know much about the man except he's not well-liked. What's going on?"

"Oh, where to begin?" Moirin rolled her eyes, then pulled her chair closer to the desk, leaning forward to rest her crossed arms on its surface. "I'm going to give you the abridged version, then come back and fill in details where I need to."

Colin nodded.

"I recently learned that Gregorian Plankett's mother was my father's girlfriend back in college. He dumped her for my mother and later came to claim he was Gregorian's father. Falsely, of course. Nevertheless, my grandfather paid her a settlement. It seems after Gregorian came of age, Dad helped him get his start in business."

Colin sat back in his chair, his face slack. "I don't know what to say. This is a lot to take in."

"That's all just history," Moirin said. "Now for current events. I knew Gregorian had been angry since we refused to give him a seat on our board here at Garret. I wish I had known the history at the time, and perhaps I would have been more diplomatic, but that's water under the bridge. He's been thoroughly unpleasant for years, and I'm afraid I grew the habit of being abrupt with him. A few weeks ago, I started working with the PEP environmental project and discovered Gregorian was on the board there. I overheard him on the phone with someone and caught only a piece of their conversation, but it caught my attention. I went down a rabbit hole of investigation, but eventually discovered he had secretly replaced one of the Garrett properties we'd offered for testing with one he knew was contaminated and would show in the testing. Worse yet, he had forged my signature at least three years ago, putting it in my name."

"He what?" Colin sat forward, slamming his hand on the desk.

"I had the intern at PEP restore the original property to the list, then my attorney took care of the liability on the fraudulent one."

"This is all unbelievable, Moirin."

"I know. This morning, Gregorian storms into my office, furious he's been kicked off the PEP Board." She shook her head. "Steffie, the intern over there, must have said something, because I certainly didn't. Either that, or one of his other nefarious deals caught up with him. He was certain, though, that it was Dad or me."

"So, are you worried now?" He drummed his fingers on the desk, venting worries of his own.

"Yes, but not about all that. He said a couple of other things that I didn't catch at the time."

"What's that?" Colin asked.

"Remember when you told me that your father had you pulling old annual reports? It piqued my curiosity, and I looked into them myself. I found inconsistencies stemming from a project called Fairway. During Gregorian's rant, he mentioned losing millions on a Fairwind project. That can't be a coincidence, can it?"

"No. No, I don't think so." Colin's face took on an ash-white pallor. "Why would Dad have been looking into something like that without mentioning it to either of us? Do you think he was connected somehow?"

"I can't imagine that, but something's shady."

"What are we going to do?"

"I don't know yet, but it seems like Gregorian's holding all the cards, and we don't even know his endgame. We're going to need to work on this together, and we'll need your dad's help too."

"Are you sure about all of this? There's a lot of history mixed in with the business and it's likely to get uglier than it already has been."

"Yes, but when it's a family company, and what impacts the family impacts the company, you know." She smiled. They had both heard that phrase often enough from their fathers.

Colin chuckled mirthlessly. "That is our mantra, isn't it? Do you want to let me take lead on it? I'm worried that this has been a string of personal attacks on you, and you might benefit from some distance."

She looked at him speculatively. He was showing a lot of patience and self-control, calmly assessing without allowing ego to creep in. She envied that. She didn't know how she would solve this new problem. She was pleased to know that, in time, he was going to make a great CEO.

"I think we should work on this together. You, Ian, and I. Keeping each other in the dark caused some of these issues to grow larger than they needed to be. I stopped by his office, but he's left for the day."

"He what? Oh, of course, Moirin, I'm sorry. You shouldn't be here either." Colin stumbled over the words, a blush creeping up from his collar over his chin.

She smiled weakly. "It's all right. This right now took precedence. I'll leave now. I have a few things to do before going to the wake."

"I understand. We'll see you there."

"Thanks, Colin."

There was nothing left to do at the office, no further excuse for delaying facing the reality. Wanda had already been sent home after her earlier ordeal. Although it was not yet noon, Moirin logged off her computer, retrieved her briefcase and purse, and turned off the lights as she left.

30

She drove first to her father's house, parking in the driveway. She walked into the house, as she had done a thousand times before. This time, a wave of floral scent accosted her even before she crossed the threshold. Flowers filled every surface in the foyer, and there were more in the living room. As she walked by, individual words jumped out at her: *Condolences, Sympathy, Get Well.*

She followed the sound of voices to the living room, where a verbal battle seemed to be underway. Her father stood nose to nose with Dorthea, apparently at a standoff.

"Dad?" Moirin approached him, trying to keep her voice calm and soothing. "What's going on?"

"Nothing, I just won't be treated like a child in my own home. Tell Dorthea to stop hovering and tell Aggie to go home. Now, get out of my way," he said, his voice echoing off the vaulted ceiling. He spun on his heel, too fast to maintain his balance. He sidestepped, catching himself with the arm of a wingback chair.

Dorthea rushed forward.

"Charles?" Aggie's voice squeaked as she entered the room.

"Enough," Moirin's voice took on the authoritative tone she used to control large meetings.

"Everyone, sit." She waited only a moment for the three to comply. "Dad, you're going to let us hover a bit. Losing Mom was a shock, and none of us has processed it fully yet. You will not traumatize us more by endangering yourself. Furthermore, you will let us take care of you so *you* can process. No argument. Aggie is going to stay here for as long as she wants, and you're not going to give her a hard time. She loves you, and you're going to need her. I'm sure there'll be some tough days coming." Her voice broke as her frustration faded, and the reality of the day set in again.

"Yes. Today is one of those days," he said in a quiet voice. He withered, his shoulders drooping as he slumped in the chair. The perfumed scent of flowers seemed to overpower the room. Violets — her mother's favorite.

"Okay," Aggie said. "Charles, let's you and I go to the garden. It's a beautiful day, and I'm sure you don't want to lie down."

Moirin crossed her arms and stared at the flower arrangements crowded on the end table.

"How are you doing, hon?" Dorthea came over and put an arm across Moirin's shoulder.

"It's surreal. I keep waiting for her to call me, to walk into a room. I don't know when that feeling will stop."

"It will take a while. I'm so sorry for your loss," Dorthea said.

"Thank you. I'm sorry for your loss as well. I know you two were very close."

Dorthea pursed her lips and nodded. "Yes, well, when you're ready, there are messages and cards on the desk in the study. I'll let you know when Edna has lunch ready. The limo will be here at four o'clock to take you, Charles, and Aggie to the funeral home for the visitation. If you need anything else, just let me know."

Dorthea's steps echoed, then faded away, leaving the house quiet.

She neglected to mention that Jace would be joining them in the limo. How had she not mentioned Jace? She started to follow Dorthea, then stopped. Four occupants instead of three wouldn't change anything. She looked around the room, the reality of the room and its current contents threatening to incite an avalanche of emotion.

No, focus.

Fortunately, there was work to be done. Moirin went to the study and sat at the desk, flipping through the pile Dorthea had assembled. As she expected, most were condolence messages. She stopped at the note from her mother's law firm. From the date and time Dorthea noted, they had called yesterday afternoon.

Partners will send someone to retrieve Iris's laptop. Contains confidential client information is crucial to pending litigation. Please contact at earliest convenience to arrange.

Moirin sifted through the pile of cards again. None from the firm. They would likely have one of the largest ones on display at the funeral home, accompanied by a card with carefully-crafted heartfelt condolences. Moirin felt a stab of pity. To have years of association boiled down to a handoff of work to your successor.

She retrieved the laptop from her mother's briefcase and powered it up. She had memorized the complicated password years ago, knowing her mother used the same string for everything. The most important elements of her life: eight-digit date of college graduation, followed by a dollar sign, then her nine-digit zip code, the letters AbC, and the eight-digit date of when she took the bar exam. Numbers, upper and lower-case letters, and a special character in an easy-to-remember twenty-nine-character password. It was simplistically complicated, just like Iris. Moirin pressed her lips together as she typed in the characters, a smile and tears warring for control.

She glanced through the emails, making notes of people she'd need to contact about her mother's passing. Iris had hundreds of clients, associates, and acquaintances. It may take weeks or months for the news to reach all of them. Moirin would need to communicate directly with those who had called or emailed, unaware that Iris would never respond. Her mother would think it rude and unprofessional to leave such communication unanswered. Moirin set a forwarding order on the email so that any future messages would be sent to her own account.

She scrolled through the files on the hard drive, starting with the photos. She transferred all personal images to an external drive, then deleted them from the laptop. Next, she reviewed the spreadsheets, then the word processor documents. She would ensure that no personal or Garrett Diversified information was left on the device when she turned it over to the law firm.

The most recently opened file was labeled *Speech*. Moirin clicked on it, and the document opened.

She stopped reading after the first line, sitting back in the chair, flooded with memories. *I am so honored to have even been considered for this recognition as Woman of the Year.* Her mother had been so uncharacteristically excited. The nominations had only been released a few weeks ago, and Iris had already started drafting an acceptance speech. The final selection was months away. Moirin laughed. It was typical of her mother's confidence, though.

That would always be a part of her mom's legacy — accolades and acknowledgments for her impressive legal contributions. She had said children were an unreliable legacy, but Moirin disagreed. Her own success reflected her mother's influence. It might be a fitting tribute for Moirin to be nominated for Woman of the Year. She should make that a goal for next year. Her mother would be proud of that.

She stopped reading after the first line, but printed the document before deleting it. She stuffed the printed page into her pocket and continued purging the computer.

When she was finished, she discovered her father was napping after all, so she quietly left the house. He'd need the rest to face the night ahead.

Late in the afternoon, Jace arrived at her condo, dressed in a dark suit with a crisp gray shirt cinched at the neck with a black and silver bolo tie. Professional. Classy. *Sexy.* Her first impressions when she opened the door overshadowed the emotions she'd been battling all day. Guilt was the first one to return. Thinking about how sexy Jace looked, dressed to accompany her to Mom's visitation. It was just wrong.

He stepped forward and pulled her into his arms. She melted into his embrace, her cheek resting on his chest. It was safe, comforting, and intoxicating. Amongst everything in her life that felt wrong, this one thing felt right.

They drove together in Moirin's car to her parents' house. No, her *father's* house. She hated making that distinction now. Too many changes, too many adjustments. None of this was going the way she'd planned. Introducing Jace under these circumstances wasn't fair to anyone.

She parked by the front door and heaved a sigh as she looked at him. "Are you ready for this?"

"I'm here for you. Right now, this isn't about meeting your father, it's about being here for you and your family." He took her hand, wrapping it between his, and squeezed.

She nodded, breathing around the lump in her throat, willing the tears to remain at bay.

They walked into the house holding hands. Charles and Aggie were in the living room. They both stood when they saw Moirin.

"Oh," Aggie said, looking from Moirin to Charles and back again.

"I'm sorry. Dad, this is the man I've been seeing, Jace Caradova," Moirin said.

The two men sized each other up as they shook hands.

"Sir, it's a pleasure. I'm sorry to be meeting under these circumstances. My condolences on your loss," Jace said.

"Thank you."

"And, this is my Aunt Aggie," Moirin said. "Aggie, this is Jace."

Aggie stepped forward to embrace Jace in a hug, raising up on her toes to reach around him.

"It's good to meet you, Jace," Aggie said.

"The pleasure's all mine, ma'am. I'm sorry for your loss."

"Thank you, dear."

"The limo's out front," Charles said. "It's time."

They arrived at the funeral home an hour before the visitation was scheduled to start. The place seemed unnaturally quiet but not silent. It lacked the mundane sounds of life yet had a hint of ethereal music. After they entered, the door closed behind them, hinges squeaking and the latch clicking like lightning crackling on a still night.

A short hallway lay in front of them. The wall on the left had two closed doors. On the right, a set of double doors was propped open. Next to the open doors, a small table held an open book, a marbled-base pen holder, and a framed portrait of Iris. Heather had chosen the perfect image, of course.

Moirin could see past the doors to a large room where folding chairs stood in rows. Huge flower arrangements, plants, and funeral wreaths were lined up along the walls and in the aisle from the door to the front of the room. A glossy mahogany casket stood at the front, flanked by more flowers, three rows deep.

"Dad, you go ahead," Moirin said. "We'll go see the funeral director." Moirin kept a firm grasp on Jace's hand, flanked by the strength of Aunt Aggie on her other side.

Half an hour later, Moirin stood looking at her mother. Iris was impeccably clad in her favorite Sapphire suit and white cowl-neck shirt with a perfectly tied silk peacock scarf. Mom would approve of Heather's selections. Iris lay there with a slight smile on her lips, her makeup flawless, and her hair expertly coiffed. She looked perfect. Too perfect. Just an unnatural waxy replica of the woman she'd been.

Tears filled Moirin's eyes. Jace put his arm around her shoulders and pulled her close. The doors opened behind them, and she heard the hushed mumble of voices. She turned. Jo, Leslie, and Heather were there, suddenly surrounding her. She heard words, but the meaning was unimportant. The feeling of love and support overwhelmed her, giving her strength.

All too soon, it was time. Moirin squared her shoulders and took her place next to her father. Aggie stood with them at the start, murmuring with family members as they arrived. Iris had been an only child, and her parents were long since gone. She had only in-laws to mourn her passing.

Ian had his arm around Felicity, who seemed to still be in shock, several times mentioning the upcoming round of golf they had scheduled. Colin was there with Brittany and their children, Ryan and Megan. Ian's daughter, Gillian, arrived with her daughter, Avery, and son-in-law, Devon, the parents-to-be.

Moirin and her father accepted condolences from an endless stream of her mother's friends and acquaintances. Some were familiar, but most were not. Those arriving to pay their respects were colleagues from work, prestigious clients from the area, couples from the club, and members of the ladies' group her mother supported. Moirin realized there were far more acquaintances than friends, and soon the similar comments began to run together.

"Brilliant attorney,"

"Sharp legal mind"

"Fierce negotiator,"

"First-rate strategist"

Moirin looked up at the pictures she and Leslie had assembled as they scrolled across a large screen. Iris, with her brilliant smile at parties, grouped with colleagues or posed in formal photographs. The informal snapshots were her favorite. There were fewer of those, and, in many, Iris held a telephone to her ear while looking toward the camera with a smile. Moirin felt the pain, sadness, and numbing sense of loss, but over the past few hours, another emotion was building.

"I guess she's a shoo-in for Woman of the Year now." A whispered voice carried louder than the speaker intended.

Moirin heard the comment, as well as several others, based on the shocked gasps. The emotion she felt earlier intensified, now recognizable.

It was pity.

Her mother had little family and few true friends, the result of her endless pursuit of professional success and public praise. Moirin ran her fingers over a folded piece of paper she had printed out hours before. A few of her mother's final thoughts, the last ideas she would ever record.

Moirin took the well-folded page from her pocket and read it for what felt like the hundredth time. Her mother was nothing if not confident. Iris had drafted a brief, questionably humble acceptance speech, complete with adjustable notes to herself on specific thanks.

> *I am so honored to have even been considered for this recognition as Woman of the Year. Each year, an impressive group of women who stand head and shoulders above their peers is selected, and to be counted in their number is indeed humbling. Having been chosen from these as this year's Woman of the Year, I am nearly at a loss for words. I have so many people in my life who have supported me, assisted, mentored, guided, and helped throughout my career. I want to thank my family for supporting me (Note them if they are in attendance — my husband, Charles, and my dear daughter, Moirin). Thank you to the nominating committee, to the membership of the league, and to our wonderful hosts here at (name of venue TBD). You have all been wonderful. I am so honored and humbled by this. Thank you all so much.*

Moirin wondered if her mother ever intended to mention the names of those who were there. What if she or her father had some last-minute, unavoidable conflict? Would she cut their names from her speech? It shouldn't matter if a person were there to witness it; appreciation should still be voiced. Unless Iris had thought that drawing attention to her daughter or husband would underscore her devotion as a mother and wife, thereby increasing her life's accomplishment. Moirin didn't want to think so. She wanted to think better of her mother.

She sniffled and murmured an apology, stepping away from her father and the endless line of people and ducking into a quiet back hallway. Jace followed close behind her. He hugged her as she took several deep breaths, willing her nerves to calm.

"You're doing great, sweetheart. It's okay to take a minute," he said.

"I had to get out of there," she said.

"I know it's hard. It's one of the hardest things in life."

"You don't understand." Moirin couldn't hold back the tears. She had stayed strong and stoic for her father and the hordes of people who knew her professionally. It simply wouldn't do to break down like an overly emotional female in front of them. But she could with Jace.

"Tell me," Jace said.

"I loved her so much. She was my inspiration, my hero. I think she always wanted to love me back, maybe cherish me as her daughter, but there was never enough time. She never had time to love. I see these people out there. They're the ones who knew her best, the ones she dedicated her time to. But they knew her as a lawyer, a brilliant mind, and a problem solver." Moirin swiped at her eyes and gasped to control her shaking voice. "So few people really knew *her*. More than the pain I feel, I just feel pity. She was so focused on achieving success that I think she missed out on life. I don't want that to happen to me."

Jace held her close. "You have a loving spirit with people close to you. You have a lot of responsibility that you take seriously. I get that. But you can find balance. Maybe that wasn't your mom's path. You have to find your own path and decide how your life goes."

"I'm not sure that's my choice," Moirin said, disentangling herself from his embrace. "But, right now, I'm glad you're here. I should get back."

She took his hand, and they walked the short hallway together before Moirin let go and made her way through the clusters of people back to her father's side.

31

Moirin looked up at the dark Colorado sky, a smattering of stars visible despite the light pollution of the city. The night air was warm and filled with the scent of pine. Orson stretched out on the patio, the flagstones still warm from the day's sunshine.

It was over. The funeral mass had been long and the graveside interment brief, followed by a luncheon at the house for family and close friends. When Jace received an urgent call back to work, Moirin seized the opportunity to leave as well, comfortable knowing her father had both his brother and sister with him. The flowers, houseful of people, and incongruous white tents set up in the backyard by the catering company were all too much. At the first possible moment, she escaped to the peaceful oasis of her condo's patio.

"Are you doing okay?" Leslie said, reaching over to grasp her hand. A half-empty bottle of wine sat on the wicker table between them.

"Hmm, yes. There's so much I've been thinking about the past week," Moirin said, staring at her wine, then speaking slowly. "Riggs from the PEP projects has called a few times. I keep dodging his calls. I haven't decided how to handle that yet. And everything with my parents." Her voice trailed off.

"I think you should take some time off. Get away somewhere. How long has it been since you had a vacation?"

"Vacation?" Moirin laughed at the idea. "I couldn't even get away on that yoga retreat last month. That was just a three-day weekend."

"You're wearing yourself out, hon. Besides, they say all work and no play makes Jack a dull boy," Leslie said.

"Really? That's the best you got for me?" Moirin scoffed. "What choice do I have? It used to just be my reputation and success on the line, but now it's everyone's. The whole family and the entire company."

"You're always trying to take on the responsibility for the world. That's not your job." Leslie wagged a chastising finger at her.

"In this case, I think it is. I need to clean up this mess. My name is on the line, and the company's reputation is at stake. We have a bid package pending for a major purchasing group, and if we experience a PR crisis now, we risk losing that business, not to mention me personally losing the vote for CEO. If the worst happens, Garrett Diversified might be in serious trouble."

"Isn't that the benefit of a family company? Don't take it on alone. Work with your dad, your uncle, and Colin to fix it with you so you can be in the business and have a life too."

"Maybe," Moirin said, taking another sip of wine.

"No maybe about it," Leslie said. "I spent some time getting to know Jace yesterday. He's a great guy, Moirin. And he's crazy about you," Leslie said, grinning. "And I saw you watching him, too. You haven't looked at anyone like that in a long time, maybe never. Don't let work rob you of a chance for love."

Moirin got up and walked to the edge of the patio, looking out at the mountains. She felt the pull of the outdoors. Leslie was right. She needed a vacation. A week at a cabin in the woods or a river rafting trip. Jace had asked her to go on a four-day trip to a team roping event in Wyoming. He told her it was part of an annual Independence Day celebration that had been going on for over a hundred years. It would be nice to say yes to a trip like that. She turned to face Leslie, leaning against the railing.

"Mom lived life on her own terms. I think she was happy," she said, giving voice to the thought circling her mind.

"I think so, too," Leslie said.

"Do you think it was all worth it? Do you think her life mattered? Her legacy, I mean?"

"Of course, her life mattered. People loved her, she made a difference in the lives of her clients, and she had a terrific family. That's her legacy. Work. You."

"She told me that children were an unreliable legacy."

Leslie laughed. "Well, maybe. I'm not sure what kind of legacy I am to my parents, but then they set the bar pretty low. I know my boys will outshine me in life. I love that idea."

"I'll never have that. I have a responsibility to my family and to the business. At this point, I'm not sure I even have a choice in that. I think sometimes legacy chooses you."

"The way you talk about legacy is like you have some idea that people need to see you and what you've done for you to know that you matter. You know, the impact you have on the world is not increased when more people know about it, nor is it decreased if no one knows. Your life does not have to be witnessed to matter. The things that you do matter."

"If it's not witnessed, how will it matter?"

"Did you ever see that movie about the women mathematicians at NASA? The work they did changed the world. Whether anyone knew about it or not, they still changed the world. Their contribution mattered. Once the story got out, people were inspired, and it was great. But once everyone knew what they had done, it didn't make their contribution any greater. The awareness didn't increase the value of their actions."

"I feel like there's a teacher lesson in there I'm not grasping yet," Moirin said.

"I'd like to think that a person's legacy lies in the things they are passionate about. Like me, I'm passionate about being a teacher. I might not be Teacher of the Year, or write a textbook, or do anything that would make me be remembered in history. But I can plant seeds. I can make a difference in a kid's life by teaching them something or inspiring them to discover what *they're* passionate about. They might remember me, but they might not. Either way, what I do every day can help change the world. Whether it's in a good way or a bad way depends on my actions."

"All my work, the company, the environment? It all means nothing? I'd like to think that my legacy will be in how Garrett Diversified does business in the future. How much of the environment is saved and protected for future generations?"

"That's true, I suppose, but way more literal than I meant. I'm not talking about the environment per se. I meant your life. Your passion for protecting the environment — does that come from your own conviction or a sense of responsibility because of your family's business? Is it really your passion, or is it penance?"

"I never gave it much thought," Moirin said.

"Maybe you should. What are the times when you feel best about yourself? Not the times when you're easing your conscience or owning up to a responsibility. When do you feel honestly feel fulfilled? Just think about that." Leslie gave her a thumbs-up and a big smile.

Moirin felt like she'd just been given a gold star for accepting the homework.

32

The board meeting would be held the following week, right after the Independence Day weekend. If the board approved her as CEO, it would be the start of a new era for Garrett Diversified. Moirin knew everything would change for her then, but for now, she vowed to take advantage of the lull in her schedule. This was her last opportunity to sample the path not chosen and create memories that didn't involve work. She wanted those memories.

Thursday morning, she called Aunt Aggie. "I just wanted to let you know Heather will be picking me up, and we should be there by noon. Heather can't wait to spend the afternoon up there."

"I'm just pleased as punch for you guys to be visiting. I've got the guest rooms all ready for you, honey."

Although Jace had originally suggested the trip to Wyoming as a chance for the two of them to be alone, Moirin didn't feel their relationship had progressed to the level of a private getaway. While the four-day trip sounded fun, it was a big step, and she was too out of practice at dating for that. There was a part of her that felt too old and uncomfortable with the thought of intimacy, but she was still ready for a brief adventure. It didn't take much cajoling to convince Heather to join.

"I'd love to," Heather had shouted through the phone when Moirin called last week. "I just couldn't stand the thought of another holiday looming that I'd spend alone."

"This will work out great, then. Although I almost wish I could snoop around and keep an eye on Jo."

"Why? What's going on with Jo?"

Moirin told Heather about Jo's new job. They continued to talk, spending almost an hour on the phone, learning there had been a recent development in Leslie's life as well. She would be spending the holiday with her sons for the first time in several years. Everyone was moving on and making changes. Moirin didn't want to look too closely yet at what the future might hold for her own life.

Moirin was happy to rely on Heather's travel planning expertise, since she had, after all, planned many family vacations. She emailed Heather the list of rodeos and team roping events that Jace had provided, certain Heather would plan the best travel routes, identify restaurants and places to stop for fuel, and handle the arrangements for accommodations.

They laughed at how much their lives had changed this year. They were planning four days and three nights traveling through Wyoming like a couple of fan girls, but instead of concerts, they were chasing ropings and rodeos. Even two months ago, either of them would have laughed at the suggestion of such a road trip.

When Heather arrived to pick her up, Moirin was ready with a suitcase, a cooler full of drinks and snacks, and Orson securely tucked into his travel carrier. He would be spending the long weekend with Aunt Aggie.

"Let's blow this pop stand, girlfriend." Heather giggled as she looked at Moirin sitting in the passenger seat. The look on Heather's face reflected how Moirin felt - as if they were two kids waking up on an eagerly anticipated Christmas morning. Nothing close to the staid and boring fifty-something-year-old women sticking to responsible, boring routines.

After a leisurely drive north, they spent the afternoon and first night at Aunt Aggie's house in southern Wyoming. They had an early but indulgent breakfast of waffles smothered in strawberry preserves and whipped cream before filling travel mugs with coffee and taking to the open road.

"I'm so glad you invited me on this trip, Moirin. I think it's just what I needed," Heather said.

"Me too," Moirin said.

"How are you doing since your mom?"

"It's still a shock. Most of the time, I still can't believe it, but every day gets a little better," Moirin said.

"It makes you stop and think about life, that's for sure," Heather said.

"Do you ever have regrets?"

"You know, I never thought I did," Heather said. "But since Tabor left, I've had a lot of time to reflect. I loved my life, my daughter, my home, everything. I thought I was happy. Tabor wasn't."

"Looking back, you don't think you should have known?"

"I don't know. Maybe there were signs, and I missed them." Heather shrugged. "Tabor said I didn't have any spark and just went through the motions of life. He wanted more."

"How about you? After your reflection, what do you think?"

"I'm getting to know myself again. I'm not a risk-taker, and there's a lot I'm afraid of, but I loved my life the way it was. Right now, I'm trying to figure out what my new life looks like."

"You've had a lot of changes. I'm looking at that myself, so let's make a pact to put all that to the side and just enjoy the next few days?"

"I love that idea. Next stop, adventure." Heather wiggled around in the seat, doing a car dance complete with jazz hands.

Heather planned their route carefully and had pages of notes indicating gas stations, restaurants, shopping, and grocery stores. Her overnight bag was in the trunk with Moirin's, but she insisted on keeping the first aid kit in the back seat. Moirin wondered what kind of emergency they'd encounter that would prevent access to the trunk but wisely decided against too much contemplation of that. Neither of them had much experience with the outdoors or backroad travel.

Moirin appreciated the irony of that. For once, she wasn't going to worry about protecting nature; she was going to connect with it and simply enjoy it. Within reason, of course. Camping, even glamping, was a bit too up close and personal. For their first stop, Heather had made reservations at a rustic cabin just outside Cody. They would meet Jace and attend the rodeo tonight, then cheer Jace on at a team roping competition the following day.

That gave them over eight hours to complete a five-hour drive. Plenty of time for a relaxed lunch, stops at a few scenic overlooks, and browsing any store that piqued their interest. They were each making up for lost time, opportunities passed up for the sake of responsibility. Moirin's to work, and Heather's to family. Who knew if they would ever get another opportunity like this?

They left the interstate and stopped at a small cafe for lunch, ignoring the reprimanding inner voice that warned against deep-fried food and sugary indulgences. They had thick burgers with hand-cut French fries and shared a piece of homemade peach cobbler. After lunch, guilt set in, and Moirin insisted on a brisk walk before continuing the drive. That turned into browsing through several shops, purchasing new hats, and an obscene amount of homemade fudge.

Once back in the car, they enjoyed the summer day, riding partway with the windows down, singing at the top of their lungs like a couple of delinquent teenagers. Moirin turned her phone off and stowed it in the car's glove compartment. In the event of an emergency, Leslie would contact Heather. There was a certain freedom from responsibility that made them both giddy. When they pulled into Cody, Moirin felt like she'd already been on vacation for a week.

The cabin was quaint but rustic. Two queen-size beds and one dresser took up most of the space. A door led to a small bathroom with a minuscule shower tucked into one corner.

"It provides the basics," Moirin said.

"Yeah, and it's clean," Heather said, checking the dust on the dresser and dropping to her knees to check under the bed, in her hygienically-obsessed mom-like fashion.

They met up with Jace and several of his friends for a steak dinner, then they all attended the rodeo together. Moirin enjoyed the casual night's entertainment, but truly loved seeing Heather bask in the attention of cowboys who stumbled over themselves to explain each of the rodeo events.

In addition to the team roping, the rodeo included competitions for steer wrestling, tie-down roping, bareback, and saddle bronc riding. They also had women's events for breakaway roping and barrel racing.

Between the fast-paced events, the entertainment ranged from music to rodeo clowns and even trick riding. Jace and his friends were good-natured, and Jace showed his witty sense of humor. Moirin hadn't laughed so much in years.

The night was over too quickly, but Moirin and Heather were both tired, ready to relax after their long day. Moirin sat outside on an old wooden wide-slat rocker with several layers of peeling paint, showing that it had once been white and another time blue. Its current coating was a mellow sandstone.

Heather sat down next to her. "Enjoying how the other half lives?"

Moirin chuckled. "The half that doesn't work twenty-four seven. But am I enjoying time to stop and smell the roses? Yeah. The office feels like a million miles away."

"That's the goal of a getaway, probably the reason we call it that." Heather clucked her tongue and pointed pistol fingers at Moirin.

"You are so dorky, Heather. That's one of my favorite things about you."

They laughed together and talked of unimportant things mixed in with heavy philosophical life questions in the way that only good friends with years of history could do. It was late when they went to sleep, but that's what one does when one is on vacation, and no alarm is set to ring the next morning.

Moirin enjoyed another leisurely morning, drinking two cups of coffee before she and Heather checked out of the small cabin. If she wasn't careful, lazy mornings could become a habit. They walked over to the café, where they'd agreed to meet Jace for breakfast. Two other men in cowboy hats were already seated with Jace when she and Heather arrived.

Moirin kissed him gratefully. They hadn't planned it, but Moirin was certain he had invited friends to make Heather feel more comfortable.

Nothing was worse than being newly single and feeling like a third wheel with a couple.

The day passed in another blur of laughter, food, and activity. The men returned to the area grounds to prepare and warm up the horses. As they left the cafe, Heather saw a flyer for a western arts and crafts festival downtown and insisted they check it out. They spent several hours poring over the products at each vendor booth and bought similar rhinestone-encrusted leather belts to commemorate the trip.

Moirin and Heather arrived at the arena in time to watch over a hundred teams compete in several rounds. By the end, Jace and his partners placed second in the roping, winning several hundred dollars each. One of the cowboys they met at dinner the previous night won first, edging Jace's team out by only two-tenths of a second. Several losers good-naturedly bought a congratulatory beer for the winning team. Moirin was continually impressed by the camaraderie everyone seemed to share in this sport.

When she mentioned it, Jace told her it wasn't the sport; it was the cowboy way. A code of conduct that they all learned young and served as the principles to live by.

"Your life rule book, then?" Moirin asked. They were sitting in the grandstands, watching a team roping event Jace hadn't entered. Moirin was sitting in front of Jace, leaning against his chest, his arms encircling her. It was a sappy moment right out of a young woman's junior high sweetheart fantasy, but Moirin wouldn't have changed it for anything.

"More principles to live by, I'd say." His voice rumbled in his chest, vibrating through to her spine.

"Are they secret, or can you tell me?" She felt silly and carefree, teasing him like she was thirty again. Like the responsibilities looming over her didn't exist.

He scoffed. "It's pretty basic stuff. Do what's gotta be done, finish what you start, take pride in your work, keep your promises, be tough if you must be, always be fair, um, listen before you talk, know where to draw the line, oh, remember that some things aren't for sale, and ride for the brand."

He paused a few times in thought as he listed out his lifestyle guidelines, tapping a finger on his forearm now and then to emphasize a point.

"Those are all good rules. I could live with those," she said. She wished her life *could* be that simple. A wish that, if she wasn't careful, could become a longing.

That evening, they snuggled together under a blanket, watching a fireworks display. Moirin couldn't remember the last time she watched fireworks on the Fourth of July. The very idea evoked images of traffic jams, parking nightmares, and crowds of people jockeying for the best position hours before sunset.

This year, she had been surrounded by American flags and banners. People were dressed in red, white, and blue, and children played with silvery whirly birds, battery-operated fans, and tiny pompoms. As dusk fell, sparklers were brought out and lit. The infectious patriotic spirit was everywhere, and Moirin relished every moment.

The following two days of rodeo events, team roping competitions, and playing tourist delighted them. Sunday morning came, and while both Moirin and Heather were ready to go back home, part of Moirin wished this trip could last forever. She had no choice, though, but to return to the life that awaited her.

Sunday morning, she stood outside the tiny motel. A month ago, she would have been working from home, likely late once more for brunch with her parents. Today, she closed her eyes, tipping her face up to relish the full morning sunshine, as a mild breeze brought her the scent of cattle and horses that grazed in a nearby pasture.

"Ugh," Heather dropped her overnight bag on the sidewalk. "It's not as strong as some of the places we've been this weekend, but that is quite an *outdoorsy* smell for this early in the morning."

Moirin laughed. "I was just thinking how fresh and natural it was. I'm starting to think it's the smell of freedom and independence."

Heather coughed, wrinkling her nose. "I have a way to go before I can agree with that."

Jace pulled his truck into the parking lot, and Moirin waved. He drove to where she stood, parking a few feet away.

"Well, you go say goodbye to Jace, and I'll get the bags settled in the car."

"Thanks," Moirin said over her shoulder, already walking toward him. He met her halfway, scooped her up into the air, and swung her around.

She laughed, pushing half-heartedly against his chest. "Put me down. I'm about twenty years too old for that kind of thing."

"Hm, if I must," he said, releasing her slowly to stop for a kiss before her feet touched the ground. "I'm going to miss you. I've gotten used to having you around every day."

"I'll see you in a few days when we're both back home."

She kissed him again, then held his face between her hands. "I love you."

His body went still as he stared, stone-faced, his eyes locked with hers. A roll of panic washed over her. Not having a response was one thing, but a heavy silence was something else altogether.

The world stopped in the silence between her heartbeats.

The words seemed so natural when they rolled off her tongue. It had been a statement of fact; an admission of emotion, spontaneous but not untrue. The words hung in the air. Now that they'd been released, nothing would be the same. She felt the impact of that now, but even in the uncertainty while she waited for the world to start spinning again, she knew she wouldn't change a thing.

He leaned down and touched his forehead to hers. "I love you too, darlin."

33

Moirin parked in front of her parents' house, her *father's* house, for a rare extended family Sunday dinner. The invitation had been more of an edict than a request, but she was relieved to join. She craved a sense of normalcy. A simple family dinner, one where she could almost pretend the events of the past few weeks had never happened. Although she already anticipated this would be far from a simple dinner. Aunt Aggie, Uncle Ian, and Colin, likely accompanied by Felicity and Brittany, would be in attendance, and the business of Garrett and long-held family secrets would be the primary topics for discussion.

She entered the house and heard the muffled voices in conversations and the clatter of dishes. The smell of pot roast and apple pie made her stomach growl as she walked into the kitchen. She heard the conversation clearly now, Aggie and Charles engaged in lighthearted banter, laughing over some sibling joke. Moirin could almost imagine her mother was just having a late night at the office, a crucial meeting serving as a thinly-veiled guise for missing a visit with Aggie. Those little character flaws and shortcomings seemed endearing now.

"Hi, honey," Aggie's greeting was bright, filled with laughter. "Help me with this, will you?" She offered a large flat basket, overflowing with dinner rolls. When Moirin accepted it, Aggie threw a pristine white cloth napkin over the top. "Take that to the dining room, will you?"

Ian, Felicity, Colin, and Brittany were all gathered in the formal dining room. The table was set with formal China and sparkling flatware, with crystal goblets and wineglasses properly positioned at each place setting.

"Moirin," Brittany greeted her as she set the basket of rolls on the table. "How was your rodeo weekend?"

She smiled. "I had a wonderful time. I was definitely out of my element most of the time, but I really enjoyed it."

"Colin says that you were with Jace on that trip. He is such a dear. I talked with him at the wake and again here at the house. Terrible circumstances to meet him, but I can understand what you see in him."

"I'll be sure and tell him, he'll enjoy knowing that."

Charles entered the room, standing just inside the doorway, and spread out his arms. "Thank you all for coming here tonight. I appreciate the impromptu family meeting."

Aunt Aggie nimbly skirted around him, carrying a platter to the table. Edna followed with two large bowls. She waved at the five of them clustered. "Come now, take a seat before it gets cold."

Charles sat at the head of the table. As soon as everyone else was seated, he bowed his head, saying a blessing over the food. Everyone joined in at the third or fourth word of the familiar prayer, synchronizing by the time they said *Amen*.

Food was passed and plates filled with a minimum of murmured conversation. Brittany, seated across the table from Moirin, asked a few more questions about the rodeo and more personal details about Jace. Colin seemed attuned to the conversation, nodding and smiling a few times as Moirin answered Brittany's questions.

Halfway through the meal, Charles cleared his throat. The other six occupants of the room looked up expectantly.

"It's been a difficult month for the Garretts. There's no denying that. We're not through the rough patch yet, but I think we're close. I want to talk a few things out, get on the same page, and close up the ranks." He looked from one to the other, nodding as he spoke.

"Of course, Uncle Charles," Colin said.

"Losing Iris doesn't change the Garrett Diversified plan. The Board's done their due diligence and completed the vetting they wanted on record. We'll have the board meeting later this week. Is there anything you'd like to discuss? Anything anyone wants to get off their chest?" He stared at Ian.

"Charles, you know I hate to do this, and I've avoided it for months now, but if you want to get into it, let's get into it." Ian's tone was icy.

Moirin exchanged a long look with Colin, who raised his eyebrow, questioning, and Moirin responded with a slight shrug.

"I had my reservations about this," Ian said. "You know I don't think she's ready. Things have been fine the past few years. I think we make a good team, her running operations with me in oversight. I don't see a reason to change it."

"That's not what we discussed. The shift toward renewable energy, changes in the industry, the tech advancements. It makes sense to step back and let a fresh face lead Garrett. It's going to position us better globally," Charles prattled the words out in a flat manner, as if we were tired of the repetition."

"Well, I've changed my mind." Ian raised his voice, slapping his hand on the table. "If anything, the last couple of months have shown me it would be a disaster for me to step away. I talked with you about it, and I've talked with her." He waved his hand toward Moirin. "I've been covering, but let's talk brass tacks. That million-dollar database had a few hiccups, we nearly had the annual reports late, the mess with the PEP project. Should I continue?

"Ian, please," Charles began, before Moirin interrupted.

"No, Dad, let me respond." She turned toward Ian. "First off, the hiccup with the million-dollar database was caused by a virus deliberately uploaded into the corporate mainframe. A virus that originated from your workstation."

Several gasps overlapped around the table. Moirin wasn't sure, but, from the shocked looks, it could have been anyone in the room. She hadn't shared that tidbit of information with anyone outside the IT department yet.

"Further, I'm interested to know *how* you found out about the PEP project. I kept that issue closely guarded, only Steffie from PEP and my own legal team knew the details."

Ian's face blanched, the color draining.

"Finally, as much as I've hated to consider it and refused to believe it, even when faced with the evidence, I cannot ignore it any longer."

"What are you talking about?" Charles looked as pale and drawn as Ian. Felicity looked like she might faint, and Aunt Aggie's eyes threatened to overflow with tears.

"You've falsified the financials," she said flatly. "Colin mentioned something in passing, and I started digging. It didn't all click until Gregorian stormed into my office. He mentioned Fairwind."

Ian swayed slightly in his chair as his face flushed. His lips pursed in anger, like he was biting back a retort.

"There's just one thing I don't know yet," Moirin said. "Were you in on it together, embezzling from Garrett, or was he forcing you?"

"I..well, no," Ian sputtered.

"Uncle Ian, I love you. You can deny it; it will just take me longer to prove, but I have enough already that I'll uncover everything eventually," Moirin said, her voice just over a whisper.

Every word was crystal clear in the silent room. The half-finished meal lay on plates across the table, food forgotten as everyone was transfixed by the drama unfolding around them.

Ian's lip quivered, then he dropped his head into his hands.

"Ian, what did you do?" Charles' eyes narrowed as his face twisted in disbelief.

"Dad?" Colin's face reflected grief and a shattered sense of respect for his business mentor.

"I was in a financial hole. That Fairwinds project was a dog anyway; we were bound to lose several million. Yes, I altered a few records and bought myself breathing room. Everything would have worked out fine if Plankett had kept his nose out of it," Ian said bitterly. "I know he had resources, or spies, inside Garrett. He was leveraged as a contractor on that deal and lost heavily. He got vindictive. He bought out all my mortgages and threatened to foreclose. I don't know how, but he found every debt, every bad decision I made, and he had it all stacked against me. I was going to lose everything."

All eyes at the table stared at him.

"It would have impacted Garrett, too. What could I do?" He looked from one person to the next, seeking support. "I couldn't have all that come out. He blackmailed me into giving him preferential contracts, insider trading information, anything that could be of use. He's been using me, forcing me to do it for years."

"Like you used me to upload a virus?" Colin bellowed. "Why would you do that? You put the whole company in jeopardy."

"Gregorian insisted it was the only way to discredit her. If the Board had enough concerns about her leadership, they wouldn't vote her in as CEO. He knew I had to stay on as CEO if I were to keep feeding him information. The whole thing was his idea. Can't you see that?" His tone had a desperate edge to it.

"How long?" Charles growled.

"Four years, give or take," Ian said, waving his hand. "Plankett is certifiably insane. He swore you should have been his father. Did you know he got a sample from you — hair or some such thing — and did a DNA test? When it came back negative, he tried coming after Moirin." Ian nodded at her. "I guess his next plan was to marry into the family. When she rebuffed him, I think he just wanted to destroy us. All of us."

"I am so sorry," Charles whispered. "All of this. All of this." He shook his head before pushing back his chair. "I need a few minutes. If you will all excuse me."

He turned and marched stiff-backed from the room. The silence broke, and everyone began speaking at once.

Moirin followed her father into the study, knowing that's where he would be. He poured a small amount of brandy into a tumbler and offered it to her. She put her hand up, fingers raised, declining the silent offer. He threw the drink back in one gulp and poured another inch into the glass. She raised an eyebrow, but he shrugged and shook his head. She wasn't going to chide him for having a drink. She knew it wasn't an argument she could win.

He sat in one of the plush club chairs, as he had many times over the years, settling in for one of their talks. This additional element of normalcy was comforting, but as he faced her, he seemed worn and tired. Moirin worried the strain of the past week, the past hour, was too much for him.

"Maybe we should talk another time," she said.

"No. We need to talk now." His voice was firm, tinged with irritation. "It's been a tumultuous time for everyone. It's even worse than I'd imagined."

An understatement if there ever was one. Moirin kept that thought to herself, allowing her father to continue.

"I have to make the decision here. I'm still Chairman, and what impacts the company impacts the family. *And what impacts the family impacts the company.*" He said the words absently, almost out of habit. He held the glass up to the light, staring at the amber liquid as if it could provide answers.

"Ian's always played the part of a bigwig who has the power to hook people up for whatever they want. He liked being in the favor-broker business. That way, powerful people would owe him favors. It's always been small, meaningless stuff." Charles shook his head in disgust.

"With Gregorian Plankett, it's far more than that."

"For years, I've tried to oversee his work and keep the company headed in the right direction. Your grandfather put him in charge when I got sick. I knew I couldn't keep up with the hours demanded of the CEO, and I was fine with being distanced from operations, but I was the face of the company, always in the public eye. I occasionally fixed a problem here and there. I always did it quietly and thought he was just careless. Our Mom used to call him a carouser, a party animal. He just cared more about a good time than being responsible."

"He's always had a relaxed approach, but I've never felt like he's shirked any responsibility," Moirin said. "I'm so sorry I didn't see it."

"In the beginning, when Ian started running things, our father was still calling the shots, so he didn't give Ian much latitude. After Dad retired, I kept an eye on things and fixed whatever needed to be fixed. When you stepped up and took over operations, I didn't think I had to do as much. You handled it all, pretty much took over from him. I knew you never needed any direction to do what was right. I just didn't see this coming."

"Neither of us did, Dad."

"The timing will work out. We'll retire Ian quietly, and you'll take over as planned. There's no way now that Ian can take my position as Chairman. I'll have to stay, but we'll need to handle the messaging carefully, especially after losing your mom. It could make things look even worse."

"I understand. We'll approach all this delicately. Ian doesn't want this made public. My only concern is Gregorian. He was already livid, and now losing his inside man isn't going to sit well."

"One disaster at a time, Moirin. Let's get through this week."

"I think I'll go home now, unless there's more?" Moirin asked, as she stood.

He shook his head.

She left, then returned to the dining room. After a round of quiet farewells, she left the house with a sigh of relief.

Once home, surges of satisfaction, excitement, and dread sent adrenaline coursing through her. Orson paced with her as she walked back and forth across the living room. She sat down. It was over. She had survived weeks of stress and worry to finally achieve success. She needed to share the news. To celebrate. She flipped her phone over in her hand, then stopped.

Her father's words came back to her. *It's going to be a lot of work, and it'll take all your time. You've been preparing your whole life to run this company.*

She recalled the conversation with Leslie days ago, when she had been nearly convinced she wanted the opposite. Was Garrett Diversified really the path where her passion led? She had made so many sacrifices in life. Giving up marriage and children, the chance to have her own family. She'd never be a grandmother surrounded by small children begging for her attention.

And now Jace was a part of her life. Just as she was coming to terms with the past, considering the possibility of a new path, she was being asked to make even more compromises.

There would be no vacations for the foreseeable future. No girls' trips and no four-day weekend to attend a century-old tradition of team roping for the Fourth of July. She would have limited free time.

She needed to talk with Jace. She had never considered talking with someone else or taking their feelings into account before taking the next step in her life.

Why was she hesitating?

What if Jace wasn't willing to date a workaholic? She had had a brief glimpse of something wonderful, and now the thought of giving that up pained her. Still raw over the loss of her mother, the thought of losing anyone else in her life was intolerable.

She wanted to have lazy weekends with Jace and have dinner at his house with only an hour's notice. Joining Jo for karaoke night or listening to her announce at a roping event. Moirin's mind kept going from one to the next, connecting with each of the people that meant more to her than Garrett Diversified.

She needed more time with Leslie and the progress she seemed to be making. Heather, who needed the support of her friends now more than ever during her divorce. Aggie and the winery. Her father and the extra help he might need now. If she had paid more attention to her mother's health, maybe she would be alive now.

That thought gave her pause. Certainly, there was no legacy worth losing a life over. If that were true, then there was no legacy worth sacrificing her own life over. Leslie's final question came back to her mind.

When do you honestly feel fulfilled?

34

Monday brought the real world into complete clarity. Moirin had one day left to reset her mind to business and prepare for the day that would change her life. After an unprecedented time off the prior week, she had a backlog of urgent issues to address. It didn't help matters that she hadn't checked her weekend emails on her cell phone as she normally did, or that last night was wholly engaged with family drama.

She left the pile of work and unanswered message, walking down the hall to Colin's office. He was hunched over the desk, typing furiously on the computer keyboard.

She knocked on his doorframe. He looked up and grinned, shifting back in his chair. "Come in, come in."

"You seem like you're in a good mood."

"It's amazing what a good talk and honesty can do to clear the air. After you left last night, your Dad stayed in the study, but the rest of us sat down and had a good talk. I don't think my parents have been that honest with each other in a long time. Maybe ever." The grin stayed plastered on his face.

"I'm glad to hear that. I just wanted to come by and chat one last time before the Board meets this afternoon," Moirin said. "Any final thoughts?"

He shook his head. "Nope. I blocked off two weeks next month to take the family on a vacation. We're letting the kids decide, and right now it's a toss-up between Alaska and Lake Tahoe." He shrugged. "Either way, it will likely be our last time with both of them before Megan goes for her semester abroad and Ryan heads off to college."

"That sounds wonderful. You'll have a great time either way." The joy he found in his family was evident in his face. For all his dedication to the company, it was clear he'd created a successful work-life balance.

"All right, I'll see you in a couple of hours then."

Moirin returned to her own office, where Wanda hustled and hovered, ready to assist, accustomed to Moirin's detailed preparations for quarterly board reports. Her schedule was always clear the day before the meetings, and Wanda typically handled numerous last-minute details. This time was different. An unusual Monday meeting skewed their routine. There were several packages of thick stapled pages that Moirin copied and collated herself. Wanda offered help several times, but Moirin politely and firmly declined.

Moirin knew Wanda would be itching for the gossip. Garrett Diversified was a privately held company, but often the Board of Directors' agenda was routine and, truthfully, dull. This time, however, the first line indicated two topics were designated as *in camera,* indicating confidential material would be discussed. Moirin was certain Wanda had wild guesses about those topics. If she only knew. But everyone would know soon enough.

It was time. She stood motionless at the door, looking at the board members assembled, seated around the table, chatting before the meeting began. She had paced in her office for ten minutes to work off the nervous energy. She needed to be calm, cool, and completely collected during this meeting. No shaking hands or twitching feet to undermine the certainty of her words.

She had never been more certain of her convictions. A few short weeks ago, her greatest desire was to leave a lasting legacy - one that included her painted portrait hanging in the CEO corridor at Garrett Diversified. A legacy that ensured people years from now would look back and revere her for her leadership. She was now poised to take that next step.

The meeting came to order. Ian, as CEO, was the first to address the board. After a few broad remarks, he stunned those assembled by announcing his retirement.

"I had initially planned to work a few more years, but my brother's health and the sudden loss of his wife, my sister-in-law, have driven home the understanding of how brief and unpredictable life truly is. I have dedicated the better part of fifty years to this company. It's in my blood and will always be dear to my heart." He took a sip of water, cleared his throat, and looked nervously around the room before continuing. "The next generation has already earned our trust, and I have full faith and confidence in their abilities to take Garrett through its next hundred years. I feel like my time here has ended, and I look forward to spending more time with my wife, children, grandchildren, and soon, my first great-grandchild."

There was scattered polite applause as his words sank in. The mood in the room was expectant, and everyone looked at Moirin, anticipating her next words. She felt the pressure of that expectation, and her stomach fluttered with excitement, along with a bit of dread. It was like the moment before marriage vows, being on the precipice of a lifetime commitment. Where had *that* thought come from?

Moirin watched her father stand and smile from one board member to another. "And we thought this was momentous because it was my last meeting," Charles said. Polite laughter tittered around the room, Charles' guffawing the loudest. "Truly, we are on the brink of a new era for Garrett Diversified. I am stepping down from the board, and my brother, Ian, is retiring as well." He placed a hand on his heart, then gestured to his brother before turning back to the board members.

"Let me put all your minds at ease. Garrett Diversified has been a family-owned company for generations, and we have no intention of changing that now. My daughter, Moirin, started here fresh out of college. She worked her way up, learning every aspect of the business, and has served as the Chief Operations Officer for over a decade. We are in capable hands with her at the helm. Moirin can lead us into the future, ensuring Garrett Diversified's success for generations to come. Moirin, come join me."

They had planned this moment. She and her father, that night in the study. How it would go, what she would say. They rehearsed how best to address the board and what words to avoid, although the Board typically rubber-stamped any decision the Garretts offered with a united front. It didn't matter how it came about. The result was the same. The achievement of everything she had worked for and all she ever wanted. Her legs wobbled beneath her as she measured the steps to her father's side. She hugged him briefly and smiled at the Board.

"I share the sentiment of my father and Ian, my dear uncle. I have been blessed to work so closely with them. I've honestly learned from the best."

She took a deep breath, looking from her father to Uncle Ian, before launching into her prepared remarks. She had practiced this speech, memorizing every word until it was ingrained in her mind. She delivered it flawlessly without glancing at her notes. While her mouth spoke the words, her thoughts went rogue.

Scenes and memories from the past month flooded her mind. After thirty years on a narrow path, she saw a glimpse of a completely different life. An alternative future she had never allowed herself to have, nor even dared to dream. That moment in the study, after dad had left her alone, she had been ecstatic about the promotion, but instantly felt the freedom to choose her life slipping away.

She had just witnessed the results of her mother's choices and the sacrifices she'd willingly made. Moirin had already made sacrifices. She hadn't regretted any of them. She had no desire to change the past, but at this moment, as her corporate self continued to deliver the speech committing her life to the corporate world, she knew it wasn't right.

The long weekend she'd just experienced wasn't something she wanted to file away in memory. It was a lifestyle she wanted to seize. That desire stopped the flow of words to the board seated in front of her.

For a moment, the room was silent.

Moirin took a deep breath and removed her blazer, casually rolling up her sleeves. That slight motion was freeing. "I love this company, the employees, and the mission we've had together, but I can't be the one to lead." It was as if someone else was speaking. She heard the words and knew they were true. She heard sharp gasps from around the room. She nearly giggled at the relief of it.

"My time here is at an end as well. With what I hope is Ian's and my father's blessing, I nominate my cousin, Colin Garrett, to take over as CEO. I'll stay close to support him, and, if it's okay with everyone, I'll take over my father's seat on this board."

Two dozen shocked faces stared at her, not the least of which was Colin. She risked a glance at her father. Most people would have called his face unreadable, but she knew him better. There was anger and disappointment in his eyes.

As the meeting broke up and people started to leave, Charles stayed in his seat. He appeared to be content watching everyone else.

When the room cleared, it would be time to face the music. The exuberant, giddy feeling was still with her, fueling irreverent thoughts. *I don't want to face the music. I want to dance to the music.*

When they were alone, Moirin sat in the seat next to her father. "I'm sorry, Dad."

He shook his head, his mouth twisting in contemplation, but he didn't speak.

"I know we had a plan, I can't explain it, but I couldn't do it. I'm sorry to disappoint you, but at the moment, I just *knew*."

"You knew what, exactly, Moirin?" The words were low. "Knew that?"

"My passion lies in a different direction, Dad." She hugged him, despite his rigid stance, and turned to leave, exercising all her inner self-control to resist the urge to skip.

She met with Colin one more time, who was still reeling from her announcement.

"Of course, I expected to run the company one day, but I thought it would be years from now," he said. "You caught everyone off guard, Moirin. Dad was nearly crazed when we got back here. One minute, he was furious with you, then he was excited; he was passing the torch to me."

Moirin smiled. "Right now, your Dad can retire. You and I will steer the ship until after your vacation. Then, we'll make the moves. Trust me, I won't let you fail. This company means too much to me to let that happen."

"So why did you do it? We had a plan. Why are you throwing that away?"

"I'm not throwing anything away. Honestly, this decision isn't about moving away from something; it's about moving toward something. It might not make sense to you, but it doesn't feel like I'm leaving, it feels like I'm arriving."

"You seem certain," he said.

"I am. I think it's something that has been coming for a while. Losing my mom at a point when things in my personal life were changing made me take stock. I don't think I realized it's what I wanted until the words were out of my mouth."

"Are you sure?" Colin looked doubtful.

"I'm absolutely certain," Moirin said. "I had already started an executive search for my position, so we'll just need to broaden that plan a bit and replace you instead. Now, let's get started. Don't worry, fresh blood is good for innovation."

"A little fresh blood, then, before we bring on more family. It's only a matter of time before Ryan comes to work here. In the meantime, we have a long and established history we can rely on."

"The company will be in good hands, Colin," Moirin said. "Besides, I'll be on the board, and both your dad and mine will be watching over things. They might be retired, but they're still going to be opinionated and won't be shy about butting in."

"What are you going to do with your time? I know you'll have a hand in things here, but after managing daily operations, serving as Chairman of the Board will be a lot less demanding."

"Oh, I have plans. There's another business I have in mind that will benefit from my experience, but I expect it to be a much lighter workload. It will leave me time for other things I've been thinking about, like mentoring, and being more involved in the PEP project." The idea that she could help young women like Steffie occurred to her after her mom's funeral, and the thought appealed to her more every day. It would be nice to have time to mentor.

"That will be quite a change for you. Aren't you worried about getting bored?"

"Not at all. I'll likely have my attorney and her team look into our friend Mr. Gregorian Plankett and his business dealings. He should be held accountable if, or when, he strays from gray areas to actually breaking the law. I don't like dishonesty, and I don't like bullies. I think he's probably both."

"Be careful there. I know he made the past few weeks tough for you, but I don't want you to have any backlash. I care about you, but I have to be selfish. You know I still need you here."

Moirin laughed. "I promise Garrett Diversified will always be one of my top priorities. I'm here for you, and one day we'll both be there for Ryan." She wasn't about to let Colin fail, but she knew she wasn't crucial to his success. She wasn't irreplaceable in the business; no one was.

Love and time with others were irreplaceable. After all these years, she finally learned that spontaneity had its place. Not everything had to be structured and planned. Some of the best things in life were happy accidents.

At the end of what proved to be a long day, she was finally alone in her office. She walked behind the desk and took down the photo of her father and grandfather, holding it in her hands. She might never have her face on the CEO wall, but her legacy was still established. She had made a lasting impact here and would be remembered by those who truly mattered.

Besides, she had another thirty years or so to create a new legacy. There were a few people she needed to see to start working on that.

EPILOGUE

The high-ceiling banquet room with its rough-hewn plank walls, exposed beam ceiling, and rough stone floor had been transformed with dazzling holiday sparkle. A ten-foot Christmas tree was decorated with ornaments made from wood, burlap, and shiny silver, intermingled with bright red ribbons. The wide expanse of windows only added to the festive air, the landscape itself sparkling with fresh snowfall. A large fire crackled gaily in the massive stone fireplace. The covered patio was lit up with tiny strands of lights, warmed by three separate fire pits and numerous standing propane heaters for those who wanted to embrace the brisk winter wonderland.

"To Hillson," Moirin held up her glass, and the room resounded with the echoed toast.

Aunt Aggie beamed as she walked into the room, each hand holding an open bottle, refilling the goblets of guests. She chatted with guests, laughing and accepting compliments from the partygoers as she meandered through the room. The first annual Hillson Wines Holiday Tasting Party was an unequivocal success.

"It's too bad your father couldn't be here," Aggie said as she hugged Moirin. "I'd love for him to see what you've done here in so short a time."

"Dorthea said he agreed to accompany her to *The Nutcracker* ballet this evening," Moirin said.

"Oh, really?" Aggie leaned away, stretching out the final word in surprise. "Is there something going on there?"

"Just friendship, from what Dorthea says. But, Dad still hasn't quite forgiven me the betrayal, so the ballet was probably the lesser of two evils."

She laughed, slapping her hand over her mouth to ward off the humor. "Oh, honey, I'm sorry. Your father will get over it in time. Colin's stepped up, and he seems to be doing great with your help. Charles just has his nose out of joint because you chose the winery."

The front door opened, bringing a ribbon of cold air and nearly a half dozen party guests into the room. Aggie gave Moirin a smile and rushed off to greet them.

"You look fabulous, Moirin. You're practically glowing." Heather sidled up next to her, linking arms affectionately. She assessed Moirin's attire —a Christmas green dress with a cowl neckline and three-quarter-length sleeves, paired with a white silk scarf featuring green mistletoe and holly tied in a simple bow around her neck, nodding her approval.

"Thank you. So do you," Moirin said. "I mean, Wowza." She drew her index finger up and down in the air at Heather's low-cut red dress.

Heather laughed and shrugged with a gleam in her eye. "So, I've amped up my wardrobe a bit. It's been fun finding out who I am on my own and growing into myself. And, a handsome new man's attention doesn't hurt my ego at all."

"Well, I love it. It's a great look on you," Moirin said.

"Thanks. Congratulations on all of this. I am so happy for you. You started out to change your own life, and look at what you've done."

In the ninety days since Moirin took over Hillson Wines management, they had experienced more success than she or Aggie could have imagined. This party was a celebration of that success. Moirin took full advantage of the opportunity by showing off the winery's new party-hosting capabilities and catering partnerships.

Aggie took every opportunity to boast of her good sense to join Hillson, knowing it was a perfect fit. Moirin had been surprised at how easily she had acclimated to her new role and lifestyle. She stayed at the winery Monday through Thursday, having moved into the manager's efficiency apartment. On the weekends, she stayed at the condo or, more often these days, at Jace's house.

As if conjured by her thoughts, Jace appeared, sliding his arm around her waist, nuzzling her neck with his lips. "Hello, sweetheart. Beautiful party."

Moirin smiled at him and kissed him. She was looking forward to the romantic week-long ski trip they'd planned between Christmas and New Year's.

"Okay, lovebirds. I'm off to find my man and drag him under the mistletoe," Heather said.

"Everything turned out perfect for tonight, didn't it?" Moirin turned in Jace's arms, leaning back against his chest, surveying the room. She rocked comfortably on her black patent leather wedge heels with the extra-padded insole. They were indulgently comfortable, and at barely two inches high, they made her feel positively diminutive next to Jace.

"You did great, honey. A perfect party for the winery, and I love the fact that so many members of your family could make it. It must be nice to know they support you in this big move you've made."

He was right. Almost everyone was here. Ian and Felicity. Colin and Brittany. Ryan was off skiing with some new college buddies, and with Megan still away on her semester abroad, the two seemed to be adjusting well to their temporary empty nest. Moirin smiled as she watched a very pregnant Avery preen under the attention of her doting husband, Ellis. Even Gillian was there with her new boyfriend. Moirin had been happy to see her finally moving forward with her life. She'd been divorced for three years now. It was time.

Jo approached them as Moirin's cell phone rang. Moirin slipped it from her pocket and looked at the caller ID before answering.

"This is Moirin. How can I help you?"

"Ah, the professional greeting, taking a work call during the party, I see." Jo wagged a finger at Moirin while winking at Jace.

Moirin pulled the phone away from her ear and stage-whispered. "I heard that. What did you expect? You've always said I thrive on work. I always will; I've just learned how to balance things now."

As evidence, she leaned over and kissed Jace. "I'll be back in a minute, love."

She waved her fingers at Jo with a grin and stepped away to take the call.

The End

ACKNOWLEDGEMENTS

It has been nearly five years since I started this book. Through countless versions, revisions, and changes to the storyline, I am immensely grateful for all the support I have received, not only for this book but also for the next three in the series that are part of this effort.

First and foremost, I want to thank my incredibly patient and talented developmental editor, Ema Barnes, who helped me identify the key themes I wanted to explore and worked tirelessly with me to create outlines for each story. Toni Robino, whom I worked with on my last book, has encouraged me, remaining a confident, mentor and friend over the years.

I would also like to express my gratitude to my critique group at Central Colorado Writers, a diverse group that consistently provides excellent insights and observations. A special thanks goes to Kelly Luce from The Writing Workshops Iceland, along with all my fellow writers there, for their invaluable input. I am equally thankful to Lara Bernhardt from the WriterCon Retreat at Canebrake, where, based on her input, fully twenty percent of the book was scrapped and re-written (greatly improving it).

I appreciate the ongoing partnership with my editors, the beautiful work on interior layout, and the brilliant covers created by Kelly Martin, who always brings even my most obscure visions to life. I feel truly blessed to have each member of my publishing team.

ABOUT THE AUTHOR

 Heidi Herman is an author of books in several genres but has a special love for women's fiction. She favors writing stories of strong women who face and overcome obstacles to live their best lives. Her passion and a common theme in her writing is her Icelandic heritage.

She started her writing journey with children's books and folklore, and in addition to fiction, has written a motivational book for adults and two cookbooks. In addition to writing, she loves cooking, photography, travel, and exploring the outdoors. She spends her time writing, researching Iceland, attending Scandinavian events, and pursuing adventure all along the way.

Website: https://www.heidihermanauthor.com

Instagram: https://www.instagram.com/heidihermanauthor

Facebook: https://www.facebook.com/HeidiHermanAuthor

If you enjoyed this book, please consider sharing your comments in a review on Goodreads or your favorite retailer. Reviews from readers like you are so important to the success of independent writers like me, and I sincerely appreciate the feedback.

OTHER BOOKS BY HEIDI HERMAN

Fiction
The Reins of Friendship (Novella)

Her Viking Heart

Non-Fiction
The Hidden Vegetables Cookbook: 90 Tasty Recipes for Veggie-Averse Adults

On With the Butter! Spread More Living onto Everyday Life

Homestyle Icelandic Cooking for American Kitchens
(with Ieda Jónasdóttir Herman)

Short Story Collection
The Guardians of Iceland and Other Icelandic Folk Tales

Children's Books
Yule Lads Legend: Iceland's Jólasveinar

The Icelandic Yule Lads: Mayhem at the North Pole

www.ingramcontent.com/pod-product-compliance
Lightning Source LLC
Chambersburg PA
CBHW011128190726
48289CB00012B/2955